In a future where schools have no teachers and no classrooms, Jennifer Calderon is the perfect student. Every day she watches her video modules, plays her edu games, and never misses an answer. Life is comfortable in the Plex, a mile-wide apartment building. Corporations and brand names surround her and satisfy her every want and need.

Then one day, her foul-mouthed, free-spirited, 90's-kitsch-wearing girlfriend Melody disrupts everything. She introduces her to a cynical, burned-out former teacher, who teaches them the things no longer taught in school. Poetry. Critical thinking. Human connection.

But these lessons draw the attention of EduForce, the massive corporation with a stranglehold on education. When they show how far they are willing to go keep their customers obedient, Jennifer has to decide what is most important to her and how much she is willing to sacrifice for it.

D1164391

AT THE TROUGH

Adam Knight

A NineStar Press Publication

Published by NineStar Press
P.O. Box 91792,
Albuquerque, New Mexico, 87199 USA.
www.ninestarpress.com

At the Trough

Printed in the USA
First Edition
May, 2019

Print ISBN: 978-1-950412-69-3

Also available in eBook, ISBN: 978-1-950412-67-9

Warning: This book contains the deaths of secondary characters and references to suicide and suicidal ideation and abuse of an adult child by a parent.

This book is dedicated to my students, who are so much more than data points.

One: Learning is Fun

The brain releases the neurotransmitter dopamine in response to certain stimuli. Eating candy, having sex, consuming drugs, even petting a dog can trigger a pleasure response. Video games, especially ones with bright lights, upbeat music, and facile accomplishments are especially potent, flooding the brain with a sense of reward. As such, they were the bane of teachers for many years. That is, until EduForce began to use these games in their products. The scourge of learning was being disguised as learning itself.

—Charles Winston, *The Trough*, p 114

Jennifer Calderón stared into the screen, slack-jawed and passive as the bright colors and shapes burst before her eyes. Her pupils traced letters and blocks as they bounced from one end of the sixty-inch screen to the next. She reached out and touched a word before it hit the bottom—GAMBOLED. The white letters lit up, neon-green, and the word whooshed across the screen to smash into another word—GAMBLED—and shatter into a shower of sparkles.

"*Same-sounder found!*" a chirpy electronic voice declared.

Dopamine squirted into Jennifer's brain in happy little jets. A smile traced the corners of her lips. Learning was fun.

Jennifer flicked her eyes to the upper right-hand corner of the screen. The figure *23/25* quickened her pulse. Two more. Two more word pairs and she would earn the Same-Sounder Achievement.

A new word appeared at the bottom of her screen. ASCENT, it read. The friendly female voice read the word and definition. Bubbles with other vocabulary terms floated around the screen. Colors whirled before her eyes and electronic dance beats filled her ears as she searched for Same-Sounders. Then she saw it. The word, in white letters on a floating bubble, drifted toward the bottom. Jennifer's finger jabbed at the screen. *Pop!* The word ASCENT exploded in fireworks. More music and chirpy voices.

"*Same-sounder found,*" the voice said. More dopamine gushed into Jennifer's brain. Her eyes flicked up to the corner. *24/25*.

CYMBAL.

Once more, Jennifer scanned the bubbles and blobs and cubes and tetrahedrons swirling in her vision. Her breath was shallow. More and more words poured onto the screen. In one moment after another, tiny subdivided fractions of seconds, Jennifer saw and rejected words she did not think made the same sound as "cymbal." Her eyes, her brain, and her hands all had to work in unison. Each level of Same-Sounder Finder was faster, more complex, and more stimulating than the last.

Then she saw it. SYMBOL.

She thrust her finger out to the screen. The little magenta gem in which the word sat was zigzagging down the screen, and she almost missed it and pressed the word TUMBLE crossing its path. But the SYMBOL illuminated, exploded, and a fireworks finale showed on the screen. *25/25*.

"*Same-sounder found,*" the voice declared, then louder and triumphantly, "*Same-sounder achievement unlocked!*"

Jennifer leaped and thrust her fists in the air as a fanfare of electronic tones rang through her bedroom. Not many students earned perfect scores on Same-Sounder Finder, but Jennifer did. She earned perfect scores on everything. She was twenty-three years old and finishing her last year of schooling, a year ahead of the usual schedule. Because of all the hours she put into learning, and because she never had to redo any of her modules, she had raced ahead of her peers, many of whom were still on Achievement Level 13 or 14. She was working on 15.

After the music died down, the screen went still. Jennifer's head was still pounding. A headache was setting in, as was a twinge of crankiness. She left her bedroom and went to the kitchen where she poured herself a cup of coffee. Her mother always had a pot brewing, anything to keep her beloved daughter focused on school. Jennifer clogged the coffee with sugar and milk, stirred it, and took a gulp. Better. She freed a couple of aspirins from their foil pouches and swallowed them with the next mouthful of coffee. She returned to her room.

Jennifer slid her finger along the screen and opened it to a new frame, one summarizing her academic progress. *Current Achievement Level: 14. 12 percent of the way to 15. 106 of 880 modules completed. Achievement Level Grade Point Average: 5.0/5.0.*

Total Progress to Completion of all Achievement Levels: 97 percent. 12,845 of 13,215 modules completed.

And then there was the final number. The prized number, the number she had worked for since age three.

Aggregate Grade Point Average: 5.0/5.0

Every assignment Jennifer had ever done, from toddlerhood into now her mid-twenties, had been flawless. Missing just one question on one task would eradicate her record—The Perfect Five. There had been students with 5.0 GPAs before, but their scores came with asterisks. Usually the student had missed a smattering of questions throughout their education, resulting in a score that would round up to 5.0 in the ten-thousandths place. But Jennifer Calderón began each module on a knife's edge, knowing one slip up would end her lunge at history. Each completed question nudged her progress toward earning Achievement Level 15, the equivalent of what was once her high school diploma. Thus far, however, all she had was poor digestion, headaches, sleep deprivation, and occasional interviews for the NewsFeed as her accomplishment became more improbable.

Jennifer left the score screen and opened a new frame to continue with a new module. She had done three Grammar Modules in a row and wished for a change, so she opened a Chemistry Module. It made no difference to her. She never understood students who had favorite subjects, who would put off Math or Writing as long as possible. She never understood procrastination. She simply worked until she was exhausted, every day, with no heed to the subject area. It was all the same to her.

To unlock the next series of edugames, she needed to watch the Chemistry vidlesson. At the opening screen, she was given a choice of several hundred different teachers to choose from. Each teacher had his or her own style. Some were brusque and businesslike, while others joked and kept the lesson light. Some had an air of wisdom and experience, while others were young and attractive. Some explained topics deliberately, but Jennifer returned to the same half-dozen teachers who explained briskly. Unlike many students, Jennifer always watched the vidlesson before the edugame. It was true "Learning Was Fun" but it was also true that "Hard Work Pays Off." *It's so easy,* she thought. *They give you all of the answers right in the lesson.*

Too easy. But the thought was fleeting, and she brushed it away.

Jennifer selected Mr. 85. She was not sure why the teachers did not have real names, but she did not dwell on it long. Mr. 85 was a favorite of hers because he spoke a little faster than other teachers. The content of what he said was the same—it had to be; the teachers were scripted—but he lingered a few seconds less on the examples and generally made his points and moved on. She wondered how many minutes of her educational life had been saved by Mr. 85's expediency.

Her stomach rumbled. *I should eat,* she thought, but instead she touched the icon for the Chemistry video and sat on the edge of her bed. The video opened. It was six minutes. *Damn. A long one.*

The introduction music came up, a familiar, infectious jingle followed by a voiceover. "Chemistry—All You Need to Know. A lesson by the EduForce Corporation." Then the camera fixed on Mr. 85. Mr. 85 was a middle-aged black man with graying hair. He never smiled. Jennifer kind of liked that. He stood in front of a display showing an elaborate chart with boxes. Each box had one or two letters inside.

"Good day, I am Mr. 85. Today we are going to learn all about Chemistry. As you remember from the Introduction to Chemistry lesson, Chemistry is the part of science that is chemicals. The chemicals have names and symbols. Today I will teach them to you."

He stepped to the right and indicated the chart. Jennifer already knew she would have to rewatch this segment of the video. Maybe the whole thing. All those boxes and letters would be difficult to remember.

"This is called the Chemical Chart. It used to be called the 'Periodic Table of the Elements,' but let's keep it simple. The Chemical Chart shows you a list of all the chemicals, called 'elements,' in the world. Little ones are on the top and big ones are on the bottom.

"Let's look at some of them. The very top one is called 'hydrogen.' Its symbol is H. The next one is Helium. Its symbol is He."

Mr. 85 pointed out about a dozen of the most common elements and their symbols. Aluminum. Carbon. Oxygen. Phosphorous. Jennifer repeated to herself everything Mr. 85 said.

"Next, we are going to look at what the elements do together," he went on. "But first, you may be getting tired. Do you find your energy dragging after all this learning? If so, why not order a box of Perk-Eez? It's the little yellow pill that keeps you shining bright!"

The video of Mr. 85 paused and was replaced with a new screen offering Jennifer the opportunity to order a box of Perk-Eez. She touched the "Yes, please!" button on the screen, and a message immediately appeared. "Thank you! Your delivery will arrive at your unit shortly. Your household account will be debited." Perk-Eez were another reason Jennifer was on track to graduate two years early.

Mr. 85 returned.

"Now that you know some of the chemicals' names, let's look at what chemicals do. They like to be together. Sometimes the same kinds of chemicals get together. One oxygen and another oxygen will get together, and they make up the oxygen we breathe. If you have taken the Human Biology module, you know we breathe oxygen."

The Chemical Chart was replaced with a graphic of two blue blobs with the letter "O" on them smooshing together.

"Sometimes different chemicals get together. A carbon and two oxygens get together and make up something called carbon dioxide. Yes, that's right, carbon dioxide, the bad thing your grandparents put into the air that almost killed Earth!"

A new graphic with two blue blobs and a red blob with a "C" all clinging together replaced the old one.

"All kinds of chemicals get together. Let's look at some combinations."

The screen showed a series of different colored balls, all with different letters, making different combinations. Jennifer shook her head, trying to maintain focus. It was a lot of new information.

As the video neared completion, Mr. 85 folded his hands and stepped to the center of the screen again. Jennifer thought she almost detected a smile.

"I hope you have enjoyed this lesson on Chemistry. Please rewatch this video as many times as you like before going onto the edugames. My name is Mr. 85 and it has been a pleasure teaching you today. This has been an EduForce vidlesson. EduForce, making learning easy and fun since 2034."

The video closed. Jennifer watched it again three times. After the second time, the doorbell rang. She accepted the delivery from SentiAid, the pharmacy delivery service. She tore open a foil packet and gobbled a couple of Perk-Eez. Almost instantly, even faster than after a cup of coffee, her brain and body were buzzy and alive.

All right, she thought. *Let's play some more edugames.*

The Chemistry edugame was called "Elementastic!!!" She read the instruction screen, then the game began. After a countdown, two words appeared on the screen:

Iron Argon

Jennifer typed in FEAR. The letters Fe and Ar zoomed in from the left and right of the screen, collided in a burst of color, and formed the word "fear," which dissolved into sparkles that floated up to the top of the screen.

Carbon Oxygen Oxygen Phosphorous

Easy, Jennifer thought. She typed COOP.

More collisions and explosions.

Tin Iodine Phosphorous

SNIP

Helium Aluminum Sulfur

HEALS

Jennifer fell into a rhythm, working faster and faster on each round. Her breathing became shallow. Her pulse quickened and her pupils dilated as the words came faster, exploded bigger and more colorfully, until finally a computerized voice—male this time—announced, "Activity Complete. Chemistry Achievement Unlocked!" and Jennifer lowered her hands, panting.

The voice continued, "To celebrate your achievement, how about downloading the new song from Tuliphead? The infectious single 'Plex Lovin'' is already breaking new—"

"Sure," Jennifer said, and the advertisement stopped. Buying was the easiest way to make the ads go away.

Even as a small child, edugames had come easily to her. She watched the vidlessons, played the edugames, and thought little of it. She learned with carefree abandon. But when she reached the age of twelve or thirteen, she became aware she was doing something unusual. Of course, she did not have classmates to compare herself to, and she had few friends to ask, but she understood she was different. Other children made mistakes, even had to redo modules they had not mastered. She had wondered what mistakes were, to have the certainty of rightness yanked out from under you.

As she grew older, she became acutely aware of her achievement. At age fifteen, she received a request for a vid interview with a reporter. She had sheepishly declined, unsure of what to say and certain her mother would not have allowed it. But over the subsequent years, several more interview requests came to her, and she began to accept them. Each time she said the same things, that she was proud and studied a lot to do the best she could. That answer was only half true. She was proud of her grade but never had to study. She watched a vidlesson, played the edugame, then moved on to the next.

A female voice emitted from Jennifer's speakers.

"Good morning, Jennifer. How are you this morning?"

"Fine," Jennifer replied. The voice was her A.I. personal assistant, or AIPA. The AIPA's user could have their assistant speak through mounted speakers, portable speakers, or earpieces. AIPAs who blurted out sensitive information was a frequent source of comedy. Jennifer's AIPA was named Carlita, one of ten thousand personalities available. Jennifer liked that the Carlita personality was efficient and organized, but sometimes she clung to the pleasantries too long.

"You have received a message. Shall I read it to you?"

"Sure. Thanks."

"You are quite welcome. The message is from Melody Park. It says, 'Hey bot, are you busy?' Do you wish to respond?"

Melody, Jennifer thought. *Always when I'm in the middle of schoolwork. Then again, I am always in the middle of schoolwork.*

"Sure. Tell her she's got a half hour."

"Do you wish me to send that message verbatim, or—"

"No, say it however you want."

"Very well," Carlita replied. She would then compose a message reply to Melody in a tone that best simulated Jennifer's own. Carlita was Jennifer's new AIPA, and it often took weeks or months of working together before an AIPA could mimic a user's syntax and diction just right. Carlita was a low model AIPA too, so the results would probably be ugly. "Before I go, can I interest you in a Lime Blast Freezie-Chug?"

"No, just send the message," Jennifer replied, chagrined that her mother did not have the money for an ad-free AIPA. Jennifer had bought a Lime Blast Freezie-Chug a month ago, and now Carlita kept bugging her if she wanted another.

"Very well. Goodbye, Jennifer."

"Bye."

Ten minutes later, the electronic tone of her doorbell beeped. Jennifer went to the door and opened it. In walked a woman of Jennifer's age. Her hair was straight black and cut with horizontal bangs. She wore blue denim jeans and a plaid shirt, and a bag sat on her back, held by two straps over her shoulders.

"What's the look this week?" Jennifer asked. "Retro to the twenty-teens?"

Melody scoffed.

"For being the girl who knows everything, you don't know jack shit about fashion history. This was the nineties!"

She walked in the room with an exaggerated swagger.

"'Jack shit?'" Jennifer asked. "Vintage cursing too?"

She grabbed Melody's sleeve and pulled her in for a brief kiss.

"So, your mom is not home?" Melody asked when they pulled apart.

"Working. Always working."

"That's good for me," Melody said. "Good for us."

"So, explain to me your new style." Jennifer said. She always wore the same styles that were popular with her peers—light fabrics, dull earth tones, and a smattering of corporate logos over everything. The more logos on the article of clothing, the more prestigious. Her hair, which was naturally curly, had been straightened into oblivion and was cut in cascading zigzags down her back. It was also the popular style.

Melody popped the collar on her plaid.

"The nineties! Kurt Cobain, Pearl Jam, heroin, blow jobs in the White House, the greatest decade! I've been listening to music from that time."

"Our grandparents' music."

Melody shrugged.

"Maybe. My grandparents were still in Korea in the nineties. And yours were still in El Salvador. Hey, I'm thirsty. Buy me a drink, sailor."

"Colombia," growled Jennifer. She did not know if Melody could not remember the country or if she was toying with her. Either way, she hated it. And liked it a little, as well. She went to the kitchen and held a glass to the beverage fountain. She selected Jazzy-Pop Grape Soda and pressed the button. Grape, no ice, just like always. No one liked grape, but Melody did.

Melody flung her bag to the floor and plopped down on the sofa while taking a long swig of soda. Jennifer's heart skipped. If her mother returned home from work to find Melody had dripped even a drop of purple on the fabric, she would excoriate Jennifer for days.

"Where did you even find those clothes?" Jennifer asked. "And that back bag. No store would sell them."

"Are you serious? There are stores that sell anything. And it's called a 'backpack.' Nineties kids loved them."

Jennifer pointed to Melody's light blue denim.

"Jeans?" Jennifer asked. "They only sell them in the grandma stores, where—"

"Exactly."

"You went shopping in the grandma stores?"

"Yes, I did," Melody replied.

Jennifer sighed and shook her head. She leaned down and kissed Melody again.

"You taste like cough syrup." Melody breathed on her.

"You are critical today," Melody said. "Making fun of my clothes, making fun of my breath. I should leave."

"Don't."

Melody smirked.

"Nah, I'll stay. Say, I had an idea. Let's get up on the roof and get drunk tonight."

Jennifer shook her head.

"Not this time. We were almost caught last time."

"Almost. Almost means we weren't," Melody said. "I've found a better spot, out of view of all the cameras. I have something very grip to show you."

"How grip?"

"Oh, you'll thank me. It's a book. Like a real, vintage book."

"Are you serious?" Jennifer hissed. "You can't get caught with that."

"Why? It isn't illegal."

"No, but it's...yech. Why would you even keep it?"

"Look," Melody said. "Do you want to see it or not?"

Jennifer glanced at her sideways. Books. Big clunky things with covers and pages, as relevant as corsets or leeches. But if Melody had obtained one, a real one, it would be the most grip thing she had seen in a long time.

"Show me," Jennifer said.

Melody shrugged. She reached for her bag and unzipped the main compartment. She reached in and pulled out a slim paperback with a plain gray cover. She held it out to Jennifer, who would not take it.

"Where did you get it?" Jennifer asked with a mixture of awe and revulsion.

"The old lady down the hall from me, Miss Hammond."

"The one whose birds you used to feed?"

"That was her."

"Was?"

"She died this week. No surprise. She's been sick for a long time."

"Oh, I'm so sorry," Jennifer said. "Did she leave you that book?"

"Not 'leave,' exactly."

Melody grinned. Jennifer grimaced.

"You didn't! From a dead woman?" she said. Melody shrugged.

"I grabbed a few things. The book, Some CDs, even though I don't have any way to play them. A Jurassic Park action figure. Oh, and her Quarantine Suit. Can't have too many of those. The book, though, that's the real prize."

Jennifer goggled her eyes at Melody.

"Oh, come on," Melody continued. "Miss Hammond wasn't going to read it again. I read the whole thing last night. It was amazing. I think you could learn a lot from it."

"What is it called?"

Melody held the book out again, and this time Jennifer took it. The cover had no graphics or images, only a matte gray background. White letters in the center read:

The Trough

By Charles Winston

"Hmm," Jennifer said. "What is it about?"

"You'll have to reeeead it, my little starfish."

"I'm not a starfish." Jennifer opened the front cover. She read the first two sentences:

> *If you were born in the twenty-first century and went to a public school, you have received an education that is worse than worthless. Your education is toxic.*

Jennifer's head started to hurt. She snapped the book shut and shoved it back toward Melody.

"I don't think I'm going to like this."

"You know what I've always loved about you?" Melody said. "Your open-minded approach to new experiences."

"I have a lot of work to do," Jennifer replied. "Maybe some other—"

"You always have a lot of work to do. You are two years ahead of me in your modules. Blow up your afternoon and read a little illicit lit. Go on, it will be a tonic for your perfectionist soul."

Jennifer examined the cover again. Her gut fluttered. Mostly, she was anxious at the thought of abandoning an afternoon of work to read an old, useless book. Part of it was anger at Melody, who was always pushing her to do things she knew she oughtn't do. But buried deeper below was a feeling like a twist at the base of her spine, a wriggle of unsettled discontent, a twitch waiting to be acknowledged. *Is learning really this easy?* She went to the kitchen, poured a glass of water, and drank the entire thing at once. It did not help.

Melody stood up.

"I'll leave you alone now. Happy reading."

Just then two distinct voices spoke simultaneously. One was Carlita, in her cheerfully polite tone. Her voice came from the massive screen in Jennifer's bedroom. The other was a gruff male voice, warped and modified to sound like a demon from the pits of hell. That voice came from somewhere in the depths of Melody's backpack. Both AIPAs said, "You have received a message."

Melody and Jennifer looked at each other.

"May I?" Melody asked.

"No," Jennifer said. "I hate listening to Bruno. I don't know why you had him modded like that."

"Are you jealous of my hellspawn boyfriend?" Melody asked, but then she said to her AIPA, "Bruno, Jennifer is going to take this."

"As you desire, my dark queen."

Jennifer shook her head. "Go ahead, Carlita. Read us the message."

Carlita gave an "ahem" before saying, "From EduForce to all learners working toward Achievement Levels 13, 14 and 15. As you know, we live in an ever-growing, ever-changing world, full of new challenges and information. For the past several years, students have been earning Full Achievement Status after completing fifteen Achievement Levels. For several years, this was sufficient. However, it has become clear to our researchers many important concepts are not included in any of the Learning Modules! Therefore, we are excited to announce a new change in the Learning Track. All students will now be required to complete sixteen Achievement Levels to earn Full Achievement Status.

"Please note that none of your current progress through your Learning Track will be lost or changed. The additional Achievement Level will give you more opportunities to develop critical real-world skills and enjoy more of our top-quality educational products.

"We look forward to working together for years to come on your learning journey. Keep working and remember Knowledge is Power!

"Best regards, Geraldine Barfield, President of EduForce Corporation."

Jennifer's lip trembled. The ground under her feet was sliding away. She gripped the sofa.

Melody slurped the last of her grape soda.

"So, another year of this shit?" she said before setting the empty glass on the floor. "Ah well."

"I can't," Jennifer said. "A whole extra year. More videos, modules, never missing a question."

"You're tougher than you know, kid." Melody slapped Jennifer on the shoulder as she slung her backpack over her own. "You'll figure it out."

Jennifer batted her hand away. Hot, angry tears rose in her eyes.

"Stop it. What do I do?"

"You know what you do?" Melody sounded serious. "Fuck studying tonight. Read that book. Meet me on the roof at eight. And we will get so shitfaced you won't remember a thing about that message. At least not for a few hours."

"Okay. Okay." Jennifer was beginning to hyperventilate as the room tunneled.

"Don't sound okay. Sure you don't want that drink now?"

Jennifer smiled weakly. She closed her eyes.

"You're just trying to get me drunk so you can get into my pants. Won't work."

Melody shrugged.

"Not now. I guess I have to wait until tonight. Just breathe, kid. You'll be fine."

"Sorry I am such a mess," Jennifer said as she embraced Melody, draping her arms around her.

"Everyone is a mess. Just your turn right now."

Jennifer said nothing for a time as she let Melody hold her. The room was returning to normal, as was her breathing. As soon as Melody left, she would go to the bathroom and take a couple of Relax-Eez. She had been taking them for years, longer than she could remember. Actually, she could remember. Back to the time she first became aware of The Perfect Five. *The Perfect Five does not just belong to me,* she thought. *I have to give credit to all of my supporters. Melody, caffeine, anti-depressants, Relax-Eez, Perk-Eez, sleep deprivation. Without all of these allies, I would not be who I am today.*

"I'm sorry about Miss Hammond," Jennifer said, her voice husky. "Were you her friend?"

Melody shrugged.

"She was a nice old lady. No kids or grandkids, kind of lonely. A little angry."

"You never told me about her. What did she do?"

"She was a teacher."

Two: The Human Touch

By 2034, education in America was unrecognizable. Gone were the brick-and-mortar school buildings, gone were local school districts, gone were classrooms, gone were grade levels, gone were teacher-crafted lessons. In was EduForce. Led by their president, Geraldine Barfield, EduForce had one more major reform to make. They could calibrate and control everything to their aims, but there was one variable they could not control—the teachers. So, they dismissed all the teachers and hired new ones. The new teachers were actors with no educational training, hired to record dynamic, engaging lessons from a script. The role of teacher had literally become a role.

—The Trough, p.77

Charles Winston knew what to do. Good sense, accepted protocol, and his contract said he must report the student.

He had been so startled when he read the essay that he'd splashed coffee on his flexscreen computer. Nothing startled him anymore, but this did. These words. *How does this girl know these words?* he wondered. Of course, he could not be sure if the writer was a girl or not. There was no way to know whether the student was male or female, twelve years old or twenty-five, living across the country or down the hall. Charles never met any of his students. They weren't even his students, though he still liked to think of them as such. He held his finger over the touchscreen, letting it hover over a red button that said, "REPORT TO EDUFORCE." If Charles touched the button, the essay would disappear, and some authorities—he never knew who—would set to action and address the issue. Charles never found out what happened to the writers of any of those essays.

Charles Winston did not touch the button. *Good sense, accepted protocol, and my contract can suck it.*

This one would be his secret.

Charles stood. He rolled up the flexscreen, which resembled the placemats his grandmother set on the dining room table decades ago, and walked from his desk to his kitchen. He unrolled the flexscreen over the sink, tore off a single paper towel, and wiped the spilled coffee. He folded the towel in half and wiped again to be sure everything was dry. He threw the towel in a wastebasket.

Charles walked to his window, a forty-eight-inch screen bolted to one wall that showed a constant video feed of outside the Plex. The screen was trimmed with a sash and a windowsill. The video stream never stopped and was fixed at one angle, so it was a very close approximation of the view outside. Charles watched trucks rolling up the six-lane road to the Plex, then pull into to the docking bays. In the distance, the solar train slid along steel tracks. He opened the window, meaning he pressed a button setting it to "open" status. A gentle, cool breeze of recycled air poured in from the vents below the window. The sound of light wind, distant birds, and downshifting trucks emanated from built-in speakers. It felt almost real, making its unreality all the more pointed.

Charles "closed" the window and returned to his desk. The words were still there.

He reread the essay again. He slid his finger down the touchscreen to scroll the text.

Extended Prose Construction Topic #7894

Achievement Grade: 13

Student Identification Number: 880056236

EPC Directions: In the text box below, please create an extended prose construction that responds to the following topic. Your construction will be assessed according to its development, organization, and adherence to proper grammar and sentence structure.

EPC Topic: Many families enjoy eating dinner together, such as a Swanford® Rotisserie Chicken and fresh Vivasprout® Green Beans. Is eating dinner together important to you and your family? Explain why or why not.

EPC Response:

A proper response to this topic is founded on the supposition that I even have a fucking family, which I do not. I am with my third family in the past six years now, and I would rather ingest my own innards and then defecate them than eat your putrid chicken and green beans. I take my own food into my own room each night, where I can banquet like a beast of prey, sullen and lonely, couching in the cave which is my lair, and—it may be— my grave.

As a response, the essay would earn a low score, Charles knew. The student did not actually answer the question and provided little development and few specifics. The use of "fucking" would ruin the score for appropriate word choice. The essay had a strong vocabulary, but that was all. However, these academic concerns faded back in Charles's consciousness. He read the essay again. Part of it did not sit right with him. *Couching in the cave which is my lair.* The phrase clung to Charles. The whole sentence did. It just did not fit with the rest of the essay. It was probably plagiarized from somewhere. Plagiarism used to be considered a grave academic offense, but now it was seen as mere sloppiness or laziness. And yet, not even that was the cause of Charles's disquiet. *Where is the phrase from?*

Charles did not know why he was so troubled by this. He read thousands and thousands of words every day. There was no evident threat here of self-harm or harm to others, nor was there any sign of fraud.

Seeking distraction, he switched his screen from Work Mode to NewsFeed Mode. Instantly, a long list of headlines, tailored to Charles's interests, career, and past history, appeared. Charles read a few of the articles, or at least the first paragraph, then moved on. He tried to be up to date on every news development, but it seemed like the same things were happening over and over. The cycle had made Charles angry once. Now he felt only numb resignation.

He shut off the screen again. He went to his sink to wash the morning dishes. There were only two—a bowl and a spoon. The coffee he had been drinking and spilling was now lukewarm, and he dumped it down the drain. Three dishes. He turned the water on and tossed in a dishwasher pellet to make suds. Washing dishes in a sink would be considered quaint and old-fashioned. Everyone had a dishwasher. But Charles thought himself quaint and old-fashioned. At fifty-four, he was old enough to remember a time when people lived in houses, teachers had actual classes with students, and people washed dishes in their sinks by hand. He was also quite sure he was too old to change any of those things.

As he rinsed the bowl, spoon, and cup, he asked himself what was really so bad about dishwashers. *Nothing. They make things easier.* Maybe that was it. Maybe making things easy could be overdone. Soon, the time would come when no one in America even knew how to wash a dish by hand. *Doing things that were difficult and original used to be our country's greatest strength,* he reflected, *and now, they are our country's most atrophied muscle.*

He turned off the water. He smiled. *Not bad. Would make a great first line of an essay. Or last line.* Not that he would write the essay. What was the point? Who would read it? There was no way to even publish it. And then there was the idea itself. Charles grimaced when he realized his parents had said the same thing in their fifties—that the current generation was lazy and unoriginal. Probably his grandparents had said it too. Maybe every generation said it. Charles felt petty and foolish, not profound.

The three dishes lay on the countertop, dripping.

I should get back to work, he thought. Washing three dishes in the middle of the morning. Charles knew procrastination when he saw it.

He sat down and reactivated the screen. He set aside 880056236's essay and moved on to the next one in his queue. Charles had no control over what responses were sent to him. Computers graded most of the essays. EduForce had designed writing assessment software that could analyze a piece of writing for its development, vocabulary, and grammatical consistency in hundredths of a second. Human readers were unnecessary.

However, the software was unable to detect nuances such as suicidal or homicidal danger. When the assessment software found a suspicious phrase or passage, it forwarded the essay to a reviewer such as Charles who would read it and determine whether or not EduForce needed to take further action. The programs detected plagiarism, but these essays were only marked off for lack of originality.

The last type of response that made its way into Charles's queue was a composition the software suspected might be fraudulent. As soon as EduForce's program went into widespread use, students would write— then sell to other students—lengthy compositions of complex and compound sentence structures with a highly sophisticated vocabulary that were utter gibberish. At first, students using these were earning the highest possible scores, until EduForce caught on and began having the software send suspicious work to teachers. "What these essays need," EduForce said in its hiring materials, "is the human touch."

The human touch, Charles thought. *Has such a salacious-sounding phrase ever been more innocuous and empty?*

Charles opened the essay file from the next student. He read it and found a passage in which the student described being "sick to death" of tofu loaf. He marked the essay *"Acceptable for Assessment"* and sent it back to EduForce, where the machines would administer their scores. Most of the essays he received were like this—perfectly benign and bland, devoid of any apparent risks or dangers, and all that happened was a simple word or phrase in the writing got caught in the program's algorithms. In his work, Charles did not award a grade or evaluate any writing. His job was to double check the work of the machines.

Charles read two more essays like this before opening one that began:

> When hierarchical nomenclature results in a salubrious valediction of malodorous dispensation, the ribald hijinks of multifarious nebulizers, being in a perpetual state of cantankerous and ancillary revocation, presume to defenestrate the antediluvian quagmire.

This was clearly one of the fraudulent essays, designed to trick the assessment software into thinking the writer some sort of linguistic genius. Charles opened the drop-down menu, marked the essay as *"Fraudulent,"* and returned it to EduForce. The student would receive no credit, thus ruining his score on the Level 14 Achievements. He'd have to take the exam over again, but Charles didn't feel bad. *That's what he gets for cheating,* he thought, though he had no idea whether the student was male or female.

Charles spent the remainder of the hour grading. His delay over 880056236's essay would cost him some free time. He had daily quotas of essays to read with bonuses for going over. But even at the height of his concentration, he could not stop thinking about the strange sentence. He went back and reread it two, then three times. *What does this person know?* For a moment, the distance between himself and the writers seemed impossibly vast. He didn't know their names, faces, personalities, histories, not even their genders. Anger flashed within him. Reporting the essay would only mean playing into the system more, and he was sick of collaborating.

What he wanted to do was leave his apartment, leave the Plex, and find that student and say to him or her personally how sorry he was about their parents. To look a student in the eyes again and engage in a conversation. *Selfish. Here I am daydreaming about talking with a student and undermining the entire educational system, even if it means putting a young person's life in danger.* He scolded himself for the thought. But it did not go away.

Charles turned back to the other essays. He commanded his AIPA to play his Baroque station he used for working. It featured Bach, Handel, and other composers whose steady rhythms and tempered dynamics settled his mind into a productive state. However, today, his thoughts could not stay focused on his work. The music was distracting, irritating. He barked a command to switch to the metal station. The speakers poured out heavily distorted guitar, blast beat drums, and vocal snarls and growls. Charles used the music to block out the distracting thoughts, but even after he barked, "Raise volume! Raise volume!" at his AIPA until the apartment thundered with sound, the troubling essay cut through his mind clearly. The harder he tried to concentrate, the more that sentence forced itself on his consciousness. *Where I can banquet like a beast of prey, sullen and lonely, couching in the cave which is my lair, and—it may be—my grave.*

Charles stopped typing and leaned back in his chair. He stopped fighting and let his mind daydream about the mystery student. She was shy and timid, the offspring of two oppressive, perfectionist parents. They demanded she earn fives on every Achievement Level, and when she earned a four one year, she was beaten ruthlessly. She had a wild imagination, so she kept a secret file on her flexscreen for a diary, which she showed to no one, and vowed never to reveal. Now, she was going to send her rage out into the world, not caring who read it, not caring that her actions would sabotage her own GPA.

Charles laughed at himself and shook his head. It was all so romantic and predictable, the quiet, troubled kid who lived a secret, imaginative life—

Romantic.

He bolted upright, nearly falling flat with remembering. He told the AIPA to shut up, and the stereo went quiet. Charles scrambled across the suddenly silent apartment, falling over his feet as he came to his tiny bookshelf. A bookshelf was the embodiment of unnecessary archaism in 2051. The truth was Charles could not whittle down his book collection any further. During the Recycling drives, he had been unable to part with these titles.

He paused for a moment as he touched the gray covers of the book he had published a decade before. *The Trough.* He had been proud of it at the time. It was his dream that every teacher in America would read it and wake up, but it received crushing silence in reception. He had not written since.

Charles ran his fingers along the spines until he came to "Anthology of British Romantic Poetry." He opened the covers, feeling the pages flick between his fingers. He could not remember which poem that line had come from, or which poet had written it, but he knew as soon as his eyes hit the right page—one of nine hundred in the volume—he would remember.

And there it was.

The Lament of Tasso by Lord Byron. He remembered the poem from college. It was about an Italian poet who was locked in an insane asylum. Byron had imagined the cruelty of being imprisoned, stifling his wild imagination. The poem had haunted and inspired Charles as an undergraduate, even causing him to write some bad imitative poetry himself.

How does this student know Byron? Charles asked himself, then he asked the question aloud to his empty apartment.

I have to find out who this kid is. The need was urgent, beyond reason, beyond all the prohibitions and restrictions. But there was no way to contact or interact with the student. Students and essay reviewers were kept strictly anonymous and separate.

No, Charles thought. *There is a way.*

He scrambled back to his feet and hopped in his chair. Thinking back to when he was first hired by EduForce sixteen years earlier, he opened the file for the EduForce essay reviewer manual. He could have asked his AIPA to locate the instructions, but using the disembodied voice never came naturally to Charles, and he knew it never would. His eyes scanned the flickering pages for the instructions he sought.

He soon found them.

Sec. 7.a. Providing Advanced Feedback to Students

In most cases, the Assessment Score of 1-5 is adequate feedback for student writing. However, if an Essay Reviewer feels additional explanations would benefit the student, the Reviewer may write an explanation of no more than two hundred words. All explanations must address elements of the essay only and should not elaborate beyond the scope of the writing task. Be aware that EduForce may monitor any messages sent through the Additional Explanation feature.

Charles then read the directions for opening the text box. The software did not make it simple or clear. Charles never left additional feedback for students. The sheer volume of essays he had to read—usually a couple of hundred per day—made taking even two or three minutes to write feedback unfeasible. And besides, he would never see or speak with the students anyway, and they would have no opportunity to make any changes to their composition. He might as well have thrown the time and words into a giant pit.

Charles followed the directions from the manual and brought up a small text box on the screen. *Now what to write,* he wondered. He was not sure what to say, and he knew EduForce would read whatever he wrote. It would have to be clever, oblique, encoded.

Charles stretched. He shook out his hands, as if to awaken them.

What do I say?

QWERTY keypads were another relic of the past, now nearly everyone used an AIPA, but their layout comforted Charles. The words flowed better from his fingers than from his lips.

Well, let me start typing. See what comes out.

You know Byron? Great! Let's meet for coffee and discuss poetry! Sincerely, Charles Winston.

Charles chuckled to himself as he reached for the "delete" key. It had been fun just to type. He tried again, seriously this time.

You have provided an interesting take on this essay topic. Your use of Byron is an unorthodox approach. Further development would make this a stronger essay, and your use of profanity is not appropriate for academic writing.

Charles deleted this one, as well. Even if the student read his message, what would he or she do about it? He knew he needed to leave some clue, some call to action. But it would be a violation of EduForce policy, of Federal education laws, and of basic appropriateness to even try to have a conversation with a student.

Who cares? Things were not always this way. Why must they be this way now? What do I have to lose? I know exactly what I have to lose.

He drummed his fingers on the desk. If he was going to send the student a message, he would have to be smart about it. Smarter than the people at EduForce.

And then he realized.

He didn't have to be smarter than people. People would not be the ones who would catch him. It would be computer programs. Algorithms. Software.

When hierarchical nomenclature results in a salubrious valediction of malodorous dispensation. Charles remembered the sentence he had read that morning. That student had been foolish. The software had known immediately it was not writing. So, Charles would have to be smarter.

> *If you want to call or meet to discuss Lord Byron or any other poets*

Charles deleted the line. The software would surely be checking for phrases like "want to call" and "meet." More subtlety needed.

> *If you are of a like mind, then*

Then what? How would he actually get the message through?

> *If you are of a like mind, then you might enjoy this poem:*

Okay, so a poem it is. How can I tell her how to reach me without really saying it? Then he remembered a puzzle a teacher had shown him years before.

> *Tiger oh cat*

> *Fascinating tiger pussycat*

> *Oh, oh, pussycat...*

Almost there, Charles thought. That last word was a tough one. His mind raced through all the long words he knew, no matter how absurd or unusable.

indefatigability

Charles counted on his fingers, smiled, and leaned back in his chair and reviewed his poem. It was not perfect. It made no sense, and the software might get suspicious over the last word. But not many words would fit what he needed. So "indefatigability" would have to stay. He scrutinized the lines many, many times, considering and reconsidering whether he was making an awful mistake. Or whether the student who received the message would understand it, or even bother to look at it. There were so many "ifs," so many ways his wish would go unfulfilled. But the longer he delayed and second-guessed himself, the more certain he was of his mission. It might not work. He might even suffer severe consequences just for attempting. But failing to attempt would be the most humiliating defeat of all. It would mean EduForce, and everything it stood for, had won forever. He held his finger over the "*Submit Feedback*" button on the screen. He stared at the words again. He touched the button.

There, he thought. *Stick that up your algorithm.*

He abandoned any hope of getting work done that day and powered down his flexscreen. He knew this rare bout of unproductivity would come back to harm him. Reviewers were paid based on a ranking system, and they were ranked based on how many essays they graded per day. This one lost day of work would drop his ratio for the week, and the following week his paycheck would be smaller. The scholarly version of piecemeal, sweatshop labor.

Charles went to his bookshelf and pulled out a tattered paperback. The book was one of the few he had saved from the Recycling Purges. The title was *Border Patrols*. It was a thriller, almost fifty years old, and its spine held together with tape. It had been a book he bought and read while in middle school. It was about a poor, working father who becomes involved with a drug smuggling operation in southern California to get unapproved drugs from Mexico for his sick children. Charles had not been quite the right audience for the book when he read it. There were a handful of mild sex scenes and some rough language that shocked and titillated him. The car chases, interrogations, and gunfights had burned in his imagination. He had reread it every few years since then.

As he grew to be a better critical reader, and was exposed to the classics, he came to realize the novel was riddled with weaknesses, flat dialogue, and unbelievable characters. It was just not very good. But in Charles's personal canon, the constellation of books that deeply impacted him as a young reader, few novels had a greater impact on him. It was not the plot or the characters, but the moral core of the story that held him. Up to age thirteen, in all his reading experience, protagonists truly were "good guys" who did good things to achieve good ends. No one broke rules, or if they did, they were swiftly forgiven in light of the positive results. But in *Border Patrols,* the main character violated laws to protect his loved ones and mete out justice. As a young teen, Charles was stunned to learn the world did not always operate neatly. He could not imagine himself breaking laws, not even to save his family. So, the book buried itself into his consciousness, and every few years he reread it, each time recalling how the author had so swiftly pulled his moral certainty of the universe out from under him.

He turned to a random chapter in the middle—by now, he knew the book so well it didn't matter where he started reading—and entered the story. But after ten pages, he jolted upright at the sound of an alert from his flexscreen. An incoming message, then another. He climbed off the sofa and turned the screen on. The first message was from an unrecognized number. Had the student figured out his poem so quickly? Was this a reply? His heart leaped in his chest. Trembling, he opened the message.

> *I think we are "of a like mind," like you said. That poem you sent, "Tiger oh cat" was pretty easy.*

Charles was amazed. He had thought his puzzle would be too difficult. "Tiger oh cat." Two syllables, then "oh" for zero, then one syllable. Area code 201. Charles doubted one student in twenty thousand, a hundred thousand, could figure out a puzzle like that anymore. He read on.

> *I live in the Tiger oh cat. You must too. Within the Tiger oh cat, I am indefatigability territoriality. You?*

Indefatigability territoriality, Charles thought, counting syllables on his fingers. *Eight-seven. The student must live in Plex 87, too. What are the chances?*

Breathless, he hit "REPLY."

Me too.

Charles sent the message. He was floating, suspended in anticipation. Now they both knew they lived in the same Plex. Could they meet? If so, where? In public? If he was seen with a student—and there was not an inch of space inside the Plex that was out of range of a camera—then he would be fired.

He did not have a chance to follow up his message. About two minutes later, he received a reply.

Tonight, at indefatigability. Under the stars and behind the sun. North wall. Byron will be there.

Meet at eight, Charles reasoned. *But under the stars and under the sun?*

He thought about it. Under the stars, certainly. It would be dusk at that time. While he mulled over that puzzle, he opened the second message. It was a vidmessage, so he played it. The video featured a young man in a suit in front of a neutral background. The man, whose face was pleasantly nondescript, seemed poised between gentle smile and stern scowl. Charles played the vidmessage.

"Hello, Charles Winston. I am Mr. Chambers, your personal EduForce agent. You recently sent advanced feedback to a student in response to an essay prompt. Please be advised any extra-educational communication between students and teachers is expressly forbidden. All EduForce resources are to be used for solely educational purposes. Any deviation from the scripted educational process will be prosecuted. Thank you for your dedication to our students!"

Well, I'm on their radar now. But the thought thrilled rather than intimidated him. *I'm going to meet a student today, for the first time in sixteen years. We are going to talk about Byron. And I am going to break the rules.*

Three: Molding the Minds of America

EduForce claims to produce engaging lessons that are finely tuned to modern educational standards. Through celebrity testimonials, expensive advertising campaigns, and other forms of propaganda, they have brainwashed an entire generation to believe EduForce education is the only education. Exploring beyond approved materials is irregular, pointless, and dangerous. The rotten truth is that all EduForce products and curricula are bent toward five aims:

1) Create a permanent, semi-educated, shallowly skilled class of workers.

2) Segregate that class into inferior Plex colleges, distinct from the elite in their prestigious universities.

3) Promote a facsimile of critical thinking while in fact disabling critical ability.

4) Dissolve the autonomy of districts and states in education policy.

5) Make students into gullible, reliable consumers.

　　—The Trough, p.6

Jennifer refused to read *The Trough*.

　　She set the book on her desk and stared at it with contempt. *How could Melody bring that into my apartment?* she thought. If her mother found it, there would be trouble, no doubt about it. Probably a bilingual tirade, probably a backhand or two. She could hide it from her, but not forever. She was good at hiding things. She had hidden Melody for three months before her mother realized they were together. But then her mother found a package of cheese puffs in the kitchen she didn't recognize from any of her grocery orders. It had resulted in a lot of cursing and yelling and *¡Dios mío!* and a slap that left a bruise on Jennifer's cheek. The discovery of a book from Melody? Jennifer shuddered to think of the consequences.

They are not illegal, Jennifer told herself, but it brought little comfort. Books didn't need to be illegal. Between the financial incentives to Recycle and the social pressure to get rid of every shred of paper in a household, keeping an old book was seen as foolish.

Jennifer had fond memories of Recyclings as a child. Gathering on the lawn outside the Plex, everyone piling books into a dumpster, the scent of cotton candy and barbecue wafting through the air as music blared on the PA system. She had carried an armful of old paperbacks that had belonged to her recently deceased great-aunt and tossed them in with the rest, then went to claim her reward—two dollars per book, twenty-four dollars in total. It was terrific fun, especially for the children of the Plex. Now there weren't Recycling parties very often anymore, maybe once a year, but nearly every book in Plex 87 was gone. A sense of great community pride came with that accomplishment. Everyone knew Recycling was good for the environment.

Back to work, she thought. She could shut out distractions like few of her peers could, which made it all the more frustrating when Melody and *The Trough* lingered in her awareness.

She stared at the words on the screen. Her words. Her finest words. Her application essay for the Scholarship.

> *In the following essay, I will elucidate three primary reasons why I, Jennifer Calderón, should be awarded the extremely prestigious honor of The Merit Scholarship. My first reason is that I am a very hard worker and will do all of the modules and edugames assigned to me in university. My second reason is that The Universities are very prestigious and honorable and I would like to be a part of them. My third reason is that I am a Perfect Five. That is my most important reason. I will now explain to you each of these reasons in the following essay.*

It had taken her nearly a week to compose the introduction, and she beamed with pride as she stared at the words glowing on her screen. *They are good words,* she thought. Not just the words, but the arrangement, was what she admired. The crisp clarity, the neat ordering of thought, the strict adherence to essay format: in so many ways it was the embodiment of a perfect essay. One sentence in the introduction—"That is my most important reason"— deviated a little from essay format. But she thought it was such an important idea it needed to be highlighted. It might be the little nudge that would set her essay apart from the other, more pedestrian ones.

Still, she knew it needed work. The vocabulary could always use improvement. Vocabulary replacement was the easiest way to accumulate points. She replaced "hard worker" with "diligent pupil." She deleted "do all the modules" and wrote "complete all required modules and assessments." Jennifer double and triple checked her sentences to be sure they were error-free and complete.

Jennifer sat on her bed, leaning against the wall. She folded her arms in satisfaction as she chewed a Perk-Eez. The essay introduction was certainly the finest thing she had ever written. And she had not yet begun the body paragraphs. She trembled with anticipation at how grand the final piece of writing would be.

Still, *The Trough* sat there on the desk, inert and threatening.

I have work to do, she thought. *So much work now.* But work could wait. It would wait. She would be bad instead. There were different kinds of bad. There was getting drunk on the roof with Melody bad, and there was reading a book bad. The second one was worse.

She opened *The Trough.*

The Trough: A Manifesto

If you were born in the twenty-first century and went to a public school, you have received an education that is worse than worthless. Your education is toxic. You have been force-fed a steady diet of lies, misdirection, and false hope. You have been led to believe that by completing your education, you will be a better thinker, a better citizen, and a better employee when you enter the job market. You have been told studying and working hard and performing well on your exams should be important to you because these challenges will one day reap benefits to you in your career and your life. You have been told knowledge is power. You have been lied to.

She tried her hardest to read, but her eyes seemed to slide all over the page, unable to latch onto any words or meanings. She had little experience reading on paper. The screens she read on were responsive and user-adapted. On EduForce reading programs, if her retina lingered on a word, a definition and synonyms would appear. If she reread a line, the screen would offer to read it out loud to her and to analyze the sentence. These words, however, sat limply on the page. Jennifer could not remember ever exerting so much effort to make sense of a paragraph. And it did not adhere to proper paragraph structure: topic sentence, supporting sentence, and three supporting details. Whoever Charles Winston was, he was clearly not a skilled writer.

"Hi Jennifer," Carlita interrupted. Jennifer snapped the book shut and shoved it under her pillow. "You have a new message. Shall I—You have two new messages. Shall I read them to you?"

"Sure."

"Both are from Melody Park. The first one says, 'Oh shit oh shit oh shit. Jen pick up I have the most grip news ever to tell you.' The next one says, 'Never mind I'm coming over. See you in a minute.' Do you wish to reply?"

The flat electronic tone of the doorbell sounded in the house.

"No, Carlita. That's fine. Thank you."

"Always a pleasure. By the way, I notice twenty-four days ago, you ordered a new mod-skin for your flexscreen. Would you say you are satisfied with your purchase?"

"Uh, yes. Bye, Carlita—"

"Can I interest you in other accessories for your flexscreen or—"

"No, 'lita. Go away."

The AIPA paused briefly. In the silence, the doorbell chimed again.

"Very well," Carlita said in a tone Jennifer thought was a little terse. "Enjoy your day."

Jennifer opened the door and Melody burst in. She had dyed her hair in the few hours that had passed since they last spoke. Now, slightly off center, a pink streak cut through the black.

"You get my message?"

"Yes, I just—"

Melody held her hands up.

"I. Found. Him. I found him!"

"Who?"

"Him! The guy! Charles Winston."

"Oh."

"And we're going to meet him!"

"What?"

"You sound like a Neanderthal. All monosyllabic and whatnot," Melody said.

Jennifer shook her head, still confused.

"The book I gave you. You read it, right?"

"Part of it," Jennifer said after a moment's hesitation. Melody threw her arms in the air.

"What are you waiting for?"

"It's been less than a day! I can't read a book in that time."

"Pshh."

Jennifer sighed. Sometimes when Melody got like this, she would blurt out idea after idea, racing from one thing to the next, reading entire books and talking to strangers and planning booze and drug binges on the roof of the Plex. Jennifer became frustrated, unable to keep up with her lover's imagination and whim, but she had to admit those manic outbursts were what she loved most about her.

"All right," Jennifer said. "Start from the beginning. What happened?"

"I wrote some bullshit essay for some bullshit I-don't-know-what module. Something about family dinners and I just let it rip, really let loose. I can't stand those petrol ideas, all Norman Rockwell families around the table, man in a tie and wife in an apron. It's 2051! So, I guess I let it rip too much and my essay got flagged, which happens a lot but what the hell. Except this time, I get a message through EduForce from some reviewer. You know how we usually just get the score back and that's it? Well, this guy read the essay and wanted to ask me about it. I quoted Byron which really threw him off. Anyhow, he was all secretive and made up a clever code to help me figure out where to meet. Seems like a smart man. Except I don't know if *he* knows that even though he didn't tell me his name, the EduForce message included it, so unless there are multiple Charles Winstons out there, all working in education, I think we will get to meet my new hero!"

Jennifer shook her head, struggling to keep up.

"What if it's a trap by a serial rapist or something?" Jennifer asked.

"I knew you were going to ask that. That's why you're going to come with me. We can back each other up."

"And who is Byron?" Jennifer asked. When Melody had said she quoted him, her attention had perked up. Quoting any source in an essay was an instant points boost. Maybe this Byron guy would be a help.

"Oh, Byron is this poet from the 1800s. But don't worry. He's old but not petrol. The man could express the whole spectrum of human emotion."

"Okay, you've used that word twice now. 'Petrol.' What is it and where did you get it?"

Melody rolled her eyes, then her shoulders, as if her entire body was coursing through with energy and she could scarcely stand still.

"Some of my British friends."

"You have British friends?"

Melody smiled devilishly.

"I have many mysterious friends. Some of them are British. 'Petrol' was what they called gasoline way back when."

Jennifer wrinkled her nose.

"That's terrible. Why would you name anything after gasoline?"

"Exactly."

"But no one uses gasoline now!"

"Exactly."

Jennifer shook her head.

"Well I'm not calling anything 'petrol.'"

Melody shrugged.

"That makes *you* petrol. Irony. Wanna fuck?"

As Jennifer started to wave her off, Melody stepped in and hooked her arm around Jennifer's waist. Her mind squirmed and wriggled in a frenzy of anxiety, frustration, and sexual excitement. Melody's breath was hot and smelled like grape soda. Her muscles trembled under the fabric of her T-shirt. Jennifer pushed her away.

"I'm not in that kind of mood," she said. "I'm working on my essay."

"You're always working on that thing. But opportunities like this..." Melody's voice was husky with suggestion. Jennifer had seen her like this only a few times, and Melody was always irresistible and irrefutable in those times. But she didn't listen, either.

"The Scholarship is important, Mel. It's everything. It is my only way out."

"I hate when you call me Mel. You know that. It sounds like the name of the Plex Head Plumber or something."

"You don't hate it."

"I do. And to prove it—Bruno?"

"Yes, my dark queen?" Melody's AIPA asked in an unholy growl. Melody often put Bruno on the speakers and observed people's reactions. She could send the voice to her earpiece, instead, but rarely did. Jennifer had never understood her ideas on privacy and discretion.

"Next time Jennifer calls me 'Mel,' I want you to tear out her spine and devour it. Got it?"

"I do not think I can do that, my liege. I would like to notify you that the package of Fresh 'n Free Cleansing Wipes you ordered has arrived at your home. With it comes an offer of half-priced Fresh 'n Free Intimate Lubricant. Are you interested?"

"Go back to sleep, Bruno," Melody said.

"As you command." Bruno fell silent.

"Sorry," Jennifer said, softening her voice. "I'm flattered, I just—"

"Flattered? Fuck you. We've been together almost a year and you treat me like I just asked you on a first date? If you don't like who I am or how I am, tell me. I can find someone else who isn't busy with her head buried in her ass."

"I'll be on the roof tonight." Jennifer hoped for conciliation. "I promise."

"You'd better be," Melody growled, striding from the room. Jennifer thought she was safe, but Melody turned and faced her one last time. "You know, that scholarship is a waste of time. You'll never get it. There are fifteen universities left in this country offering fifteen spots to a couple thousand people just like you. Probably smarter than you and nicer than you and better qualified than you. I am here. I am real. I am so goddamn real you don't even understand, but you keep looking at that screen and typing your stupid words on there. For no reason."

Then Melody was gone. Jennifer was shaking, so she went to the bathroom and popped a couple of Relax-Eez from their foil pouches and gulped them down with a mouthful of lukewarm, sugary coffee. She sat on the edge of her bed, staring at the huge screen.

They are good words, Jennifer thought. *Melody is wrong. She was just mad. I will write the most extraordinary essay the Scholarship Committee has ever read.*

Still, doubt lingered. Melody was right. There were indeed only fifteen spots for thousands of entrants. Each of the remaining universities in the country—all top tier, elite schools—offered one full scholarship each to a public-school student. It was the only way for an ordinary citizen to afford university. To earn the Scholarship, students had to submit all their academic histories, be video interviewed, and write an application essay.

Jennifer knew her academic history was her strength. She was a Perfect Five, a true Perfect Five, the nation's first. She had practiced for the video interview for dozens of hours, studying tutorials and mimicking the eye contact, gestures, and intonations of the interview coaches. For the essay, however, she was on her own. She had always earned the highest scores on her writing, but this was different. This was something a human being would read, someone with prejudices and beliefs and attitudes. Surely, an essay that earned a high score from a computer could also earn a high score from a human reader. She hoped. She hoped she was as smart as she thought she was. She hoped she was as smart as the people in the news said she was, though she would never be as smart as her mother wanted her to be. And she hoped she could do this extraordinary thing, to be accepted into a University.

University was not college. Everyone could attend two years of Plex College for free. "College Opens Doors," or so said Geraldine Barfield in her videos. And free college opened doors for everyone. But Jennifer was certain she was not everyone, that she was destined for something greater. How many Perfect Fives were out there, after all? Even the ones with asterisks. Perhaps a hundred? No one had ever done what she was doing. If that did not usher her to the top tier of Scholarship candidates, she did not know what could.

With that thought, Jennifer hopped off the end of her bed. *I can do this. Will do this,* she thought, and she said aloud to her AIPA, "Carlita! I want to finish this essay."

"Are you referring to the essay for the Scholarship?" Carlita replied from the speaker.

"I certainly am. Let's pick up where I left off. Write this: 'The first reason I should be given the Scholarship is because I am a diligent pupil.' No, wait. Replace 'given' with 'awarded.'"

The words appeared on her screen, and Jennifer smiled.

"Damn, this is going to be good," she said aloud, then, "Don't write that down, Carlita."

Carlita obeyed, and soon Jennifer was building the essay, word by word, sentence by sentence, paragraph by paragraph. She knew where each part belonged, how each part fit into the overall scheme and structure of the essay. Writing essays was more difficult than answering questions in the edugames. It was not as much fun and there were a lot of parts to remember. But it really came down to remembering the right essay formulas and constructing each sentence to fit that formula. Topic sentence restating the argument, another sentence further explaining the topic sentence, three sentences providing an example or giving an illustration, then a concluding sentence restating the topic. Deviating from that would not only endanger her score, it would also be a senseless waste of time. The essay formulas were easy to follow. She simply had to plug the right words into their places.

Writing the introduction had required several days. But the body of the essay was finished in a few hours. By that time, much of the Perk-Eez and Relax-Eez had worn off, leaving Jennifer feeling dull and listless, but the sense of accomplishment at finishing the Scholarship essay overpowered that. She thought of setting it aside and continuing it another day, but the productivity swelled her with a sense of momentum. *What better time than now?*

"Carlita, what time is it?"

"Five thirty-eight," the AIPA responded. Jennifer went out to the kitchen to make another pot of coffee. If she was going to the rooftop with Melody to meet this kooky old writer tonight, she figured a little more caffeine was necessary. As the coffeemaker gurgled, Jennifer found the anger at Melody rising in her. *This is dangerous. Could ruin my chance at the Scholarship. Mel has nothing to lose. She doesn't care. Why does she drag me into these ridiculous stunts?*

Because I like it. A little bit.

Gurgle, gurgle. Drip, drip. Jennifer's emotions rushed up at her, and she fought to keep them down.

I could lose everything if we get caught. All of my work, lost, because of Melody's crazy ideas. She's going to destroy my future.

But Melody never gets caught. I would get caught, but not Mel.

The admiration and resentment mixed and swirled inside her, and as she poured sugar and milk absentmindedly into the cup of coffee, she could not decide exactly how she felt.

Everything in my life makes sense. I know where everything stands. I know what is good and what is bad and what to do and when to do it. But then there is Melody. The one thing I cannot control or even understand, and I keep her too close to me.

Jennifer shook her head. Thinking like that caused her discomfort. She slurped the coffee. It was time to get back to the essay. She replaced a few words and smoothed over a few awkward wordings she had formulated in the first draft. But Jennifer was good at writing essays and she knew it. She didn't even really need drafts. She had so perfected the insertion of words and sentences into proper slots that, by following the plan, the essay was basically complete.

No need to delay, she thought. *This essay is ready. It will never be better.*

She asked Carlita to bring up her application for the Scholarship. The long document appeared on the screen, along with all the filled-out and checked and rechecked fields. Jennifer had reviewed the entire thing so many times, she knew she had double and triple checked every line. A sudden urge to action coursed through her. On every page of the application, she told Carlita to submit, and one by one, the pages disappeared and whisked away across the currents of wireless internet connecting the country. Finally, Jennifer came to the last page, the essay, and as confidence swelled within her, she told Carlita once more to submit, and the essay vanished into the ether.

The screen sat blank. Her application was done. Her head hurt.

The time was five fifty-eight, leaving about two hours before the meeting on the rooftop. She did not want to go, but it was for Melody. And Jennifer dreaded when Melody was mad at her. Melody was an intensely close friend and an equally intensely harsh enemy. *Go up, meet the old man, come home, and Mel and I can be good again.* The meeting, then, would be a peace offering, nothing more.

Jennifer was tired and thought to take a nap, but as soon as she lay down, her flexscreen bleeped an alert.

"Jennifer, how are you?" Carlita asked. Jennifer groaned. *When will she drop these annoying manners?* she wondered.

"Fine. Tired. New message?"

"Yes. You have a new message from Geraldine Barfield at EduForce. I am sorry to hear you are feeling tired. Would you like to purchase some more Perk-Eez, the little yellow pill that—"

"No. Just play the message."

Maybe I'm being too mean, Jennifer thought, but before she had any longer to reflect on her treatment of an artificially created persona, the video began to play. It opened with the EduForce logo, the company name in block letters, superimposed over the Earth. EduForce's jingle played, the notes coming in rapid-fire tripled eight and quarter notes: *Molding the minds of America. Molding the minds of America. Molding the minds. Molding the minds.* A children's choir sang the lyrics, and with a few flourishes of harps and horns, the tune caused a feeling of warmth to wash over Jennifer. The logo and the jingle had been part of her life for so long they permeated down to the nerve tissue in her brain and spine. The rhythm, the tune, the timbre, the graphics, the logo, all these elements did their familiar, comforting work in Jennifer's brain. She knew whatever was coming next in the video was important, was meant for her, would make her better and smarter.

The shot zoomed into and through the center of the logo before fading into a woman sitting before the camera in a tasteful office chair. She wore a sand-colored suit and pearl earrings. Her moussed hair sat obediently in place. Her fingernails were lacquered and pointed. *She's pretty,* Jennifer thought. Not sexy, but pretty, confident, and self-assured. Put together.

Barfield smiled for the viewers, her teeth brilliantly white. She stood and paced around a staged office, never breaking gaze with the camera as she spoke.

"Welcome. I'm Geraldine Barfield, here with an important message for you from EduForce. Here at EduForce, we have promoted the most innovative technologies and forward-thinking ideas in education. The best teachers in the country all work for us, here, at EduForce, and for you, in your homes. When I first began this company as a little startup business twenty-five years ago, I was trying to make a small difference in the world. I wanted my company to make its mark on education, whatever that small effect might be. Today, EduForce *is* education."

Jennifer smiled. Even though she deleted most broadcast messages, she always watched the ones from EduForce. Partly, she wanted to stay informed about the company that dictated so much of her life. But mainly, she admired Geraldine Barfield and loved watching her speak. She admired the woman's confidence, her poise, her fierce determination that did not diminish her femininity. Jennifer aspired to be as bold and successful as Barfield in her career, whatever it might be. The Scholarship would be the requisite first step on that path.

"Since I founded EduForce, I have guided this company from a small, independent-minded teaching company to the world leader in teaching resources. And as proud as I am of all I have done, it is time for me to move forward."

Anxiety fluttered inside Jennifer. Was Barfield retiring? She seemed so strong and vibrant. Jennifer could not imagine a world in which Barfield was not guiding her.

"I am here today to announce my candidacy for President of the United States. President Alvarado has been a great ally of EduForce and of America's young people. Now that his term is expiring, we must continue making America the smartest and most productive nation in the world. I urge you all to watch your NewsFeeds closely in the coming weeks. America's future is its present, and the present is in the hands of you, our nation's young people. I am confident that with your EduForce education, you will know the right choice to make."

The camera shot zoomed out, the smiling Barfield in the center, before the screen went black. Jennifer did not dare move. Geraldine Barfield, her idol. Businesswoman, educational reformer, and soon, president.

There would be no naps now. Jennifer tidied her room and checked some messages and NewsFeeds to keep her mind busy until the meeting. As she did, she found herself humming the EduForce jingle. *Molding the minds of America. Molding the minds of America. Molding the minds. Molding the minds.*

Four: The Rooftop Readers Club

The Plexes are models of efficiency and environmental consciousness. Single-family homes, heated with gas or oil? Gone, along with the rest of our shameful, wasteful past. With exteriors built of solar-harvesting tiles, the entire building powers itself with no fuel needed. Low-level Plex workers sort organic and recyclable materials from general trash. Gone are the days of shoving everything into a plastic bag and leaving it in a can on the street. Cremation of the deceased is standard practice, saving thousands of acres of land that only a generation ago were filled with corpses and tombstones. In the Plex, even death is green.

So, for environmentalists, the move into Plexes was a victory. But the sudden advent of Plexes did not occur because of care for the Earth; Plexes have always been a tool for the ultra-wealthy elite to keep the populace in big boxes. Contained people are easier to control. And easier to forcibly educate. If it is not already evident, the work of EduForce, the might of corporations, and the wishes of the elite function in concert.

> *—The Trough, p.49*

Charles felt like a fool, standing before his mirror trying on clothes, trying to pick an outfit that would create the proper impression. Professional? Casual? Friendly? Serious? He tried on shirts and pants and ties, almost chose a jacket and tie, then reminded himself the meeting would be after dark, and the mysterious student would probably not see or care what he was wearing anyway. In the end, he chose khakis and a plaid shirt, but no tie. It was the sort of arrangement he might wear if he was at school but not teaching, perhaps chaperoning a dance. Not that there were dances anymore. Or chaperons. Or schools. Or teaching.

As he sat in his apartment all afternoon and evening, whittling at the time until 8:00 P.M., he wondered if perhaps there was no student. Perhaps EduForce had set a trap for him. *You sound paranoid. Realistic, but paranoid.* He pushed the thoughts away. He was going on that roof. *But to do what?*

He played out the meeting in his head. He would introduce himself. She would introduce herself. Then what? He thought of bringing something to discuss, but what? Family pictures? There was no way he wanted to talk about family. *The Trough?* He would love to share his book with someone, to find even one person who could understand what he had written and why he had written it but doing so might be coming on too strong. *Hi, nice to meet you, I wrote a book!* He decided not to share his own work, not yet. But another book, perhaps?

He pulled his Robert Frost poetry anthology from the shelf, and it fell open to a familiar page. There sat a few photocopies of a poem he had wedged in years earlier for his introduction to poetry classes. Charles nodded. *This will do nicely.* He also took a stack of filler paper and a handful of ballpoint pens from a closet. He doubted she had her own paper and pens. Few people did anymore. In a single generation, loose-leaf paper had gone from classroom staple to a cringe-inducing symbol of waste and excess.

By 7:40, he had dressed and paced around his apartment and passed an hour or two distracting himself on the Internet. He had run out of ways to procrastinate, so he decided to leave early. He slung a bag over his shoulder, containing the pens, paper, and Frost anthology. Under his arm, he tucked his flexscreen. This was the most vital. Without it, he was never getting to the roof.

Charles walked down the corridor, adopting as casual a demeanor as he could. *Just walking to the grocery store,* he told himself, hoping his body would project the lie. *Just an old man, not the least noteworthy, going for a stroll around the corridor.*

Finally, he arrived at a staircase. It was marked "*Maintenance Only.*" Charles peered down the hall to be sure he was alone, then unrolled his flexscreen and turned the screen on. Instantly, a file called "*Prospective Brunch Menu*" appeared. Charles was about to open the file when a woman and her daughter approached. He bent down as if to tie his shoe. He smiled and nodded as they walked past. Then, when they were out of sight and Charles was alone in the hall, he turned the screen back on and opened the file. It did not contain a brunch menu but had been labeled that way to shield the contents from possible hackers.

The file was an ultra-high-definition image of an eyeball. A light-blue iris gazed up at Charles, magnified in such detail that the striations of brown and gold radiating from the pupil were like a sunburst around the perimeter of a black hole. Charles held the eyeball image over the retinal scanner. The magnetic lock released, and Charles pushed the door open.

For as long as retinal scanners had been the standard of security in Plexes, the black market for images of approved irises had thrived. It was illegal but commonplace. Charles thought back to his days in high school and the ease with which he obtained his first fake driver's license to buy beer. The eye file Charles had used on the maintenance door was relatively cheap; it had cost him fifty dollars and would likely have to be replaced before the year's end, when Plex Security identified the iris as fraudulent and blocked it. But there were always new eyes to buy; if a low-level maintenance worker wanted to make some money on the side, he could go to an eye dealer, have a quick picture or two taken of his eyeballs, and leave a few hundred dollars richer. The eye dealer then sold the image dozens of times until Plex Security caught on.

But eye files were the crudest and cheapest tricks. They fooled maintenance doors and the average locks on a Plex apartment door, but banks, businesses, Plex control rooms, or any other secure site would have more advanced iris detection. To counteract this, eye dealers—depending on their skill level and willingness to take risks—could manufacture customized contact lenses, eyeglasses capable of projecting a holographic eyeball, and in some cases, actual prosthetic eyeballs.

In a highly publicized case the previous year, infamous bank robber One-Eye Wasserman had been arrested after stealing nearly $70 million from various banks over a period of years. He proudly went by the name One-Eye because he had paid a surgeon to replace one of his functioning eyes with a highly sophisticated prosthetic, one so realistic not even medical students could distinguish it.

For over three years, One-Eye Wasserman held the news media's attention as he siphoned money from one financial institution after another. He became the Jesse James of the Plex world, except his robberies were bloodless and he never touched a dollar in cash. He would lean into the retinal scanner of a bank window, make a few commands, and funnel millions of dollars into his account. Since there were no municipal police in the Plexes, the bank hired Silent Strike, a private investigation and security corporation, to track him down. They finally caught Wasserman by tracking down the model for his prosthetic eye—a disgruntled, ousted bank executive who had sold the likeness of his eyeball to an elite eye dealer as vengeance against his former employer.

Charles had to climb five flights of stairs to get to the topmost floor. Though he exercised three times a week in the Plex gym, usually riding the elliptical machine, there was nothing quite like huffing and straining up an eternal set of winding stairs. By two flights, his thighs were beginning to burn, by three, he was short of breath, and by five, his forehead was slick with perspiration. *Are you too old for this, old man?* he thought. Now, with no more stairs to climb, Charles stood facing a metal door with the words *"Roof Access. Maintenance Only"* on a red plaque. Again, Charles opened the door with the eye file.

The air at dusk was warm. It startled Charles; his Plex was set to sixty-eight degrees all the time, a perfectly neutral temperature for him. The humidity and airflow rate were all regulated, as well. Even for someone who had grown up in the pre-Plex days, outside air was strange and uncomfortable. *You are getting too comfortable and soft,* he reflected. *The Plex mindset is getting to you.*

Charles admired what a feat of engineering the Plexes were. The roofing material under his feet, as well as the siding material that comprised the exterior walls, was solar-harvesting. Lined along the roof were rows of twelve-foot wind turbines, spaced far enough apart that the blades would not collide, not even if they had to twist in a windstorm. By using every inch of the roof space for generating power, the Plexes were entirely self-sufficient for electricity. Massive batteries, located in a dozen equidistant places on the roof, stored energy at times when little was in use. Whether it was sunny or overcast, and whether the wind was gusting or calm, the batteries held enough energy for almost a month of use in the Plex. Charles admired the soft whir of the turbine blades and the hum of power under his feet.

A female voice cut through.

"Get down!"

Charles ducked. *Cameras,* he thought. Even with two sets of locked doors, the Plex security systems surely had video monitors on the roof, as well, watching for his face or an identifiable portion of it to transmit to Plex Security. He crawled behind the massive solar batteries and wove among the columns holding up the turbines. He moved toward the voice.

"Over here," the voice said. She sounded near, perhaps only ten feet away. Charles was nearly at the north wall of the Plex. For another moment, he allowed himself the fear and self-doubt—what if he was crawling into a trap? *Well if you are, the hook is already in your throat. There is no going back now.*

The woman, in her early twenties, sat cross-legged next to a battery-powered lamp. Her hair was black with a streak dyed pink, just off the center of her part. She wore jeans, which had not been fashionable for many years. What was most striking about her, aside from the pink hair, was her T-shirt. A shoe line called "Shocks" was among the most popular in the nation. In the advertisements, young people would leap toward a basketball hoop or take off from the starting block or break for second base, and when they did, lightning bolts shot from under their feet and electrocuted everything around them. At least, this was what Charles picked up from advertisements and occasional references in student essays. The girl had a "Shocks" T-shirt, black with neon-green letters, but she had peeled the "Sh" from the shirt and used fabric paint to write "Schlocks" instead.

"Nice shirt," Charles said. "What are you doing, sticking it to the corporations?"

"Nice shirt yourself," she replied. "What are you doing, chaperoning a school dance?"

How does this woman know what a school dance is? Charles wondered. *How does she know about school?*

Charles pointed to the sky.

"Under the stars. That was easy. I knew to find you somewhere up here, on the roof, by the north wall. But behind the sun?" he asked. The woman tapped the metal casing she was leaning against, a block five feet high and fifty feet wide. A solar battery. Charles smiled. *She is smart,* he reflected. *Smarter than me.*

"I'm Charles," he said, stepping forward and offering his hand. She did not shake it.

"Mister Winston," she said.

"How do you—"

"It was on your messages. You aren't as good at sneaking around as you think."

Charles grunted. The girl shook his hand.

"You're a teacher, Mister Winston?" she asked.

"I am. I was. I suppose."

"I'm Melody Park."

"Do your parents know you're up here?" Even though she was an adult, it was reasonable to assume she still lived with her parents. Without passing her Achievements, she would not be hired anywhere. And then during college, she would most likely stay at home too. It was very rare for children under the age of twenty-five to live on their own. *This is all the doing of our education system. The infantilization of America.*

"Foster."

"Ah."

"They're cool. Cool, that's what your generation said, right?"

"Yes. I suppose I should ask if your foster parents know you are up here. If anyone knows you are up here. Because of the risk—"

"Just you and me," Melody replied. "And, well..."

Melody motioned to the shadows, and another young woman crept into the circle of light of the lamp. She was tall and lean, like a runner, with flat, straightened hair and designer clothes. She looked as if she had been plucked from an advertisement.

"This is my girlfriend, Jennifer," Melody said.

"Hello," Jennifer said tentatively. Charles felt betrayed, irritated about the unexpected company.

"What is this, an ambush? The more people up here, the bigger the risk."

"I know," Melody said. "But Jennifer is a great student. Much better student than me."

"Oh, stop," Jennifer said.

"What makes you such a magnificent scholar?" Charles said.

"Excuse me?" Jennifer's face twisting in indignation.

"What makes you so great?"

"I'm a Five," she replied.

"A Five?"

"A Five. A Perfect Five. The only one. Maybe you're aware—" Jennifer snapped.

"In that case"—Charles shook his head—"I feel pity for you. You may be an outstanding student, but you cannot be very smart."

Jennifer stood.

"I told you this was a bad idea. I'm logout. See you later."

Melody grabbed Jennifer by her pants leg and pulled her back down.

"Give him a chance."

"No. This man is—what was the word you used—petrol. He'll get us caught and I'll lose everything."

"I won't get you caught," Charles said. "I haven't much experience in sneaking around, but I am not a fool."

"Well, I do know about sneaking around," Melody said. "I know where the cameras are on this roof. There's an area right here, about twenty feet across, that none of the surveillance cameras will see. I come up here to drink all the time. I don't need to, of course. I'm an adult. But I like to think. Actually, to not think. To drink and not think."

"And what about that camera at the entrance?" Charles asked.

"I used to be neighbors with a guy who worked in the camera room for the Plex. He told me not all the cameras record all the time, you know, for budget reasons, and rather than remove some of the cameras, each one goes offline for about an hour a day. They just don't tell people which ones and where. Well, I know for a fact that camera is off from 7:55 to 8:55 each night. Also 7:55 to 8:55 A.M. I think he told me because he wanted me to take him up here and screw him. Which I did not."

"Well, then," Charles said. "Melody and Jennifer. I must ask. Why are you here? What do you want?"

"Let me tell you," Melody burst in. "I have not taken a single learning module that taught me a single thing I wanted to know. I will tell you what happened. See, I am not a good student. Like, at all. I don't do the work if I don't see a point in it, and I don't see a point in any of the assignments I have to read or the essays—excuse me, extended prose constructions—I have to write. So, you know, I don't pass many modules, or if I do, it's barely. But I'm not dumb. I. Am. Not. Dumb. I just couldn't find anything interesting to me.

"Then, with my last foster family, we moved into an old apartment where the tenants had left a lot of trash. That included a book—a real, actual book. The cover was ripped off and it was water damaged, but it was the first actual book I'd ever seen, other than in a museum or in a video. So, I kept it. It was called *Anthology of British Romantic Poetry*. I thought it might have been love poems or something, but mostly it wasn't. So, I read the whole book in one night. That was a year and a half ago and I've probably read each poem in that book ten times since then. So, I know there's more out there, more than these goddamn modules and videos and assessment scores.

"And it's the same thing with writing. Every essay they make us write is boring. It's stupid. A retarded monkey could answer those questions. There is no thinking, no creativity in them. So, I write my own poems and my own essays and my own word puzzles just because. I do them in the 'Enter Text Here' boxes on the Module Tests. I create. I destroy. I thought there was something wrong with me until you found my essay and sent me the message. I want to know everything."

Charles could only stare at Melody. Her eyes glistened in the lamplight. Her cheeks were flushed.

"Jennifer?"

Jennifer shrugged, then leaned back against the battery.

"I'm here because Melody asked me. I thought it was a bad idea. I still think it is. Do you want to know what I did today? I submitted my application for The Scholarship. It was a couple hours ago and—"

"Don't do it," Charles said.

"Excuse me?"

"The Scholarship is a fraud. A lure. Worse than the lottery. You'll never win."

Jennifer set her hands to her hips.

"Who do you think you are? You know nothing about me. I bet you haven't seen me on NewsFeed. I am The Perfect Five. I am not just anyone. I am different, and I am going to get the Scholarship and go to Princeton or Harvard or Stanford or somewhere. Are the chances bad? Yes. But I like my chances. I would pick me over any student in this country."

"No, it's just..." Charles began, but then he hung his head. Someday he would talk to Melody and Jennifer about their education, but not today. Not here, after just meeting.

He looked into the eyes of the two women. Melody's, eager and hopeful, begging for connection. Jennifer's, hard and cold, glaring with defiance. Charles understood now how long it had been since he had seen a student's eyes, and how much of teaching, real teaching, was transmitted through the eyes.

He pitied the actor-teachers who had to share knowledge through a camera lens. A real teacher—a real teacher who was very good and was sensitive to his or her students—could receive everything clearly through a student's eyes. They could read a "Thank you" or "Fuck off" or "I am trying to pay attention, but I haven't eaten in a day and a half," all in the eyes. They could tell the difference between "I don't understand but am too afraid to ask for help" and "This is really easy, and I already understand, but I'll humor you anyway." Maybe the eyes were the windows to the soul, as the old saying went. Or maybe they were the keys to the soul.

Two impulses battled in Charles's mind. His instinct, compassion, and experience urged him to proceed. *They need you,* the impulse said. *Do not let fear win.* But the other impulse was fear, fear of EduForce and the Plex and of losing his only source of income. *Leave. Go back inside and forget this meeting happened,* the fear said. *You are too old and need this job too much. Besides, you can't change anything.*

"Let's go," Jennifer said, standing. "This old man is going to waste our time or get us in trouble, and I can't afford either."

"Wait," blurted Charles. "I—I have a poem."

"Show me!" said Melody.

He pulled the book from his bag and opened it. He handed a copy of the poem to each of the women. Jennifer looked at it uncomfortably, but she sat down again.

"I don't like reading paper pages. They give me a headache."

"Chill," Charles said. "It isn't long. It's just a short poem."

Melody squinted at the page.

"What kind of a poem is this?" Melody asked. "It's too short."

"Not at all," Charles said. "A poem can be as short or as long as the poet makes it."

"*Fire and Ice,*" Jennifer scrunched up her nose. "This isn't like any article I've read before."

"That's because it isn't an article. It's a poem. It's called *Fire and Ice,* by Robert Frost."

"We don't read poems," Jennifer explained.

"I read poetry," Melody said. "But nothing that looks like this."

"Would one of you care to read it out loud?" Charles asked, but suddenly, both Melody and Jennifer fell silent. Charles smiled. Even in a class of two friends, reading aloud makes even the boldest bashful.

"I'll start us off," he said. "But I can't do all the work myself."

So, he read:

> *Some say the world will end in fire,*
>
> *Some say in ice.*
>
> *From what I've tasted of desire*

I hold with those who favor fire.

But if I had to perish twice,

I think I know enough of hate

To say that for destruction ice

Is also great

And would suffice.

His voice died out, drifting over the wall of the Plex and dissipating over the surrounding sea of concrete. Melody uttered a thoughtful, "Hrm."

"I don't get it," Jennifer said.

Four words Charles knew well. It tingled him, thrilled him, to hear them. Every student's mind presented its own challenges, obstacles, and talents. The path from "I don't get it" to "I got it" was never the same from one student to the next.

"Well, Frost is setting up a contrast—" Charles began.

"Like a compare and contrast?" Jennifer interrupted eagerly.

"Sort of."

"So. this is a compare and contrast essay!" Jennifer declared.

"No," Melody said. "It isn't an essay. It's a poem."

"I don't get poems."

"That's why we're here," Melody explained.

"Melody," Charles said. "What is the contrast Frost is making in the poem? It's right in the title."

"Between fire and ice," she replied.

"Good. Now, Jennifer, how are fire and ice different?"

She rolled her eyes.

"One is hot, and one is cold. Is this really all poetry is?"

"Hardly. But this is how we start. Find the obvious, then use it as a light to guide you through the obscure."

"I don't get that, either," Jennifer said. "Is that a metaphor?"

"Yes," Charles said. *She can identify metaphors but doesn't know what to do with them. But why would she?*

"Ah, okay."

"So back to the poem," Charles continued. "Frost sets up a contrast, between fire and ice. Then what does he say in the first two lines?"

Jennifer reread the lines.

"Oh! I think I get it now. I read an article about the different ways scientists think life on Earth could end. Asteroids, diseases, things like that. So, Frost is talking about different theories about planet-wide extinction. Maybe global warming or a new ice age. Right?"

"Could be," Charles said after a diplomatic pause. "But fire and ice are also metaphors."

"There are more of those things?" Jennifer said.

"Always," Charles said. He wondered if Melody was going to participate soon. She simply sat and stared at Jennifer, watching her struggle. *Is she letting her flounder? Letting her try to succeed? Daydreaming?*

"Metaphors are a pain in the ass," Jennifer sighed.

"That expression is, itself, a metaphor," Charles said with a smile. But Jennifer frowned.

"It is? I don't get it."

How is this girl a Perfect Five? Charles wondered.

"Let's look at what each one represents," he continued. "He says it right in the poem. You're right, the poet is talking about how the world ends. But he isn't talking about scientific theories. He says, '*From what I've tasted of desire, I hold with those who favor fire.*' So, what does fire represent?"

After a pause, Jennifer said, "Desire?"

"Right! Now, ice?"

"Wait," Jennifer interrupted. "Why does he think desire will be the end of the world? Isn't desire love and isn't love good?"

"Well," Charles said after a pause, "he doesn't say. That is left up to the readers."

"But isn't good writing supposed to back up statements with explanations and reasons? You can't just say things and make the reader figure it all out. This must not be a very good poem."

"It's actually considered a profound poem. Simple on the surface but with a lot to say. The rules you are expressing only apply to essays. And I shouldn't say that because essays can come in a variety of forms, as well. They only apply to essays that are written for tests, which aren't really a form of writing at all. A poem isn't going to come out and say what it has to say."

"Why not?"

"That's what makes it a poem. You have to think *into* the poem."

"Whatever," Jennifer said, crumpling her copy. "This is dumb."

"It is not dumb. It is difficult," Charles replied. Jennifer made to throw the paper ball over the edge of the roof, but Charles grabbed her wrist. It went against every one of his teaching instincts—never, ever touch a student—but for an instant his anger and fear overruled his sense.

"Now that, that would be dumb," he growled.

"No one will care," Jennifer replied.

"Wrong. Most people won't care. But if someone who works for EduForce finds it, they'll become sharks with blood in the water. Sorry, another metaphor. They'll know something prohibited is taking place, and they will swarm over every inch of this building. They'll find us, and I'll lose my job and you will lose your academic standing. Melody, do you want to take a crack at this poem?"

Melody stretched her legs out in front of her.

"Fire is desire and ice is hate. Too much desire can destroy the world. So can too much hate. The poet has experienced both desire and hatred, but he doesn't seem to be very judgmental about this. I mean, he says 'suffice' for hatred, like, 'yeah, sure, this will be fine.' He's not warning or begging or threatening destruction. He's sort of telling us, 'Look, there are two ways the world can be destroyed.' The two ways seem like opposites, like fire and ice, but it doesn't really matter which one ends up destroying the world because, well, The End."

Charles sighed.

"Succinct, but that's about it," he said, then he fell silent. The two impulses still battled within him, but he knew which side had won. *You are a foolish old man and you are going to get caught,* he told himself.

"Do you want to learn?" he asked. "I mean, really learn, not watch vidlessons and play edugames?"

"Yes!" Melody said.

Jennifer shrugged.

"You have a lot to lose, I know," Charles said. "As do I. But we also have a lot to gain."

"Teach us," Melody said. "Please."

Charles could not recall a time in his career, ever, when he had heard a student say those words aloud. *This is how bad things have become.*

"I'll tell you what," he said. "Keep your copies of the poem. Don't show anyone. Take the night and think about them a little more, and tomorrow we can meet and discuss."

"Could I borrow your poetry book?" Melody asked Charles. "I want to read some of Frost's other poems. See what he's all about."

Charles held the book to his chest and hesitated. But the thrill at having a student request more material was too strong. It always had been. He knew he was a sucker for any student who showed even a little interest over the minimum. He handed her the book.

"Be careful with it," he said. "Don't lend it to anyone. Don't let anyone else see it."

"Obviously," Melody replied.

Then Charles handed each of them several sheets of paper and a pen.

"Bring these with you and write down your thoughts about the poem. Any thoughts at all. Writing about what you read will help you clarify your feelings."

Both girls looked at the pens and papers with disdain and confusion.

"What do we do with these?" Jennifer asked.

"Write," Charles replied. "Keep the pens. I have hundreds."

"My mother might know how to use them," Jennifer said. "I don't."

Charles was nonplussed.

"You don't know how to use a ballpoint pen?"

Jennifer shrugged.

"Like I said, my mother might. Is it like typing?"

"Forget it," Charles said. "Just reread the poem. I'll figure something out."

"Are you mad?" ventured Melody.

"Not at you," Charles said. "Not at you. Look, I cannot promise much. I cannot change your home life. I cannot change your inborn intelligence. I cannot change what you do with what we learn. I am a teacher, and what I have to offer you is learning. I will give you an education, the best one I can in our circumstances. I can show you stories, real stories, not the EduForce manufactured ones. I can show you poetry. I can show you how to think."

"I can think—" Jennifer protested. Charles held up his hand.

"No. Not yet. But you will someday. We cannot change the world, or the system, but we can have our own little reading club right up here. How often? Once a week at 8 P.M.?"

"Every night," Melody said. "Every night, we are up here, reading and writing. I want to know absolutely everything there is to know. About everything. I stare up at the stars—well, I'm guessing it's the stars behind all the haze and beyond all the lights—I stare up at the stars and all I can think about is how vast space is and how far is the distance between the Earth and the Moon, and how that is only a fraction of the distance from the Earth to the Sun, and the sun is huge to us, but is just an average star, and the numberless billions of stars and galaxies out there, unimaginably far apart, except we can see them, we can see them, Mister Winston, and the light they spit out way back when Julius Caesar was emperor is just now hitting our eyes. I want to know everything from that time up until now."

"All right, then," Charles said. "Every night at 8 P.M. The Rooftop Readers Club."

"That sounds retarded," Melody said.

"Please don't use that word," Charles said.

"Fine. That strikes me as retarded."

Charles rolled his eyes.

"What if we can't make it?" Jennifer asked. "How do we let one another know?"

"Are you coming back?" Charles asked.

"For now."

"Good," Charles said. Melody would be his eager student, waiting to learn. There was usually one in every class. Jennifer would be his recalcitrant one, daring him to teach. There was almost always more than one in every class. "We do this the old-fashioned way. Same time, same place, each day. No messages, or EduForce will catch on."

Even though the messaging system was independent of EduForce, EduForce monitored everything at all times. Or at least they were capable of it, which was essentially the same.

"We won't use flexscreens or any electronics EduForce can track," Charles continued. "Just paper."

Jennifer grimaced.

"So much paper! Don't you know Recycling is good for the environment?" she said.

Not wanting to antagonize her further, Charles said, "I know you are trying to be green, but—"

"In the Plex, even death is green," Melody said. Her words stunned

Charles, because they were not her words. They were his, from *The Trough*. He could barely form his next question.

"You—you read my book?"

Lonely hope, like that of a shipwrecked sailor seeing his first companion in years, surged in him. His words had spanned the gulf of time, distance, and censorship to reach a reader.

"What did you think?"

"Incredible," Melody said. "Is all of what you said about education true?"

Charles checked the time on his flexscreen. It was 8:48.

"We don't have time to talk about it now," he said. "But yes, all of it is true."

"Will you tell us about it?" Melody asked. As she and Jennifer stood, Charles saw their hands intertwine.

"Someday," Charles said. "Someday."

Five: Eres Me Todo

As families moved into Plexes, they often had to greatly reduce their possessions. Books are one of the most space-consuming luxuries in a household. With the rise of the flexscreen, paperbacks and hardcovers were obsolete. In the fervor of environmentalism and efficiency, the Plexes sponsored 'Recyclings.' Families could bring all hard copy reading material—books, magazines, old papers, anything with paper—to The Recycling and deposit it. Recyclings were parties, with food and music and tossing books into dumpsters. Participation was not legally required, but it did not need to be. The social pressure was far more effective. Plex managers didn't force people to hand over their books at Recyclings. They made Recycling so much fun that people looked forward to relinquishing the books.

EduForce was instrumental in the Recyclings. They didn't destroy books. They destroyed the desire to read. And Geraldine Barfield didn't kill anyone's intellectual curiosity. She simply fed that curiosity with distractions, advertisements, and vapid games disguised as educational tools.

> *—The Trough, p.51*

Jennifer could not slow the thoughts and emotions that overwhelmed her mind as she lay on her bed, staring into the dark. She took a pair of Relax-Eez, but the usual soporific effect never took hold. She tried to control her breathing and sort her feelings. *I am angry. Angry at Melody, even though she grabbed my hand at the end to try to make things right. Angry at Mr. Winston. That arrogant old man, acting superior to everyone. I bet he wasn't a Perfect Five. Probably wasn't even a Four. Angry at Mamá, who I lied to about going out and lied to about coming home. Angry at—angry at me. Why am I letting myself get pulled into this mess?*

Jennifer thought of the things she had done with Melody—drinking on the roof, stealing from the convenience store, sleeping together in Jennifer's bed while her mother sat fifteen feet away in the other room, oblivious. They had been irresponsible, slightly illegal, and against Mamá's wishes. But they were nothing that could threaten Jennifer's future. This was different.

You like it.

The thought rolled into Jennifer's head.

She tried to expel it, to deny it, to pretend it was someone else's thought. Useless.

"*Bonita?*" called a voice from outside her door.

"*Sí,* Mamá?" she shouted back.

"*Aquí, aquí.*"

Jennifer sighed and slung her legs off the side of her bed. She trudged out to the living room. In the dimmed light, the frame of her mother, Rosa, was draped on the threadbare brown sofa. Jennifer thought the sofa was ugly, but it had belonged to her father.

A glass of sparkling water sat in Rosa's hand, effervescing quietly. The hand holding it was bony and witch-like. Rosa stared ahead into empty space, not acknowledging the entrance of her daughter. Jennifer kissed the papery skin of her mother's cheek. She felt the stiff bristles of cheek hair against her lips.

"I love you, Mamá."

"*Eres mi todo,*" she replied, but Jennifer shook her head.

"No, Mamá. Practice the English."

Rosa sighed.

"You are my everything."

"I know, Mamá. How was your day?"

"Long."

It had not been a day, but rather thirty consecutive hours of shifts. Eight hours of data entry for the Plex 87 Loading Dock, twelve hours in the laundry for their block, and ten hours vacuuming the endless corridors. Sitting, standing and walking. Coordinating all of the shifts between the different employers was an act of balance. Working them all was one of endurance.

"You should sleep," Jennifer said.

"You like that, no?" Rosa said, a trace of ire in her voice. "I know you waiting for me to go to sleep. Then you go with your Melody again."

"No, Mamá. I have to study."

"*Mentirosa!*" Rosa replied. Now her eyes moved. They fixed on Jennifer, who found herself unable to move or speak. "You a liar! You tell me you go to the gym, but I know you go with Melody. To lie to your mother? A shame."

It was true; Jennifer had lied to her mother about going to the gym. It had been the last thing she'd said before going to shop for jeans with Melody at what Jennifer called the "grandma pants" store. She had lied again upon returning a little over an hour later. When Rosa asked why she did not appear sweaty or flushed, Jennifer had said the gym was too crowded, so she went for a walk. The smell was most likely something her mother imagined. But this had happened the previous week. *Is Mamá losing her mind?* Jennifer wondered. *Or just too exhausted to know what day it is?* She tried to feel pity for her.

"Can I go study?" Jennifer asked. Those words were her only escape.

"I get another shift at the laundry from Maria. She still sick, so she ask me to work. I go back in six hours. It give me a little time for to sleep and to eat."

"You should. Can I make you some food?"

"Make yourself some. Look at you. Too skinny," Rosa said, little more than a skeleton herself.

"*Sí*, Mamá. I am too skinny. If I make us sandwiches, would you eat one?"

Her mother's eyes moved back to their fixed position, straight ahead.

"No, no. Are there any empanadas left? The ones you made last night?"

Jennifer frowned in thought. *I did not make empanadas last night.* Then she remembered she had made a batch over a week ago, but they had long since been eaten.

"No," she replied, not wanting to tangle with her mother about food, memory. or time. Rosa did not question her further. The bubbles in the sparkling water were diminishing.

"I have some good news," Jennifer went on. "I applied for the Scholarship today."

No motion in the eyes, nor the hands. It was as if she said nothing at all. Jennifer went on.

"I won't know for a few weeks. The application has to go through many steps. But I wrote a very good essay and I think I have a strong chance."

Still nothing. The urgency in Jennifer's voice began to rise.

"I really want the Scholarship, Mamá. I need it. I could go to a really great university, not just the Plex 87 college, and not only will I get an elite job when I graduate, but I will bring such great honor to our family. I want to win it for you, and for *Papá*—"

"*Cállate*. Do not speak of your father or of what he would want. You did not know him."

With a remarkable effort of her arms, legs, and back, Rosa stood. She pushed away from the sofa, set the glass of water on a table, and shuffled wordlessly to her bedroom. The door clicked shut behind her, and Jennifer knew within half a minute, she would be deeply asleep. Her mother had three states: deeply asleep, dimly awake, and briefly, violently furious. Jennifer hoped for her to be asleep as much as possible.

Papá.

He was not in the room, yet his presence hung in every corner and crevice. Jennifer did not believe in ghosts, but if she had, she would believe her father was haunting them. He had not even lived in current apartment—the Calderón mother and daughter had moved through five different units in the past twenty years—but he was there, nonetheless. He was in the furniture and the food and the silences in conversation.

Jennifer had no definite memories of her father. What she did have was a photograph, a single, printed photograph, like from the old days when people had them developed. The photograph showed Jennifer, at the time three or four years old, grinning and standing on the railing of a stairwell. Her father, Juan Carlos, stood behind her, smiling too. Rosa had taken the photo, standing on the landing a flight of stairs below.

Juan Carlos had also left his daughter a couple of short videos. In them, he said: *Know that I love you more than anything. I wish I could be with you and I want you to be proud of your Papá. I did it all for you.* When Jennifer had been old enough to understand those words, she had asked her mother. What did Papá mean? Then Rosa spilled all to her daughter.

Her father, Juan Carlos Calderón, had been a Federal agent tracking down a drug cartel. He used his old connections in Colombia to bring down some of America's and Colombia's worst drug lords. He had been highly decorated, even received a medal and a handshake from the American president. But his heroic acts had made him many enemies, and he recorded the videos while he knew he was being pursued by them.

He had been found shot in a storage shed in El Paso, leaving a toddler-age daughter and overworked widow to live on without him.

Rosa, when she was not worked to the point of exhaustion, and when she was not treating her daughter with suspicion and resentment, would tell Jennifer stories of Juan Carlos. She told her about his arrests and the criminals he had caught. She told him about the long hours he worked for the family, and the nice apartment they had had when first married, a corner unit in the Plex with two real windows overlooking the solar train tracks. She told her about his gentle spirit and the sweet words he would speak to Jennifer in her crib. These stories, the pictures, and the videos he left created a composite of Juan Carlos Calderón as real and vivid as any flesh and blood man.

Jennifer retreated to her room. She thought of the poem Mr. Winston had forced her to read. *Fire and Ice. What sort of nonsense was that?* she thought. But the nonsense would not go away. As she lay on her bed, staring at the ceiling and waiting for her thoughts to spiral into darkness, the words of the poem, the memories of her father, and the anxious anticipation of the Scholarship swirled around inside her head. Her breathing slowed. She needed no Relax-Eez.

Melody is the dark spot in my brilliant life. My beautiful, beloved, dangerous dark spot.

The strange image appeared in Jennifer's mind. She had never had one like it before. She marveled, and feared, what was happening to her brain.

When Jennifer woke, her mother was gone. Her extra shift at the laundry began at four in the morning, and she had slipped out of the apartment she worked so hard to pay for and had so little time to spend time in.

Jennifer rose and went to the kitchen to make coffee. Her mother's glass of sparkling water still sat on the arm of her chair, now completely flat. *I will not become that. This is why I need the Scholarship.* She had read profiles of all the past Scholarship winners, many of whom had gone on to high-paying administrative positions. They worked as doctors and lawyers, as designers of EduForce's curriculum and solar tech experts. In some cases, they even managed entire Plexes. Jennifer did not know precisely what career she wanted. She could decide after she began her university education. But she knew she wanted a good job. Not like the ones her mother took.

Jennifer opened the refrigerator. Takeout leftovers, an unfinished gallon of milk, and a few other dribs and drabs of old snacks populated the shelves. *We should get a proper grocery order in,* she thought as she took out the milk. *She and I can make a real dinner and sit and eat it. I'll use a recipe.* But she knew it would never happen. When would her mother ever be around? And when was the last time either of them had cooked or followed a recipe? Jennifer had done it before, and she found it easy. Following directions always came easily to her. Spending time with her mother did not.

I have to get to work.

Work. Always more work, and after the previous day's announcement, an entire new Achievement Level. Jennifer had been on track to complete Achievement Level 15 in a few weeks or months, but now she would need nearly a year, depending upon how many modules and assessments were in the new level. She did not question the need for it. She had heard somewhere human knowledge was increasing exponentially. It made sense that another Achievement Level was needed. Besides, if Geraldine Barfield insisted it was necessary, it was necessary. Still, she was disheartened. And then there was the threat to The Perfect Five. Every question she answered endangered her record.

She spent the rest of the day in her room, working through module after module, watching videos and answering questions and playing edugames. Percentage point by percentage point, she crept closer to completing Achievement Level 15. She waited for a message from Melody, but by that evening had heard nothing. *She's in one of her moods again,* Jennifer decided.

So, she went to the Plex Your Muscles, the Plex gym, and ran a few miles on the treadmill. Then she showered and went home. Still nothing. Her mother was still working. She could not remember if she was on a vacuuming shift or if her next shift at the Loading Docks had begun. She stopped trying to keep track. She was twenty-three years old and could take care of herself. She could order a meal and adjust the temperature in the apartment and knew how to contact Plex Alert, the emergency services subcontractor. She was practically an adult.

THAT NIGHT AT eight, Jennifer walked to the roof entrance. After a glance to be sure the corridor was empty, she waved an eye file over the retinal scanner, then pushed the door open.

She crept to the usual spot behind the solar battery, where Charles was speaking in hushed excitement with someone in a Quarantine Suit. She paused and listened. The voice was Melody's.

"The entire thing?" Charles said. "You read the entire Frost anthology in one day?"

"One night, actually," Melody said. "I reread some of my favorite ones this morning and then wrote a couple this afternoon."

"Wrote?"

"Sure."

"Could I—could I read them?" Charles asked. Jennifer approached them.

"Are you sick?" Jennifer asked.

"Are you well?" Melody replied.

"Why are you wearing your Q-suit?"

The Quarantine Suit was bulky and made of some impermeable material; Jennifer wasn't sure exactly. She did know Q-suits were airtight and covered the entire body and face, with antibiotic and antiviral filters around the mouth and nose to prevent the spread of disease.

In the Plexes, one of the primary dangers that first made itself known was the spread of illness. In contained environments where the same air and water circulated for thousands of people, an airborne illness could become an epidemic in little time. So, all Plex residents who had been diagnosed as contagious were legally required to wear the suit until the infection passed, and anyone with even so much as a cold was strongly encouraged to wear one, as well. The fear of infection grew so great for some that they would wear the Q-suit all the time when leaving the apartment, and only the intervention of a psychologist could break a patient of the neurosis.

The problem with Quarantine Suits for the Plex security was they obscured too much of the face for the recognition software. So, each Plex resident had his or her own unique suit. When the suit was distributed, Plex security programmed and embedded an identification chip that the software could read upon scan.

Melody removed the hood and visor.

"Don't you ever want to be somebody else?" Melody asked.

"Huh?"

Melody extended her hand.

"Tonight, I am Miss Beverly Hammond. Pleasure to meet you."

She took Ms. Hammond's Q-suit, Jennifer remembered. The old neighbor who had died. Of course, this was a crime, as Melody's actions were tantamount to identity theft.

Jennifer shook her head and could not suppress a smile.

"You're twitchin'," she said, "but I love you."

Charles made a confused expression.

"Twitching?"

"No, twitchin'," Melody said. "As in crazy, out of control."

The confused expression did not go away.

"Moving on," he said, "Jennifer, Melody was about to show me her poems."

"Oh, I can't," Melody replied. "No, I put them in a text box for an essay on the water cycle or something. I don't know. It was the only place I had to write."

"I must find both of you some place to write that can't be seen by EduForce. I wish I could teach you writing by pen and paper, but that would take months. I don't even know how to teach it."

"Well, show me," Melody said. She sidled up next to Charles, and Jennifer felt a pang of jealousy. *Why would I feel that?* she wondered, but she moved over and sat next to them.

Charles drew a sheet of paper and a pen from his bag.

"Recite your poem to me, if you remember," Charles said. "I'll write it down for you. Watch my hand as I work."

Without preamble or shyness, without even an *ahem*, Melody recited:

> *"I looked upon the falling snow*
>
> *And wondered where my life would go.*
>
> *The whipping wind and seething storm*
>
> *Revealed to me my psyche's form.*
>
> *My spirit's basking in the sun*
>
> *But beware it when the winter comes."*

Charles nodded and grunted approval. He handed the sheet to Melody.

"See? Your words. You created that."

Dizziness swept over Jennifer. She had always thought of Melody as "creative" or "different." But to have these words, these images in her, she seemed almost superhuman. Jennifer herself tried to think of a phrase or description that would suit her feelings.

"Melody," she finally said, nearly choking on the words, "that was...really good."

"Thanks," Melody said, bowing her head shyly. It was a gesture Jennifer had never seen her do.

"You managed the meter well," Charles said, "and did a decent job with the rhyme, though you cheated a little in the last couplet. Still, we aren't here to dissect poetry. Not yet. I want to thank you for having the courage to share. For taking the words and images from your heart and your mind, speaking them aloud, and allowing me to record them. It has always been an honor for me to be a part of a student's creative process."

"Twitchin'," Melody said.

"Did you have any other poems?" Charles asked. Melody lowered her eyes.

"One. But I don't want to share it. It's about Jennifer."

Jennifer tingled with wonder, fear, and disgust. She thought *Melody wrote a poem about me!* and *How dare Melody write a poem about me!* simultaneously.

"Very well. Some secrets perish when exposed to the world. Let's begin. I've brought a story for today. Since I know paper reading is difficult for you, I'll read the story to you and we'll discuss it. The story is called *The Hunger Artist*. It is by a German author named Franz Kafka."

Irritation gnawed at Jennifer. Melody did not have any trouble reading on paper. Only she did, yet Mr. Winston treated them both the same. *This is why the video modules are so much better than this old man. Those are personalized for me, and Melody's are personalized for her.*

Yet she listened as Charles told a story of an artist who starved himself, which for some reason was entertaining to people. Then the public stopped being interested in public starvation, but the artist kept starving himself. Then he had some sort of confession at the end. It was all horribly confusing to Jennifer. She followed the words and the plot well enough, but she could only articulate her confusion with a single question.

"What was the point of that story?" she asked. "What was the main idea? The lesson?"

"Not all stories have main ideas or lessons," Melody said.

"At least real stories don't," Charles added.

Jennifer's annoyance at the pair increased.

"What do you mean, 'real stories?'" she asked.

"Real stories by real writers," Charles explained.

"I've read lots of real stories."

"For your modules?" Charles asked. Jennifer said yes. "Then they aren't real. They are sham stories created by EduForce."

Jennifer folded her arms.

"I don't believe it."

Now Melody folded her arms.

"You would if you had read his book," she said.

"All right." Charles held his hands up in a sign of truce. "Jennifer, tell me one story you read recently."

"Fine. *The Education of Marla Mackenzie.*"

"I don't know that one. What is it about?"

"I read it a couple of weeks ago. A girl is living in a Plex and she wants to sneak out and live in the forest. Her friends and family tell her to stay but she disobeys and sneaks out. She hears a lot of scary sounds in the forest and so she returns home."

"That's it?" Melody said.

"Yes, that's it," Jennifer snapped. "You would have read the story too if you were following your modules. It's a good story with a clear message and symbolism."

"What is the symbolism?" Charles asked.

"The sounds in the forest. They symbolize the danger outside of the Plex."

Charles paused.

"That's—that's not quite how symbolism works."

"Oh yeah? Well I got the question correct on the assessment. Obviously." She stood abruptly. "Stop treating me as though I'm stupid. I'm the smartest one here and both of you are trying to make me feel stupid."

Charles held his hands up again.

"I'm not trying to do that at all. I greatly respect and admire your achievements in your Achievement levels—"

"That is a lie," Jennifer yelled. Melody motioned her to quiet down. If she shouted loud enough, distant audio recorders might pick up her voice.

"That is a lie," Jennifer said again with more restraint. "You even said in your damn book my education is worthless. 'Worse than worthless. Toxic.' That was what you said. So, don't insult me and then lie about it to make me feel better."

"I just want you to understand that—" Charles started, but Jennifer threw her hands up.

"I'm logout. Mega-logout."

She stomped off and slammed the roof entrance door behind her. *I am smart,* she thought. *Why am I wasting my time with them? With the old man and Melody, my Melody, my dark spot.*

A WEEK PASSED. In that time, Jennifer refused to go to the roof or speak to Melody. Yet a strange feeling undercut her anger. Curiosity. It was not a feeling she readily recognized. She had only ever cared for her assessment score, but the content was not interesting or important. Everything she had learned, from her earliest modules to the present day, was simply fuel for her quest to maintain The Perfect Five.

But now, she found herself thinking about the words of Charles Winston, and even of Melody, though she was furious with them both. Not all stories have lessons or main ideas. Sometimes people write poems too personal to share. The stories in her modules were not really stories. So much of what she understood and trusted was being assaulted with doubt.

In that week, Jennifer underwent emotional turmoil unlike any she had ever known. Relax-Eez did nothing to settle her thoughts as she lay in the dark, asking herself questions she had never dared ask, never even thought to ask. *What if I am not smart? What if I have not learned anything, not one thing in twenty-three years? What if I am not in control of my education? What if knowledge is not power? What if I am just being used?*

During that week, Jennifer was unable to hold her focus on more than one or two lessons before the self-doubt returned. She had always been able to work no matter the conditions. She had worked through colds and flus, even though a bout of mononucleosis. She had worked through moving from apartment to apartment and through Plex construction taking place right in the hallway outside. But this reflection made her afraid she might lose her concentration and accidentally answer a question incorrectly, so she would stop. Her room, already comfortably messy, filled with used dishes and garbage as Jennifer's mind wandered far from daily obligations. For hours, she sat on the edge of her bed and let the thoughts flow around her. *Flow around me, that's a metaphor, I think,* Jennifer noted, feeling not so much pride as awe at the potency of a single image.

On the last day of that week of isolation, Jennifer reached under her mattress and pulled out *The Trough*. For almost an hour, she sat on her bed and stared at the cover. *Why is reading this so hard? Why is it so frightening?* Part of it was the act of reading on paper. Without popup definitions and synonyms, without interactive software and scrolling text, the words simply lay on the page, inert and forcing the reader to do all the work. But now as she stared at the plain gray cover, she began to understand her struggle was deeper than that. The last time she had tried to read Winston's book, the actual words had frightened her. She had not wanted to read them but had read them anyway. Jennifer could not recall the last thing she had read that was not provided to her by EduForce. In that stare-down, her thoughts moved from *why should I read this if I don't have to?* to *the main reason to read this is I don't have to.*

Jennifer opened to the first page. Already, the static page intimidated her, but this time, she vowed she would not surrender. After scanning over the first page she had read last time, she read on:

> *In 2038, in a routine data breach, a memo from the EduForce was leaked to the public. Here is an excerpt of that memo:*
>
> *"The newest set of NACS standards may not be perfect, but they are good enough for our purposes. As always, the timing is as important as the content. Every two years, EduForce needs to create new standards for new curricula, new modules, the whole line of products. The system only works if it keeps moving.*
>
> *"As I have noted in some of our Board meetings, I feel like not everyone in the EduForce Corporation has the right approach to these standards. There are still too many who cling to this outdated idea that each standard needs to be calibrated to the needs and ages of the students, and we have to be sensitive to regional and cultural differences. We've all heard the bleeding-heart bullshit. Look, these are the educational standards for public education. These kids aren't eating fine cuisine at a French restaurant; they're at the trough, and they will eat what*

is served to them. The trough does not have to be good, but it does have to be full. So, for the slower-moving members of your divisions—remind them of EduForce's goals."

These are the words of Geraldine Barfield, President of EduForce. This was an internal memo, sent to the members of the Board.

When this memo was leaked, you might expect a horrified public outcry. Here was the President of EduForce, the organization solely responsible for the education of our nation's children, speaking of 99 percent of those children like they were pigs, belly up to a slop trough. But the leaked memo went virtually unnoticed. Why? Because no major news networks reported on it. And the few independent ones who did said it was probably a typo, that Barfield probably meant "tough," because the standards are so tough and rigorous. A typo! Yet the populace has been force-fed this slop so long, they lacked the critical faculties to notice how they were being duped. And unless everyone starts waking up to what has been done to them by a few people with a lot of money and power, the American people will keep their faces shoved into the feeding trough for the foreseeable future.

The concentration Jennifer needed to read those two pages was extraordinary. She touched her hand to her forehead and realized she had begun sweating. The sweat was not just from exertion, however. It was also from fear. Geraldine Barfield? The woman was a hero to the nation's students. Her smiling, ageless face popped up almost every day before or after the video modules. Quotes about success and achievement, attributed to her, streamed through Jennifer's NewsFeed, as well as the NewsFeed of every student in the country. Jennifer had a hard time believing the woman whose face conjured up inspiration and encouragement could really be calling America's students pigs. Could be calling her, Jennifer, a pig.

And then, Jennifer realized the trough too was a metaphor. Not a beautiful image, like the ones in the poems Charles and Melody enjoyed. An ugly one, an insulting one. She started to understand. *Metaphors aren't just tricks authors put into their stories. Metaphors are everywhere. The better I understand metaphors, the better I'll understand everything.*

And at that moment, Jennifer decided she would give Mr. Winston another chance. Melody too.

She immediately sent a message to Melody, who did not reply. Jennifer was not surprised. After a week of silence, a little retaliatory silence from Melody was perfectly fair. At 7:45, Jennifer closed the door on her slovenly room and walked down the corridors of Plex 87. She walked the hall with confidence, even with excitement. As she walked, her limbs shivered with anticipation. She feared the reactions of Melody and Charles, but more than anything, she wanted to learn. To really learn.

She came to the maintenance door, scanned her eye file, and ascended the staircase. The air that night was hot and muggy. *Ugh. Weird.* She had only ever known one type of atmosphere in her life, and air was not supposed to be so warm or wet. Crouching low, she made her way to the usual spot behind the solar battery.

Melody was not there.

Did she forget? Jennifer wondered. Of course, she didn't. She would meet with Charles twice, three times a day if she could. She heard footsteps behind her. She snapped her head around and saw Charles.

"It seems our friend is late," he said.

Jennifer shook her head. "Melody is never late for things she cares about," she explained. "Never on time for things she doesn't."

"That's well phrased. Maybe there's a poet in you yet."

"Where's Melody?" Jennifer demanded. Charles shrugged, appearing casual, but Jennifer thought she detected some anxiety in his motions.

"She and I have continued to meet all week. Her appetite for literature is...remarkable. But where have you been? I thought maybe you had given up on me."

"Given up on *you?*" Jennifer asked.

Charles shrugged again.

"What we are doing up here takes courage. You have a lot to lose if we are caught. Do you think Melody realized this and got spooked?"

Jennifer rubbed her temples.

"No. No, nothing gets her spooked. She's just having one of her moods."

"Ah."

"She'll need a few days. Maybe a week. We can try then."

"How will you know?"

"She always sends a message when she's back. I know to stay out of her way."

"Ah."

"Mister Winston? I read your book. Well, part of it. I tried."

Charles smiled.

"Good."

"I don't know if you're lying about Geraldine Barfield, or maybe you don't know enough about her yet. But she is not who you say she is in that book."

Now, Charles folded his arms and glared back at Jennifer.

"You're probably right," he finally said. "I don't know if she is a monster personally. I only know what she has done to education. And what's she's done has been..." He shook his head. "Never mind. Let's give Melody until a week from today. Reconvene then?"

"Good," Jennifer said. "It usually takes her a couple days."

"See you then," Charles said before turning his back and walking away.

Back inside the Plex, Jennifer was not ready to return to her room. All the thought and confusion and excitement had caused much nervous tension to build up. Her legs twitched with the desire to sprint as hard as they could down the corridors. But running in corridors was against Plex rules. She knew she would never do that anyway. Instead, she went to the Plex Your Muscles, ret-scanned in, then went to the locker room and changed.

For an hour she ran on the treadmill, going at a steady pace. When her nervous excitement surged, she would increase the speed on the treadmill until it was as fast as she could handle. Her legs became a blur as she pounded the tread faster and faster, the soles of her sneakers only touching long enough to keep her upright. In those bursts of sprinting, her mind seemed to go blank for a few seconds, as all her attention went into the run. After twenty or thirty seconds, she was winded. Then the speed came down to a jog and her thoughts returned. A few minutes later, when the thoughts and excitement built up again, she sprinted.

Over and over, she jogged then sprinted, not with any preset plan or prescribed workout, but simply to run, to obliterate the stream of unceasing thought for a brief moment and to purge the energy and tension that never seemed to leave. Men sometimes stared at her, but on the treadmill she didn't care. She didn't care if they were staring in admiration or lust or curiosity or fear. On the treadmill, as in her academics, she felt dominant, invincible, unstoppable.

Later, at her apartment when she was exhausted, showered, and refreshed, she thought of sitting and reading a few more pages of *The Trough* before heading to sleep. *Unless Mamá is home. Then she will want "family time." Even if that means sitting in the living room not talking.*

Mamá was home.

Jennifer knew even before she unlocked the door with her eye. She heard the muffled sounds of furious cleaning inside.

Uh oh.

Jennifer opened the door and saw her mother with a wastebasket in one hand and a latex glove on the other. She was muttering to herself in Spanish as she stomped into Jennifer's room.

"Mamá!" Jennifer said. "What are you doing?"

Her mother whirled around. Her wild, burning eyes were ringed with dark circles. She appeared to be even more gaunt than usual. *She looks like a hungry animal,* Jennifer thought, amazed the image just popped into her head.

"Am cleaning. You such a pig."

Jennifer sighed and rolled her eyes. She liked when Mamá left her alone, and generally she did, but every few months, Rosa would come home from work ready to clean. Jennifer knew her mother did not drink, but when she got it into her mind to clean her daughter's room, Rosa moved with drunken fervor and unfocused intensity.

"Fine, Mamá. Do whatever you—"

"*¿Qué es esto? ¿Qué es esto?*" screamed Rosa, raising *The Trough* in the air and waving it. Her voice pierced Jennifer, who trembled. Her mother seemed like a madwoman, stomping around the apartment waving a book around her head, demanding to know what it was. Jennifer shrank back against the wall.

Rosa strode over to her. If she had looked like a hungry animal before, now she seemed to be like one moving in for the kill. She raised the book high over Jennifer's head and then brought it down, the spine smacking her daughter in the head, again and again. Each blow came harder, more brutal, than the last.

"*¿Un libro? ¡Un libro!*" she screamed.

"What's wrong with un libro, Mamá?" Jennifer cried.

Rosa did not pause once. Her words came in short bursts between her blows.

"I work three jobs. Work so hard for you, and you hide a book? We have to Recycle! This book could bring money to the family, but you hide it. You are so greedy. Always so greedy. When I had twenty-three years old, I already have a job and a baby. *¡Egoísta! ¡Perezosa!*"

Bruises began to form on the crown of her skull. Her instinct was to put her hands up and block the attacks, but she had been hit enough to know that fingers broke more easily than skulls, so she huddled with her face between her knees while *The Trough* struck her on the head. The blows were diminishing a bit, and Jennifer hoped her mother's fury was subsiding. It usually only lasted a few minutes. Or rather, the violence only lasted a few minutes. The fury never left her.

"Mamá. Mamá. *Perdóname, perdóname.*"

Forgive me. Forgive me. Jennifer had been using these words as far back as she could remember. They often stopped the beatings. But this time, they made Rosa strike harder. She mixed in several kicks too.

"Out!" Rosa screamed. "I no take care of a baby any more. Go with Melody. *¡Puta! ¡Puta perezosa!*"

Jennifer moved. She scurried out from under her mother's assault and into her bedroom, now clean and organized. She grabbed several changes of clothes and threw them into her gym bag, along with her most prized electronics. Of course, the wall-mounted screen would stay, but she had her flexscreen. Jennifer looked around. *Will I ever see this room again?* she wondered. She stuffed her gym bag, zipped it shut, and ran from the room and the apartment. The last thing she saw before the door slammed behind her was Rosa, short and bony and shaking with rage, hurling the battered copy of *The Trough* at her. Jennifer picked up the book, shoved it into her bag, and ran.

Six: The Point of Poetry

Reading is a complex activity that each person accomplishes a little differently. In their efforts to turn reading a set of testable skills, the framers of modern educational standards destroyed reading. Is it important for a reader to be able to identify a main idea in a piece of writing? Of course. Should a reader be able to read an unfamiliar word and tease out a meaning from its context? One would hope. But putting together these skills does not make one a reader. The standards took reading, dissected it, and reassembled it into a sort of zombie of reading—all the parts are there, yet it is not really alive. Students were learning a set of reading-related skills for tests, but were still, after everything, terrible readers.

—*The Trough*, p.22

What have I got to lose?

Charles had asked himself the question before sending Melody that first message. He had meant the question rhetorically, at first, in the flippant way that implies the correct answer was "nothing at all." *You only live once,* Charles thought, though as time passed, he reflected if he had even done that.

Framed photographs hung by his desk. Old photographs, printed on paper, relics. There were two. One was of a short, Indian woman, with glowing, dark brown eyes and an easy smile. She was standing on the beach in San Juan, her hair blowing in the breeze as the midday sun blazed overhead, a tiny white ball in an oppressively dark blue, clear sky. Charles remembered the vacation well. He remembered the wriggling feeling he had in his stomach the whole time, because while he and his wife, Shaaya, were doing all the fun and relaxing things tourists in Puerto Rico were supposed to do, he was not having fun, and neither was she. The wriggling feeling in his stomach was the awareness their marriage was disintegrating, and no vacation, no matter how nice, was going to save it. The photograph was at least ten years old.

The other photograph was older with Charles and Shaaya and two girls, young teenagers at the time. They were the Winstons' twin daughters, Tamra and Clara. The girls were heavily made up and their hair was pulled back into tight buns. Each wore a windbreaker. The family sat in a big chain restaurant, their table littered with plates and glasses. Charles smiled, remembering the exact moment the photo had been taken. *Right after dinner, but before the ice cream sundaes had arrived. God, the girls had waited months for that ice cream.* It had been a celebration of the girls' ballet recital, in which they had danced together in an excerpt from Tchaikovksy's *The Sleeping Beauty.* Their teacher had pushed and pushed them to excellence, forbidding them from eating desserts or staying up late talking on the phone to their friends. In the months leading up to the recital, all their attention was to go to dance.

As a result, their performance in the recital had been the greatest of anyone's in the dance school. No one could dispute that. And so, the night of the recital, Shaaya and Charles took the girls out for dinner and ice cream, and Charles had asked the waiter to take their picture in the moments before dessert. Charles smiled. There had been no wriggling feeling in anyone's stomach that night. The smiles on all four faces were genuine and joyful.

That, Charles thought, *is what I have to lose.*

When Jennifer stormed off the roof, Charles had thought it was the last time he would ever see her. It disappointed him she would give up so easily. He had known many students like her in his days in the classroom—high achievers who said and did all the right things to succeed but when faced with the least adversity crumpled. He knew her fate too. She would earn her score and go on to two years of Plex 87 College and then graduate and find a job and blend in with the remaining 99 percent. She might get more offers of employment or a marginally higher starting salary, but from the point of view of the ones truly in power, she would just become another unremarkable laborer.

So will every young person in this Plex. Once, I could look at young people and see future composers, lawyers, senators, quantum physicists, poets, and ambassadors. Now they are workers.

But while Charles was saddened Jennifer surrendered so quickly, he was also relieved. It was Melody, not Jennifer, whose writing had intrigued him. It was Melody, not Jennifer, who had that strange and beautiful spark of madness and creativity. It was Melody, not Jennifer, whom he wanted to work with. Yet most of his time had been devoted to Jennifer. Melody was not supposed to be his star student. She was supposed to be his only student.

With the old ways, Charles would have felt differently. All students, regardless of background or ability, would attend school together. School had been a place of convergence for everyone. An equalizer, a democratizer. Teachers had no choice in who was placed in their classrooms. Therein lay the great nobility of public-school teaching—a teacher served the community, not just the selected elite. This principle was also something Charles had explained to his friends who dismissed his profession. "Just get up and teach," they would say. "It doesn't sound too hard. Just stand up there and talk to the kids for a while."

But what they never understood was teachers were expected to help every student succeed, not just the bright and hard-working ones. This was why, despite his frustration with Jennifer, he hoped she would return, and he violated his own Rooftop Readers Club rule by sending her a message, asking simply if she was still in.

During the next several rooftop meetings, Melody examined poems and stories closely, and Charles saw in her a poetic and aesthetic intelligence unlike any he had ever seen. The way she not only understood but appreciated language marveled him. He wanted to recommend a hundred stories and poems, essays and plays and paintings and sculptures and films and all the things he loved and valued in the world. All the things that had been wiped out by EduForce, either through legislation, incentives, or social pressure. He wanted to open her to the world of beautiful art. He reminded himself during each lesson—one at a time. One poem, one story, one idea.

But she needed no motivation. He had never seen a student with such fervor for learning. Back when he taught, even the strongest students seemed to have a limit at which they had learned all they could learn for a day. And it was not like Jennifer's motivation, which was based purely on maintaining her Perfect Five. Melody's desire to read and learn seemed infinite. She was like a fire that consumed every bit of knowledge fueling her, and with each bit of fuel, her need grew larger and stronger.

But Charles had noticed at times, when he was reading a passage, her eyes would be fixed into the darkness. It was only a fleeting observation, like one of thousands a teacher made every day. But then the evening came when Melody had not been on the roof, and Charles met Jennifer, who said to him that sometimes Melody got in a mood. *Ah, the poetic temperament,* Charles reflected. He would give her a week.

His AIPA alerted him: "You have a vidmessage."

Charles powered on his flexscreen and opened the vidmessage. It was another video from young Mr. Chambers, his personal EduForce agent. His face showed that enigmatic expression, neither hostile nor welcoming, and yet both. The video played, and Mr. Chambers spoke.

"Hello, Charles Winston, Mister Chambers here. Do you remember me? I sent you a message recently regarding using advanced feedback to contact a student in response to an essay prompt. Please be advised any extra-educational communication between students and teachers is expressly forbidden. All EduForce resources are to be used for solely educational purposes. Any deviation from the scripted educational process will be prosecuted. Thank you for your dedication to our students."

Well then, Charles thought with an equal mix of fear and thrill. He was not surprised. He knew EduForce monitored everything he did. He was their employee. He would have to tread a little more carefully. Notebooks, binders, and piles of paper from years past lay sprawled around Charles. He laughed. Over the years, he had saved almost everything. Lesson plans, graphic organizers, sample essays, worksheets, articles, even notes from students. He did not know if he could use any of it anymore, but the memories these artifacts resurrected were vivid and potent. When he had lost his teaching job and begun to work for EduForce, he had filed them into boxes and stacked them in a bedroom closet. They sat there, largely forgotten, for sixteen years.

Now, in this deluge of paper and three-ring binders, he sought ideas for the next lesson, and for the lesson after that. He began to imagine a whole curriculum, a roadmap for a difficult journey with his class of two students. The last lesson had been a failure, but that had been his fault, not theirs. He knew he had assumed wrongly about their knowledge, interests, and abilities. The next lesson would be clearer, more concrete, more accessible. This lesson would provide an entry into poetry and imagination that even a student in 2051 could comprehend.

During the week, his queue of essays for EduForce grew longer and the warning notices accumulated. He spent an hour or two per day reviewing essays, but he worked without motivation. He figured he would work a few marathon grading sessions later. He had never procrastinated that way before. But he was giddy with this new love, which was really an old love, of teaching. The ideas for lessons buzzed in his mind. He envisioned the conversations that would happen, imagined the quiet "oh" students emit upon sudden understanding, and wrote questions designed to tease out new levels of comprehension.

Jennifer's problem, he realized, was she was an ideal EduForce-era student. She could classify and identify and crank out thoughts according to a formula. But when it came to making imaginative leaps—even small ones, like a simple metaphor—she was hopeless. Not hopeless. Charles always believed teaching depends upon hope, even a tiny sliver of it, that people could change. If you believed people never changed, why bother teaching?

For Jennifer to change, I have to change. I should have started with appreciating poetry, not mining it for meanings.

Charles had always loathed that term, "Poetry Appreciation." A squishy term. Even the word "appreciate" was insultingly bland and polite. *Poetry shouldn't be appreciated, it should be savored. Devoured. Ravished. Throttled. Seduced. Seduced by. Danced with. Enveloped in.*

The night before he returned to the rooftop, Charles had a dream. It was a recurring dream, one that pounced on him once or twice a year, particularly when his work for EduForce was not going well. He had the dream almost nightly after Shaaya left. In the dream, his daughter, Clara, was performing *tours jetés* around him. They were on the shore. Charles knew with dream-certainty it was Ocean City. Clara was young again, fifteen. She danced her routine to *The Sleeping Beauty,* but the music was in her head. Charles heard only the vacuum of silence. *Assemblé. Plié. Pirouette on demi-pointe.* As she glided over the beach, her feet moving so lightly as to not displace a single shell or grain of sand, Charles noted the tide coming in. He shouted for her to come back. No words came from his mouth. He waved and shouted but Clara danced in oblivion, the water rising rapidly around her ankles, lapping at her knees. As she danced, she drifted out into the sea. Charles ran after her, but she had drifted too far, and finally her head vanished below the waves. And then he too was under ten feet of water. Before him, Clara performed a perfect *grande jeté* in the aquamarine.

Charles woke. *The dream again.* Sometimes the details changed. Sometimes Clara danced in fire, not water. But in none of the dreams could Charles save her. He wondered why he never dreamed of Tamra, Clara's twin sister. Tamra had always taken after Shaaya, and in fact lived with her in the same Plex several hours to the north. Clara had always taken after Charles. And Charles had been the one to put her in Hopespring Home for Intractables. *The madhouse,* Charles thought. He knew it was not the strict truth, but it was truth enough.

"WHO ARE THESE people?" Charles demanded. As soon as he had pushed open the propped door and stepped on to the roof, he saw four figures sitting under the lamplight, not two. He stood still, fear making his legs like lead.

"Mister Winston, come over here!" Melody said, and Charles jogged over to the circle of light. Melody sat in her usual spot, leaned against the solar battery casing. She wore jeans again, and this time a decades-old T-shirt that said "PETA: People for the Eating of Tasty Animals." Charles remembered the joke from his youth, but what really puzzled him was Melody had said before she was a vegetarian. Jennifer sat cross-legged next to her, looking less miserable than usual.

Next to her sat a boy, younger than the girls, probably thirteen or fourteen. He was a skinny little white kid, with a thin neck and eager eyes popping out behind his designer glasses. Charles also noticed the kid wore brands most Plex kids rarely could afford. His pants probably cost his family two hundred dollars and his sneakers were easily four hundred.

Next to the kid was a big, hulking young man who appeared to be older than the girls. He looked down, as if embarrassed to be there with the others. His shoulders drooped, his hair hung over his face, and his mouth frowned with apparent apathy.

"The kid is Peter. He recently moved to our Plex," Melody said, indicating the younger boy.

"I'm not a kid," Peter said.

"How old are you?" Charles asked.

"Fourteen."

"You're a kid."

"He's smart," Melody said. "His family didn't live in a Plex until recently. They owned a house!"

Charles shrugged nonchalantly, but inwardly, he was surprised.

"And the other guy here is Jean Paul Alvarez," Melody continued. "I've known him for years. Bizarre, right? Cause I move so much. But when he lived with his parents, he lived in the old Plex I used to live in. Now he lives with his grandma, and I moved to be with my new parents, and here we are together again!"

"A pleasure, Jean Paul," Charles said, offering his hand. Hesitantly, Jean Paul shook it. Though his demeanor was languid and soft, his grip was forceful.

"Hey, you didn't shake my hand!" Peter said, and Charles offered his hand to the kid, who shook it with an eager pump.

"Melody," Charles said, "while you are generous to share your experiences with your friends here, were you perhaps confused about 'keeping these meetings a secret?'"

"You can trust these guys," Melody assured him. "I've known JP for years. And I've only known Peter a couple of weeks, but you can trust him. And since he went to private school his whole life, he might know more about poetry and stuff no one else knows!"

"Private school?" Charles asked.

Peter nodded and grinned.

"Since I was a baby. Yeah, we never had to do any of the stuff you guys do in your screen schools. That's what we called them."

"What do you mean?" Jennifer asked. Charles held up his hand.

"Some other time. Look, gentlemen, I had only planned on two students today, so you will have to share with Melody and Jennifer. All of us could get into a lot of trouble for meeting up here, so you can tell no one. Not your parents, not your girlfriends or boyfriends or best friends, no one. All I am trying to do with this club is expose you to a few ideas you might not have seen in regular classes. A few off-the-record things to read, a few different ways to write. You in?"

"Absolutely!" Peter said.

"Fine," Jean Paul mumbled.

"Okay," Charles continued. He had been standing, but now set his messenger bag on the roof and sat, facing the semi-circle of students. "Ladies, did you give some more thought to the Frost poem we read last week?"

"I did," Jennifer said tentatively. "I mean, I think I see what he was doing, with the whole compare and contrast between fire and ice. I don't understand why he could not tell us what he thinks about desire and hate. Just, you know, get to the point."

"Are you asking me what is the point of poetry?"

"Yeah. Yeah, that's it."

"Well," Charles said, scratching his chin, "people have been asking that for decades. Centuries, maybe. Some people think the only things worth learning are the things that will get you a job later. And those of us who are interested in beauty and art have never been able to mount a defense of art that satisfies them. We say, 'art is important because without it, we don't have a civilization,' and then the practical-minded folks pat our hands and slash our budgets."

"Woah. Deep stuff, Mister W," Melody said.

"Please, Mister Winston."

"But W is easier."

"Is it?" Charles asked. He had fought this same battle with students years before. Though he sounded fed up, inwardly he was bemused. "W is more syllables than Winston."

"I think we're getting off track," Jennifer reminded them. Charles nodded.

"So, poetry. Let me show you how poetry is valuable. You said anything that can be expressed with a poem can be just as well expressed in an essay."

"Well, I didn't," said Jennifer defensively, "but I agree."

"Okay," Charles said. "Have you ever been punched in the nose?"

"Me?" Jennifer asked.

"Yes."

"Never."

"Okay, then hit it really hard. Maybe into a door or something."

"Sure."

"Remember that tingling feeling in your sinuses, where everything is raw and stinging, like fireworks being lit behind the bridge of your nose?"

"Oooh, yeah," Jennifer said, nodding with memory.

"Good," Charles said. "Now, explain that feeling to me in essay form."

Jennifer sat silently.

"I can go on," Charles continued. "With a single image or phrase, a poet can share or reveal an experience in a way a thousand words of prose would struggle to accomplish. Write an essay about the vacuum of numb horror at learning a loved one died. Explain the first kiss with a true love.

Find me the main idea of biting into a fresh piece of honeydew melon. Reading and writing are more than the transmission of information. If we treat it that way, we become little more than hard drives."

Charles trembled. *Where is all this coming from?* he wondered.

"Yeah, Mister W! Er, Mister Winston. Keep going!" Melody said. Charles shook his head.

"No, I'm rambling like an old man today. I reflected on our first lesson. It did not work out as I had planned, to be honest. And the fault is not yours; it's mine. A poem challenges the reader. It dares the reader to enter. And rather than guide you in, I think I pushed you into a strange house, locked the door behind you, and shouted, 'Good luck!'"

Charles paused with a frisson of delight, power, and eagerness as eight expectant eyes gazed up at him.

"That was a metaphor," Jennifer said. She said it without confidence or joy, but Charles sensed she was seeking his affirmation.

"Yes," Charles replied. "What do you think it means?"

"He's saying that—" started Peter, but Charles held up his hand for silence.

"Let her respond."

Jennifer furrowed her brow, then looked away, then looked down. Charles noticed her fidget.

"That..." She started then after a deep, steadying breath, continued. "That means the poem is...is a house. And you were supposed to show us around the house, that is, to explain the meaning of the poem, or at least I guess to show us how to figure it out, but you didn't, and that's why we got lost—well, I got lost; Mel was fine—and by lost I mean I had no idea what the poem was about, which by the way was pretty embarrassing, so thank you for that."

"I imagine it was. And for that, I apologize," Charles said.

"Mistress," growled Bruno, causing everyone to jump, "the girl Jennifer has called you 'Mel' again. Shall I tear out her spine and eat it, as you have commanded?"

"What in the hell is that?" Charles gasped.

"Bruno, my AIPA," said Melody. "Want to pet him? Bruno, stand down."

"As you command, my consort to the midnight moon," he said.

Charles shook his head, then handed them each a sheet of paper. "So tonight, I will show you around a more familiar house."

"What is this?" Melody said with a sneer.

"Read it," Charles said.

"It's for babies," she said.

"Read it."

Melody groaned.

"Humpty Dumpty sat on a wall. Humpty Dumpty had a great fall. All the king's horses and all the king's men couldn't put Humpty together again. Wow."

"What do you mean, 'wow'?" Charles said. "This is poetry."

"No," Melody insisted. "Poetry is deep. It is about what is in your soul. Poetry is the razor blade that slices in your vein, and poetry is the blood that pours out. This is...silly. And dumb."

"I agree," said Jennifer warily. "My mom read me this when I was, like, three years old. I think I outgrew it by the time I was four. Aren't you taking these meetings seriously?"

"Very," said Charles. He suppressed another grin. "This is just as much a poem as Milton's *Paradise Lost*. It has rhyme and meter and all the elements of poetry we seek. But let's not get into all that quite yet. Let me ask you: who is Humpty Dumpty?"

"An egg," said Jennifer.

"Where does it say that in the poem?"

Jennifer reread the poem, scrunching her forehead.

"I always thought that..."

"Always watch your preconceived notions. They will blind you to what is right in front of you. Nothing in the poem tells us Humpty Dumpty is an egg. In the illustrations to Lewis Carroll's *Through the Looking Glass*, he is depicted as an egg, but that was an artist's rendering of a character in a novel who was based on the character in the nursery rhyme. There is no egg in the poem we are reading now. So, let's examine the poem again. This time, Humpty is just a guy."

"Who is he?" Jean Paul asked.

"The poem doesn't tell us," Charles went on. "Some scholars think he is based on a historical figure, even King Richard III of England, but of course there is no way to prove that. So, for the sake of the poem, let's say he's a guy sitting on a wall. Why would he sit on a wall?"

"To wait for his drug dealer!" said Peter.

"He's peeking into someone's window!" said Melody.

"What a perv!" said Peter.

Jennifer shook her head.

"I don't get any of this. Where in the poem does it say he is doing anything? He's just sitting on the wall."

"As my generation would say," Charles said, "he's just chillin'. Is that what you mean?"

"Sure," replied Jennifer.

"The poem does not tell us anything beyond 'Humpty Dumpty sat on a wall.' We don't know who Humpty is, what his motivations are, or any other context. He might just be a bum, or some average guy, but if 'all the king's horses and all the king's men' are called in to fix him up, we might assume Humpty is a pretty important guy."

Grunts and nods of dawning comprehension rumbled through the group.

"So, we have a character, someone important, who suffers a 'great fall.' Now, what does that mean, literally?"

"That he had a lot of fun on Halloween and stuff!" said Peter, snickering.

"Maybe," Charles replied, remaining diplomatic, and not wanting to discourage anyone's participation. "What else?"

"It just means he fell off the wall," Jennifer said.

"One meaning, yes," Charles said. "What else can be a 'great fall?'"

"A fall from grace," Melody said. Charles smiled.

"Yes. A fall from a height of power or stature. Humpty's 'great fall' might mean he literally fell off the wall, and many people—well, horses and people—tried to heal him. Or we could take it to mean he was in a position of power, or he was a great moral figure, and after he fell to the level of everyone else, the best efforts of the best people in the land to restore him were useless. He is irreparably damaged. The story of Humpty Dumpty is a tragedy."

"But if you're one of the regular people on the ground," Melody said, "it could be a triumph."

Now Charles was at a loss for words. He could only nod in admiration.

"All this from a dumb kid's rhyme?" Peter said.

"It's hardly dumb," Charles said. "In fact, in 1946, Robert Penn Warren wrote a novel called *All the King's Men* about a popular politician who tries to do great things for his constituents and is eventually brought low. The novel won the Pulitzer Prize, was adapted for film a couple of times, including a version that won the Academy Award, and is considered by some to be the greatest novel ever written about politics and morality. Now, all of that is a side note to this poem, but the potential is there. Within the five lines of this silly children's nursery rhyme is the potential for sweeping epics and tragedies, magnificent stories about goodness, evil, strength, and weakness."

Jennifer shook her head.

"What you're saying makes sense," she said. "But none of that is in the poem."

Charles sighed. *This was going to be a great discussion,* he thought. *If I can't break through to her with Mother Goose, what else can I do? Maybe this is all a waste of time.*

"Enough poetry for now," Charles said, checking the time. Only ten minutes remained. His flexscreen flashed a new message from a number he did not recognize. "I'm going to give you an assignment for next time."

"What?" Peter cried.

"Nothing difficult," Charles said, holding up his hands in reassurance. "Nothing graded, nothing you have to turn in. I want you to think of a nursery rhyme or other simple poem, and then during the week, think of a story that might be behind it. Just like we did with Humpty Dumpty. And next week, we will share what we came up with. Can you do that?"

Apart from Melody, who assured him she could, the students mostly grumbled and shrugged. Charles smiled. *Like old times.*

"I have to know," he went on, addressing Peter and Jean Paul, "what brought you here? You know what you are risking. What do you have to gain?"

"Melody invited me," Peter said. "She said we do fun stuff up here and that since I used to go to private school, I probably know a lot of smart stuff to share with everyone. No one at private school said I was smart, but I bet people here in the Plex will think I'm smart."

"Well I'm sure we will," Charles said, not addressing the insult the boy had just leveled at everyone around him. Already, Charles was anticipating and evaluating what he knew about Peter. *He shows arrogance, coming from off-Plex to here, but who wouldn't? He will have a hard time the first time I tell him his answer is wrong.*

"Jean Paul?"

The big young man looked up. His eyes were wet with tears. Charles had been so engaged in his Humpty Dumpty discussion that he hadn't even noticed.

"I'm so dumb," Jean Paul said. "I'm thirty and I can't get past my Level 12 test. A twenty-year-old should pass that. But I study and study and I can't remember nothing. Like Melody said, I've known her a long time and she says what you do here isn't like regular modules. So, I thought, 'Hey, maybe I can learn in a different way that makes sense.' That way I can pass my Level Twelves and get a job."

Level Twelve. The lowest Achievement Level anyone can pass before dropping out. And he's thirty? Learning disability? Drug abuse? Not laziness; no student would be so lazy as to fail a level for a decade because it was too difficult. EduForce cripples the students at the top and abandons the students at the bottom.

Charles put his hand on Jean Paul's shoulder. He did not know how the gesture would be received, but the young man did not flinch. Indeed, he seemed to relax at the touch.

"I know you can do it."

"How?" he replied. "You barely know me."

"I know students," Charles replied. "If you have the courage to come up here with me, against all the rules, then you have the strength to pass that test."

Charles did not know if Jean Paul had the strength or not. If he had a cognitive impairment, no amount of courage in the world would allow his brain to process knowledge correctly. But he would do all he could.

Charles scanned the horizon. *An odd landscape,* he thought. Other Plexes made rectangular silhouettes against the twilit sky, and Charles knew thousands more lived there, as well. The Plexes were connected by solar train rail lines and the paved roads only shipping companies could use. Interspersed between the monolithic Plexes were the decaying remains of the old neighborhoods. In the building of the Plexes, contractors had dismantled and reused materials from the old infrastructure to build the new. Now, the remains of the old world rotted. Concrete debris lay in the unused avenues and streets, while the rows of foundations and basements had filled with garbage, foliage, wild animals, and little enclaves of off-Plexers.

A sudden idea came to Charles. It was a wild, idiotic idea, foolish for him and for them. But if the students were ever going to think and imagine and dream beyond the confines of EduForce—to think outside the Plex, as it were—then they would have to *go* beyond those confines. If only—

"Mister W, it's time," Jennifer said.

With less than two minutes until the cameras would reactivate, the Rooftop Readers Club hustled down the staircase and into the corridor. They agreed to meet in twenty-three hours.

Back in his apartment, Charles's mind buzzed with ideas. He had planned the lessons out, but now would adapt them for Melody, for Jennifer, for Peter and Jean Paul. Each student would access the text in his or her own way. He thought especially about his last idea, the really crazy one. He smiled at his audacity. *Experiencing is a better way to learn than listening. Just hearing about the past is not enough.*

Just then, he remembered the message he had received. He powered on his flexscreen and read it.

> *Charles,*
>
> *This is Shaaya. I have a new number that you probably do not recognize. I need to meet you to discuss something important. I live in Plex 291 now. I hope you can afford the train trip here.*
>
> *S*

The feeling of his heart leaping in his chest was soon replaced by the feeling of his stomach wavering. It was the first message he had received from his wife in nearly five years. He had not seen her in over ten.

Charles turned off his flexscreen. His hands moved so swiftly, it was as though someone else was doing it. He did not trust himself to touch "REPLY." If he did reply, he did not know what he would write. *What could I say? What could she want?*

Feeling jittery, Charles walked into the bathroom and flung open the medicine cabinet. But when he did, he was closer to the door than he realized, and it smacked him on his nose. Charles cursed. The feeling of tingling and fireworks and raw nerves burst behind his eyes. *This feels...this feels like...*he began, then he looked in the mirror. He laughed, despite himself, and despite the lights dancing before his vision. *Maybe I should write a poem to describe that feeling.*

He reopened the cabinet more gently and located the Relax-Eez. He kept it because it was one of those things everyone had around, like tissues or toothpaste, even though he almost never used them. But today he popped two of them from their foil pouches and he flung them into his mouth. There the capsules sat, their enteric coating starting to soften under his tongue. Charles stared at his face in the mirror. *Remember the teaching? You felt ecstatic a few minutes ago. Now look—a pathetic old man. What happened?*

Shaaya. Shaaya had happened. She could always do that to him, send him from the depths of the valley to the top of the mountain, and then down again, with a few words. *Should I reply to her?* he wondered. *What do I do?*

He spat out the Relax-Eez into the sink, then ran the tap to flush them down.

Seven: The Dark Spot

So now all three parts of the three-part attack were in place. One, all students are force-fed standards to prepare them for Plex college. Two, Plex college is made free to all students. Three, the cost of universities grows so absurd that every mid-tier school closes. Meanwhile, the wealthy send their children to a few elite universities. These institutions teach students the most advanced and challenging coursework, preparing them to take leadership roles in America. The graduates then become business leaders and politicians who proceed to make more decisions that further secure the power of the ultra-wealthy. The ivory tower of scholarship grows taller and more inaccessible with each passing year.

> *—The Trough,* p.70

Jennifer lost track of what pills she took, and how many. She sprawled on Melody's bed, with colorful tablets and capsules sprinkled among the wrinkled comforter. Each one created new sensations—spinning, flying, falling, fading in and out. When the room and the Plex and the Scholarship and The Perfect Five came into focus, she reached out and felt around until her hand settled on a new pill. Fist would close around pill, and then fist went to mouth and pill went down the throat with a gulp of water or of Melody's grape soda, which Jennifer hated but she did not care. The pills were both legal and illicit, easy to obtain either way. Certainly, cheaper than booze. The garden of pharmacopoeia in which Jennifer and Melody lavished was cheap and plentiful.

"Don't dwell on it," Melody said, her voice floating through the room. "In the grand scheme of...and all."

"Dwell. To abide. To reside," Jennifer said.

"Rhyme. Poetry."

Silence hung between them. Jennifer's eyes scanned over the walls of Melody's room, which were plastered with digital posters of her bizarre, old-fashioned idols. Their visages stared down at them. Wynona Rider. Brad Pitt. Monica Lewinsky. Courteney Cox. The Teenage Mutant Ninja Turtles. Kurt Cobain bent over his guitar. Jennifer closed her eyes. The firm support of the mattress faded away, and gradually she felt as if she were hovering a few inches over it. As though wrapped in cotton and vapors, Jennifer's body grew dull to sensation.

Some seconds or minutes or hours passed between them.

"Jen?"

"Hm."

"Jen?"

"Hm."

"Your mom loves you."

"Hm."

"I never had that love. Hard mother love. Seventeen mothers, a new one every year or two. No mother love."

"Hm."

Jennifer contemplated this, or the best she could with a brain that was floating in fog. The love, if it was there, was hard to feel.

Jennifer popped a new pill, and after another thirty seconds or minutes, a bright hot sun burned her fog away and left her mind bleached in blistering sunlight. She opened her eyes. Everything was overexposed with faces in negative.

Her flexscreen was blinking. New message.

It was from EduForce. That was not exceptional. EduForce radiated messages to students every day: news updates, policy changes, strategies for success, student profiles, warnings, congratulations, reminders, and deadlines. The lives of students orbited around the information from EduForce, waiting for their futures to be illuminated by the little photons of guidance from that omnipresent and omnipotent organization.

The subject of the message was "Regarding Your Recent Scholarship Application."

Jennifer plummeted.

"What is it?" Melody asked. Jennifer could only point. Melody lurched over to the flexscreen.

"Carlita, read it," Melody said.

Jennifer had enabled Melody's voice to activate Carlita, but before the AIPA could respond, Jennifer said, "Carlita, don't." Then to Melody, "What if it's bad?" Her voice sounded far away from her ears.

"Then it's bad. What if it's good?"

Jennifer was too addled to have any will. She felt like cascading water.

"Carlita, go on. Read me the new message."

In the moment between asking that question and Carlita's affirmative reply, a moment of lucidity shone through to Jennifer. *This is the pills. If I were sober, I would wait.* But she wasn't, and she didn't. Typically, when she went drinking and pilling with Melody, she locked her EduForce account. The last thing she needed was to drunkenly watch a video and botch the edugame, ruining her score. She kept a barricade between her work and recreation. But she had forgotten this time.

"Certainly," Carlita replied through Melody's speakers. "It says, 'Dear Miss Calderón, Thank you for your recent application for the Scholarship to Elite Universities Consortium. Your application was one of many impressive ones for this very competitive and very selective program. While your academic record is strong, we regret to inform you your application has not been selected to move on to the next round of—'"

A great vacuum of sound filled Jennifer's ears. Carlita's voice vanished. Everything began to go dark.

When she came to consciousness again, Melody was straddled over her. Concern was written on her expression.

"How long?" Jennifer croaked.

"The fuck should I know?" Melody said with equal parts exasperation and relief. She looked like she was about to slap Jennifer, but then she leaned in and lay next to her.

"I am so sorry," she said, wrapping her arm around her. Jennifer had no defenses, no self-control. Tears shimmered.

"Nothing left now. The Scholarship was all."

Melody stroked her hair.

"Just going to be average," Jennifer said. "A Perfect Five and I'm going to be average."

Melody remained silent for a few moments before replying.

"Me too. Me too."

If there was any indignation in her tone, Jennifer was too far gone to recognize it.

"Gimme more...something," she groaned. She groped around the bedspread. Melody's hand was on her own. She thought for a moment it was an attempt to restrain her. Instead, it was to steady her. Melody pushed two pills into her palm.

"Take these. You'll feel better."

Jennifer brought her hand to her mouth, like a man dying of thirst scooping from a fountain. The two pills rattled in her mouth, clung to her teeth, then tumbled back toward her throat. She tried to gulp them down, but they were sticky. Halfway down her esophagus, the two pills stopped moving. Jennifer pointed at her throat. Melody handed her a cup. The last thing Jennifer tasted was grape soda before the darkness closed around her.

This time when she woke, she knew she had been out for a much longer time than the last blackout. Those pills, whatever they were, had been powerful. Melody was asleep next to her. All the electronics in the room had gone into hibernation. The room was dark, like twilight. Jennifer listened for the sounds of Melody's foster parents outside the door. She heard nothing. Jennifer had only met them a few times; they made themselves scarce in Melody's life and scarcer when Jennifer was around. At first, they had thought Jennifer would be a good influence for Melody and put her back on a more respectable, responsible path. But that was not the nature of their relationship. Melody would be Melody, regardless of who she loved. Jennifer never lectured her about drinking or drugs or neglecting homework or breaking rules. Never wanted to.

Melody is the dark spot in my brilliant life. My beautiful, beloved, dangerous dark spot.

There was the thought again. Jennifer knew she would never change Melody, but Melody had changed her. Rosa had cultivated Jennifer, sheltered and protected and prodded her to greatness, though she herself was one of the lowliest workers in Plex 87. *What are other dark spots?* Jennifer wondered. Shadows. Freckles. Cancer. Dirt. Black holes. Fleas. Smudges. Rosa used to force Jennifer to polish the dishes, to seek out and eradicate every last streak and smudge. Melody was just another smudge to Rosa, but a dangerous one. *Is Melody dangerous? If she is, is that good or bad?*

Jennifer sat up. Not wanting to wake Melody with her voice, she touched her flexscreen to activate it. It lit up, revealing the EduForce message Carlita had read to her. Jennifer checked the time and estimated she had been out for at least sixteen hours. *Sixteen hours I have been essentially dead, and the world went right on without me.*

Jennifer checked her NewsFeed and found it longer than usual. Of course, there was an endless stream of news. Information from the most egregious massacres to the inanest celebrity gossip spilled before her eyes. Information saturated her world, drowned her world, to the point where to be cut off from it was to be cut off from air, water, or food. Information was the brine in which humanity soaked, at first surrounding, then penetrating, and ultimately altering it. Ignorance, once a tragic result of inequality, now required a force of will to maintain.

One story dominated the NewsFeed:

Barfield Projected as Early Favorite in 2052

The latest polling predicts an 82 percent likelihood EduForce President Geraldine Barfield will win the Presidential Election in 2052. With the election only eighteen months away, Barfield recently joined an already crowded field of contenders. Experts say, however, that her high profile and experience negotiating business and government make her the frontrunner.

Though she entered the primary for the Republican Party, her ideologies and skill set would play well in either party, says Ralph Homberg, our network political consultant. "Barfield has it all—experience, image, style, and a track record of using her power to do good."

In her announcement, Barfield said, "America is the greatest, smartest nation in the world. For decades, I have been molding the minds of America, and now, I am prepared to mold the rest of the world to see that."

Jennifer closed the report and opened her EduForce account. The familiar screen came up, beginning with a smiling image of Geraldine Barfield, along with a message of encouragement. Jennifer opened her statistics page. Current Achievement Level: *14. 21 percent of the way to 15. 13,009 of 14, 113 total modules completed. Achievement Level Grade Point Average: 5.0/5.0.*

She stared at the numbers with a clear but deadened feeling, the sober flatness coming off the previous night's intoxicated lows and highs. *They are all just numbers.* Then she saw her name. Jennifer Calderón. Next to it was her identification number. 343410761. *I am just a number. We are all just numbers.* She was not sure what the thought meant, or even if she believed it to be true. But it sounded true and felt true in that moment.

Numbers feed machines. What breaks machines? Bad numbers.

The thought was like something Melody would say, but again, it sounded true and felt true. *Melody may be my dark spot, but she understands things I do not.*

Maybe Melody is smarter than me.

Jennifer had always taken it as a given that she was the smarter of the two. But now she felt dumb, duped, and angry.

She opened a new edugame. She picked an easy one, Alge-bonanza. Algebra always came extremely easily to her. Everything that looked tangled and complex could, through reliable processes and formulas, be made simple.

Alge-bonanza was a first-person point of view game. The user was a gold miner, and had to select gold, silver, and gems from a rock bed. Each precious material contained an algebraic problem. If the problem was solved correctly, the gold or silver nugget or gem would vanish, and "money" would appear in the player's account. This "money" could be redeemed for real products from companies that were EduForce sponsors. Jennifer had purchased countless bags of candy, song and movie credits, and games with the money she had earned from the edugames. She had conquered every level of Alge-bonanza save the last one. She resumed her progress.

Her flexscreen showed an animated tunnel, supported with wooden beams and with little carts, the types used in old mines in the West in the days of the Gold Rush. Jennifer navigated deeper into the cave. Downward she plunged, her avatar winding past already-mined rock faces. She recalled her earlier sessions in which she had picked swaths of rock clean, leaving the cave empty and her money purse full. It had seemed so rewarding at the time. Now she felt empty and foolish. Still, her avatar moved into the bowels of the mountain, down ladders and shafts and over underground rivers and through cenotes and over great abysses of darkness. Finally, she arrived at one of the inner chambers.

The wall glittered in the light of her avatar's headlamp. Emeralds, rubies, diamonds, and other crystals protruded from its surface. Great veins of gold ran parallel to the ground.

Jennifer clicked on a gold nugget the size of a basketball. The head of a pickaxe came down, striking it. A question burst out of the gold.

$15 = x3 - 8x - 17$

A few mental calculations, and Jennifer typed in x=4. The burst of golden light, the explosion of electronic melody, and Jennifer was a few credits richer. The gold nugget vanished, and she moved her avatar onto the next challenge. Her brain buzzed with the familiar charge of dopamine and adrenaline that accompanied every feat in every edugame. But now she could sense the reaction happening in her without believing in it. *This is a response I am having to a game,* she thought, the clarity making her feel cold and free and cynical. *This is just a feeling. This is not me.*

She came to a silver nugget. This was a smaller one. The question would be shorter and simpler and less valuable, but every gem and ore had to be mined for the edugame to be complete. She swung the pickaxe onto the silver.

$4=3x+1$

The answer was 1.

It was an easy question, laughably easy. An Achievement Level 9 sort of question. Such questions were often sprinkled in among the rest, an easy way to accumulate wealth and feel a cheap sense of victory. But as Jennifer realized this, she became filled with a rage that had been swelling inside her since her rejection from the Scholarship the previous day. *To tell the truth, it has been growing in me much longer than that. Maybe since I first met Mr. Winston. Maybe since I first met Melody.* The question was a cheap one. An easy one. One meant to make her feel good and push her further into the game, so she could click on more rocks and gems and crystals and accumulate more fake money and feel more cheap victory. All her life, Jennifer had focused on the victory. Now she focused on the cheap. What little joy her accomplishments provided. She had worked hard all her life to achieve something no other student in the country had ever done, and while she felt proud and smart and superior and sometimes invincible, she did not feel joyful or satisfied. Every question she answered only fueled her to go on to answer more questions, even though it was all unchallenging and predictable.

The answer was 1.

She hated the easy question. She hated the sound effects and the graphics and constant feedback and statistics and the ridiculous names of the edugames. She hated EduForce. She hated Geraldine Barfield. She felt vastly insulted and humiliated. What purpose was the Scholarship? How could she not have won? Mr. Winston had started to warn her about it, but she had cut him off. *Why?* She wondered. *The Scholarship was everything to me. Why didn't I at least listen?* But she knew the answer. She knew Charles knew something she did not, something that would expose all the lies her life was built upon. It would expose EduForce as a fraud and her as a dupe.

Now she wanted nothing more than to find Mr. Winston, sit with him, and hear all he had to say. His ideas may have sounded like garbled nonsense, but now she craved garbled nonsense. She craved something obscure and challenging and uncomfortable and frightening. She wanted to learn something that would keep her awake at night, and not because her body was flooded with adrenaline and caffeine. She wanted to read through the night and read a real book. She wanted to punch a brick wall with her fist as hard as she could. She wanted to climb on top of Melody and make love with her. *No,* she thought, *I want to fuck her silly.* She wanted to run to the roof of the Plex and howl like an animal straight out of the Pleistocene.

The answer was 1.

But Jennifer typed 2.

No explosions of color or sound. The screen went ever-so-slightly dim. "Sorry, try again," the screen suggested.

Did I really do that? Jennifer wondered. She exited the game and went back to her profile with all her statistics. She looked at her score.

5.0*/5.0

The asterisk. Her score rounded up to 5.0, probably to the hundred-thousandths place. But that asterisk meant everything to her. *That beautiful, dark spot,* she thought. *A little smudge that means so much.*

Jennifer looked up. The room was still dimly lit, and Melody was still asleep. She felt weird, and good.

"I'm ready to learn now!" she said aloud to no one in particular.

Eight: Machine Parts

Thus far, it might seem my thesis is anti-technology. Perhaps I come across as a curmudgeon and a Luddite. Not so! In my early career, I embraced the power of technology. I have seen inner city students watch live video feeds of a moose giving birth two thousand miles away. I know of students in the most rural hinterlands who took virtual tours of the world's greatest art museums. I once observed a class of six-year-old students map the stars with the aid of computer programs. Technology can bring the remote and inaccessible to any child. It is when technology makes us believe we do not need moose, or art museums, or the stars any longer that we have gone too far.

—The Trough, p.83

Mr. Chambers had another message for Charles.

"Good morning, Mister Winston. How have you been feeling? If you are ill, have you been to a clinic? We at EduForce are concerned about your health and your recent drop in productivity. Your completion rate has fallen by ninety-one percent in the past week. If you are ill, please report to a clinic and as a thank-you for your years of dedication, EduForce will reimburse you ten percent of the medical bill. If the reason for this drop in production is non-medical, you must resume work immediately to retain your position in EduForce. Your current backlog is one thousand, eighty-four essays. Please be advised we are monitoring your work and will have to redistribute your workload to other EduForce Reviewers if the backlog is not cleared in three days' time. Thank you for your dedication and service to our students!"

Then the fadeout, and the theme song. *Molding the minds of America. Molding the minds of America. Molding the minds. Molding the minds.*

Charles daydreamed about sometime meeting Mr. Chambers, wondered what he was like in person. He seemed so devoid of originality, so much more like a corporate product than a person, that Charles desperately wanted to humanize him. Did he own a cat? Maybe he cultivated cacti or listened to Slavic folk music or had once broken his sister's arm. Of course, there was almost no chance he would meet his Personal EduForce Adviser face to face. Mr. Chambers probably lived in Washington in a Plex but with a slightly better apartment paid for by his video work for EduForce. Charles thought of vidmessaging him—all of Mr. Chambers's messages included contact information—but playing the scenario in his head even once, he saw it would not work. *Hello, Mr. Chambers? This is Charles Winston. You send me all of these wonderful videos and I have to ask—do you play in a polka band? Please tell me you play in a polka band.*

Charles shook his head and smiled, but it was not enough to erase the monumental task before him. One thousand essays. Three days. He activated his flexscreen and signed onto the EduForce portal.

For a moment he was caught by surprise at the ease of modern technology. He remembered when he was a boy and had to search for connections to wireless networks. To access the Internet outside of these zones required the purchase of expensive data plans. Back then, wireless networks—Wi-Fi, it had been called at the turn of the century—existed in little oases, each house and family and store and school with its own password-secured link to the Internet. None of those terms were even in use anymore, as they were utterly obsolete. Wireless Internet connectivity was free and open for everyone, provided as part of living in a Plex. Asking for a Wi-Fi password in 2051 would be like asking for a password for air.

Charles looked at his EduForce queue and his shoulders slumped. The backlog might take weeks to make up. And if the essays were not reviewed, he did not get paid. And if he did not get paid, he could not fulfill his promise to his family.

So, he began reading. EduForce touted its workflow as "self-paced," but there was only one pace: constant and relentless. Charles had heard of essay checkers who missed a single day of work because of a cold, and never received the same volume of essays. It was all determined by data and algorithms. *If I don't work like a draught horse every day, I go to the glue factory,* he reflected.

All-nighter. The term conjured up memories of Charles's college years, grinding out research papers that were due the next day at 8:00

A.M., his brain pickled with black tea and energy drinks and long passages of scholarly text. He knew working non-stop for a full day and night would be bad for his health, both mental and physical. He knew the work would not be his best. But an all-nighter was the only way to clear out that queue before his career was threatened. So, he worked all morning and afternoon, then past dinner, idly munching on crackers to sustain himself. He dozed off for a few hours, the words swimming before his eyes as he slumped at his desk. When he awoke, he shuffled over to his coffee maker. It was an old model, a traditional twelve-cup percolator. It had a plugless adapter, as no appliances used outlets anymore, but in all other aspects, it was the same as the coffee makers his parents had used, and he had used. He heaped spoonful after spoonful of grounds into the basket, filled the pot to the brim with water, poured it into the reservoir, and pressed "start." Charles leaned against the cabinets as the coffeemaker gurgled and bubbled. The sound comforted him.

He looked at the coffee package. "Colombian Hills" was the brand, the one Charles liked best. It tasted the closest to real coffee that he had ever found. He read the side of the plastic pouch ruefully.

> *Start your morning with a fresh, lively cup of Colombian Hills coffee product. Our proprietary blend of natural coffee colors and flavors, along with the extra boost of Perk-Eez to keep you going strong all morning long...*

Real coffee, true coffee made from beans imported from South America, was now a drink for the ultra-wealthy Off-Plexers. The ersatz coffee most people drank was a water-based product with coloring, flavor and smell designed to replicate coffee perfectly. The higher quality brands, such as Colombian Hills, were nearly indistinguishable from the real thing. The added Perk-Eez only gave it a bigger kick than the caffeine alone. Charles longed for the authentic thing even though his mouth and stomach could not discern the difference.

The percolator finished. He poured a cup and took a drink. *My mouth thinks this is real. My brain does not. Which is right? Does it even matter?*

Charles carried his mug of wannabe coffee to his desk and began work. He opened his EduForce work queue and started reading. Usually, he at least showered and dressed before starting his daily work. The routine had always kept him in a professional mindset, but he didn't care now. He would work unshowered, unshaven, and in his pajamas today. And every other day, for all it mattered. EduForce did not care about his hygiene. They cared about his productivity. So, Charles opened essay after essay, checking for signs of cheating, or of potential danger, and sending the essays back to EduForce. He slurped coffee, stared into the flexscreen, and his mind filled with poisonous resentment. He cursed EduForce and kept working. He cursed Geraldine Barfield and kept working. He cursed Shaaya and Tamra and even Clara and kept working. He cursed himself and kept working. He worked fast and sloppy and did not care. *So, what if I miss a cheater?* He thought. *Good for the cheaters. All of education now is a game of lies and sneaky algorithms, so why shouldn't some kids figure out how to beat the game?* His only care was speeding through the greatest volume of work in the smallest amount of time. *This is what EduForce wants. A machine. Well then, I'll be their best goddamn machine.*

Around mid-morning his pace slowed. The dregs of the coffeepot swam at the bottom, now cold. Charles got up, dumped the pot, and made twelve more cups. His hands trembled as he did. Though he usually saved them for moments of pressing need, Charles broke open four Perk-Eez pouches and chewed the tablets, washing down the acrid debris with more coffee.

After four hours of work, he had completed a typical full day's workload. He thought of rewarding himself for his hard work by taking the rest of the day off. *No,* he thought. *I'm making up lost ground here. Work all day. Maybe all night. Drink coffee till my teeth chatter. Tomorrow, maybe I can work on lessons for the Readers Club.*

This thought, though, pulled him from his focus. He imagined what his class would be like with a classroom and without having to sneak onto the roof. He thought of his early days of teaching, back when he was in his twenties and overworked but excited, back when he had no idea what changes were in store for him and for his profession. He had even believed the lies and propaganda from government and business at that time. He had believed in changing the standards and pressuring school districts to meet them and on holding teachers accountable for the results. He had believed blindly in the virtue of reform.

Charles worked through the afternoon. He did not feel hungry at lunch. By early evening, he was trembling and ragged. He had not even changed out of his pajamas or brushed his hair. But he had reviewed more than four hundred essays in a day, almost twice his typical rate. He knew he still had a lot more to do, but now he knew he could do it. He glowed with pride. Here he was, a man of over fifty, working with an intensity that was only present in frantic graduate students. He had not worked as hard in decades.

So, he did it again the next day. After a few hours of turbulent dozing, every moment of which was against his will, Charles arose in the early morning and returned to his flexscreen for more EduForce work. Coffee brewed all day. The coffee, which at first was a stimulant to maintain his energy, had become like a whip with which he struck his brain.

By the end of the second day of essay reviewing, his eyes were bleary, and his brain felt dull and dead. His only break on the second day was for a short walk down the corridor to his corner store, where he purchased two more bags of Colombian Hills and several bags of Naturia Falls trail mix. He could have had them delivered, of course, but what he really wanted was the walk. On the second day, he worked until he wavered in his computer chair. He had reviewed almost seven hundred and fifty essays in two days. He typically did a thousand in a week. Charles calculated that after a few hours of sleep, he would rise the next morning and complete the backlog of essays by noon. Then he would spend the afternoon crafting a lesson for the Readers Club.

He dozed again that night, but he had so much caffeine and adrenaline in his system his sleep was like the skipping of a stone across the water. He dreamed vividly but in short, jagged fragments.

By 5:00 A.M., he went to work. As he passed eight hundred, then eight hundred fifty essays over the past three days, his pace began to lag. Charles would stare at the flexscreen for several minutes, reading the same passages over and over. More coffee, walks around the apartment, splashing water on the face, nothing helped. He turned on his window and looked outside at the traffic coming and going from the loading dock. Charles yelled at himself, cursed, and pounded his fists on the desk. *I have to get a thousand. I have to get a thousand.*

He briefly entertained the idea of stopping. Eight hundred and fifty was also productive. But he would not let himself fall short of that goal. He would get a thousand. And yet, the harder he pushed himself, the more excruciating each essay became. He scarcely even looked at the words. Tears began to well in his eyes as helplessness overcame him. He looked at his hands. They were shaking and crooked. He looked at his reflection in the bathroom mirror. Face unshaven, hair unbrushed, eyes wide with exhaustion and ringed with dark circles, he looked less than human, certainly less than civilized. He began thinking streams of violent thoughts. Of murdering Geraldine Barfield. *Wouldn't change a thing,* he thought. He thought of taking a train to Washington D.C. and blowing up the EduForce headquarters, though he knew nothing about explosives and was certain EduForce would have more than enough security to stop him. *And EduForce is like the Hydra,* he reflected. *No, like Proteus. Always shifting, multi-faceted. Blowing up one building would not stop it. It is both a gargantuan monster and a tiny parasite. I am helpless to stop it. I am helpless to please it. I cannot reach one thousand essays today.*

Then a thought came to him that startled him.

I do not care.

That exhaustion-addled moment brought Charles brilliant clarity. He did not care about pleasing EduForce. He did not care that he might not read one thousand essays. He did not care that what he did made no difference to anyone other than to himself, and perhaps to Clara, as his income kept her in Hopespring Home. But he was useless, superfluous, and therefore liberated. He smiled and laughed at his insane face in the mirror, then he scrambled back to his flexscreen to continue reading. He blazed through one essay after another. If his job did not matter and no one cared how well he did it, there would be no consequences. Sometimes, he gave the essay no more than a brief glance before clicking "ACCEPTABLE FOR ASSESSMENT." He found new stores of energy within himself, energy fueled by his own apathy and resignation. Meaninglessness was liberating.

Finally, around one thirty in the afternoon, Charles reviewed essay number one thousand eighty-four. He did not even power off his flexscreen as he staggered to his bed. He was asleep before he knew his eyes closed.

Charles awoke many hours later. He had left the window turned on, and it was night. Glancing at the clock, he saw it was after ten. Stiff and ragged, he poured himself a glass of water and vowed to return to bed for more sleep. *You can't do this to yourself, old man.* But first he went to his flexscreen, which he had left on overnight. Checking the flexscreen was always the first thing he did. Sometimes he told himself to set it aside and not be a slave to it. But he had grown up with screens and engaging them felt natural to him. Besides, Plex life was sufficiently dull that one always had to look to the online world for engagement. The networked world gave him a constant itch and a way to constantly scratch it.

Right at the top was a vidmessage from Mr. Chambers. *We've been seeing a lot of each other recently, haven't we?* Charles thought, feeling a sense of dread undercut his glib observation. He opened the message. There was Mr. Chambers, seated at a desk, that non-smiling, not-frowning expression fixed on his face. *Insipid,* Charles thought. *That's the word for this guy.* The strange urge to meet him renewed.

> *Hello Mr. Winston,*
>
> *As per our previous conversation, we at EduForce have been monitoring your work closely in recent days. Upon a recent quality review inspection, several discrepancies have come to our attention in a recent set of essay reviews you completed. An unusually large number of essays you marked "Acceptable" were later discovered to be suspect or fraudulent. As I am sure you are aware, all flagged essays are reviewed by at least two independent reviewers.*
>
> *We are deeply concerned about the quality of work done on our students' behalf. EduForce policies explicitly forbid "speed passing" large numbers of tests without actually reading them. Our guidelines recommend spending no less than two minutes of review per essay, preferably five. If it is discovered you are passing a large volume of exams without properly reviewing them, you are subject to termination from EduForce employment.*
>
> *Thank you for your dedication to our students!*

Then the fadeout. Then the jingle. A cocktail of nervous fear, angry resentment, and hollow futility splashed into Charles's blood. *Of course, there would be a second reader.* It was easy to forget, secluded in his Plex apartment, working in complete solitude, that anyone else cared or checked on his work.

He slinked back to his room, turned off the light, and crumpled into his bed.

Upon waking the next morning, he felt rested, but scooped out and weather-beaten. *I can't do that again,* he thought. *Maybe in college I could have pulled off a work session like that, but not now.*

He showered, shaved and dressed. He looked at himself in the mirror again. *Almost human.* His mood a little improved, Charles made himself a bowl of cereal and sat at his kitchen table. For a full minute, he sat there in silence, listening to the sounds of his Plex apartment. A faint whir of the overhead air filter. The whisper and hum of electronic life. The slow absorption of milk into his cereal. Then he powered on his flexscreen, feeling a little more relaxed, a little more balanced, a little more hopeful.

There was a fresh message from EduForce, delivered less than an hour previously. Mr. Chambers again. This time, he was frowning.

> *"Mister Winston. Due to your recent failures to maintain the rigorous pace demanded by employment at EduForce, and also due to your recent spate of inaccurate reviews, your position with the EduForce Corporation has been terminated. Effective noon tomorrow, you will no longer be an employee of EduForce. Your final paycheck will be deposited directly into your account at the conclusion of the next pay period.*
>
> *If you feel this message has been sent in error, please contact us immediately."*

So that was it. Charles had not been without a job since he was a college student. His first response was a bubble of panic. Clara. How would she stay in the home? Her remaining there depended entirely upon his paycheck. Would she be kicked out, sent to live as a destitute off-Plex? And what about finding a new job? There were jobs available, no doubt. The year was 2051. But there was that saying about teaching old dogs new tricks, and Charles knew if he did not learn a new trick, he was without a job, his apartment was lost, and he would be cast out of the Plex.

There was only one option. *Shaaya,* he realized.

Charles had never replied to her message from several days earlier. Partly, he had forgotten. Mostly, he had procrastinated. Now he composed his wife a message, not dictated through an AIPA, not a vidmessage, but a plain old text message, like they would have done years earlier, during their courtship. His first version was vague, hoping to leave some mystery to his purpose for meeting after these years of separation, hoping the intrigue would motivate her to go. But then he erased the message. He knew Shaaya well enough to know mystery and intrigue would annoy her. He simply wrote that he had received her message, had since lost his job and wanted to meet to discuss arrangements for Clara. He suggested a date and time. He sent the message. Two minutes later, he received the reply.

Fine. See you then.

WHERE IS THE old man? they wondered.

Melody and Jennifer sat on the rooftop, the summer night air sweltering. Heat radiated up from the roof. Peter leaned against the warm metal casing of the solar battery. Jean Paul appeared impervious to the heat, sitting and sweating a few feet away. It was 8:15, and Charles had never been late before.

"Maybe he had too much work tonight," Jennifer said. Though the pill binge—and The Perfect Five—had ended two days ago, she still felt foggy-headed and dull. "Reviewing all of those essays must be hard work."

Melody shook her head.

"He would never skip these lessons. Those essays are his job, but this is what he loves."

"Maybe he died," Peter said, looking around to see if anyone laughed. They did not. "He is pretty old."

"Shut the hell up," Melody said. Peter grinned.

"Did anyone bring their flexscreen?" Jennifer said. "Let's message him and see if maybe he forgot."

"He said don't," Jean Paul warned. "No messages."

"Yeah, we can't do that," Melody agreed. "He would be cranking mad if we did that."

"Let's go in then," Jennifer said. "It's too hot."

"Wah wah. Boo hoo," Melody mocked. "Come on. We can do this. I even found a poem to show Mister W, see what he thought."

Peter inched closer.

"A poem? Can you read it to me?"

"Sure," Melody said. "Some of the words I don't know, though. It's a really old poem."

"Who wrote it?" Jennifer asked.

"Shakespeare. Ever heard of him?"

Jennifer shrugged. Jean Paul did too. Peter nearly leaped to his feet.

"I remember him. My teacher at my old school taught us about him. I was only in eighth grade, so we only read one play by him so far. It was called *Romeo and Juliet*. It was this romantic love story. I thought it was kind of boring, but my teacher said it was important."

"I think *Romeo and Juliet* is beautiful," Melody said.

"Me too!" Peter continued. "It's my favorite. Anyway, my teacher said that Shakespeare lived in England way back a long time ago, and–how did she say it? We owe everything in our modern literature to him."

"What is eighth grade? Jennifer asked.

"Well, each year you are in a grade level. You go up to the next grade the next year, as long as you pass. If you fail, you have to repeat."

Jennifer scrunched her face in confusion.

"So, it doesn't matter how fast or how slow you do the lessons?"

"Well, the teacher teaches the lessons. That's how fast you do them."

Jennifer folded her arms.

"That sounds stupid."

Peter shrugged. "That's what school was like for me."

"So this Shakes guy. England? A long time ago?" Jennifer said. "He's not some petrol poet, is he?"

Melody smiled and said, "You used 'petrol' correctly. Good for you, trying to act your own age. And no, he's not petrol at all. Mister W probably knows more about him than I do, but he wrote a bunch of poems and plays and a lot of them are really famous."

"Famous?" Jennifer said. "I haven't read any of them. I haven't even heard of this Shakes guy. If he's so important, why haven't I heard of him?"

"Read *The Trough*!" Melody cried. "Mister W reveals everything. He uncovers the lies and the deception. What he's teaching us up here, this is real. This isn't one of those fake eduproducts."

Jennifer fell silent.

"Read us the poem, Melody," Peter said. Melody pulled a crumpled sheet of paper from her pocket. Jennifer twinged with discomfort. *She should Recycle that,* she thought automatically.

"It's called *Sonnet Fifteen*. I don't know what all of these words are, but anyhow...

When I consider every thing that grows

Holds in perfection but a little moment,

That this huge stage presenteth nought but shows

Whereon the stars in secret influence comment;

When I perceive that men as plants increase,

Cheered and checked even by the self-same sky,

Vaunt in their youthful sap, at height decrease,

And wear their brave state out of memory;

Then the conceit of this inconstant stay

Sets you most rich in youth before my sight,

Where wasteful Time debateth with Decay,

To change your day of youth to sullied night;

And all in war with Time for love of you,

As he takes from you, I engraft you new."

"Huh?" Peter said.

"Why do those words sound like that?" Jennifer asked. "Presenteth? Debateth?"

Melody frowned and shrugged. "I can't say," she replied. "Maybe that's how poets wrote back then. But look at—"

"I thought you said Shakes *wasn't* petrol," Jennifer went on. "I can't even understand what he wrote. Why should I care?"

"Just listen!" Melody urged. "This is important."

"Says you," Jennifer replied. "If it's important, why hasn't Mister Winston introduced it to us?"

"I—I don't know!" Melody shouted. Peter and Jean Paul looked around anxiously, as her voice carried over the rooftop. "Just stop asking so many questions and listen!"

The meeting that night, and the next two nights, continued in the same fashion. Melody proved to be a terrible teacher. After every line she read to them, she stopped to say "ooh!" or "that reminds me of—" and her sentences would break off as her eyes shot up into the stars, recalling some other passage in another work none of them had read either. Jean Paul soon lost interest. Jennifer did, as well. Peter remained fixed on Melody. The two of them discussed many of the strange books and poems they had both read, and Jennifer felt an odd pang of jealousy. The boy's intentions were clear, even if they were entirely hopeless. Jennifer almost felt embarrassed for him, except it seemed Melody enjoyed the attention and connection.

On the third night, Charles returned to the roof. He seemed weary and distant. He did not look at the four students but gazed out toward the horizon. Jennifer wondered what he was contemplating.

"Were you sick, Mister W?" Melody asked.

"I have been relieved of my employment," he said, before proceeding to tell them how he had fallen behind reviewing essays, then rushed to complete them in two days, and when his work had been found to be inadequate, been terminated by EduForce.

"I feel awful," Melody said. "You fell behind because you were working on lessons for us, didn't you?"

Charles shrugged. "This group is my real work. This is where I make my difference."

Melody leaped up and embraced him. Charles stood there, passively receiving the hug without participating in it. Jennifer felt a twinge of guilt. Charles had lost his job for them, but he hadn't been forced to. He had been irresponsible and neglected his work. *Irresponsible, like sabotaging one's own grade for no apparent reason?*

As if reading her thoughts, Melody turned to Jennifer.

"You'll be proud of Jen, here. She just had an important first experience, a ritual to usher her into womanhood. You'll never guess."

"Do I want to?" Charles asked.

"Jennifer here, Jennifer Calderón of The Perfect Five, answered a question wrong." Before Charles or Jennifer could reply, Melody added, "Intentionally."

"Int...but...why?" stammered Charles.

Jennifer could only shrug. She did not have the answers for herself, let alone for him.

"Well, I am sorry to hear that," Charles said. "You still have an excellent grade, I am sure. There are still many doors open to you."

Now ice water poured into Jennifer's veins. She hated him for saying it. "Do you really believe that?"

Charles looked down. "No. There are no doors opened to you. EduForce has one door out, and it leads you right back into the Plex, where you will toil away until you die."

"Mister W, please. I read *The Trough*. Jennifer's going to read it, aren't you?" As she said this, Melody glared at Jennifer. "I want to know more. I want to know everything. What was school? Why was it so bad? Why don't we have it anymore? What does it mean to learn?"

As Melody said these things, something stirred in Jennifer's chest. Melody's ranting and rambling about truth and knowledge and learning, topics that usually made Jennifer tune out and roll her eyes, suddenly sounded profound. She wanted Mr. Winston to share all he knew. And she vowed to herself to read *The Trough*.

Charles smiled. It was a smile Jennifer thought was sad, then humble, then mischievous, and finally maniacal.

"I have had a tumultuous few days. And I have yet more ahead of me. I fear a lengthy stay here in old Plex 87 might not be good for my health."

"Where are you going?" Melody asked.

"Me? You should say 'we'."

"We?"

"My pupils, have you ever heard of an ancient practice called a 'field trip'?"

Nine: Personal Business

Following World War II, the availability of cars and cheap fuel, along with the flourishing of interstate highways, led to suburban sprawl. Then, seventy years later, cars and fuel became expensive and the highways became unsustainable. Like a star collapsing in on itself, people abandoned their furnace-heated homes, their yards, their two-car garages. Enterprising developers scooped up entire neighborhoods, sometimes entire cities, and raised apartment mega-complexes. With self-sufficient energy from solar and wind power, and all the amenities one could need accessible within walking distance, the Plex became the standard for modern American living. Reverse suburbanization.

    —*The Trough*, p.46

Five A.M. came very early for the students.

Charles was ready at one of the exit corridors of Plex 87, holding a large nylon bag that was stuffed full. He had a backpack slung over his shoulder. One by one, his four students arrived with bags of their own, as instructed. He had not told them what they would be doing or where they would be going, only that they would be learning about learning. He had told them to pack for a long day trip. It was only after giving the instruction that he realized none of them even knew how to pack for a day away from the Plex. They'd never had reason to leave.

Jennifer had not spoken to her mother since their fight, so she had no need to explain her absence to anyone. As for her modules, she would make the work up upon her return. Jean Paul did not say how he would explain his absence to his *abuela*, who by his telling was a devoted, doting Dominican woman who disliked when her baby went out on his own. *Her thirty-year-old baby,* Jennifer thought.

Peter was pointed in telling how he had deceived his parents. He had told them he was going to an art museum in New York, and they'd assented. If they had known the least thing about the module system, they would know an art museum could be experienced in a virtual tour. But they had sent their son to private schools with field trips, so they did not question his departure.

Melody had a more difficult time. Though generally, her foster parents ignored her comings and goings, on this occasion they demanded to know where she was going and why. Melody refused to tell. After a half hour of screaming, Melody slammed the apartment door with a shout of, "You petrol bots will never see me again!" She met Jennifer in the corridor. A snooping neighbor tried to appear distracted and inconspicuous.

"Well," Melody said, her voice sing songy, "that's that."

"Aren't you worried—what are you going to—did you mean that?" Jennifer asked.

Melody shrugged. She pushed her pink and black hair from her eyes, then slung her backpack over her shoulder.

"Don't know. They'll probably take me back. If not..." She shrugged again.

"But if they don't," Jennifer asked, "where will you live?"

"I'll talk to my social worker when we get back."

"Is that how foster works?" Jennifer asked. "Just ask for a new family and get it?"

"That's how I make it work."

Jennifer nodded. *How Melody.*

They followed the signs reading *Sol-Train Station*. Peter, Jean Paul, and Charles waited at the exit. With the Rooftop Readers Club assembled, they left Plex 87 together, triggering the double automatic doors to swing open, and a gust of humid air to billow in.

The Sol-Train station was only a short walk from the door. The teacher and students waited with nervous excitement. Eight minutes later, the train arrived. It was nearly silent, gliding on the lubricated track like an eel on the water. The train car doors opened, and they stepped in. Air-conditioning again.

Charles found five empty seats and directed everyone to sit. A screen faced him on the back of the seat in the next row. The screen had no words, only a black graphic on an orange background of a giant eyeball. Charles leaned in and opened his eyes wide. After a few seconds, the display beeped pleasantly, turned from orange to green, and the message changed to *Thank you, Charles Winston! Your fare has been debited from your account. Please interact with this Sol-Train interface to make your traveling experience pleasant.*

Charles chuckled. "Sol-Train." It had been the music of his grandparents' generation, but he was old enough to get that it was funny, even if it wasn't meant to be. He whistled a couple of notes, but when the students looked at him oddly, he stopped.

"Mister W, I thought you couldn't be seen with us. Ethics and all," Melody asked.

"Charles Winston, the EduForce employee could not," Charles replied. "But the private citizen?"

The train departed, whooshing along the tracks, gliding west. The sun climbed over the horizon behind them.

"So," Melody said, propping the soles of her feet on the seat. If an attendant or conductor came around, Jennifer knew she would be reprimanded. *Which is why she is doing it.*

"So what?" Charles said, the sad, mischievous smile returning.

"What are you doing? Kidnapping us? Selling us into slavery?"

"Well none of you are kids, save Peter, so that isn't likely—"

"Hey," Peter said.

"—and I don't know any slave traders. I don't run in the right circles. So, no. But we are going on a trip. To explore the past."

"Come on," Jennifer said. "Tell us."

"Authentic experience," Charles said. "That is what virtual tours cannot offer. Even if you have read my little book, you do not understand how it felt to walk the halls between classes, to sit at a rickety desk with profanity etched in its surface, to stand in an auditorium or cafeteria or gymnasium. And I can tell you about them, but hearing is not the same as knowing."

"Grip," Melody said.

"You'd better believe it's grip. You will see what school meant in the past, what you're missing."

"But where are we going?" Jennifer asked again.

"To my old high school," Charles replied. "Still in New Jersey, to the northwest. Less than an hour."

"That will take us all day?" Jean Paul asked. He looked up from his flexscreen, where he had been reading a technical manual for Plex solar cell repair.

"No," Charles admitted. "First, I have to attend to some...personal business."

"What does that mean?" Peter asked.

"It means it's personal," Melody snapped.

"We're starting off at Plex 291. I'm sure you can keep busy for an hour or two. Then when we finish, I'll meet you and take you to the school."

"And how will we get there?" Peter asked.

"We'll have to walk."

"Walk?" Peter whined. "Can't we get a car?"

"A what? From where?" Melody asked.

"Can't you just get a car?" Peter asked. "Call for one?"

Charles smiled.

"Your off-Plex upbringing is showing. There are no cars for people like us. It should only be a mile or so."

For a few minutes, they all looked out the Sol-Train window at the landscape, the densely packed buildings of northeast New Jersey being replaced by trees and fields. The train zipped past the crumbling, weed-choked carapaces of old department stores and parking lots. They were connected by long ribbons of broken concrete and steel snaking across the fields and hills. Single-family homes, stacked and coiled in neighborhoods and developments, sat empty and dark with windows broken and roofs caved in and yards grown wild.

"Not too long ago," Charles said, and the students turned to him. "Not too long ago, all of these places were alive. I used to drive on these roads and shop in these stores. Live in a house just like these. Seeing them fall to pieces like this feels...wrong to me. Unnatural. But really, it is becoming natural again. The forests and wetlands, the fields and streams and rabbits and deer and bees and birds, they're all coming back."

"Is that because of the Hundred Day Shutdown?" Peter asked. Charles smiled. The kid knew his history.

"Yes," he replied. "When other nations started calling in America's debts in the 2020s, our Federal government could no longer pretend it had the money it was spending. Congress declared the 'Temporary Fiscal Reassessment Recess,' but news, and now your history modules, call it 'The Hundred Day Shutdown.'" While Congress muddled around and the Federal government disintegrated, the public predicted doomsday. The news said the nation would be thrown into chaos and anarchy, with looting and burning, leaving our old civilization in rubble. Didn't happen. Our society didn't collapse; it adapted. The highway system was doomed.

"Rashid Nair, the visionary developer, piloted the first Plex in Detroit. He bought up entire neighborhoods, knocked them down, and created a single Mega-complex of apartments. It was an instant success. It was safer, cheaper, and more secure than other housing choices. Nair invited retailers and restaurants inside. Metropolitan police departments, already underfunded, were leery of using resources to station officers inside a private residence permanently, so Nair hired a private security force, setting the precedent you know today. Soon, Cleveland, Indianapolis, and other "Rust Belt" cities with large quantities of cheap, available property became the sites of the next Plexes. Other cities followed suit.

"And as for transportation between the Plexes? Major oil corporations worked with the rail companies to establish this system of solar-powered trains. Cars went from something every person *had* to have to something a few of the wealthy *chose* to have. Anyone can ride the Sol-Train, and tickets are cheap. Most of Sol-Train's profits come from advertising, not fares. Have you ever stopped and looked at how much advertising is around you, all the time?"

The students looked all around the train at advertisements on the seat-back screens, in the windows of the train, on digital billboards outside, on the doors and ceiling.

"Then think about your AIPA," Charles went on. "Always offering to help get you anything you want. They may annoy you occasionally, but the artificial intelligence they run on is adaptable and accurate. Your AIPA gets to know you because it monitors your behavior and spending habits, then offers to make purchases for you based on this data."

"What's so bad about that?" Jennifer said. "I think it's helpful. I don't have to go out and find things if I want them."

"Oh, it's helpful. And brilliant. Almost fifty years ago, companies were attempting rudimentary forms of at-home delivery and predictive purchasing. But the Plex system united everything. Anything you could think of buying is available within the four walls of the Plex. There is no more delayed gratification. Your wants and needs can be met before you even know they exist."

"Plex life isn't so great," Peter muttered. They looked to him to elaborate. The train sailed along a stretch of track suspended between two hills. Below, a car dealership rusted away, a testament to the waste and excess of the previous century. Peter pointed to it. "Well, take cars.

Cars are grip. They go fast, and they're more fun than the train. Poor people take the train."

"Everyone takes the train," Melody said.

Peter shrugged and mumbled, "I guess so."

"In some ways," Charles said, "cars are grip. They give the driver a sense of freedom, of independence, of control. This is why the corporations and governments wanted them gone."

Jennifer saw no glamor in cars. How absurd and dangerous they were! Almost anyone could get a license, fill the tank with combustible fuel, and propel the driver and passengers along poorly maintained roads from one structure to another. It sounded irresponsible and terrifying. And what about driver error or distraction? Did drivers really accept as a given risk that another driver could be using a phone or turning around to yell at his children in the back seat or drinking alcohol, and that these other drivers could crash into you and kill you? The Sol-Train system sounded much safer. The number of people killed in Sol-Train accidents each year, across the country, could be counted on two hands.

"Peter," Charles asked. "Why did your family move on-Plex?"

Peter looked away.

"It just didn't work out anymore," he said.

"What happened?" Melody asked.

"It just didn't work out. Dad's job changed. Now we're on-Plex."

"What is it like, living in a house?" Jean Paul asked. "How do you stay warm without the solar heating system?"

"It was called a furnace. It would burn something, I think some kind of gas, and keep the house warm."

"Wasn't there smoke in your house all the time?" Jennifer asked. Peter laughed.

"Of course not. You hardly even noticed it. The house stayed warm in the winter and cool in the summer."

"But how did they get the gas into your house? Where did your food come from? When you had to buy things, what did you do?"

"Well, the gas, I don't know. I think it came to us in pipes in the ground or something. If we bought food or clothes or furniture or anything, we placed the order and a truck would come from the company and bring it to us."

"Wait," Jean Paul said. "A whole truck? To your house, just to your family?"

"Yeah."

"And when I was a child," Charles added, "only some goods were delivered. Most of the time, we had to get in the car and drive to the store, buy it, then drive it home."

Jennifer shook her head. She was starting to understand why the pre-Plex system was so wasteful and inefficient. In the Plex, every shopping convenience was within an AIPA command or walking distance.

"What are those?" Melody asked, pointing out of the window. The train was passing by a row of abandoned houses huddled along an abandoned highway. The windows were boarded over, and the front doors marked with red X's.

"The red X's mean the houses were marked for demolition," Charles said. "They must have been forgotten or ignored. There have been a lot of houses to tear down in the last fifteen years. This little row along the highway must have been low priority."

"No," Melody said. "In front of them and behind them. All of those plants growing there. This place wasn't a farm, was it?"

Now Charles laughed.

"No, not a farm. Those were called 'lawns.' They were plots of land around the house where the owners grew grass."

"What was the grass for?" Jennifer asked.

"Nothing," Charles said. "It looked nice."

"No one ate it? You didn't use it to feed animals or anything?" Jennifer asked.

"No."

"But grass grows," Jennifer said. "Didn't it grow up over the house after a while?"

"That's stupid," Peter said. "The lawn service came in and cut it."

"Or, back in my day, we used lawnmowers."

"What?" Melody asked. The word came out like a chop from a hatchet.

"Wait," Jennifer said, turning to Melody. "I thought you knew about all that old stuff. Music and stuff."

"Right," Melody replied. "Music and stuff. But not lawnmowers. How did they..."

"Lawnmowers," Charles said. A slim, secretive smile came over his face. "They were machines the user would start up, and giant blades underneath would start spinning very fast, and the user would push it in straight lines, back and forth across the lawn, until all of the grass was cut short and close to the ground. Homeowners would have to do this every week or so."

"Giant blades?" Jennifer asked. "Sounds dangerous."

Charles shrugged and said, "It was. You had to watch out for loose sticks and rocks. If they were caught in the blades, they would be flung out like little projectiles. Even worse were things like glass bottles or wasp nests. It was physically demanding work, and sometimes, if someone did something risky or stupid, he lost an arm or a foot."

"But how did the blades spin?" Jennifer asked. "Please tell me they were solar powered."

"No. Way way back, before I was born, they were manual. The blades turned from the rotation of the wheels. But in my day, most of them were powered by gas or electricity."

Jennifer leaped out of her seat. "So, you're telling me that back when you were a kid, your family had a big patch of grass in front of your house that did nothing other than sit there and grow. It didn't feed anyone or add anything to the world. And to maintain it, you had to buy a big machine that could chop off your foot or send a nest of angry wasps after you. And even if it didn't do that, you had to fill this big machine with gasoline that was ruining the atmosphere. And you would do this every week."

"Yes," he replied. "And some of my fondest childhood memories are stepping out onto the lawn after my father cut it, the smell of fresh cut grass and gasoline still in the air, the uniform prickle and caress of shorn blades of grass under my bare feet. I haven't smelled or felt that in...in a long time."

Peter sighed. Melody rolled her eyes and crossed her arms.

"The past was twitchin'. Old people are weird," she said. "No wonder you guys messed up the twentieth century so bad."

"Don't blame me for the twentieth century," Charles warned, though his tone was playful. "I was born at the end of it. I've lived most of my life in the same world you've lived yours, the world of Plexes and Sol-Trains and EduForce and Recycling Binges. But I remember the world the way it used to be."

"Which way is better?" Jennifer asked.

Charles shrugged. "How is 'better' defined? The old ways were inefficient, dangerous, wasteful, and ignorant."

"Agreed," Jennifer said.

"So, if the old ways are so loathsome," Charles said, "why are we having this class?"

The only reply was silence. Jennifer looked at the ground, Melody out of the window. Jean Paul was still buried in his manual. Peter's gaze was far away. So, Charles went on.

"I've studied a lot of history. Despotic governments, the really wicked, destructive ones, they can get people to obey by manipulating the past. They can make people idealize it, then idolize it, so that nostalgia becomes patriotism which becomes nationalism which becomes jingoism and xenophobia, which can make citizens do some terrible things in the name of restoring the good old days."

"But the past was better," Melody said. "At least, look at the music. The music from the eighties, nineties, and early twenty-first century, that was real. Real instruments and emotions. Music today is garbage."

Charles smiled.

"Back then," he replied, "people were saying the same thing about the music of that time."

Jennifer held up her hands.

"Don't listen to Melody. She's strange. She likes all the petrol things no one else likes and hates the popular stuff. Personally, I'm glad the past is over. Everyone used to be so stupid and do such ridiculous things. Like drive cars. I wouldn't want to be around for that."

"Not so fast," Charles said. "It is just as dangerous to reject the past, to say everything old was bad and everything new is good." His voice lowered, and he leaned in.

"This is the time we live in now. Those in power want only one thing—to stay in power. To do this, they will make you just happy enough, just settled and content enough, to prevent you from realizing you have no power. They have built you a world with so much convenience and easy stimulation, so much distraction and so many unearned rewards that you will not ask why things are the way they are. A few thousand ultra-wealthy, ultra-powerful people keep a stranglehold on every last cent and every last vote, and all they want to do is keep themselves where they are and keep you where you are. And how do they do this? With your education. What is my job? To undo your education. Not to make you forget. Making people forget is a tool of the tyrant. No, my job is to make you unlearn. By unlearning the teachings of tyrants, you can undo tyranny."

"But we live in a democracy," Jennifer said.

"Pssh," said Charles.

"No, we do," Jennifer went on. "I learned it in my American history module."

"You mean a module designed by EduForce, a multi-trillion-dollar educational company, with the blessing of our national government. Is that where you learned it?"

"Yes," Jennifer said, feeling like she was being made fun of but not sure why. She was starting to understand why working with a teacher in person was so much different than studying the modules. A teacher in a module video would never confront her like this, never challenge her or make her question her understanding.

"Tell me Jennifer, what is a democracy?"

"Where people vote."

"Vote for what? Or for whom?"

Jennifer smiled because this was a fact she recalled from the history module.

"A direct democracy is one in which citizens vote on every issue. A representative democracy, or republic, is one in which citizens elect leaders who make the decisions for them."

"And what do we have in America?"

"A republic."

"Very good. So, you vote for people to represent you and your interests. Who ran for President in the last election?"

Jennifer thought. It seemed so long ago.

"Well, I know Alvarado won."

"He did. Alvarado has a fortune of approximately $3.5 billion dollars. Do you know any billionaires?"

"No," Jennifer said.

"No," Melody said.

"I used to," Peter said.

"Jean Paul, do you know any billionaires?" Charles asked. Jean Paul shook his head no.

"Neither do I," Charles said. "And not only does Alvarado have $3.5 billion, but he got most of that from his parents. So, he has never known a life other than the life of a billionaire. So how could he possibly represent you or me?"

Silence. Charles went on.

"Last election, Alvarado ran against Markerson."

"That's right!" Jennifer said, remembering.

"Also a billionaire," Charles said. "Alvarado's term is expiring next year. So, we have three candidates now announced. Who are they?"

"Geraldine Barfield," Jennifer said, a glimmer of admiration in her voice.

"Billionaire. Who else is running?"

"Stern," Jennifer said.

"Billionaire."

"And Kandar."

"Billionaire. Trillionaire, actually, if you include all of his property holdings. Kandar owns about twenty percent of all the Plexes in the country. So, you have three people running, though it will narrow down to two by next spring. Two billionaires and a trillionaire. You live in a Plex. One of the candidates owns nearly one hundred Plexes. Do you think any of these candidates care about your needs? Or even know about them?"

Jennifer looked down.

"Well, it is the responsibility of the electorate to vote these people in," Melody said. "If you don't like the people running the country, vote for different ones."

Charles smiled and nodded.

"An excellent point. Did you know this? Last election, Alvarado won with about forty-seven percent of the vote. Not a majority but enough to beat the other candidates. So, it sounds democratic. Except about ninety million people voted in the last election. That is about twenty percent of our country's voting population. What does this mean? This means that in this representative democracy of ours, less than ten percent of the voting age population voted for our current President.

"A survey was taken after that election. The number of people who voted on Election Day? About ninety million. The number of people who spent more than six hours playing a video game or messaging people with different applications? Two hundred million. So yes, American citizens have to shoulder part of the blame."

"But I don't care which billionaire runs this country," Melody said. "What difference does it make? My life just goes on the same, one way or another."

"Exactly," Charles said. "During election season, candidates want you to think the contest is between one candidate or another. But they are really all on the same team. Every politician's goal is to either maintain or expand his or her power. The campaigns look like vicious, dirty fights, but they aren't. If a billionaire loses an election, he is still a billionaire. But if a billionaire is dragged down from his mighty, off-Plex mansion, and forced to live near other people and learn how it feels to never have money for retirement and face the prospect of working until death, and forced to eat commercially grown food that has been injected with steroids and hormones and antibiotics to make it cheaper, and made to see that he is just as much a human being as the millions of humans who live beneath him, well then, that would terrify him.

"So, maybe voting means you are participating in democracy, or maybe it means you are participating in the illusion of democracy. Maybe being a good citizen means more than going to a voting booth once every four years and pressing a button. Maybe being a good citizen means being a little bad."

The train car door opened, and Charles fell silent. An automated snack and drink cart rolled in. It stopped near the group, and immediately Melody, Jennifer, Peter, and Jean Paul pounced on it and leaned their faces into the scanner to deduct from their account. A few moments later, pouches of chips, cookies, sodas, and energy drinks rolled out of a chute on the side. Charles did the same, ordering a seltzer water and bag of popcorn.

When the snack cart departed, the heat of the conversation had cooled. Melody read from Charles's Frost anthology. Charles pulled out *Border Patrols* and idly read a random chapter. He smiled, thinking what an odd sight they must be. Jean Paul studied solar batteries in a manual on his flexscreen. Jennifer worked on her next EduForce module. Perfect Five or no, she had work to do. Only Peter stared out of the window.

"What are you thinking about?" Melody asked him.

"Lawns," he replied, and said no more.

THE SOL-TRAIN ARRIVED at the Mahwah/Ramapo/Ringwood Station, a few miles from the New York/New Jersey border, about an hour later. A small Plex, 291, stood only a few hundred yards away. Charles led the group to the entrance. Most of the Plexes followed the same design schematics, and so aside from the choice of paint and carpet colors, or the particular arrangements of stores in the shopping areas, each Plex was interchangeable with every other.

"All right, Mister W," Melody said, "what are we doing here?"

Charles spread his arms.

"Whatever you like. Just don't get into trouble. Buy clothes, eat food, go to a sun booth, I don't care. Just stay out of trouble and be back at this entrance in...three hours. Ten o'clock."

Melody scowled.

"But what are you doing?"

"Don't you remember?" Peter said. "Personal business."

For a moment, it looked as if Melody might punch Peter. He blushed.

"Three hours," Charles said, already walking away. "And don't be late!"

Charles walked through the main corridor to the shopping area that lay at the heart of the Plex. He did not stop and browse the stores. The same dozen corporate chains were present in every Plex anyway, so he would not find anything here in Plex 291 that he could not find in Plex 87.

He climbed the stairs to the second floor, avoiding the easy convenience of the elevator. He looked around until he saw the sandwich shop they had agreed to meet at. Charles scanned the tables and immediately saw Shaaya. She looked much like she had the last time Charles had seen her five years earlier. Short, sharply dressed, radiating professionalism. Perfect posture. A powerhouse. Dark, dark eyes that glowed. *She hasn't aged a bit. She even looks younger.* Charles doubted the same could be said for himself. He had transitioned from "middle-aged" to "old man," from "salt-and-pepper" to "gray," from "weathered" to "wrinkly," and "lean" to "skinny."

Shaaya was not alone.

Charles did not see the other person at first, as he had been transfixed by the sight of his wife. But Shaaya, who was four years younger than Charles, was sitting by a man who was probably ten years younger than her. He smiled a lot as Shaaya spoke to him, and his teeth were brilliant white. The man also sat with excellent posture, and when he moved, he seemed to be brimming with vigor. *He has the look of a man who has not put on a pound since high school. I bet he still swims a mile a day and works out with weights.*

Shaaya looked up and noticed Charles. *That gaze.* It was why her students had respected and loved and feared her. It was why Charles had respected and loved and feared her. It was a gaze that could tear through any problem. When the man's gaze joined Shaaya's, Charles felt small and defenseless. The twenty steps to the table seemed to take a long time.

"You're here," Shaaya said.

"Yes," Charles said, "I took the train."

"Obviously."

"It's been a long time."

"Some time," Shaaya said, swishing her coffee in its cup. "Some time, yes."

"You look good."

"This is Martin."

She said it "Mart-*teen,*" and Charles wondered if the man or his ancestors were Latin American. Or maybe it was an affectation. Either way, the man extended his hand. Charles debated shaking it, but then did. It was firm.

"Pleasure," Martin said, his syllables like jabs. Charles grunted. He had not expected Shaaya would be seeing anyone else. Charles had never seen anyone. He and Shaaya had never formally split—she had left, and he had waited, and had waited now for five years. The thought of her spending time with another man, kissing him, taking him to bed—he forced himself to stop the thoughts.

"That's some grip," Charles said. "You an athlete?"

"I swim a mile each morning," Martin replied.

"And he lifts weights," Shaaya chipped in.

Goddamn it. No way.

"We were about to order," Shaaya said. "Take a menu. Our treat."

Charles took the menu tentatively. "Our treat" sounded like a trap.

"How have you been?" he asked Shaaya, pointedly directing the question to her and not to Martin.

"I am well," she replied. "You?"

"Same as always."

"That bad?" Charles wasn't sure if she was attempting a joke or being critical. He had never been sure.

"What line of work are you in?" Martin asked. *He must know already.* If Martin had been dating Shaaya for any length of time, she would have already mentioned Charles and his work. *He's trying to get a dig in at me. Or maybe he's being polite. I cannot tell with this guy.*

"I'm a teacher," Charles replied. Martin beamed.

"So am I!"

Shaaya opened her mouth as if to cut Martin off and avert an awkward conversation, but Charles replied too fast.

"What do you teach?"

"Oh, anything," Martin replied. "Anything they give to me."

Charles understood. He frowned.

"You're not a teacher," he said. "You're—"

"Enough," Shaaya said, and both men fell silent. "Enough talk about work."

"What about your work?" Charles asked. "I saw a little write-up in my NewsFeed about your research. Still at the University?"

"Yes," Shaaya said, "Well, vidconference lectures. And don't start with—"

"Still helping the rich get richer?"

"Goddamn it," Shaaya exhaled. "Don't get me started on this."

"I'm saying I've worked for decades—and worked longer hours for less money and less respect each year—to steer as many young people as I could toward good books and good writing. And I recognize what I do now is only a shadow of what I once thought my career would be. But this guy—" Charles pointed to Martin with the menu. "This guy here, with his tanning bed tan and bleached white smile, thinks he can slide in front of a camera and talk like a parrot for six minutes and call himself a teacher. He's an imposter, a mannequin with a good handshake."

"Martin is my fiancé," Shaaya said, and Charles could not have been more surprised if she had pulled a gun on him. Martin stood up.

"I'll order. What do you want, dear?"

"Usual," Shaaya said without breaking eye contact with Charles.

"I'm not hungry, darling," Charles snarled.

"Oh come, now," Shaaya said. "You traveled all the way out here. The least we can do is buy your lunch."

Charles had another angry reply on his lips, but instead he looked at the menu. He really wasn't hungry, but his eyes went to the highest priced item he could find.

"The lobster bisque with a crab salad and the deluxe flounder sandwich. With an extra-large iced tea."

He thrust the menu to Martin, who took it and walked off to the ordering kiosk. Shaaya's glare revealed she knew exactly what Charles was doing. He hated seafood.

"How can he be your fiancé?" Charles asked, his voice hushed and angry. "We are still married."

"Are we? In what way besides legally?"

"That's the way that matters," Charles said.

"Tell me what you want, and I will tell you what I want," Shaaya said. Charles resisted the urge to lower his head in humility. Shaaya would only see that as cowardice.

"Very well," he said. "I lost my job with EduForce. I cannot pay for Clara's residence anymore. I need you to take over the monthly payments."

Shaaya gritted her teeth.

"When we put her in Hopespring, you said—"

"I remember what I said."

"You said 'I will take care of it. I will pay for her stay.' She should not suffer because your incompetence at your job—"

"It was not incompetence—"

"You said 'I promise.'" Charles had no reply. Shaaya threw up her hands. "You are outrageous. Now it is my turn."

Shaaya reached into her bag and brought out her flexscreen. It was a bigger, faster, newer model than Charles's, but he was not surprised.

She unrolled the device, turned on the screen, and brought up a document. Then she slid the flexscreen across the table to Charles.

"Petition for Divorce"

They were the only words Charles could read. They were the only ones he needed to read. The sandwich shop started to close in around him.

"Why?" he stammered.

"Why? How many reasons can I give you? We have not spoken in five years or lived together in ten. You stubbornly refuse to listen to me or make any changes for our family—"

"You know I was stuck at that job—"

"But you *like* being stuck. You call it 'stuck' but it really means 'hiding.'"

Ouch, Charles thought. *Her mind and tongue were always like a surgeon's scalpel. And she always knew myriad ways to carve me up.*

"We've discussed this. I need to teach," Charles said. "I'm not skilled to do anything else."

"When did you even try?"

Silence fell between them. It was a fight so tired, so worn out, and repetitive neither of them felt like dragging themselves through it again. Charles looked over. Martin had ordered the food and was waiting at the counter.

Charles looked back at Shaaya. She really did look younger. Even when she was mad at him, she was beautiful. *Especially when she was mad at me.*

"How are the girls?" Charles asked.

"Well, Tamra is married now—"

"Married, really?"

"Yes. They live on the other end of this Plex."

"Here?"

"And her son was born last year."

"A son?"

"Do I not enunciate properly for you?" Shaaya asked. "His name is Daniel. Very healthy. Their family is getting on well. I had hoped she would stay home with him after the birth, but she said it was not realistic. She went back to work two weeks later."

This did not surprise Charles. Few citizens could afford to stay home and raise their children. Two weeks was the standard healing time most employers allowed.

"Is she still a Sol-Train driver?"

"Yes. I think she is up for a promotion next year."

Charles squirmed with discomfort at hearing that.

"And Clara?"

"Still in...in the home. The doctors say she is well behaved but not improving."

Charles squirmed again, and Shaaya noticed.

"Why don't you go and visit her, then? Get out of your damn apartment and take the train out to Poughkeepsie and visit the home and see your daughter. God, I have not seen you in five years and you still want me to go out scouting for you. Do you really want to know what made me realize I need this divorce? Our wedding vows."

"Our wedding vows?"

"My God, you are like a parrot sometimes. Yes, our vows. In them, you said I was your anchor. How nice. But I am not the anchor. I am the engine. I am the wind in the sails. I am the paddlewheel. I thought for a while you were the anchor, but then I realized it was not true, because anchors can be pulled up. You are just dead weight. So please sign the document now, and you can go back to your life, and I can go on with mine."

"With Martin."

"With Martin."

As if on cue, Martin arrived with two trays of food. He set one in front of Charles and one in front of himself and Shaaya. Charles did not even look at his meal. Instead, he rose from his seat and slung his drawstring bag over his shoulder.

"Not today," he said to Shaaya. "Give me time."

"Time? How much time do you—"

"And thank you for lunch," Charles said to Martin, before picking up his tray of seafood, dumping it in the trash, and walking out of the restaurant.

WHILE ALL PLEXES followed essentially the same design, Charles could tell the section of Plex 291 Tamra lived in was not as well kept as the rest. The old, infrequently cleaned carpets smelled of chemicals and body odor. Overhead lighting flickered in the hall. And when he stopped at a directory, it ran sluggishly, as if its software had not been updated in some time. Nevertheless, he soon stood at his daughter's door, knocking, preparing to see her for the first time in five years.

He was not prepared. He had not been prepared to see Shaaya, who had grown stronger, more graceful, and more beautiful in the interceding years. But time, it seemed, had not been so generous to Tamra. Tamra was tall and lean, and had fairer skin than her twin sister, Clara. As a teen, she could have been described as "willowy" and graceful. She had a physique her ballet teachers had quivered to see.

When Tamra opened the door, Charles could tell she had not treated herself well in the past five years. She was, perhaps, only five or ten pounds heavier than when he had last seen her, but it was distributed oddly, making her look paunchy and unkempt. Her hair strayed out in frizzled strands from a messy bun. Her eyes no longer glittered, as they had when she was a child. They were tired and dull. She looked at Charles the way she might look at a sandwich she had forgotten about in the refrigerator.

"Tamra!" Charles exclaimed, hoping false cheerfulness could turn into the genuine thing.

"Charles," she returned, and he knew he was in for trouble.

"May I come in?"

Tamra stepped aside, and Charles walked into the apartment. It was larger than his own—he rented only a tiny studio—and immaculately kept. Tamra had always been the tidier of the twins, but this place looked like a showroom. An elegant vase with a single flower sat on the dining room table, gleaming stainless-steel appliances lined the kitchen, and even the pillows on the sofa were symmetrically arranged.

"What a beautiful home," Charles said. "You didn't have to clean up like this for me."

"Huh?"

"You must have spent hours."

Tamra waved her hand dismissively. She walked into the kitchen.

"Cleaning takes whatever time it takes, I guess."

Then Charles realized: *She does this every day.*

"That was quite a train ride," he said, looking at the framed art on the walls. All of it was the sort anyone could buy at a retail store. "I remember back when you were kids, we took a trip up to Boston. We all piled into the car and drove up I-95. Except there was a terrible accident on the Connecticut border, and traffic was so backed up that we all turned our cars off and walked around. There were a couple of teenage boys in the car next to ours, and you shared your road snacks with them. I think you girls thought that part was more exciting than the time in Boston! Do you remember that?"

"Can I get you a glass of water?"

"Sure."

Charles sat at the dining room table on a polished, high-backed chair. He would have been more comfortable on the sofa, but Tamra brought two glasses of water to the table, set them at opposite ends, then sat down.

"You look good," Charles said, fighting against the silence.

"Thank you," she replied tonelessly.

"How have you been?"

"Well."

"What have you been doing?"

"Working."

"Oh, really?" Charles said. The words came out of his mouth sounding condescending, but he had not meant them to. He wanted to sound interested. "Doing what?"

"I am a Sol-Train driver," she replied. "Still."

"Wow!" Charles said, and scolded himself again for the inflated tone. *I sound like I am listening to a three-year-old showing off his teddy bear.* "Have you gone anywhere exciting?"

"I am only a regional driver. Interstate runs are for the veterans. I have four more years to go before I will be considered for that."

"Well, that's something to look forward to," Charles said.

Tamra shrugged. "The driver's seat looks the same whether you're in there for a half hour or five hours. But the pay is better."

Charles took a sip of water.

"That sounds nice," he said.

"Why are you here?"

"Why? I'm your father. I wanted to see you."

"But you haven't wanted to the past five years?"

Charles fell silent again. He felt foolish and unprepared.

"Have you even looked at my mantel?" Tamra asked. Charles turned his head to the wooden mantle around the artificial fireplace.

"It's a wonderful fireplace," he said, and Tamra groaned.

"Not the fireplace. The mantel. The pictures on it."

Charles's mind was dragging through mud. His own daughter had adopted the tone of an impatient parent. He rose and walked over to the fireplace. There was a row of digital framed photographs. Tamra and a man, short and squat, not particularly handsome but genial enough. Tamra and the man in front of Faneuil Hall in Boston. Tamra and the man in skiing gear on a windswept mountain. *Probably VR vacations.* Tamra and the man at an altar, before a minster.

"You're married."

"Yes. You figured it out."

"But I wasn't there!"

"Gabriel and I did not invite you."

"Why not? I'm your father!"

"Not much of one," Tamra replied. Her tone was icy. "Not for what you did to Clara. Not for shutting Mom out."

"I...I didn't—"

"Look at the rest of the pictures," Tamra said.

Charles did. More of Tamra and Gabriel. Then one of Tamra and Gabriel in hospital scrubs, proudly holding a squalling newborn. Then pictures of just the baby. Charles looked down to the end of the mantel at a photo narrative of a little boy, from birth, to bassinet, to crawling, to standing in the kitchen, to the last picture, the boy making an awkward swing with a tee-ball bat, probably at a game in the Plex sports complex.

"Tell me about your child."

"A little boy named Daniel. He will be four in a few weeks."

"And I'm a grandfather."

"If you want to call yourself that, I can't stop you."

"Tamra, I am trying to get my bearings here. The last time I saw you, you were a little girl."

"I was twenty-two."

"Still, no husband, no children, just your future ahead of you. And now—do you still dance?"

Tamra laughed acidly.

"Do I dance? Look at me."

"Dancing is in your heart," Charles pleaded. "Don't give it up."

"Wrong. Dancing was in my head. It is in Clara's heart."

"But you were so good!" Charles explained. "To throw that away…"

"I didn't throw anything away," Tamra said. "I just made smarter choices. Realistic choices. I reached an age when I realized even if I was a good dancer, there was no way to make a life from it. It was like being highly talented at making pipe-cleaner animals. Who cares? Then I saw what pursuing dance did for Clara, and what you did for her, and I made some smarter choices. You were nowhere to be seen, and Mom was a mess, so I found Gabriel, we had Daniel, and now he's old enough for childcare, I drive. Not a bad life. We are comfortable and content. I doubt you can say the same."

"I had to put Clara in Hopespring," Charles said, repeating what he had told Shaaya, Tamra, and himself countless times.

"Had to," Tamra replied. She did not say it as a question, but as a challenge.

"It was that or send her out of the Plex. Have her live in the shadows with bandits, lunatics, and child molesters. She couldn't work at a job, so I—"

"Wouldn't work. She was immature, not mentally ill. But hey, it's your paycheck from now until death that will keep her in Hopespring. You could at least visit her."

I can't tell her about my job. He looked at his shoes.

"I think I should go," he said.

"It's what you do best."

"That's not fair."

"Just do one favor after you leave."

"What can I do for you? Anything."

"Not for me. For Mom. Sign the papers."

Charles grumbled.

"She talked to you?"

"Of course. Unlike you, she still talks to me. She called me before you came here. She told me about your meeting, and about how rude you were to Martin."

"I was not rude. I was...cordial."

"Sure. Did Mom tell you about her job?"

"No."

"She is getting promoted."

"What?" Charles said.

"To full professor. No more vidconferences," Tamra explained, with pride in her voice. "She and Martin are moving to Plex 440, in New Haven. She'll be teaching on campus at Yale."

"Huh," Charles said, feeling like a fool. Shaaya's career had just lapped his again. There were probably no more than a hundred professors in the country who taught on campus.

"So," Tamra continued, "just sign the papers so she can move on. So you can too."

Charles was not sure what that last comment meant. But he left Tamra's apartment, his glass of water still half-full on the dining room table.

CHARLES SAT ON a bench in the Plex 291 corridor by the Sol-Train exit. The time was 10:15, and the Readers Club had not returned yet. *Border Patrols* sat open on his lap, unread. He thought of the train outside and imagined Tamra buckled into the conductor's seat, her long legs bent as she sat at the controls. She was so tall and graceful, a dancer so talented and skilled her teachers said she had nearly unlimited potential as a ballerina. There was no stage she would not be able to conquer. Now she was twenty-eight, married with a child, and crammed into the conductor's seat of a train.

And then there was Clara, Tamra's twin. The dance instructors had agreed that though Tamra's technical skill was superior, Clara was the dancer with more passion and spirit, the one who lived and embodied the emotions of her characters.

Now she was in Hopespring Home for Intractables. *I really should visit her,* he thought, then felt guilty that he never thought the same of Tamra. But even thinking of the home, of the day he and Shaaya left her there, filled him with shame. Thinking of Clara in the home brought a dark cloud over his mind. His frustration and anger hardened.

I would take care of her. I had promised.

But now the situation had changed. He could not take care of himself without a job, much less his daughter in an institution.

When we get back to Plex 87, I will find a new job, no matter how dull or dreary. These woods are lovely, dark, and deep, but I have promises to keep.

Ten: The Field Trip

No system designed for the controlling of humans is 100 percent efficient. Those who do not fit, whether by nature or by will, are always going to threaten the system. In difference lies resistance, and in resistance lies hope.

　　—The Trough, p.194

The road from Plex 291 wrapped around the hill and curved out of sight. The group had to be alert as they walked. Since roads were largely unused, they were largely unpoliced. If a driver for AmeriHaul decided to cut some time off a run by traveling back roads at one hundred miles per hour, or if a wealthy off-Plexer decided to take one of his Mercedes for a carefree spin in the country, neither driver would be looking out for pedestrians. If Charles or one of the students was hit by a vehicle, they would be dead before the engine was turned off.

But there were no cars or trucks on the road. The roadbed was cracked and buckling, the result of never having been repaved in a decade. Highway infrastructure, as with most services once municipal, was no longer the province of the government. The wealthy off-Plexers who used it for recreation and AmeriHaul who used it for shipping paid for the upkeep, and thus could use roads as they pleased.

Off-Plexers came in two types. One was outrageously wealthy and able to import goods and generate their own power and utilities. Often, their homes were more like compounds, fortified estates supporting a staff of dozens and guarded against outside intruders. The other type was stubbornly unconventional, subsisting beyond the fringes of civilization on their own survival skills. This breed of off-Plexer was a constant source of contempt and ridicule in Plex entertainment. In films and television programs, they were bearded and missing teeth, speaking bizarre mountain dialects and wearing smudgy old clothes. In literature—or at least the EduForce short stories that were manufactured for testing—Off-Plexers were psychologically disturbed, drug addicted, and hopelessly flawed. They lived in tiny communes, and the men and boys penetrated every female, old and young, mothers and sisters, humans and animals. Charles and the students huddled a little closer walking up the road.

Half a mile ahead, around a wooded bend, sat a brick building in a clearing. Rows of windows, all dark, sat in stillness as tall weeds grew wildly against the walls and a solitary flagpole pierced the sky. Trees stood watch in the courtyard and in the parking lot. The lot was empty, save for a row of yellow school buses, rotted with rust, parked near the side entrance.

"This," Charles said, "was a school."

"It looks..." started Jennifer.

"Empty?" Melody said.

"Well, of course," Charles said. "No one has used this building in fifteen years. But years ago, this place was a wonder. Every morning, children and young people from all over the region would pile into buses, or arrive in the cars of their parents, or walk, if they were close enough. Everyone would pour into the front entrance, and the building came to life with the energy from all of these youths. Their teachers waited in their classrooms, ready to teach. The children would then disperse to their classrooms, arms full of books and notebooks and pencils. And in those rooms, there were no distractions. No cameras watching you, no advertisements popping in front of you in the middle of a lesson, no lights and sounds jarring you for every little thing you do. There was the material, and there was the student, and there was the teacher who was a conduit between the two. That was what learning and teaching were all about."

"Bullshit," Melody said. Everyone else turned and stared at her.

"That's bullshit, Mister W," she went on. "I read *The Trough*. Schools had plenty of problems. How did you say it? 'Education was a mess everyone felt someone else had made and was someone else's to clean up.' You talked about kids being bored and falling asleep and parents who wouldn't cooperate and politicians getting in the way and drugs and gangs and guns and—"

"Okay!" Charles said. "Okay, I get it. Schools weren't perfect. But the student-teacher connection was still alive. Not now. Not with your video modules and automated assessment games. From Plato and Socrates all the way up to 2034, teachers and students had to face one another. Challenge one another. Probe. But with your recorded lessons, you don't have a guide. You don't have someone to say, 'You're wrong.'"

"What are we waiting for?" Jean Paul said. "Let's go!"

The Rooftop Readers Club walked up the broken sidewalk toward the main entrance. Jennifer stepped over buckling cement, fallen tree limbs, and empty liquor bottles. Most of the bottles were dirty and clouded. The school must have been closed for so long that the site had long since lost its appeal even as a hideaway for nearby kids to sneak off and drink. *Probably more convenient for them to go to the roof,* she thought.

They approached the front entrance. The brick façade surrounded three pairs of steel doors, once painted red or brown, though most of the paint had peeled and flaked off, leaving the dull gray below. Small, square windows sat high and close, like the eyes of a troll. The glass in them appeared to be an inch and a half thick.

"Inviting," Melody said.

"Safety," replied Charles. "These doors were probably one of the last improvements made to the school before it closed. By 2034, nearly every school was equipped with steel doors and bulletproof windows. Didn't help, though. Most attacks began from inside."

He did not have to say the name of the place to evoke the images and memories. *Scarsdale.*

Jennifer stared at the blank surface of the steel door. A school was archaic, wasteful, and apparently dangerous. Why build an entire structure, dependent on heat and electricity, to and from which students and teachers had to ride in petroleum-fueled cars and buses, and which was even closed for a quarter of the year, and which could become a massacre site in a moment, when a child could learn from home with a flexscreen and an EduForce account? But now, standing before the huge edifice, there was something remarkable about a school, something important and...sacred. The word made her uneasy. She did not know if it was the right one. But it felt close to what she wanted to express. She wanted to enter this strange temple and see the past, see and feel the halls that once held teachers and students and all they shared.

Jennifer reached for the door and pulled. It was locked.

She looked around for something to pry the door open, but all she found was garbage, sticks, and other useless debris. Even if a crowbar had been lying at her feet, she doubted she would have had the strength to wrench the door open. She turned and faced Melody, Charles, Peter and Jean Paul.

"Locked. I guess there's no way in."

Melody rolled her eyes. She stooped down and picked up a large rock. She strode over to one of the first-floor windows, but Charles stopped her before she could smash a window.

"Look more closely," he said, pointing to several broken basement windows. "We aren't the first to get in here."

"Do you think there are alarms?" Jennifer asked.

"I doubt it," Charles replied, stooping down to scoop dead leaves from the window well. "Even if there were, the power was cut off years ago. No, right now this is a big brick box. I have no idea what is inside. Maybe it was pillaged years ago. Maybe it has been untouched. Let's go see!"

He is a crazy old man, Jennifer thought. *But very grip. I hope I can be like that when I'm old.*

Then Jennifer tried to imagine herself as old and could not. Not after losing the Perfect Five and missing The Scholarship. It was as if her once-destined future had been wiped away, and only blank obscurity would greet her in years ahead. She could become anyone she wanted in the future. She could be anyone she wanted now. Today, she would be a trespasser.

Following the other four, Jennifer climbed in through the broken basement window. It took her eyes a few moments to adjust to the dark. When they did, she saw she was in some sort of storage room. Rickety metal shelves held stacks of empty notebooks, unused boxes of pens and pencils and loose-leaf paper. Broken chairs and student desks sat in jumbled, mangled heaps. Long lines of old computers, both monitors and CPU towers, sat shrouded in dust. Textbooks and workbooks had been stacked against the concrete walls like prisoners awaiting the final shot.

Jennifer looked around at all the supplies and equipment, some so old she could not identify them. *What a terrible waste. All of this paper could be Recycled. But it sits here in this basement.* She knelt before a pile of textbooks and brushed the dust from it. *Our Living World: Foundations of Biology.*

She opened the cover, the pages slippery with dust. The page she turned to showed a diagram of the nitrogen cycle. She compared it to when she had completed that module in her own studies. The lesson had featured animated graphics, with links to all of the challenging vocabulary and a teacher reading the text of the lesson over the video. This was just a picture. Static, not remotely interactive. In her module, Jennifer had watched the animated nitrogen molecules move through the air and land, whereas the diagram in the textbook had only some arrows to indicate the process.

"Try picking it up," Charles said to her. Jennifer lifted the book. It was much heavier than it appeared.

"Now imagine toting that around in a bag on your back all morning," Charles said. "Then imagine having similar books for four other classes, along with notebooks, pens and pencils, and anything else you would need throughout the day."

"Were students always treated like goddamn freighters back then?" Melody asked. Charles shrugged.

"It was the way it was."

"Well, what happened when new information was discovered?" Jennifer asked. "The words in a textbook never change. What would the school do when the textbook became too old? Just buy hundreds of new ones?"

"That's pretty much it," Charles replied.

"Sounds like a money-making racket to me," Jennifer said, slapping the cover of the biology book closed, sending little puffs of dust into the still basement air.

"It was," Charles replied. "It still is. You of all people should know. Do you know how much money EduForce will generate by having added a sixteenth Achievement level? Billions, that's how much. Billions of dollars in advertising by giving you more work to do. All they had to do was generate more modules and edugames. More products."

"But I don't get how they make money," Jennifer asked. "I guess I never really thought about it."

"You would have if you'd read *The Trough*," Melody said.

"I will, I will," Jennifer groaned.

"It's pretty simple," Charles said. "In my time, education companies made money by making products—textbooks, workbooks, video tutorials, things like that. They sold them to school districts."

"What was that?" Peter asked. Jennifer had forgotten the kid was still there. Jean Paul was in the dim distance, inspecting the ancient boiler.

"A district was a collection of all the local schools. They worked together as one entity. But by the 2030s, state and local governments were useless middle management. The Federal government had once tried to assume total control over education, but by 2034 it managed the military and little else. The development of Plexes went right along with this. If every Plex was the same, why did every school district need to be different? School districts dissolved, but since there were no more school districts for producers to sell their products to, EduForce incorporated advertisements, product placements, and other marketing devices to make their money. Soon, companies were paying millions of dollars to have their brands and products prominently displayed before the gullible, innocent youth.

"That's why your math word problems don't ask how many hamburgers someone can buy, but how many Tyson-Montford hamburgers someone can buy. Or you'll be in the middle of an edugame and an advertisement will pop up asking you if you need any Perk-Eez. They track your purchasing past and your habits and market to you individually."

"So?" Jennifer said. "Companies have been doing that for years. Even in your time."

"True. But not in schools. Up until thirty years ago or so, school was seen as a place for learning. Not for selling. If anything was sold in a school, it was for the benefit of the school and the students—fundraisers, class rings, things of that sort. The corporate world, the world of commerce and marketing, was kept out. Marketing to school children was seen as crass and inappropriate. The school space was sacred once upon a time.

"But things changed, schools became weaker and corporations grew stronger. They crept in. At first their appearances in schools were subtle and indirect. A local company might sponsor a school dance. A school board would not approve a new gymnasium, but Nike or Adidas would, provided their name was on the gym, just as happened with professional stadiums. It always, always came down to the money. The corporations had money and needed customers. The schools had a continual supply of customers, compelled by law to be there, but desperately needed money. It was a natural union.

"Over time, the corporate infiltration of education became complete, to the point you have today, where a lesson on geometry is almost indistinguishable from a deodorant advertisement. It was once unthinkable to allow companies to sell products to children as their minds were open to learning. Now our education system would not even function without it."

"Did you hear something?" Peter asked, his ear cocked toward the ceiling. For a moment they went silent, but then Peter shrugged, and the conversation resumed.

Melody asked, "I don't understand why companies were even allowed to advertise in the first place. If everyone was opposed to it, why did it start?"

"Money. It always, always came down to money. The impoverished school districts, the dysfunctional ones in inner cities and distant rural towns, were the first to succumb. Underfund a school and they become desperate for money. And anyone desperate for money will compromise any integrity to solve the problem."

"Heed your advice well, old man," Melody said, tossing a book at Charles. "You've been unemployed less than a week. Let's see how your integrity holds up when you can't pay the rent."

To this, Charles had no reply. He caught the book and dusted off its cover. He held it up to the others.

"Anthology of American literature," Jennifer said, reading the cover.

"There are more over here," Peter said, pointing to several stacks of books. "British literature. World literature too."

Charles unslung his stuffed backpack and opened it to reveal numerous empty tote bags.

"You may never have another chance like this," he said. "Let's start a trend. We'll make the bookshelf fashionable again."

Charles picked up a copy of each of the three anthologies, dusting each one off with his sleeve. He stacked the books in his bag, then added several empty notebooks and a box of pencils. He put his hands on his hips, surveying all the stacks of abandoned books.

"I'd take them all home with me if I could," he said. Jennifer, Peter, and Melody were all staring at him. Jean Paul was still admiring the antique HVAC system.

"What?" Charles said, his tone both innocent and roguish. "Some helpless, homeless books."

"You're weird, Mister W," Melody said.

"And coming from her, that means something," Jennifer said. She looked at the rows and rows of stacked books and could only think of how much money the books would fetch at a Recycling. *If I could put all of these books in a Recycling, Mamá wouldn't have to work again. We could even move to a nicer apartment.* The problem, of course, was there was no way to transport hundreds of textbooks somewhere hours away. Even carrying three or four home would be heavy, not to mention it would draw the attention of everyone on the Sol-Train. But still the potential hung in her mind, a fantasy of lavish wealth sitting there unattended in the basement of an empty school. She began filling her bags with books, as well.

"Hey everyone," Jean Paul called. "I think I found something."

The rest of the group went to him. Behind the steel bulk of the boilers and water heaters, Jean Paul stood over a gray heap of ashes. Closer, Jennifer could see colorful wisps of paper at the fringes of the circle and strange, twisted forms on top.

"Someone made a fire here, I think," Peter said.

Melody stooped down and picked up one of the pieces of paper.

"I think they used textbooks. This has half of some math equation on it."

"What are those other things on there?" Jennifer asked. *Bones,* she thought with a chill. Jean Paul picked one up and whacked it against the concrete floor. It rang out metallically.

"Used to be a chair, I think maybe. Or a desk."

"Like I said," Charles added, "After fifteen years, we certainly can't be the first ones to think of breaking in here."

"The fire. It...it isn't still warm, is it?" Peter asked, stepping back.

"Of course not," Jean Paul said, brandishing the chair leg he had pulled off the ashes.

"Relax," Charles said. "I doubt anyone is here now. Let's go up."

With their bags full of books and supplies, the group mounted the staircase leading to the first floor. Without the dim light from the window wells, the darkness closed in.

"I can't see anything!" Jennifer hissed as she mounted the second and third stairs.

"Just keep walking," Charles said. "One step then the next. I'm in front, so if any of the stairs are missing, I'll find out first."

Jennifer's grip on the handrail tightened with each step. She wished now someone had thought to bring a light.

All her life, Jennifer had known light. From her birth in the brightly illuminated hospital room to the ambient glow that peeked under her door when her mother fell asleep watching television, Jennifer was surrounded by brightness. There was no time when light was not present or readily available. So, to be plunged in darkness, even for thirty seconds, was to be plunged into a different world, a land of negation and uncertainty. When she set her foot on the top stair, entering onto the well-lit first floor of the school, she was already trembling and sweating.

Charles led them along a hallway lined with dented, mint-green lockers. Jennifer had never used a locker like these, never had to hold a combination in her head and turn the dial until the tumblers fell into place and the latch released. Every locked door in 2051 was secured with a fingerprint, retinal, or facial recognition scan.

"This reminds me of the Plex," Melody said. "I mean, everyone in a Plex gets the same apartment, for the most part. Every student gets the same kind of locker. Doesn't matter if you are rich or poor. Very democratic."

Charles looked at her with a thoughtful, wry expression. "I never really thought of that. I suppose it is."

A few of the lockers hung open, the locks broken. Peter slammed one shut, the metallic bang reverberating down the long, tiled halls. Everyone turned and glared at him. He grinned.

They walked around the main lobby, where Charles explained to them the many features, and each one amazed, amused, and horrified the students, aside from Peter. He showed them the principal's office and explained what a principal's role was in a school. They struggled to understand, and assistant principals were even more confusing. When he showed them the in-school-suspension room, he had to explain that students were expected to behave in particular ways in class, and if they failed to do so, they could be removed from class and placed in ISS. Jennifer could not comprehend anything mattering other than one's Achievement Score. Peter snickered and muttered about that room being his home away from home.

At the metal detectors and security desk at the front door, everyone remembered the somber litany. Columbine. Virginia Tech. Sandy Hook. Scarsdale. No one spoke. Jennifer recalled the EduForce history module on school violence. The videos, the audio recordings of 911 calls, the pictures of victims. It had given her nightmares for a week.

"Come, it looks like the cafeteria is up at the end of this hall. I'll show you," Charles said. The lockers were soon replaced by long rows of floor to ceiling glass. Inside sat rows of unstable-looking Formica tables with folding benches.

"Is this like a Plex café" asked Jennifer.

"Sort of," Charles explained. "Except every student had to eat here."

"Also sounds democratic," Melody said.

"Not as much as you'd think," Charles explained. "True, all of the tables look the same now. But when filled with students, this cafeteria is as stratified and rigid and hostile a society as you'll find anywhere. Certain groups and cliques of students always sat together, fending off students they didn't think belonged. There were tables for popular students, tables for band members, tables for athletes and tables for student government. Loners and outcasts scattered around into the unseen corners, at the ends of benches. Or they avoided the cafeteria the whole time and waited in silence in the bathroom. Everyone had a place and was expected to behave according to his or her station."

"Harsh," Jennifer said. "I can't believe the school would force them to do that."

But Charles shook his head.

"No one forced them. It was an entirely self-determined society. One could even argue that it is human nature to cluster with those who are like us."

"Tell me about those kids who waited in the bathroom," Melody said. "Did they get in trouble?"

"If they were caught. Usually no one noticed they were missing. After lunch period, they would go up to their next class."

"What's a lunch period?" Jennifer asked.

"A designated time to eat lunch. In some schools it was thirty minutes, some forty-five, some an hour."

"But what if you weren't hungry then?" Jennifer asked.

"You didn't eat," Charles said. "You had to eat at the assigned time."

"That's weird," she mumbled.

"I remember," Jean Paul said. "Long time ago. I eat in a cafeteria when I was a little boy. First grade, maybe."

"What was it like?" Jennifer asked. Jean Paul shrugged.

"I no remember too much. I like it now. If I'm hungry, I get food. I pee whenever I have to. In the school, we have to ask permission to go. But now is not so good because I don't have no friends. Except you."

Jennifer had always wondered about Jean Paul. She knew nothing about him besides his mere presence. Now he seemed to emerge before her, lumbering and sad and vulnerable. She wanted to do something to reach out and connect to him, to show him he was not alone, he was not alone in feeling alone, and someone else understood him.

"Anyone hungry?" Charles asked. He swung open the cafeteria doors and the group followed in. They chose a table in the middle of the room, withdrew all their snacks from their bags, and sat down to eat. Their crunching echoed against the cavernous ceiling and glass walls. Jennifer imagined eating communally every day, trapped in the jostle and din of hundreds of other students, all eating and talking together, the food smells and noise all jumbling together.

"Hey, look!" Peter called. He had eaten fastest and was now snooping around the buffet counter. He lifted a box and carried it over to the table.

"Cheese and crackers!" he announced. "My favorite. Anyone want one?"

Melody wrinkled her nose. "Are those any good? After fifteen years—"

But Peter passed plastic-wrapped packages of crackers around to everyone at the table. "These things never go bad!" he said.

Melody refused to open the package, but everyone else tried the crackers and agreed they tasted fine. Melody glowered at all of them. "Doesn't it bother you to eat food made more than fifteen years ago? That you aren't all sick? I don't know if that is a worse indictment of you or of the food."

"Oh, come now," Charles said, spraying crumbs. "They're just crackers."

But now Melody's anger rose, and she pointed right back at Charles.

"You, most of all. I mean, after what you wrote in *The Trough*. How can you even touch those things?"

Charles paused.

"What did he write?" Jennifer asked. Melody whirled on her.

"Read the book!" she cried.

"What book?" Peter asked, but Melody cut him off.

"Tell them about the cheese, Mister W. Tell them about the cheese."

Charles set down his package of crackers. His appetite was gone. *She's right,* he thought. But he said nothing. Melody reached into Jennifer's bag and pulled out the copy of Charles's book. She waved it in the air.

"I'll find the passage and read it myself," she threatened.

"No," he said. "I remember. I wrote it after all."

"What are you talking about?" Jennifer asked. Charles looked around at all of them.

"Do any of you like grilled cheese sandwiches?"

They all looked around at one another and agreed. Everyone loved grilled cheese.

"What are the ingredients?" Charles asked.

"Butter. Bread. Cheese," Jean Paul replied.

"What kind of cheese do you use?" Charles asked, holding back a smile. The students shrugged.

"I don't know," Jean Paul admitted. "Just the stuff in the plastic wrapping."

"That isn't cheese," Charles said.

"Of course, it is," Peter said, but Charles shook his head.

"Close your eyes and think carefully about the packaging. All of those individually wrapped slices of something, they aren't cheese. What are they?"

The words appeared in Jennifer's memory and she said, "American processed cheese food. What's the difference?"

"The difference," Charles said, "is the difference between food and not food."

Jean Paul shook his head and said, "So? It still tastes good."

"But it isn't food!" Melody said. "It just resembles food. And does it really taste good, or does it just taste familiar? That's why we're here! That's what we're learning about! That EduForce garbage we have to complete, that is the American processed cheese food of education. Looks like education. Kind of tastes like education. But it is a processed product. Mister W is letting us taste the real thing. Authentic. It might taste or look strange or unusual, it might not be comforting or familiar, but it will open us up to a whole new world of flavors and experiences. Did I get that right?"

Charles nodded and chuckled. "Almost word for word. Come on, let's look around some more."

Everyone rose to throw away their wrappers in a trash can, making it the first refuse to enter the can in a decade and a half. Before throwing the plastic wrap in, Jennifer glanced at the packaging. A chill shuddered through her.

"Hey," she said weakly. Her knees trembled. "Hey!"

They turned and looked. Jennifer pointed to the words printed on the plastic.

"It says, 'Packaged January 2051. Use by January 2052.'"

"So?" Peter asked.

Now Charles and Melody's faces became grave.

"So," Charles said, "these crackers aren't fifteen years old. They were made this year."

"But who bring them to the school?" Jean Paul asked.

They heard a noise.

All five heads turned toward the source of the noise, something shuffling or scurrying down the poorly lit hallway.

"A rat, maybe?" whispered Jennifer.

Jean Paul shook his head. "No rat. Too big," he said.

THE SOUND ECHOED down the halls again. Charles realized that for all his forethought to bring snacks and tote bags, he had not even considered self-defense. No guns, no knives, no tasers, or pepper spray. Even the desk leg Jean Paul had picked up in the basement was something. *Plex life has made you soft,* he thought. *Safe to the point of foolishness.* He signaled to the group to silently retreat.

The shuffling sounds moved in their direction.

In the poor lighting, they tried to both watch their footing and the approaching threat. Melody tripped, and Jennifer reached down and yanked her to her feet. The sound of one person was joined by several others. Charles looked left and right. This had been his high school, but that had been years ago. He did not know if he was leading the students to safety or a dead end. *Not dead end. Don't think that.*

He led them around the cafeteria to a long corridor that seemed to run along an exterior wall. Sunlight shone through glass at the exit at the far end of the hall. Safety.

Just then, two figures leaped out into the hall in front of the exit and ran toward the group. Charles shoved open the nearest set of double doors.

"In!" he shouted. The students ducked inside. Charles slipped in after them and pulled the door shut. Charles made out rows of upholstered seats on each side of an aisle. Looking up, he could barely make out a balcony overhead.

"What is this?" asked Melody.

"This is our home!" called a voice. "You are trespassing. Explain yourselves."

No more trespassers than you are, Charles thought. Now all sets of auditorium doors opened, and several of their pursuers entered on all sides. *Trapped.*

"Approach!" demanded a voice Charles could only think of as magisterial. The students hesitated.

"Do it," Charles grumbled.

They walked down the aisle of the auditorium until they stood in the pit before the stage. Five lanterns, filled with fire and fueled by some unknown substance, hung from rolling coat racks. *Pilfered from the costume closet for the theater department, no doubt.* These lanterns revealed three people sitting in leather rolling chairs. They were dressed in choir robes, and a large laminate desk sat in the middle of them. He looked around. Their pursuers from the hallways were dressed in jeans and sweatshirts. Each of them held some weapon—a few had knives, one had a plumber's wrench, and another held a length of rope. One even held the metal leg to a student desk.

"I am waiting for your answer!" declared the one with the magisterial voice. "Take their bags!"

"You haven't asked a question yet," Charles blurted as the armed men and women yanked the bags from his shoulders. *No weapons, no weapons but our words and wits.*

This time, one of the others of the three spoke; a woman of middle age.

"You must be a teacher? All my teachers were dickheads back when I was in school. You must be a teacher."

"He's our teacher," Melody said. "But he's not a dickhead. He's grip. Well, sometimes he's a dickhead, but it's just to prove a point to us or make us understand something better. I would say he is a dickhead maybe only a quarter of the time. A third, tops."

"Thanks," Charles mumbled.

"A teacher and his students," the apparent leader said. He was old, older than Charles, though the ragged beard and shaggy hair on his head could be adding a few decades to his appearance. "How quaint. Come here on a pilgrimage?"

"Yes, of sorts," Charles replied. "More of a field trip. I'm teaching them about—"

"About the old ways," said the third woman, also older, but with a more measured, softer voice.

"Yes," Charles said.

"The old ways still live," she replied.

"Say no more to them," the leader said. He gave her a stern glare, but her return glare made it clear she would not be moved.

"You are not from here, are you?" the woman asked.

"No," Charles replied.

"I can tell because you dress like Plexers. Few people even know this building exists. Fewer try to enter. Mostly young people, seeking escape. Is it escape you seek?"

Charles tried to speak but could not think of an answer. What could he say?

"We are looking for the way back," Melody replied. "To how school used to be."

"There is no way back, not for you!" the leader declared. "Your minds are too Plexed, too feeble to handle the rigors of learning from a real teacher."

"Our minds are not feeble," Jennifer said, and Charles looked at her in astonishment. "I was once, but our teacher has shown me how to read and think. He risked everything to bring us out here and see."

The three stared down at her from the stage.

"I want to hear more," said one of the pursuers standing in the pit. He was young, around Jennifer and Melody's age, with a wispy beard. A length of chain hung in one hand. "I want to hear about Plex life."

"Absolutely not!" declared the leader of the three. "You know all you must know. To hear anything more would be poison to your mind."

The young man fell silent.

"Well, I want to hear more about you," Melody said. "I want to know all about off-Plex life. All I have ever known is life in those boxes, and I want to hear how you survive. How did you become so wise and so liberated?"

Charles could see, even from their distance apart, that the tiniest glimmer shone in the leader's eye. *Melody is a genius. I tried defiance and that didn't work. I tried subservience and that didn't work, either. But flattery, that was the weak point.*

"You are bold, child," he said. "You trespass into our home and cause damage. You have brought fear to everyone here, and now presume to know about our ways. Do you know what happened to the last trespassers we caught?"

When no one answered, he went on.

"They were two youths, perhaps fifteen or sixteen years of age. We knew by their shabby manner of dress that they were from The Devils of Stag Hill. That is the name of another group of unboxers who live north of here, beyond the mountain. They came to this place looking for a place to copulate away from the disapproval of their parents. Our sentries caught them in mid-coitus, atop the bed in the nurse's office. They dragged the pair to the Square of the Just. I questioned them. I did not like their answers. So, I had them strung upside-down, naked, from a second-story window. They yelled and screamed and cried for help for perhaps a day and a half. Eventually, the pressure of all the blood in their heads must have strangled their brains. Then they hung there purple headed until the crows and vultures picked them apart. That was two years ago, and we have seen no one since."

The leader leaned in now.

"First," he said. "I will ask you the questions. I hope, for your sake, that I like your answers. Then, if I am satisfied, you may ask your questions. I will tell you a little of our way, of the proper way. And only you"—he indicated Melody—"may speak, unless I address one of the others. I am Francis Mallory Wieland, Protector of the Liberated Peoples of Mahwah and Ramsey. My lands reach from the Fields of MacFarran to the base of Houvenkopf Mountain, from Darlington Lake to the Ruins of Suffern. I rule all within that realm, but my court dwells with me here in Castle Mahwah."

Wieland asked Melody why they were in the school and what they wanted. She replied that they wanted to see what a school was like and they wanted to take nothing, just to look around and talk to their teacher. He asked where they were from and she replied Plex 87.

"That means nothing to me!" bellowed Wieland.

"May I?" Charles asked, and Wieland nodded to him to speak. "We are from the east of here, in what used to be Jersey City."

Wieland nodded knowingly. Though the towns and cities of America had never been formally dissolved, few still used their names. He then asked Melody what they knew of life out of the boxes, and she replied that they knew almost nothing, which was why they were visiting. Finally, he demanded to know who sent them.

"Sent us?" Melody asked.

"Yes. Who told you to come here?"

"Just our teacher," she said, indicating Charles.

"Liars!" cried the youngest of the three. "Boxers don't know how to do things without being ordered to do so. No initiative. That is why they are so easy to catch!"

"No, it is true!" Melody said, cutting off Charles, who was ready to interrupt again. "This started as his idea, but we wanted to come. We know how dangerous it is. If we are caught, we will lose everything. Homes, status in school, privileges, everything you can think of.

"Ah," said Wieland, leaning in, a fox's smile on his lips. "But you are caught. By us. And we can do far worse things to you than that."

The weapon-wielding guards closed in.

"This action must go to the Decision-Making Task Force. The DMTF will discuss your fate. Remain here. We will now recess."

The three leaders rose from their chairs and retreated out of the circle of light and into the darkness. Charles could hear only their muffled whispers and the shuffling feet of the sentries. He looked up at the walls of the auditorium. Much of it had disintegrated over the years, and insulation and wires dangled in the dark.

He thought back to his days in the classroom, to the screechy band concerts and the cracking voices of teenage choirs. Teachers would mock the performance afterwards, bemoaning the waste of an hour. Charles would smile and laugh with them, not wanting a disagreement, but he always felt the student musicians and actors had brought the school together. When the audience cheered afterwards, they were cheering for their peers. Nothing like that existed now. Every student was alone. The only cheering was from little cartoon figures in the edugames. And worse, Charles thought, no one was making art.

And then there was the ballet.

Charles recalled the upholstered seats and vaulted ceilings, the house lights and velvet curtains, and dangling microphones and cameras in local, regional, and national stages all over America as he and Shaaya followed Tamra and Clara, who were pursuing their dreams. From high school stages to Lincoln Center, the girls had danced on them all. Charles had never stopped to reflect how much of his life had been spent in auditoriums, listening and watching as vibrating strings, breath-blown reeds, horns, and hammered piano wire combined with the interplay of muscles, tendons, and bone to create magnificent things, art that soared above the physical bounds of its creation. Charles remembered a life that had once been saturated in art. Now, he awaited his fate in the tomb of that memory.

The DMTF returned to their seats. Wieland sat, impassive, without indication of the verdict on his face. He leaned forward.

"It has been decided," he said, "not to kill you. Not immediately. The DMTF prefers to put you to some useful purpose, something to serve the school and its needs. Should you fulfill your task, you will be set free on the condition that you never return, and you make it known to the Boxers that we want to be left alone. Fail, and you die. Understood?"

Everyone murmured assent except Melody.

"Wait," she said, "you said you would tell us about yourselves if we told you our story. Now it's your turn. You owe us that—"

"We owe you nothing! Who are you but a band of feebleminded Box dwellers who came to our home on some misguided quest? You broke into our basement and you walked the halls. All you must know of us is this, when society was reformed and the feebleminded ran off to their Boxes, we remained. This school is sacred, and we are the Keepers of the Knowledge.

"This is your task. The Devils of Stag Hill live on the mountain to the northwest. Their barbaric ways offend us, and they know where we set our traps for the Boxer freight trucks and set up their own ambushes up the road. The trucks are ours but because they live like animals with no home or shelter, they roam about the land freely. Their leader is Moseley, an arrogant little snipe with no scruples. I want you to infiltrate the Devils of Stag Hill. Allow yourselves to be caught; you seem to be quite good at that. Moseley will be curious about you. Use that to set your trap. Kill Moseley, cut out the eyes, and bring them to me. If you bring me the eyes of Moseley, I will not only allow you to live, but declare you a friend of the Liberated People of Mahwah. I will tell you our tale. If you fail, then you will be brought back here, hung upside-down naked from the Square of the Just, and left to die as the blood pools in your brains."

"Tell them of Kenny Pulasky," the younger woman next to Wieland said. She laid a hand on his arm and her lip curled in what looked like twisted delight.

Wieland shook his head. "There is no time for tales, Noreen."

"But they must know what the Devils can—"

Wieland held up his hand, and the woman named Noreen went silent.

"You are correct," Wieland continued. "They must know of Kenny Pulasky. Kenny was a member of my court, strong of arm and swift of foot. He was also among the cleverest of us. Some years ago, when I first deemed the Devils of Stag Hill to be our greatest enemy, I sent Kenny on such a mission as yours."

"Tell them what happened!" Noreen cried.

"Kenny never returned," Wieland said. "Killed by Moseley as a spy. Let us hope you are stronger and swifter than he was."

"We don't accept!" Peter called out. Everyone turned and looked at him. Charles winced.

"This is not an offer," Wieland said with surprising calmness. "It is your command."

"It hardly seems fair," Peter went on. "You lose, you tell us a story. We lose, we get tortured and killed. Seems to me, your risk should be as big as ours—"

"Preposterous."

"—unless you're too scared," Peter finished, and this silenced the leader. The two other members of the DMTF—the older and younger women flanking him—looked to see his reaction. His expression darkened.

"I am many things," the leader finally said. "But I am not afraid. Certainly not of you. Very well. One way or another, blood will water the Gardens of the Square of the Just!"

With a hand signal from their leader, the sentries prodded the them from their places in the pit, urging them up the aisle and out into the hallway.

The sentries did not speak to the Rooftop Readers Club, did not even look at them, as they led them out of the school, along a broken sidewalk, and away from town. Charles looked around at the sunken roofs and broken windows. They passed a coffee shop, now an empty shell, as well as a caved-in sandwich shop. Electronics stores and post offices and banks rotted. He wanted to point these things out to his students, to tell them what it was like to go out shopping or spend a summer evening eating ice cream from a stand outside on a warm summer evening with fireflies under the glare of streetlights. But their captors said nothing and allowed nothing to be said. They passed a luxury hotel, Charles could not remember which company, that was charred and hollow. In the distance to the northwest loomed Houvenkopf Mountain, surrounded by wooded green hills. The group continued for another mile, then turned off and walked up a gravel road choked with brush. As they ascended the slope of Houvenkopf Mountain, the trail dissolved in a mess of trees and scrub brush.

Finally, the guards halted at an overlook, halfway up the mountainside. Surrounded by brush and weeds, there was no discernible trail.

"Good enough," one of the guards said. She pointed up to the top of the mountain. "We are taking you no further. Go to the top, then continue down the other side. It's going to be messy, a lot worse than this side. But if you keep on in that direction, you'll come to some more trails and those will lead to the camp. Hard to know where they'll be. They roam all over these hills. Could be watching us right now. You know your orders. Do not return without the eyes of Moseley."

With that, the guards turned and walked back down, finally disappearing in the brush and the sun-drenched landscape.

"Let's go back," Jennifer said, keeping her voice low in case it carried down to the ears of their captors. "This fight is none of our business."

"But it is our problem," Charles said. "They have all of our bags. They will be watching the town. Even if we try to sneak past the school or skirt around it to get to the Sol-Train, they will be waiting for us. We didn't ask to be here, but we cannot run now."

They continued walking up the mountain. There was no trail, at least none they could discern. Charles was proud of the students. He doubted any of them, save perhaps Peter, had spent more than a few hours outdoors in their lives. Yet none of them complained. Wordlessly, with Peter scampering ahead in the lead as the self-appointed outdoors expert and Charles in the rear, they made their way to the summit.

When they crested the mountain, the group looked out over the valley below. None of them could speak. The slope rolled down below them, cut by the crumbling road, then continued toward a distant river. The empty town looked like a painting. Far in the distance was the high school, a tan and brown box. Domed over all of this was a pristine sky, the air unfiltered and brilliant. The blue was no mild-mannered pastel, but a shade darker and more vibrant than any of them thought possible. Cumulus clouds floated above, fluffy and perfectly formed.

"I've never," Melody said breathlessly. "It's... I've never seen so far away."

"Yeah," Jennifer added. "I mean, I've done the VR tours, but this..."

"Exactly," Jean Paul said.

Peter shrugged.

"This isn't anything. You should stand on Mount Marcy. My parents took me there once. The view was—"

"Shut up," Melody said. Peter shut his mouth and folded his arms.

Charles recited,

> *"I wandered lonely as a cloud,*
>
> *That floats on high o'er vales and hills,*
>
> *when all at once I saw a crowd,*
>
> *a host of golden daffodils;*
>
> *beside the lake, beneath the trees,*
>
> *fluttering and dancing in the breeze."*

For a few more moments, they stood atop the hill in silence, watching the dynamic stillness of the afternoon and listening to the buzzing of insects and chirping of birds.

By the time they heard footsteps, it was too late.

A foot crunched in the leaves and twigs behind them, and they turned. They saw no one.

"Who is it?" shouted Charles, feeling idiotic. No replies.

"Come out!" called Melody.

"Put your hands up!" shouted Peter.

Then, from the bushes, a chuckle.

"Maury," said a female voice, "would you listen to these guys?"

More footsteps approached, and soon an older man, scruffy and wild-haired, dressed in dirty khaki pants and a half-unbuttoned denim shirt, emerged from the brush.

"A little band of explorers," he said. "Some conquistadors from the land of cubicles and screens."

"You don't know a thing about us," Melody replied.

"Look at you," the woman said, emerging from the bushes behind them. They had walked right past her and not even realized it. Charles noticed a mixture of anger and humiliation cross over the face of Peter, who had appointed himself lead explorer and the eyes of the group.

The woman was also older, around Charles's age. Her manner of dress was much like Maury's—plain, rugged, and old fashioned. Her weather-beaten skin and a layer of dust on her skin could not hide the playful, incisive eyes that scrutinized them. A head of dreadlocked hair surrounded her face in a way that struck Charles as royal, even divine, like the aura surrounding a saint in a medieval painting. She smiled, and it seemed to Charles the smile was either playful or predatory, or maybe both.

"Look at you," she said, striding to them. "Your clothes are too neat and too impractical for someone who lives free. You come stomping up this hill, making a racket, and with no idea where you were headed. Why, you didn't even bring anything to eat or drink. Come with us; we've got some water back at camp. Not much food on hand, but we're going on a hunt tonight and if it goes well, you are welcome to join us for the feast."

"Aisha, wait," Maury said, holding a hand up. "How did they get here? Why are they here? You can't bring them into camp, unvetted."

"I can't?" she said, cocking an eyebrow.

"What I mean is..."

"I know what you mean," she said, her tone patient and maternal. *She waits until he finishes speaking,* Charles noticed. *She never cuts him off, even when she easily could.*

With that, Maury and Aisha began walking down the far side of the hill. After fifteen paces, Aisha stopped and turned to the group.

"Are you coming? Or going back? Or staying put? Hell of a view up here, but the coyotes won't want to share it."

As they descended the far side of the hill, down toward another valley, Charles began to wonder how and when they would return to the Sol-Train station and to Plex 87. He had planned for their field trip to last a single day, but the midday sun was becoming afternoon sun, and they were moving away from the train line, not toward it. The longer their absence, the greater the suspicion they would draw back at home. Peter's parents were surely waiting for him and would hire police if he were not returned to Plex 87 soon. *Not that we have much choice. I wanted these kids to see beyond Plex life. I wanted them to break away from everything they knew and expected. Well, it doesn't get much more broken away than this.*

"Tell us about yourselves," Aisha said.

"I'm not telling you a thing," Jennifer said. "I'm your captive."

"Captive? I invited you. We don't take prisoners. If you don't want to join us, feel free to turn around."

"They told us about you!" Peter declared. "They told us what animals you are."

"Peter, shut up," Melody said.

"Who told you what about us?" demanded Maury.

"The—the—I don't know their names," Peter said. "But they said you were like animals without a home and that you ambush freight trucks. They called you the Devils of Stag Hill."

"Goddammit, Peter!" Melody said, punching his arm. Maury whirled around on the group, looking as if he might strike Peter. Aisha held up her hand, and he restrained himself.

"Do not use that term," Aisha said. "Ever."

They walked in silence for a short time.

"So, did someone pay a visit to our local high school?" Aisha asked, then laughed as the group remained silent. "Sounds like old Frank is up to his usual nonsense."

"Frank?" Charles asked, and then he understood.

"Francis Wieland. Short fellow, our age, shrill kind of voice. Never talks when he can yell. Last I had heard, he was spending his days on the auditorium stage, yapping at his minions and shouting for blood. Sound familiar?"

Again, their silence seemed to confirm what she said. They neared the bottom of the hill and entered some thicker forest. If there was any sort of trail under their feet, Charles could not tell where it was.

"Not talking much, eh?" Aisha said. "Let me ask this. Did you find us on your own, or did Frank send you here?"

Again, the group was silent, and again, Aisha laughed.

"I don't know what you folks do in your regular lives, but I hope for your sake it isn't espionage. You might be the worst spies Frank has ever sent our way."

"We aren't spies," Jennifer said.

"Then what are you?" Maury asked.

"Lost," Melody said after a hesitant pause.

"Where were you going? Where were you coming from? How did you get on top of the hill?" Maury asked. The group could only stammer in reply. Aisha tsked.

"Frank should have at least given you a decent cover story. He really wasn't preparing you for success. He's always been like that. Demanding the impossible of people, giving them no support, then berating them when they fail. What is the penalty if you fail?"

In that moment, Charles succumbed to their collective failure. If the Devils of Stag Hill knew why they were there, then obviously they would never get close enough to Moseley to take his eyes. *Not that any of us have the stomach for that sort of work.*

"He said we would be strung upside down from our feet in The Square of the Just until we died because the blood pooled in our brains. So, you can understand we aren't keen on failing," Charles said.

The smile on Aisha's face disappeared as she looked to Maury.

"Again?" she asked.

"Seems so," he replied.

Aisha stopped walking. She turned to face the group.

"Whatever fears you have, whatever he told you about us, about me, don't believe any of it. Come and eat with us tonight. We have a hunting party out now. If they are successful, we will be feasting tonight. I'll tell you all about Frank Wieland. I can tell you what he likes, what he dislikes, who he trusts, who he doesn't, and what his goals are."

"How do you know so much about him?" Charles asked.

"I used to be his boss," Aisha said.

THE CAMP LAY deep in the forest, a mixture of shanties built from corrugated metal and plywood, and tents. A stream ran through the middle. People of all ages, dressed in old fashioned clothing of the early twenty-first century, walked around, talking, cleaning, laughing, and working. *These people live and work together,* Charles thought. *Face to face and side by side. In the Plexes, everyone is alone. In Plexes, we only see faces through screens, if ever.*

"Welcome to our home," Aisha said.

"So, this is where the Devils of—" Melody started. Maury glared at her. Aisha took a step closer.

"We don't have a name for ourselves," she explained. "We're just us. But do not utter the name 'Devils of Stag Hill' in this camp. Frank still calls us by that name, and that's reason enough not to use it."

"And what do you call Frank and his people?" Melody asked.

"Assholes," Maury said.

"Come," Aisha said. "I see the hunting party has returned, and it looks like a success. When's the last time you had an honest feast? No guest of ours leaves hungry."

Soon, they were sitting on blankets and logs in a large circle near the stream, waiting for the food to arrive. They had not eaten since having snacks on the train, many hours earlier, and now hunger made its demands.

"I wonder what we've having," Peter said. "She said a feast. I hope it's turkey and mashed potatoes and gravy and corn, just like at Thanksgiving."

"That's ridiculous," Melody said. "Turkey, maybe. If turkeys live in the forest, then maybe they caught one. But do you think they grow corn and potatoes out here? Could they even make gravy on a fire?"

Jean Paul rubbed his stomach.

"I don't need nothing fancy. Just some *arroz con frijoles,* maybe a can of Coke, anything, man. I'm so hungry."

Aisha sat next to them. She seemed to have some position of importance, as she was constantly in conversation with one person or another. But if there was a hierarchy in the camp, it was impossible to tell. Everyone seemed to be getting along.

Aisha stood. So did the other dwellers of the camp. Following suit, so did Charles and the rest of the group. In walked a parade of servers, carrying steaming pots and pans. Charles looked around and noticed everyone around them held out forks, knives, and spoons, as well as plates made of aluminum or plastic. The servers brought the pots and pans around, and each person reached in with a spoon and scooped a portion onto his or her own plate. When the serving train came around to them, Charles found extra plates and utensils being pushed into his hands. "We travel lightly," whispered someone in his ear, some unknown benefactor. "But there is always an extra place setting for a stranger."

Charles had sat at dozens of Thanksgiving dinners, countless meals at friends' and family's homes, awards dinners and parties. This dinner was distinct from all of them. There was no head of the table; indeed, there was no table. The group, or tribe, or whatever they wanted to be called, numbered between sixty and eighty people, Charles estimated. They sat in little clusters and groups on logs and lawn chairs, balancing their plates on their knees and eating with wide smiles and loud laughs.

The person behind Charles nudged him.

"Use the spoon. Help yourself."

Charles peered into the pot. Corn. He smiled and scooped a large helping onto his plate.

"Hey," Peter said, peering into another pot. "Are these really mashed potatoes?"

"Instant," said the server, "but they are real, and they are mashed."

"How did you—" Peter started to say, but he was shoveling mashed potatoes into his mouth and his words were smothered. That is, until a second server came by with a pot of gravy, and Peter held out his plate.

"Plee," he said from the corner of his mouth that was not busy eating.

Within minutes, everyone had a plate of food. Conversations dwindled, replaced by the clatter of silverware. Even Charles, normally a parsimonious eater, was scraping every morsel.

"I hope our simple meal was satisfying," Aisha said, rising and joining the group. "We don't have much here."

"This was marvelous," Charles said. "We cannot thank you enough."

"It was not easy," Aisha said. "Nothing out here is easy."

"But I thought you were going hunting," Melody said. "No deer? No turkeys or squirrels or something?"

Aisha smiled.

"We hunt trucks. Big haulers. They drive between Plexes using routes 287 and 87, the only highways still being maintained. They transport food and goods from one place to the next. Every so often, we stop one and take what we need."

"Do you kill the driver?" Peter asked, grinning.

Aisha shrugged.

"We try not to. Sometimes we let him or her go free. It's only an eighteen-mile walk to the next trucking station. It used to be easier, but the companies started arming the drivers and if they put up too much of a fight, we have to look out for ourselves. But we hunt smart. Trucks carrying furniture, computers, things like that, we let go. Really, food is what we look for. Canned goods, things that don't require refrigeration or a kitchen. We store the food in stashes all over these hills. No one in our tribe ever goes hungry."

"Still," Jennifer said, looking around. "This doesn't look like much of a life. No offense."

Aisha glared at her, and Jennifer fell silent.

"The life we've made here is ours," Aisha said. "Here, we are free. We look at you in your Plexes and laugh. You're like prisoners of war, waiting for the Red Cross to bring supplies. Utterly dependent."

"That's a simile," Jennifer said with hollow pride.

"It is," Aisha said.

"And if I follow what you're saying," Jennifer went on, "you destroy the Red Cross trucks that are supposed to feed prisoners. Not very noble if you ask me."

Aisha seemed to give the idea some thought. Then she shrugged and stabbed a forkful of canned asparagus into her mouth.

"Every creature eats at the expense of another," she said. "Teamwork helps. All of us here care deeply about one another and understand our survival depends on one another. But anyone not in our tribe—can live or die for all I care."

"How did you get here?" Charles asked.

Aisha waved her hand vaguely.

"We're from all over. Many of us worked in town. A few wandered from farther-off places. Some fled the Plex authorities. We have schizophrenics, manic depressives, paranoids among us, people who don't fit. Most of us are just...you could call us 'free spirits.' The type of person who refuses to be put in a box."

"Which are you?" Charles asked.

"I'm unemployed." She reached into a pocket and produced a battered, scratched ID badge thirty or forty years old. There was a photo of a much younger Aisha, then in her early thirties. Above the photo read "Mahwah High School Staff." Below it read "Aisha Moseley, Principal."

"You're Moseley," Charles said.

"I am."

"I think we're here to get something from you," Melody said.

"Good old Frank Wieland," Aisha said. "He and I were both vice principals. He was five years older than me and had been there longer, but I had taken more courses than him, done more for the district than him, and honestly, out-taught and outadministered him at every level. When the former principal retired, I leapfrogged over Frank and went from the junior assistant principal to full principal. He didn't take it too well. The man you met in that school building is older and scruffier, but otherwise no different than the little Napoleon who used to work for me. What does he want?"

"Your eyes," Melody said. Aisha nodded thoughtfully.

"He's getting more poetic. Last time, he just wanted me dead."

"Kenny Pulasky," remembered Jennifer aloud. Moseley laughed.

"Kenny's a lovely young man. One of our best hunters. Great sense of humor too."

"Wait," Peter asked. "Frank Wieland said you caught him and killed him."

"Killed him? He defected to us. I remember the day he entered our camp and begged us to save him from Mister Wieland, who had gone nuts. Look, you are free to make your own opinions of people, but Frank is some combination of liar and lunatic, and I'm just not sure what the proportions are of each. I didn't believe a word he said when we worked together twenty years ago, and I believe him less now than I did then."

"This sounds like quite a compelling drama," Charles said. "But we want to get back to the Sol-Train to return to our Plex. These youngsters have families waiting for them. They have modules to take; that is to say, school. We have no way to get back, and it's nearly dark."

"I might be more amenable to helping you," Aisha said, "if you tell me what it is you're doing out here. Poor, lost Plexers, lost in the woods."

Charles balked. Telling Moseley of their rooftop meetings and their reading together could not cause any harm. But he could not loosen his grip on the secret. *Tell her just enough,* he decided.

"I am a teacher. An English teacher. These are my students. I wanted to show them outside of the Plex."

Moseley waited for him to continue, but when he did not, she said, "Your answers create more questions than they answer. But that is wise. Tell me this, do you want to return? To your Plex?"

Not one of them could respond, affirmatively or negatively, for some time. Then Charles realized, *To me, this is a terrible inconvenience. To them, this is an adventure. Their first adventure outside of a Plex. Is it for me to deny them?*

"I think," Melody said, "I think I want to see the forest."

The other students nodded eagerly.

With the meal finished, Charles noticed people washing their dishes in the stream. He and the students rose with Moseley, and they waited their turns to wash, as well.

"We break camp tomorrow morning. We do not like to stay too long in one place, especially after taking down a truck. Sometimes the shipping companies hire mercenary squads like Silent Strike to teach us a lesson. Haven't been caught yet! You may come with us if you want. Who knows, maybe you won't want to go back. Become savages like us."

"There is not much light left," Charles said. "Can we give our answer in the morning?"

"I'm not sleeping in the forest," Jennifer said, folding her arms. "After all, didn't that Frank man say there were coyotes out here? Are there coyotes out here?"

"There are," said Moseley. The group now took their turns bending by the water, scraping and scrubbing the food debris off the plates and silverware until everything was clean. The little particles of food drifted and bobbed down the stream, carried further down into the valley.

Jean Paul agreed. "I'm not crazy. I don't want to spend a night out here. I miss my home. I miss my *abuela*. I miss my own bed."

"But this is like camping!" Peter whined.

"Shut up," Jennifer said. "You're too little. You don't get to vote."

"But—but—" Peter sputtered.

"What do you think?" Jennifer asked Melody, whose expression was enigmatic and thoughtful as she stared into the trees.

"These woods are lovely, dark, and deep," she said.

"And I have promises to keep," Charles said. "We all do. One night, but in the morning we return."

"Very well," Moseley said. "But think beyond your immediate want. You want to get back to your little prefab den, good for you. I cannot and will not stop you. But what then? What are you returning to? Why are you returning to it? Even one night in the forest can change you. How will you be changed?"

The sun set on the forest and the band of outcasts. Campfires dotted the forest floor. Stillness settled in the trees. Not the asphyxiating quiet of the eternal indoors, not the cotton ball and electronic vacuum of sound that comes with an isolated, windowless life. But stillness. Everything became hushed and clear, human activity diminishing until the people in the forest seemed to dissolve into the forest itself. Human voices grew softer as the sounds of the night overtook them. Soon, the music of birds and crickets and running water filled the air.

Charles sat by the fire with Moseley and his students. Two tents were set up for the Plexers. Melody excused herself and retreated to the tent even before nightfall. Charles wondered if all the walking and fright that day had worn on her more than she let on. Jennifer remained by the fire for some time, though she spoke little. Charles tried to guess what she was thinking or feeling, but she remained uncommunicative. *Is she angry? Scared? Overwhelmed?* he wondered. *She's lost her way since losing the Perfect Five. She's acting like she doesn't care but she lost the one thing that set her apart from everyone else.*

Charles thought about Jean Paul, who did not seem at all comfortable in the forest. *He doesn't care about trees and schools and breaking free of the Plex system. He just wants to get his Achievement level and start a job.*

Then Charles looked to Peter, who peppered Jean Paul with conversation, though Jean Paul clearly had little interest in talking. Charles wondered what motives and what desires stirred Peter. His fixation on Melody was clearly, awkwardly apparent, but beyond that, he was not sure what Peter wanted. *Maybe Melody is it. He is a fourteen-year-old boy, chasing a girl.* But he could sense in Peter another world, hidden below the hormones and immaturity on the surface. What was in that world, though, he could not tell.

Moseley nudged him.

"Old man, you still awake?" she asked. Charles had been staring into the flames.

"I'm not that old," Charles replied.

"If you insist. I'm surprised you stayed awake this late."

"I'm young at heart," Charles said.

"Ugh. I'm going to bed," Jennifer said before standing, stretching, and then ducking into the tent with Melody. Jean Paul and Peter sat on the opposite side of the fire, talking about some video game they had both played. When he had been a teacher, Charles stayed abreast of the interests of his students by proximity. He knew the pop songs and the games and movies by overhearing conversations. Now, though, the world of popular culture was alien to him.

"I admire what you do for these students," Moseley said. "I really do. When I was principal, I always encouraged teachers to plan field trips. Yes, it was a pain in the ass. Yes, there was a lot of paperwork and liability. Yes, fundraising was an even bigger pain in the ass. But for some of these kids, a school trip to a theater was the only time they would ever see a play. A trip to a museum was the only time they would ever see a museum. You would hear 'it starts with the parents,' but it ends with the parents too. If parents can't or won't take their kids out to expose them to everything—art, theater, history, culture, all of it—then who does it? Some parents were too poor. Some were just shitty parents. But it fell on us to replace that best we could."

Charles nodded.

"Of course, I was never taken hostage on a field trip before, nor did I take refuge with a group of woodland bandits. So maybe this trip has been the biggest pain in the ass of all."

"Ah, you love it," Moseley said. Charles smiled.

"I would not take back this trip for anything," he said. "Though I really wanted the kids to see more of the school. I'm afraid their impressions will be tainted by Frank."

"Don't let that bastard harm any more students—" Moseley said before cutting herself off.

"What does that mean?"

Moseley looked down for a time, unable to meet Charles's eyes.

"You're an English teacher. You've read *Lord of the Flies*. Sometimes, free of supervision, people restore good. Other times, they turn into Jack and the choirboys. In the big education reformation, no one needed principals. We received offers to work for EduForce. Frank asked me if I was going but I said I would rather gouge my eyes out, no offense. He said he wasn't going, either. When Plex 291 went up, I wanted to stay in my house. I liked my house. But then the power lines were redirected, the utilities shut off, and the roads abandoned.

"After three or four months of heating the house with wood fires and having no grocery stores, my husband called it quits. He moved to the Plex. I couldn't. Couldn't do it. I had worked hard to pay for that house, and I was still young—in my thirties—and I had wanted to raise a family in it someday. Now I was all alone in a powerless, cold house. I grew bored. A little scared too. Then one night I awoke to the smell of smoke. My beautiful house was burning all around me. I tried to open my bedroom door, but it was scorching hot. So, I smashed out my window and jumped from the second story. Got banged up but didn't break anything. I looked up. There was Frank Wieland, surrounded by a few people from the school. He was holding a gasoline can and a butane torch from the chemistry labs. You know what he said? 'Now I get to be principal!' Then they ran off.

"I wandered the forest for a few days. In those early days as the Plexes went up, there were a surprising number of people who didn't live in them. I'm sure you remember. They resisted. They held out hope their resistance would mean something. Did you resist?"

"I went right to the Plex," Charles said. "I don't know if I've ever resisted anything."

Moseley scoffed. "You're too modest. Resistance is what you're teaching these kids. Anyhow, back in those days, there were hundreds, even thousands of people wandering the roads, scraping by on their own. Some of them died from exposure or murder. Most of them gave up and went into the Plex. A few, like me, wouldn't quit.

"Over time, I fell in with a few others. Maury was one of the first. He worked for the National Park Service and when he learned he would direct virtual tours of parks from a screen inside a Plex, he snapped and hit the road. Our group grows and shrinks. Sometimes we're as big as a few hundred. We've been as small as two dozen. We're at sixty-three right now, which is a good size for us. We get by. But it gets harder, not easier, each year, though we've been at it for many years.

"There's almost nothing left to scavenge within a hundred miles. We've talked about making a permanent move to somewhere else that hasn't been picked clean, but no one knows where to go. Each time we go hunting, we risk getting caught and killed. And there's Frank, holed up in the high school, waiting to kill us at every opportunity. He only has ten or twelve people there, but they are ruthless. There aren't enough of them to attack us, but we don't dare get close to the school. So, we have a nice little standoff now."

"What was that about harming students?"

Moseley stared into the fire.

"Frank likes to be in command. But he also likes hierarchy and levels. So even though there are only a dozen people in there, he made himself the head of a three-person council."

"The DMTF," Charles said.

"Madeline Silva was our guidance counselor. She was young, like us, but was already recognized as the best leader in the school, even better than any of the principals. Headed lots of committees and things like that. Won an award from the county once too. I suspect Frank knew he had to bring Maddy on the DMTF to secure everyone's obedience. And then there was Noreen."

"Who was Noreen? One of your teachers?"

Moseley shook her head.

"Noreen Ditchard was a student. Terrible home life, junkie dad, five little siblings she had to care for, one of those stories. We—the principals, teachers, Maddy—all felt for her. Wanted to help her. Reported the parents, but there wasn't much more we could do. Frank was especially protective of her. Keep in mind, this is a man who would pull students from class in the morning to inform them a grandparent had died but would not let them leave until they had completed the full school day. Every time Noreen came in crying, Frank ushered her into his office, shut the door, and didn't open it until she was done crying."

Charles felt icy and queasy.

"Don't tell me he was..."

"While we were working there?" Moseley replied. "No, I don't think so. He loves having power, but even more, he loves having titles. He would not risk his title of Vice Principal for something like that. But Noreen was a student twenty years ago, and our school dissolved and Frank took over seventeen years ago, with himself as the leader, Maddy as his co-council, and Noreen as the third part of the DMTF. She gave birth to a daughter less than a year after that, then a son less than a year after that. She never had a boyfriend any of us knew of."

Charles looked into the fire. Peter had curled up into a ball on the ground. Jean Paul looked down at him, then lifted the scrawny teenager in his arms. He set the boy inside the second tent, who then waved goodnight to Charles and Moseley. All around the camp, the fires were dwindling and extinguishing, the voices diminishing. The weight of darkness and nighttime din of birds and insects and bullfrogs settled over all.

"It's late. Do you want to come to my tent?" Moseley asked.

"I don't know if that's a good idea," Charles said, with no idea why he was saying it. *Of course, it's a good idea!* he thought, but Moseley shrugged, and the conversation continued without any awkwardness or interruption. They talked about her life, about life in the forest, foraging off the abandoned scraps of old civilization and preying on the trucks that crisscrossed the country to supply the Plexes. They talked about New

Jersey, what it used to be like, and what it was now. They talked about the parks, landmarks, stores, and malls they knew in common, for in the days of cars, the two of them had not lived impossibly far apart. Not like now. Now, Charles and Moseley were separated not by miles, but by worlds. Moseley talked a little about her husband, whom she had not seen since he moved into a Plex. They had had no children, and she had no children in the forest, and she confessed to having always wanted one.

"These woods are no place to raise a child, though," she said. "Do we have more freedom than in the Plex? Sure. But we have more infant mortality too. A few children are born among us each year. Many don't make it. If we could find a wandering doctor to join us, I think we'd declare him king."

Charles told Moseley about his days as a teacher, about Shaaya and Clara and Tamra. He told her about hanging on as a teacher until he became the degraded version he was until recently. He told her about writing *The Trough*. He told her about how he found Melody and Jennifer and the two boys and the lessons they had held together. Each story he told, he revealed more of himself, stripping down one layer of secrecy after another. The night deepened. He unspooled himself before Moseley, releasing himself from all the lying and deception and fear that had kept him bound. She listened, letting him pour his frustration and anxiety into her. She nurtured with her eyes and her patient listening. The hours in the night were unhinged from the mechanized time of clocks. Time was a tidal pool, reflective and infinitely deep. It seemed to never end, and in its infinity, it seemed to pass by in a single moment. Charles was weary and hoarse. He looked around. All the fires were out, had been out for three of his stories. Now, it was just him and Moseley.

"You have to go soon," Moseley said to him, her voice husky. Night was at its densest.

"Soon. Not right away."

"Would you like to do something together?"

"What?"

"Hunt."

"Trucks?"

"No."

For how long they walked from camp, he could not be sure. An hour? Two, perhaps? Guided by only a single lantern, they penetrated into the thickest trees. He tried to breathe as quietly as possible, though he was a one-man band of crunching on leaves and heavy breathing. Finally, they found a spot in a forked tree, overlooking a stream. There, they sat and waited.

"The deer will come," Moseley whispered.

Both of them held bows. Moseley had one she had made from PVC pipe. It stood almost six feet tall and when Charles tried to draw it, he could barely move the string. Moseley had given him a compound bow, one with a much smoother draw. Charles had shot once or twice at renaissance festivals, long ago, but admitted he knew nothing about deer hunting.

"Physically, it will not be hard," Moseley said. To prove her point, she made him nock an arrow and draw, and he mastered it with only minor adjustments. "But to hunt, to kill, requires a mastery of the mind. Maybe of the soul, if we have souls. In mentally healthy people, there is a great resistance to killing. But if we do not kill, we do not eat. The first time you cross that barrier will not be easy. It does get easier, though. You've learned a lot in your life, Charles. You've learned to read and write and use a computer and use a credit card and to stifle your frustration and rage into a little four-hundred square foot apartment. This morning, you will learn to kill. To wait patiently, find your shot, and take a life."

So, Charles sat in the crook of the tree in silence with Moseley. Neither of them was camouflaged, but the clothes they wore were dull and brown or gray, so he supposed they were as hidden as they could be. They did not speak. The creek gurgled and dribbled below them.

Gradually, in excruciatingly tiny increments, a glow of pink rose in the east, at first so dim that Charles thought he imagined it. But a little at time, the sharp contrast of moonlight and dark faded with the encroaching sun. No deer. Still, Charles waited. Time, unshackled from clocks and alarms, seemed to swirl around him in eddies and sinkholes. They had been out most of the night and now it was almost morning. Was it four hours? Six? Eight? A month? A decade? Time, in the early dawn in the crook of the tree, moved not in one direction but in all directions and none. Charles tumbled back to a time and place when men and women lived as life saw fit, not as the way it was molded to be.

A twig snapped.

Charles focused his eyes on the creek. He could see no movement. He widened his vision, trying to take in the entire forest. He heard more crackling leaves and breaking twigs. He held his breath and looked to Moseley. She nodded.

In the stillness, a shadow moved.

Imperceptible at first, the moving shadow in the trees blended seamlessly with the trees around it. But Charles could see now, a nose and a head and a rack of antlers.

The buck lifted its head. The eyes, dark pools on the tan face, probed the trees. *He too seeks answers in the forest.* For a moment, Charles felt deeply intimate with the deer. *Each of us knows the other is here.*

Moseley nodded again to Charles. He lifted his bow. His fingers trembled as he nocked an arrow. He exhaled. The buck bent his head to drink from the stream. Charles drew the bowstring back to his ear. His heart was pounding in his throat. His skin prickled. *One, two, three!* he thought. But he did not release. *One, two three!* Still, nothing. He relaxed his arm. He drew again. Moseley looked at him. *One, two, three!* But again, he did not draw, and he relaxed. As he did, the arrow slid from the bow and tapped the branch below with a sharp tick. The deer's head sprang up. His muscles bunched as he prepared to bound away.

Moseley moved with swift brutality. She lifted her bow, drew, and released in a single, effortless motion. The arrow struck the deer as it leaped, hitting with such force that the animal staggered back. It fell to the ground, rose, stumbled, and staggered into the brush. Moseley slipped down from her perch and ran after her prey. Charles tried to follow, but he lacked her grace and strength. By the time he had shimmied his way down to the ground, Moseley was a few hundred yards away, crouched by the deer's side. She held a long, serrated knife to her prey's neck. After whispering something unintelligible, she drew the blade across. Blood gushed from the open throat and into the water. Charles could not look. Instead, he stared at the red water, flowing down into the valley.

"Charles!" Moseley said, snapping Charles to awareness. "Just a little buck fever. Even happens to experienced hunters."

"But not you," Charles said. He was beginning to regain control of his emotions and faculties. Shame at being unable to shoot filled in the void left by the panic.

"Not me. But I've been at this a long time. Come. Help me carry him back."

That, Charles could do. Now the sun had risen fully, the way along the forest floor was easy to see. The two of them slung the bows over their shoulders, gripped a hind leg, and dragged the buck toward camp. The flow of blood lessened. As it did, the deer became lighter to carry. Charles had never touched a deer before. Its fur was surprisingly bristly for an animal that appeared so soft. He gripped the leg above the shins. There was something intimate, again, in gripping the bone of the leg. *This deer and I, we have shared something. The exchange of life, the eternal dance of living and dying. Today, I lived, and he died. One day, I will die too. I took his life. No, I could not do it. Moseley had to do it.* He did not know which would haunt him more, killing the buck or being unable to kill the buck.

When they returned to camp, it was already fully light. The camp had awoken, and small morning fires dotted the span of forest. Already, the preparations for their departure were underway. Some of the tents had been broken down, and the dozens of forest nomads were eating breakfast cereal and granola by the handful as they bundled their few possessions into packs.

Maury strode up to them, his expression displeased.

"Where were you?" he demanded.

"I was doing my taxes," Moseley replied. Maury did not smile.

"We have to get moving. One of our sentries thought he saw a couple of Frank's minions prowling along the road."

Moseley waved a dismissive hand.

"They always stick to the road. They don't dare venture out here. Relax. We'll be packed and ready to leave within the hour."

Maury pointed to the dead buck.

"And what are your intentions with that?"

"I will have him home by ten, sir. No funny business."

Maury ignored the comment and turned to Charles.

"You and your friends have to go. We are leaving this camp and there is no room for hangers-on. I am having a difficult time getting any of them to wake up."

Charles smiled.

"You were young once. Surely you slept in whenever you had the opportunity."

Maury's frown remained fixed on his face. "I have not lived a life of comfort, nestled in a little box somewhere. On the roads and in the forests, we wake early every day."

Moseley rolled her eyes.

"Give me ten minutes. I'll dress the buck and pack my tent. I'll even carry the carcass myself. Have you scouted our new location?"

"I have."

"And?"

"I'm not going to talk about such things in front of someone who may go right to Frank Wieland. If we are still here by the time he gets down there, that little devil will send his death squad up here."

"Let them come," Moseley said. "We have bows. We have greater numbers. We have hiding places."

"But you know him all too well! How do you know he won't bring guns? How do you know he won't capture and torture one of us? Just remember what he did to Kiara and Amir."

Moseley nodded, grave for the first time in the conversation. She looked at Charles.

"Are you going to Frank? After we fed you, took you in, and brought you on your first hunt, are you going to scurry back to Frank Wieland and bring him the eyes of Moseley?"

The deer, which was becoming heavy, slid down off Charles's shoulder and onto the forest floor.

"Of course not," Charles said, rolling his shoulders loose. "After what you told me, we will not come within five hundred yards of that school and that sicko inside."

Moseley put her hands on her hips. "Well, I think you should."

THAT AFTERNOON, CHARLES stood at the auditorium doors in Mahwah High School, escorted by two guards dressed in old band uniforms and bearing two-by-fours with nails. The students fanned out behind him. He knocked on the door with one hand and held a coffee can in the other.

One of the guards knocked on the auditorium door.

"Enter," said a loud, shrill male voice from within.

Charles and the students walked into the auditorium again. After their eyes adjusted to the low light, they saw Frank Wieland in his seat in the center of the stage. To his right sat Madeline Silva, former guidance counselor. To his left sat Noreen Ditchard, one-time student and at least two-time lover of Wieland.

"Approach!" Frank declared, and the Rooftop Readers Club walked down the aisle. When they stopped, they stood in the pit, staring up at the former vice principal.

"We have returned," Charles said, hoping to match the imperious tone. Wieland pointed to Melody.

"I will speak only with her, the wise one with the pink hair."

Melody, whose eyes had been cast at the ground, looked up. *She's been really sullen the last two days,* Charles realized. *Was she upset about going into the woods? Or about being taken away from them?*

"He may speak for me," Melody said without much force behind her voice. "He is my teacher and I trust his wisdom."

Wieland rose from his seat and strode over to them.

"I did not expect you to live. I thought you to be cowards, cowards who would scurry back to your train and into your little rat boxes where you could feel safe again. I did not expect you to go into the forest. Perhaps you are to be commended for your foolhardiness."

Charles wondered if that was the closest Frank Wieland could allow himself to a compliment.

"We did go into the forest. We also met with the bandit, Moseley. And have returned to tell about it."

"Moseley was always a schemer and trickster," Frank said, almost as if to himself. "Always more style than substance. Never saw the value in harsh, swift discipline. That is what children want, not compassion. They want to know the limits and must be shown them with no softness. Mustn't we all?"

Madeline Silva, the former guidance counselor, kept a stoic face, though Charles thought he detected a twinge around her eyes.

"Moseley has done nothing but torment me since the day we first met. Living out among the animals, as an animal, she will surely come to her fate sooner than I. But I speak too much. You have acquitted yourself well, Boxer. Leave now and return to your home."

"But we have completed your task," Charles said, stepping forward and proffering the coffee can. "We bring you the eyes of Moseley."

"What?" hissed Frank.

"We allowed ourselves to be captured, as you instructed. Then, in the night, we slew her and cut out her eyes with the spoons she used to serve us stew. During the shifting of the sentries, we snuck out of their camp and returned to present you the prize."

"Impossible!" roared Frank. "Moseley has escaped my grasp for over twenty years, and you catch and kill her on your first attempt? Impossible! Tell me, what color were her eyes?"

"Brown," Charles replied.

"What did she look like?"

"Tall, strongly built, dark skin," Charles said.

"But you know not who she was, or what a danger she was to me and my people here," Frank said.

"She was once principal of this school," Charles replied coolly. "What your feud was with her, I cannot say and do not care. I simply did as you asked."

Frank's look of anger was replaced by one of admiration.

"Show me," he said.

Charles pulled the lid from the coffee can. Frank leaned over it, peering down into the metal cylinder. He caught his breath.

"Oh my," he said. Without asking, he put his hands on the coffee can and grabbed it from Charles. He showed it to Madeline, to Noreen, and then to all the armed thugs. At the bottom of the can sat two eyeballs, glistening brown orbs at the end of a trail of gristle and optic nerve.

"But...but...Moseley killed Kenny Pulasky, the best among us! Did these soft-brained Box dwellers do what he could not?" Wieland said. It almost sounded as if he were about to cry.

Charles caught his reply in his teeth. *Kenny Pulasky lives,* he wanted to say. He wanted to watch the rage wash over Wieland as he learned that the young man had betrayed him.

"Moseley boasted of murdering Kenny Pulasky," he said instead. "Now she is dead, and her eyes are yours. And we slew her. So perhaps you should stop insulting us, and honor your promise, as these soft-brained Box dwellers accomplished what the best among you could not."

"So what?" said Noreen, her voice almost screeching. "You are still our prisoners. You killed our enemy. We can still kill you. How do you like that?"

"You could kill us," Charles conceded. "But you won't."

"Why not?" Noreen asked. Charles looked at her for a wordless moment. *She looks like a broken person, not properly mended.*

"Because we killed Moseley. We did what you could not. What you respect, what Francis Mallory Wieland, Protector of the Liberated Peoples of Mahwah and Ramsey, respects above all is power. And right now, the five of us are the most powerful in this room, in this school, in this entire valley."

"He is right," Frank said, turning to the DMTF. "These travelers, though they were raised in the soft world of Boxes and electronic screens and pampering, have shown great mettle. We must send them from our home with our blessing and commendations."

The court cheered. But the quintet did not move.

"Not yet," Jennifer said, as planned.

"What?" hissed Frank.

"We made an agreement," Jennifer went on. "If we failed to bring you the eyes, you would hang us up in your courtyard."

"The Square of the Just," murmured Charles.

"The Square of the Just," said Jennifer, much louder. "And if we did, what happens? Don't you remember?"

Silence hung over the auditorium.

"What happens?" said Jennifer again.

"You cannot expect me to willingly hand myself over," Frank said.

"Why not? You made a deal."

Frank smiled. He waved his hand out at the auditorium and the dozen armed followers.

"Because at a signal, I can command my followers to bludgeon you into pulp. A waggle of my finger, and in less than two minutes, you will be carrion for the coyotes. That is why I need not honor your silly bargain."

"You won't do that," said Charles, in a tone that suggested a *coup de grace*. "Because once we are dead, your followers will see that you are dishonest and will renege on any arrangement once it becomes distasteful to you. You hold power over us because you have an armed guard. But you only hold power over that guard because they trust in you. If you kill us, you kill their trust in you too."

Frank rushed to the edge of the stage. He was pulsing red in the face as he leaned down and jabbed his finger at Charles.

"That wager was not made in good faith! You deceived us!"

"How?" Jennifer asked coolly.

"You are strangers! You don't belong here!" shrieked Frank. "You trespass into our home and then strike a crooked bargain to deceive us and then dare to humiliate me publicly! I ought to have your intestines ripped out and strung along the bleachers! I should peel your skin from your bodies and fly it up the flagpole for all to see! I can do that!"

Charles wanted to continue goading Frank, but he was becoming nervous. He had hoped to use the bargain as leverage, but for that, he needed Frank to be rational. A hysterical tyrant was perhaps even worse than a calculating one. Then he recalled something Frank had said the day before. He stroked his chin as if in contemplation.

"Perhaps...perhaps an alternative can be reached. One that will allow you to keep your power and us to claim our victory."

"Victory," Frank grumbled, but then added, "what is your proposal?"

"You are the Keepers of the Knowledge," Charles said. "You told us this yourself. Well, we are Seekers of Knowledge, and in our sad little Boxed lives, there is so little knowledge. Let us say this—we will spare your life, which you want, if we may bring some of the Knowledge back with us to our Box. What a trove of books you have in your possession! Surely you can spare a few of them to spare your own life. What is your answer?"

Charles watched the spectrum of expressions crossing over Frank's face. At first, he appeared disgusted, then intrigued, then frightened, then pitiful. Madeline Silva coughed and half stood.

"Perhaps this is a matter best discussed by the DMTF—"

Frank whirled around on her. "No! This is my life. I get to decide. No DMTF."

Now Noreen jumped from her chair.

"Do not give them the knowledge! These shit heads are blackmailers! Kill them!"

"Sit down, Miss Ditchard!" barked Frank. The armed followers began to close in on the stage. Charles was unsure if they were moving toward him or their leader on stage.

"Yes!" Frank cried. "I agree. That is a fair arrangement. Give them back their bags! They may take whatever they can carry, and never again return to this land. Lead them out!"

The guards wavered for a moment, but finally looked to one another and nodded.

"Come," said the apparent leader of the squad to Charles and his students. "This way."

The squad led them to the basement again. Charles and the students filled their bags with literature anthologies and grammar textbooks, but also science and history books. Charles told each of them to pick one book that interested them, so everyone could have at least one personal reading choice. They grabbed dogeared and worn paperback novels that had long since stopped being published. Finally, the group selected five laptop computers.

Frank's squad of thugs escorted Charles and his students back to the Sol-Train station, speaking to them little. They stopped out of sight of the station, gave them directions for the rest of the way back, and scuttled back up the road toward the school. Charles and the students waited on the platform, sweaty, exhausted, tired, and proud. Charles smiled, and was overcome with a sublime feeling, one unique to teachers. *The pure love of a teacher for a student is unlike any other in the world,* he thought.

He looked over the young people. So much potential, so much hope. It manifested as a feeling of strain from deep inside him, an ache of hope for them. *I really do love these kids.* It was a privilege to play a part in helping them grow up. Their connection had, he hoped, made a change in their lives. It had certainly made one in his.

Teaching was mostly a slog, mostly drudgery, mostly disappointment. Most teachers rarely saw a change beyond the acquisition of a paycheck, and most students rarely saw a change beyond the acquisition of skills. But sometimes, very rarely, with the right teacher and students, the change happened to the teachers and students themselves, and there was magic in that.

Moseley's plan had seemed brilliant, with a chance to humiliate Frank and come away with a magnificent haul. But it was built on a significant risk. The risk was that Frank Wieland, who had been a music teacher, hopefully knew little of biology. Fortunately, for Charles and his students it seemed to be the case. Two brown eyes lay in the bottom of a coffee can, and Moseley's eyes had been brown, so Frank assumed they had belonged to her. Not to a whitetail deer that had been shot earlier that morning.

That part of the plan had been executed flawlessly. But now they were on the Sol-Train, lugging around as many textbooks and computers as their bags and arms could carry. The train was lightly occupied, but the five travelers drew many stares. Once they reached Plex 87, Charles knew, it would only be more difficult to remain inconspicuous.

"I was thinking about garbage," Jennifer said.

"Huh?" was all Charles could say.

"Garbage," Jennifer said, her tone forcefully sunny and nonchalant. "You know, how much garbage our Plexes produce. I wonder if it could be reduced."

"Uh, I guess," Charles said, feeling like an imbecile.

"Why do you care about garbage?" Peter asked.

"Oh, I don't. I don't think anyone does. That's the point," Jennifer said.

What is she getting at? Charles wondered. But he would let her get there.

"Think about what happened with Frank," Jennifer went on." What was he looking for in the coffee can?"

"Eyes," Peter said.

"Right. But was he looking for a coffee can?"

"No, of course not," Jean Paul said.

"Exactly!" Jennifer said. "I think that could be the answer to our problem."

Hiding things from probing eyes is part of the nature of being a Plexer, Charles thought. *She is certainly better at it than I am.*

"Go on," Charles said. Jennifer could not help but let a little smile slip.

"Frank was looking for the eyes. We brought them in a coffee can. But we could have brought them in a box, in a dish, or in a plastic bag. That didn't matter. He didn't see the coffee can. Where did it come from? Probably from one of the trucks Moseley hunted! We brought him his prize in a container his enemy had claimed from him."

"Go on," Charles said again. Now he was smiling too.

"Well, what we're carrying is interesting. But what we carry it in doesn't have to be. And who we are doesn't have to be. Boxes on carts aren't interesting. Neither are garbage pickers."

DISCARDED CARDBOARD BOXES lay in heaps all around the loading bay of Plex 87. While the interior of the Plex was carefully maintained and monitored, garbage and waste often went ignored by all but low-level workers or vagrants. As a result, some Plexes had vast landscapes of old boxes, broken crates and pallets, and even old trucks or parts of trucks that had broken down and been deemed too expensive to tow. Charles,

Melody, and Jennifer hid at the corner of the loading bay, watching workers roll up the ramp and toss aside empty boxes. When the truck engine roared and the loading bay crew went back inside, no one was watching the garbage heap.

Charles snatched a few packing boxes. He tossed them back to Melody, who was waiting. Jennifer spotted a hand cart with one warped wheel leaning against the concrete wall. It rolled badly, but it rolled. "Good enough," he mouthed, and he turned to go back to the dumpster.

Before him stood a security guard.

"What are you three doing back here?" he asked, more tired than menacing.

"We're just—it's going to get cold come autumn," Melody said, adding a pout and a bat of eyelashes. The security guard squinted with doubt.

"These boxes, this cart, they aren't yours. You can't just come and take other people's property."

"Please," said Charles, adding a wheezy rasp to his voice. "I just need a couple of boxes to break down. For the floor of our home."

"Our?" said the security guard. He looked to the old man and two young women who seemed to be obeying him unquestioningly. "Ugh. You dirty off-Plexers are vermin. Someone ought to have a roundup and gas all of you. Get out of here. I don't want to see you again."

"Yes, sir. We apologize, sir," said Charles, and the trio scurried away, back to the dumpster.

Peter and Jean Paul waited outside the Sol-Train station with the books and laptops. Jean Paul would bring the cart inside. He not only looked the right age to be pushing a cart as part of his job, but he was the strongest of the group, and the heavy load on the cart made the tricky wheel that much harder to move. The other four entered Plex 87 at staggered intervals and split in different directions.

Jean Paul entered one of the loading bay entrances. He kept his face stony, in the way of one who is weary of his job and does not want to speak or be spoken to. He brought the cart in the freight elevator to the floor of Charles's room, and followed the directions to the apartment. Charles, who had entered the Plex first, was waiting for him. Within fifteen minutes, all five of them were crammed into Charles's little apartment, along with a broken cart and cardboard boxes full of old textbooks and outdated computers. They felt as sneaky as bandits and as rich as kings.

Eleven: The Reason for Running

Looking back, it seems surprising that parents would so easily allow the privatization and watering down of their children's education. Why did they not resist? Two reasons, chiefly. For one, they deemed their children safer at home than at school. Free from bullies, gangs, and school violence, children completed their school work under parental supervision, and could be counted on to do more housework and run errands. 'It brings families together,' EduForce argued. More significantly, the dissolution of local school districts meant the end of school taxes. Citizens did not foot the bill of educating children; EduForce did, fueled by private advertising. Society determined that it valued low taxes more than it valued the education of our children.

　　—*The Trough*, p.90

Jennifer sat on the floor in Melody's room, gazing into her flexscreen. Mr. 85 was on the screen, explaining about something called "civics." Jennifer was a little nervous. She did not even know what the word "civics" meant, and the uncertainty made her feel anxious about getting something wrong. Then she remembered it did not matter even if she did, because the Perfect Five was no longer perfect. *Does anything matter?* she pondered, before deciding *Yes, but not this.*

　　"Every person in America who is eighteen years old or older—this means you—has to do four things. The first is to pay taxes, though these are very low. No one likes taxes! Taxes pay for the salaries of our President and the people working in our government. The second is to serve on a jury. Juries are like poll groups who decide whether a person on trial did the crime or not. Simply watch a short video about a crime and take a poll afterward. The third thing is to always watch your NewsFeed, because Knowledge is Power. Last is to vote for a president every four years."

At this point, the video cut to a campaign advertisement for Geraldine Barfield. In the background, she was not in her typical office setting, but was in front of one of the many edugames she had created and popularized. Colorful graphics splashed behind her. She was smiling, as always.

"Young people of America, I hope you are enjoying your educational experience today. Remember, Learning is Fun! The edugames are like the candy coating to a lesson—the lesson is what makes you smart and strong, but the edugame is what is fun! You know what else is fun? Voting. Don't forget to vote for me, Geraldine Barfield, next November. I'm going to go now, so you can get back to work. Remember, Hard Work Pays Off!"

Then the outro, and the jingle. *Molding the minds of America. Molding the minds of America. Molding the minds. Molding the minds.*

Candy coating to a lesson, Jennifer thought. *That's a simile.* But what did the simile mean? The edugame made the lesson more enjoyable. There was no doubt about that. But if Learning was Fun, why did it need to be made fun with a game? Playing edugames was fun, or at least it used to be, but was she learning? She compared it to their field trip from a few weeks earlier. Taking a Sol-Train to a different town, breaking into an abandoned school building, then being taken captive and sent on a mission to murder a tribal leader, then befriending the leader and returning to trick the captors—had that been fun? No. But she had learned more in that day and a half than she ever had before.

Besides, what happens to someone who only eats candy her entire childhood? What happens to our generation?

She had lost focus and needed to watch the second part of Mr. 85's video again. But he was just going over his earlier points in more detail. Jennifer suspected there was a lot more information out there to know—what were taxes really for? What did juries do? Why do we vote for a President? She decided maybe those things would be explored more in a later module.

After the lesson came the edugame, one called "Surfin' Civics." It had a promising start. Jennifer could choose and customize her own surfer avatar. Though few people actually surfed anymore, almost anyone could experience it on a VR vacation, and so Jennifer was familiar with the suits, the boards, and the feel of wind and waves. After choosing her avatar, her character went out into the water. A question flashed on the top of the screen. *What is the first part of civics?* A series of waves came in to shore, each one with a phrase on top of it. Jennifer steered her avatar toward one that said *Pay taxes.* Her character rode high on the wave, and with a splashy blue explosion and a guitar riff, the screen lit up *Right answer! Surf's up!*

Jennifer finished the edugame with ease, answering each question correctly. At the end, her cumulative statistics showed on the screen. There was that 5.0*/5.0. The dark spot, the meaningful smudge. She turned off her flexscreen, feeling nothing.

"Mel?" Jennifer said. No reply. "Mel!"

"Hm?" Melody lay on her bed, facing the wall.

"You hungry?"

"No."

"Let's take a break from this studying," Jennifer suggested, though Melody had done no work for EduForce in weeks.

Melody did not reply.

"Well, I'm taking a break," Jennifer said. "Can I get you anything? A grape soda?"

"No."

Jennifer left the room and went to make more coffee. Melody's parents, despite their shortcomings, always kept the coffee supply well stocked. Jennifer stood next to the machine as it gurgled and hissed. *Melody and her moods.* When she and Melody had first started seeing each other over a year before, Jennifer noticed the moods and put up with them. If the occasional week of grouchiness and one-syllable responses was the price for her good moods when she was gregarious, quick-witted, and sexually insatiable, Jennifer would gladly pay.

But now, Jennifer realized she did not tolerate Melody's bad moods. She embraced them. Adored them. Fetishized them, even. *Riding through life with Melody is like riding into a storm,* Jennifer thought, proud of herself for the simile. Such images had been coming to her more and more frequently. The storm that was Melody Park was Jennifer's personal antidote, personal resistance, to the relentlessly illuminated, sunny world of EduForce, of Plexes, of Perk-Eez and Relax-Eez and AIPAs.

"Hello, Jennifer," said Carlita, as if on cue. The polite voice of the AIPA chimed in her ear.

"Hi, 'lita. What do you have for me?"

"A new message, from Jean Paul Alvarez. May I read it to you?"

"Jean Paul? For me?" Jean Paul had never sent a message to Jennifer before. She peered at Melody's bedroom door. Still shut.

"Go ahead."

"Very well. The message says, 'Jennifer, I need your help. I am gonna take the level 12 Achievements again in two weeks. Can you help me study? I really got to do good on them, 'cause I don't think I can take failing again.'"

Help him study? she thought. She had never done anything of the kind. There was no need. EduForce provided hundreds of support tutorial videos. *Why me?* she wondered. *To help someone? To teach someone?*

"Okay," she said aloud. "Carlita, tell him okay."

"Should I say that verbatim or should I—"

"Say however I would say it," she said. When was this AIPA going to adapt to her already and figure out what she wanted?

"Very good," Carlita said. "Message sent. Is there anything else that I can—Jennifer, a reply from Jean Paul Alvarez has arrived. Would you like me to read it?"

"Please."

"The message says, 'When can you start?' Would you like to make a reply?"

Jennifer looked at the coffee pouring in the pot. She grabbed the pot, triggering the auto-stop, and took a travel mug from one of the cabinets. She doubted Melody's parents would miss it for one evening. She poured the contents into the mug.

"Can he meet now?"

Carlita paused for approximately two seconds. *She is learning and adapting,* Jennifer realized.

"Jennifer, I sent a message in your wording on your behalf. I hope that is—Jean Paul Alvarez has sent a reply. The reply says 'Now is good. I am in unit 4775.'"

UNIT 4775 WAS only a seven-minute walk from Melody's apartment. She had told Melody through the bedroom door where she was going but had received only "all right" in reply. When she arrived at the door, she rang the bell and waited. A few seconds later, a shriveled old woman with a jovial smile and less than a full set of teeth opened the door.

"*Bienvenidos!*" she said. "Come in! You are the...girl? The girl student?"

"*Sí, señora. Por Jean Paul.*"

"*Bueno,*" she said with a relieved gush of a sigh, as though she had held her breath from the moment Jean Paul had told her she was coming. She welcomed Jennifer in, offered her a drink, which Jennifer declined, indicating her coffee mug, and showed her to the kitchen table, where Jean Paul sat, his head bent over a book.

Jennifer could not help but notice the similarities between the Alvarez home and her own. The layout was similar, and the same beige carpets and walls which came with every Plex apartment served as the background to everything. But they had decorated with a few photographs and handcrafts from the home country. In her own home, those had been things from Colombia. Here, they were from the Dominican Republic. Like the furnishings in her home, the Alvarezes made a little go far. The couches were worn, the dishware chipped, and the mirrors cloudy. Yet something about this home gave a feeling of warmth, of old furnishings worn down with love, whereas her own home felt only cold and shabby.

"Hi," she said as she sat across from the big man. He did not reply. His eyes were red.

"You all right?" she asked.

"I can't get these fractions," he said. "They don't make no sense to me. Why some numbers over other numbers? I got to know fractions."

"Okay, fractions," she said, feeling daunted herself. "So, you have a numerator and a denominator. The numerator goes into the denominator so many times. It's divided by it. So, you divide the numerator by the denominator. Sometimes it's even, sometimes it isn't. That's how you do the fractions."

"Huh?"

"Well, the top number is divided by the bottom number."

"Why?"

"I don't know," Jennifer admitted. "That's just what fractions are."

"What are they used for?"

Jennifer thought. Word problems and applications were always a little tricky for her, a little fuzzy.

"Do you ever bake?"

"No."

"Me neither," Jennifer said. She thought hard about what Jean Paul might be interested in.

"Cars," she said, as much to herself as to him. "You like cars, right?"

"Yeah, I do!"

Almost no one drove cars anymore, but there were plenty of aficionados who studied them, collected photos and videos of them, and took virtual reality drives.

"Okay, I don't. But let's think of a car dealership. They have ten cars."

"That wouldn't have been much of a dealership," Jean Paul said with a little chuckle.

"Okay, whatever. Just for the sake of our problem, ten cars. The dealer has ten cars to sell. Ten is the denominator."

"Okay," Jean Paul said hesitantly.

"Someone comes to the dealership and buys three of them."

"Three cars?" Jean Paul said. "Must be rich."

"Uh, sure," Jennifer said. She felt foolish picking an example she really didn't understand herself. "So, the three is the numerator."

"That the one on bottom?"

"On top."

Jean Paul sighed and hung his head.

"Just hearing these numbers, looking at them on the paper, it's all a big confusing jumble. You can keep explaining it, but I'm just too stupid to get it."

"Don't say that," Jennifer said. "We'll figure it out somehow. I wish I had ten of something to show you. Spoons, or Perk-Eez tabs, or—"

"I got an idea! Can you excuse me a moment?" Jean Paul asked.

"Uh, sure," Jennifer said, and Jean Paul hurried into his room. Jennifer heard some rummaging, and when Jean Paul returned, he had two handfuls of Matchbox cars.

"Are there ten?" Jennifer asked. Jean Paul nodded yes. Jennifer lined them up.

"Ten cars."

Then, using her hand as a blade, she spaced three of the cars off from the rest.

"These three get bought."

"Seven left!" Jean Paul said. Jennifer smiled.

"Yes, but that's subtraction. Out of the ten cars total, three are purchased. So how many cars are there? Altogether?"

Jean Paul paused.

"Still ten?"

"Right! That's the denominator, the one on bottom. How many were bought?"

"Three."

"That's the numerator. The top number. So, when we look at a fraction, it's the top number"—she held up the three cars—"out of the bottom number." She indicated all ten cars.

"Ah. I think I understand now."

"Really?"

"Yeah! You tell me numbers, I won't remember. But with the cars? *Comprendo!*"

"*Muy bien!*" Jean Paul's grandmother said from the fringes of the room. Jennifer laughed.

"Muy bien," she agreed. Jean Paul stood up from the chair and embraced her. "*Gracias.* You taught me. Better than any video."

"I... I guess I did," she replied.

"How does it feel, teacher?"

Jennifer did not know. She had only ever been the student.

Over the following week, she met with Jean Paul every day. He had skipped a number of modules on a variety of topics, mostly mathematics. For Jennifer, the idea of skipping lessons that were too difficult was foreign to her. Learning with video modules had been easy. Watch it once, remember it, play the edugames to test it. She could not understand not understanding. But Jean Paul almost never understood, at least not by watching the modules. She would watch them with him, and she could remember everything the teacher said, whereas he could barely even recall the topic. But she found that when he had something physical in front of him—ten Matchbox cars, cubes, candies, anything to illustrate the point—he remembered.

Jennifer came to realize that if not for her specialized lessons, Jean Paul would never surmount the tests standing in his way. Even better than watching his progress, she relished watching his confidence. Each day, he became less afraid of learning. "There are never any surprises," she explained to him. "You can always know what's coming up next." This alleviated his anxiety.

One Tuesday morning, while helping Jean Paul navigate the perils of reading *The Hard Choice*, a short story by Chandri Coleman about two children and what to do about a homeless man they find, Carlita announced, "Good morning, Jennifer. You have a message from an unfamiliar sender. It does not appear to be spam. Shall I read it to you?"

"Go ahead."

"The message is from Juan Carlos Calderón."

Jennifer's heart chilled. She switched Carlita from her personal speakers to her earpiece. No need for Jean Paul to hear what was coming.

"The subject line," Carlita went on, "says '*Este es tu padre.*' Do you require translation?"

"No," Jennifer said softly. "No, I understand."

Has to be an imposter. Or a mistake. Papá is dead. He was a Federal agent and some drug lords found him and killed him in El Paso and now Mamá has to raise me all her herself.

"Read it," Jennifer said, her voice thick with fear, suspicion, and curiosity.

Carlita's voice rolled into her ears, but as it did, Jennifer found the voice morphing into the voice of a man, an older one, one who had loved her and cared about her once, and about Rosa too. It became the voice of a hero, of a quasi-mythic figure whose absence was the bedrock of her life. Carlita delivered the message, but it was Juan Carlos Calderón who sat nestled in her ear, speaking from the grave.

"Darling Jennifer, if you choose to receive my message, I thank you. Surely you are fearful and suspicious of such a message. I do not know what your Mamá, Rosa Calderón, has told you about me, but I promise you I am not dead. You will know this is true because I left for you a photograph, a real photograph printed on paper, of you at the age of two years old standing on a railing over a stairwell in our old apartment building. It is my hope you still have this photograph.

"I have made many choices in my life, some of which I do not regret, and some of which I do. Leaving you and your mother was one of the latter.

"Speaking of making choices, you will now have to make the choice if you will meet with me in person. I would like to see you again. I heard of your remarkable achievements in academics in my NewsFeed. After some thought, I decided it was time for me to find you. Your mother does not know this. You are an adult woman now and do not need your Mamá to make your choices for you. If you do not wish to meet me, I understand. Perhaps my message brings you pain. If you do wish to meet me, I am filled with joy. Please take the time you need. I await your reply. *Todos amor,* Juan Carlos Calderón. Your *Papá"*

Jean Paul gently nudged Jennifer's arm to return her to him, his kitchen table, and his question about a vocabulary word. Jennifer answered it for him, but she was far away. Her ears, her head, her whole being was in the grip of her father's message. She thought the message was like the claws of a great bird, grasping her and pulling her into the air.

Another metaphor, she realized, amazed.

Papá is alive. Of this, she had no doubt. Even without the proof of the photograph, something to the words cut through Jennifer's doubt and resistance. She had learned from an early age that all strangers are dangerous. Sexual predators used personal messages all the time to lure children to isolated places. But these words were the words of a real father. *And I am no child.* Juan Carlos had called her an adult woman. She could not think of any time anyone else had ever called her that. She knew she was an adult, in a legal sense. But she wondered what being an adult felt like.

She answered another question for Jean Paul, then returned to her thoughts. She was curious about meeting this man without a doubt. But curiosity was not the same as a wish. She had so many questions for him about what he was doing, where he had gone, why he had left, and why he had chosen to send her a message twenty years after leaving.

She was not sure she wanted the answers to those questions either. He had been absent for nearly her whole life, but that absence was a steady presence. She could always count on her father not being there. That he had died as a hero was even more stabilizing. She had missed him at times, and at other times had resented him, but the truths of *my father is dead* and *my father died as a hero* were always by her side. Her mother had used these truths more than once to push Jennifer to greater success and to work harder. *Abused these truths, to tell it straight.*

Then there was Mamá. Plenty of questions for her too with answers equally unpleasant waiting to be spoken. Perhaps she was ignorant about Juan Carlos Calderón, as well. Perhaps she thought he was dead. But if she had known the truth, then the message made Jennifer loathe her mother more, resent her more. Her father may have left, but her mother had lied to her for two decades, had let that lie live with the two of them. Perhaps it was not her father's ghost she had felt living in their apartments all those years. Perhaps it was her mother's lie.

Once again, Jean Paul had to jog her out of her reverie.

"Maybe we should stop," Jean Paul said, and Jennifer snapped back again. "You don't seem too good."

"No, no I'm..." Jennifer could not finish the sentence.

"I'll be fine. I think I got this," Jean Paul said.

Jennifer excused herself and left his apartment. She wandered the halls of Plex 87, heading to nowhere in particular. She didn't want to go back to Melody's. She thought of going to Charles, but he had warned them numerous times about meeting him in person where cameras could see. She finally, after nearly an hour of meandering, found herself standing in front of the one place where she could find understanding. She walked into Plex Your Muscles, scanned in, and went to the locker room. Through all of this, she still did not feel as if she were in her body. So, she opened her locker, changed into a pair of shorts, sneakers, a sports bra and a tank top, tied her hair in a ponytail, and went to the treadmill. The treadmill, where she had always run.

She set it to a moderate pace, enough to get moving, but as she warmed up, her stride widened, her heart rate increased, and the sweat began to break on her skin, she increased the speed a tenth of a mile per hour at a time. Thoughts of her past streamed through her mind, of her mother and of her father, of school and the Perfect Five, and her deliberate failure. Of a memory of standing on a stairwell railing for a photograph which could have been an authentic memory or one her mind had fabricated from years of looking at the picture. Of crying silently for any reason, for no reason, of crying in front of Mamá and being slapped, of being called ungrateful and lazy and a disgraceful deviant, all *en español,* of course. Of Melody, of her hair of varying shades and her warped smile and her deft fingers and hot tongue and her thick, dominating hips, and of her cruel silences and dark moods, and of the times they had slept together and the times they had fought. And of how sometimes Jennifer would sob into her pillow at night about where was Papá, mostly when she was a little girl but even on occasion to this day. Of how she was still not an adult and yet still loved and hated and yearned for and resented and was curious about and felt no pity for but could not understand the enigmatic man who just reemerged into her universe with one message that came to her as a bolt of lightning from a clear blue sky, Juan Carlos Calderón.

The treadmill was careening, nearly out of control.

Jennifer glanced at the control panel: 10.4 miles per hour. Less than a six-minute mile, she calculated. Her legs were spinning, scissoring, flying along the tread as the machine hummed loudly. She lowered the speed a little. She glanced around and noticed a few of the other gym patrons had stopped to look at her. One man, an older guy with a stained T-shirt and a thick gut, was staring a little more intensely.

She eased her pace back, now her thoughts were under control again. But she pushed hard. She wasn't there for a relaxing jog. She wanted her sneakers to tear the treading apart; she wanted to devour the miles, to use the miles to obliterate her confusion and pain in a blur of sweat and exertion and motion. She wanted to put distance between her past and her present. She could waste no energy on thoughts or daydreams. *Boom-boom-boom-boom-boom-boom* her feet went, each stride hitting the tread as hard as they could. Her feet were a blur, her legs were a blur, her problems were a blur, her past and present and future were a blur as the mileage and calorie counters blipped higher.

Usually, she kept meticulous records of mileage, heart rate, and other variables to constantly improve her performance. This time, she ran until she was so tired her legs wobbled, her chest was heaving, and she could scarcely step off the machine. She turned the display off without looking at the numbers. She staggered over to a bench, sat, sipped from a bottle of water, and mopped her face.

The old man who had gaped at her earlier lowered himself from his stationary bike. He strolled over to her.

"You all right, miss?" he asked. Jennifer nodded wordlessly. "I could give you some exercise, if you want."

Jennifer stood. She was not sure how many miles she had just run. Maybe ten, maybe fifteen, but the condition of her legs told her it had been long.

"I'm sorry," she said. "I couldn't hear you."

The old man grinned. He was not getting his cue.

"You and me. I wouldn't mind taking you for a spin."

Jennifer nodded. "Ah. That's what I thought you said."

She slugged him in his fat gut, hard. He wheezed and his knees buckled.

"Bitch," he hissed. "I meant that as a compliment."

"Oh, you did?" Jennifer said. Then she punched him in the gut again. "The first one was for being a pig. That one was for being an idiot."

As Jennifer showered and dressed, she reflected on what she had done. She had rebuffed lecherous men in the past. She had dismissed them, turned her back on them, flipped them off, and occasionally cussed them out. But two gut shots? That was Melody's style, not hers. *Not that the creep didn't deserve it,* Jennifer reminded herself. But she worried. *What is happening to me? Who am I becoming?*

She had always been a Perfect Five and imagined a future where her identity circled around that. Win the Scholarship (which did not happen) and tout her Perfect Five (now tarnished) to a successful career to escape Mamá and her tiny apartment and narrow ways. Melody, on the other hand, had never deliberately tried to be anything. She was just...Melody.

Sitting in the locker room, recovering, she powered on her flexscreen. Several messages appeared. She hoped none of them were from her father, though part of her wished one was.

"Carlita, what'd I miss?"

"Hi, Jennifer. I see you have recently been exercising. Are you in need of some Energ-aid? The electrolytes and pH balance will restore your body's energy naturally."

"No, thank you. I—"

"Perhaps your sneakers are beginning to wear out. A new pair of AeroCloud Racers can bring your feet relief from the heavy impact of running. With AeroCloud, your feet will be on the ground, but your head will be in the sky."

"No thanks, 'lita. Would you please just read me my—"

"Then perhaps you'll consider a membership in the Plex 87 Runners Club. They meet every Saturday weekly in the Plex Your Muscles North Gym to talk running, shoes, technique, and arrange treadmill races. First month free trial membership!"

"No. Thank. You," Jennifer said. She reminded herself again to ask her mother to upgrade to the ad-free AIPA, though judging on how recent weeks had gone, Rosa might not be willing to do her many favors.

"Very good. Your first message is from Blam. An offer for fifty percent off—"

"Delete."

"Very good. Next message is from Chin Lu Cosmetics, bringing you the best in—"

"Delete," Jennifer sighed. "Delete all spam."

"Are you sure?" Carlita replied. "There may be valuable offers and savings in these messages."

Another effect of the low-cost AIPA. They make everything in life easier except for throwing out your junk mail.

"Yes, I'm sure. What's left?"

"A message from Geraldine Barfield. Subject line: Your Academic Achievement."

A message from Geraldine Barfield? The EduForce messages were always vidmessages, rarely text.

"Are you sure it's not a generic EduForce message?"

"Based on the content of the message," Carlita said, "I am almost certain this message was composed expressly for you."

"Well, let's hear it!" Jennifer said.

"The message says, 'Greetings, Jennifer. Recently, you incorrectly answered a question in one of your learning modules, and as a result your Achievement Score dipped below 5.0. This event comes as quite a surprise to us here at EduForce. Your progress through the achievement levels has always been of great interest to us, so much so that your incorrect response was a cause for some ordeal here in our offices. I am highly interested in meeting with you personally. Your intelligence and mastery of our modules can be a model of excellence for millions of other EduForce customers. Please respond immediately to inform us about your availability. We look forward to meeting with you soon. Sincerely, Geraldine Barfield.' Would you like to send a reply to Geraldine Barfield?"

Geraldine Barfield. Writing to me, personally. Could be a secretary, but maybe not. Wants to meet. About what? Am I in trouble? Are they mad? Dozens of thoughts zipped around in her mind. Her thinking, usually so organized and ordered, was sent into a frenzy at the mix of idolization and fear at the thought of meeting Barfield. One thing was sure. This was not the time to make a decision.

"No," Jennifer said to Carlita. "I'll write one later."

"May I point out that the message does say to reply immediately?"

"Yes," Jennifer snapped. "I know. I will when I'm ready."

She gathered up the rest of her belongings and walked, still weak legged, out of the Plex Your Muscles, and back toward her home. To Mamá.

Maybe it was still too early to return to her mother. Maybe it was too late. But she was going home, and that was that. She walked through the Plex corridors, feeling too worn out physically and emotionally to think about how scared she was.

Waiting outside her door were Charles, Jean Paul, and Peter.

"There you are!" Jean Paul said. "We messaged you!"

"Several times!" added Peter.

"'lita," Jennifer asked her earpiece. "Did we finish going through my messages?"

"No, Jennifer. You still had—"

"Were any from Jean Paul Alvarez?"

"Yes. Several," Carlita said, and Jennifer wondered if her AIPA was letting a little snark creep into her tone.

"What is it?" Jennifer asked. "Is everything all right?"

"Have you heard from Melody?" Charles asked.

"One of her moods," Jennifer said. Charles nodded. Jennifer noticed he was carrying one of the cardboard boxes from outside the Plex. It looked heavy.

"Eight. Tonight. You know where," Charles said. "And take this."

He opened the top of the cardboard box and pulled out a laptop computer. He had taken the laptops with him after the field trip to solve the passwords. Now he set it in Jennifer's hands, an impossibly heavy and blocky artifact from an era in the distant past.

"What—what do I do with it?" she asked.

"Take it home," Charles said. "Turn it on. Computers back then had big, visible power buttons. There were no retinal scans, either, just passwords. The password is 'password,' so you should be able to sign on without a problem."

Jennifer laughed.

"The password is 'password.' But isn't that illegal?"

Charles smiled.

"Back then it wasn't. People were given a lot more lenience for being stupid back then. Anyway, just...play around. Click on whatever you want. These are ours. Get your fingers nimble for tonight. For tonight, we write!"

He said this with such an enthusiastic and devious smile Jennifer could not help but be charmed. He put something smaller in Jennifer's hand, an adapter that was cylindrical on one side and flat on the other.

"Adapter," Charles said. "I had a few in my apartment. I still use my old laptops from time to time, and these adapters are the only way for them to get the free plugless power. It goes in a jack in the rear of the computer. You're smart; you'll figure it out."

Jennifer leaned into the retinal scanner on her door. The display chirped and blinked green. She had no idea if, when she opened the door, her mother would be away at work or sitting in the living room waiting for her, or even if her own belongings were still there. What if her mother had already sold Jennifer's remaining possessions to get what little money she could for them, then turned the bedroom into a storage room?

She opened the door. Rosa was not there. Jennifer walked the few steps to her old bedroom and went in. All her belongings were exactly where she had left them when she had frantically packed her bags for Melody's all those weeks ago.

Jennifer flopped down on her bed. She did not turn on her flexscreen. She did not check her messages. She did not power on the large screen in her room that she used to do her video modules and edugames. She instead put the plugless adapter in the back of the laptop, then lifted the lid. She looked over the black screen and the keyboard. She giggled. The individual keys, looking so delicate and yet clumsy, were individualized bits of plastic that could surely be plucked off or broken too easily. The thing had hinges and hard edges and little metal grate speakers. The whole contraption looked ludicrous, and yet there was a charm to it. Melody was always going on about kitschy old things from the 1990s, but with this laptop, she was beginning to feel a little of that appreciation. It was a sense of nostalgia for something about which she had no living memory, for it had been before her lifetime. *This is how people did things way back then,* she thought with a bit of admiration. They lugged these machines around with them to work and to school, back when people went away to other locations for work and for school, risking breakage or theft every time. Why, she had lost track of how many times she had spilled coffee on her flexscreen or dropped it in the sink or in the shower. Yet she looked at this old, decrepit laptop computer from decades before. Most likely, a tablespoon of water on the keyboard could be enough to cripple or destroy the entire device.

Jennifer knew enough about the history of computing to know that when this computer had been made, probably sometime between 2010 and 2020, the storage of information was a clumsy and slapdash procedure. Terms like hard drive, disk space, flash drives, compact discs, floppy disks floated in her memory. How did people integrate these things? How did they switch from one storage device to another? What did they do if one computer had one form of storage but not another? It must have been awfully inconvenient and awkward, she decided. This was replaced by "cloud computing," but by Jennifer's time, that idea was so pervasive it did not even need a name. "Writing in the cloud" sounded like the ramblings of an ancient, narrow-sighted mystic.

Charles had been right. The power button was easy to find. A big silver square, front and center on the keyboard. Jennifer touched it. Nothing. She pushed down on it with what seemed like a dangerous level of pressure. The button depressed.

Laboriously, the laptop powered on and booted up. For nearly twenty seconds, Jennifer waited and watched with anticipation, annoyance, and bewilderment as various screens appeared. One listed manufacturer's information. Another one showed the operating system—a real, classic logo, from the Microsoft corporation that was long ago a titan of the industry and was now a chapter in one of her Computing History video modules. Then finally, after the agonizing and awkward wait, a login screen appeared.

The user was set to "Guest." The cursor—a feature which had not changed in the intervening decades—sat blinking on the password. Jennifer typed P-A-S-S-W-O-R-D and felt a little thrill of playing with antiquity at the pressure beneath her fingertips, the slight resistance of the old-fashioned keys. She pressed the Enter key, the login disappeared, and, after another interminable wait, the home screen appeared. Again, Jennifer remembered from her class that this screen was once called a "desktop," from the absurd idea that a computer was some analogue for a physical desk, and the little icons were somehow on the desk. She found herself wishing for a moment she was doing this with the rest of the group so they could share the experience together. But it was pleasant too, perhaps more so, exploring alone.

She touched the screen with her finger, and nothing happened. Then she remembered. In the old days, users used touchpads and even a device called a "mouse," which was flat-out confusing. When she first moved her finger over the touchpad, the little arrow seemed to dart and dance all over the screen. But after a little practice, she was able to control its motion, and she began clicking on the icons. Each time she did, a new screen appeared. She remembered from her computing history module that these were called "windows," named after the operating system. Why, she could only imagine. Soon she was overwhelmed with countless windows, and she didn't know how to make them disappear, but she was enjoying playing with the clunky old machine.

Finally, she discovered a program for writing text. It was what she had been looking for all along, but now she had it, she did not know what to write. She stared at the blank white screen and the blinking cursor for a long time, contemplating.

She had to remind herself no one was watching her. Her computer was connected to nothing. It felt scary and dangerous and exciting. She typed.

Lies

A Poem

Dedicated to Juan Carlos Calderón

Just then she heard the front door to the apartment open. She deleted the words she had written, then set the laptop on her bed and threw the comforter over it.

"Who is here?" said a voice in the entry. It was Rosa.

"It is me, Mamá," replied Jennifer. She stepped out from her room. Her mother looked more haggard and even leaner than before, if that were possible.

"Where have you been?" her mother asked.

"Who was my father?" Jennifer asked in return. And there it was. No introductions, no buildup, no arming for battle. Just a standoff that picked up where they had left off weeks before.

"Where have you been?" Rosa repeated.

"I have been here and there."

"You will have to do better than that if you want to know about your father," Rosa said, straining the limits of her English. She went to the refrigerator to get a seltzer.

"With Melody. With friends."

"Staying out of trouble?"

"Mostly. None of your business."

"I have been thinking while you were away that it would be for the best if you moved away forever." Rosa plunked down in her threadbare chair.

"Perhaps you are right," Jennifer replied.

"I know I am."

Silence fell between them again. Silence or words, Jennifer did not know what was worse. She reached into her pockets and fished out a pair of Perk-Eez tablets in foil wraps. She popped them out and swallowed them. They felt dry and acidic as they made their way down her throat.

"Always with the pills and the coffee," Rosa said, shaking her head. "No bueno."

Jennifer sighed and rolled her eyes. "I am an adult, Mamá. I can take care of myself."

Rather than argue, Rosa shrugged.

"I know you have taken care of me my entire life." Jennifer went on, "And I thank you. I thank you from my very spirit. You raised me from a little baby into a woman, and for that I can never repay you. I know now that you have also raised me with a lie. A beautiful, touching, tragic lie that nurtured me as much as your breastmilk, as much as your *sopa de pollo* and *empanadas*. And that lie grew me into a strong woman who works hard to overcome her obstacles. But I learned today it was only a lie, and so I grew up strong but crooked. And I want to know the truth, even if it hurts me, even if it breaks us both to splinters."

Tears were pouring from Jennifer's eyes now, but Rosa's were dry. Jennifer realized she must have only understood a portion of what she had said, so she translated it into Spanish.

In Spanish, Rosa replied, her words jagged with tears of her own. "How do you know of your father? It is no concern. You are a woman, and so you shall know. Juan Carlos Calderón was not a Federal drug agent. He was being pursued by one. He was such a smart and handsome man, but he looked to make his money in the wrong ways. The heroin. Never used it, but sold it, moved it from state to state.

"During the day he made dry cleaning deliveries and would hide the heroin in the company truck. I told him to stop because he had a little baby on the way, but the men who misused him paid him much money. Then you were born, and he did not stop. He did it more, to save more money for you in the hope of you someday going to a big university.

"One day when you were only two years old, he came home from a three-day trip, packed a suitcase, and kissed me on the cheek. He gave me a little slip of paper with some numbers on it. He kissed you on your cheek as you slept in the crib. He placed that photograph of you two, the one in the stairwell, by your side. Then he walked out of the door, and I have not seen him since.

"I doubt he was captured. There would have been arrests, trials, maybe we would have been deported. But *los Federales* were not the only ones looking for Juan Carlos. He was probably killed by a rival many years ago. But I will never know. I think it is better that way, better for me and better for you. Did I tell you the truth of your father? No. That was my gift to you. As I wept in those first days after he left, I decided that to have no father is a bad thing, but if it must be the way, then let the father be a hero. I wanted your father to be the light you would grow to. And you did. You have made more of your youth than I could ever wish."

"I forgive you," Jennifer said. Her voice was raw. The truth was not making her feel free. It made her past close in around her, like an overcast sky, lead-gray and heavy with the threat of rain. *I made a metaphor,* she thought dimly. The image arrived, unbidden. She did not have to make the poetry. The poetry made itself.

"Forgive me? You ought to thank me," Rosa said, becoming yet more animated. She rose from the chair, which she never did after returning home from work. "You are who you are because of me, and because of Juan Carlos. No, because of who I made him. Without my lie, you would be the bastard daughter of a dead drug runner. Instead, you are one of the brightest students in America."

"He is not dead."

"What?"

"He is alive. In Mexico. He sent me a message today."

"That cannot be true. Why did he not send me a message?"

Jennifer shrugged.

"Dios mío. Well, what did he want from you?"

"Nothing so far as I know."

"He just wrote you a note after twenty years to let you know he was alive?"

"I think so."

Rosa huffed a cynical laugh.

"How do you know it is really him? Is not some identity thief or rapist or worse? You should know better than to trust a message like that."

"He spoke of the picture on the apartment stairwell. The picture in my room. The only one I have of him. Who else but him could know of that photo?"

Now Rosa shook her head vigorously, angrily.

"I don't care!" she cried. "I cannot believe it. It must be a lie."

"You are an expert in those," Jennifer said. She did not care how much she hurt her mother. What had started as an attempt to bridge some peace between them would now be a final, scorched-earth battle. "My father may not be here. Maybe you're right. Maybe he really is dead.

But he is the better of my two parents. He was the light I grew to. You were the shadow. All of my accomplishments have been to honor my father, but also to spite my mother. To show I could be so much better than you. And I think I have succeeded."

Jennifer thought Rosa would go into another tirade, a violent outburst that would leave her with bruises, even a trip to the clinic. Instead, it was Rosa who was beaten. She slumped back into her chair. She tried to lift the glass of seltzer, but it slipped from her fingers and fell to the floor, then bounced on the carpet and soaked in. Jennifer thought for a panicked second that perhaps her mother was having a heart attack or a stroke, but Rosa waved her hand and said, "Go. Go. Go. Mentirosa. Puta."

Jennifer returned to her room. She packed her laptop and the last few belongings she wanted to keep, though after weeks away, she realized how easy it was to let her things go. She found the copy of *The Trough* and stuffed it in her bag. She left the apartment without saying goodbye.

Evening came upon her. She sat in a café for a while, checking her NewsFeed updates. Geraldine Barfield's entry into the Presidential race had created an immediate impact across the country. Most pundits called her a shoo-in, even over a year from the election. The rest of the field was so weak and unappealing, not to mention Barfield had the endorsement of outgoing President Alvarado, the other candidates would have virtually no path to victory. Barfield was popular with the youngest wave of voters who had come of age under her company's video modules and edugames, and with the older voters who admired how she had rescued public education from the arcane systems it once relied on. Jennifer stopped caring. If Barfield won or lost, she had already made her mark on the world.

Jennifer resisted the temptation to take out *The Trough* and read, and also to power up the laptop and work on her poem. Not in the sight of others. Strangers would watch.

She was about to power down her flexscreen when one new alert appeared that stopped her. Her breath caught in her throat as she read the headline:

Bounty Offered for Disgraced Former Teacher

Authorities are asking for the cooperation of anyone who knows the whereabouts of Charles Winston, a former employee of

EduForce, who is alleged to have had an inappropriate relationship with as many as four students. Authorities have been tracking his actions as he communicated with the students outside the classroom, perhaps even meeting them in person.

Winston, a resident of Plex 87, was terminated by EduForce one month ago. However, sources have revealed to police that he has been using messenger systems to communicate with students, and even arranged in-person meetings.

"Such contact with students is not only prohibited by EduForce policies," said a spokesman for EduForce, "but it also constitutes a gross violation of boundaries. The teacher-student relationship is a treasured one. Unfortunately, from time to time an adult may take advantage of this relationship, and such people must be stopped."

Authorities will not speculate on Winston's motives, but they ask the public's help in locating him. A reward of $250,000 is being offered for reliable information about his location."

Jennifer sat there, paralyzed in the café chair. Her mind swirled with questions. *What had Mr. Winston done? Who knew about their meetings? Had what he'd done been wrong?*

Twelve: The Trough

Student writing is distinct from, and inferior to, 'real' writing. This is not to say that students are bad writers, but rather, they compose with both eyes on the teacher, making every decision to meet one reader's idea of what is good. Such writing cannot hold up in the outside world. Real writing must communicate to a larger, often unknown audience. And it must also reflect the writer's own sense of what is good, sometimes in the face of harsh criticism. Real writing is an act of generosity and faith, with one eye on the hearts of her readers, and one eye on her own.

    —*The Trough*, p 19

The summertime meetings were distant memories. The air was cool, the surface of the roof windswept, bits of debris cutting through the air as the Rooftop Readers Club sat in a close circle. The time was 8:02 PM.

"Your assignment was to finish your poems," Charles said, looking around. "Did any of you?"

None of the students met his eyes. He smiled.

"Just like the old days. Well, no matter. Let's share what we have."

Melody shook her head. Her eyes seemed to be drowning.

"Poetry is personal."

"It is," Charles agreed. "But it's communal too. What is the purpose of a poem that is never shared?"

"Is your question rhetorical?" Melody returned, her voice dark and edgy. "Cause I'll give you an answer you won't like."

A male voice, reedy and nondescript, emanated from Melody's speakers.

"Melody, you have received a message. Would you like me to read it?"

"No, Lyle. Leave us alone."

"Very well," the voice said.

"New AIPA?" Jennifer asked. "What happened to Bruno?"

"Deleted him. He bored me," Melody said, and everyone fell silent. The air was colder that night; Jennifer was sure of it. Autumn was approaching, of course. But the darkness felt darker than ever before, the night sounds above Plex 87 were a little more stilled, a little more hushed as if in anticipation. *Why is no one talking about this?* Jennifer wondered. *We all have NewsFeeds.*

"I'll go first!" chirped Peter. Charles gave him a magnanimous wave of his hand, and Peter cleared his throat once. Staring at the glowing screen of the laptop, his voice carried thinly over the roof.

"The poem is called *The Boy from Avalon.* It's a limerick. I learned about limericks in...in my old school."

"Good," Charles said with a smile. "Let's hear it."

"Okay. The poem goes, 'There once was a boy from Avalon, who once liked to play in his lawn. His dad got screwed up, the family packed up, and soon the poor boy's lawn was gone.'"

"That's very nice," Charles said. "Good work with the rhythm and meter. In your next draft, see if you can find a way to avoid rhyming 'up' with 'up.' Now the Avalon reference. Are you making an allusion to Arthurian myth? If you are, then I'm curious about the lawn, and who the father figure is. The poem really leaves me contemplating a lot of possibilities."

"No," Peter said finally. Jennifer thought he sounded a little hurt. "Avalon is the town where I used to live. My family had a real house, all to ourselves, right on the ocean. Now...now we don't."

"Ah, autobiographical," Charles said. "Very nicely done. Keep working on it; you have something there. Jean Paul, do you want to read next?"

Jean Paul's face made it appear that he did not.

"Can I go last?"

"The old refrain," Charles said.

"What does that mean?" Peter asked.

"It is a line every teacher who has given presentation projects knows all too well," he replied. "Very well. Jennifer, can you read?"

Jennifer stared down at the screen of her laptop, whose glow lit the world around her. The words of her poem seemed to take on life and personality of their own. Defiant and willful, as if acknowledging that, though she had formed the words, they were no longer hers to control.

Jennifer shook her head. *Crazy thoughts.* But the thoughts were not going away.

"Okay, I tried to make a poem. I don't know if it's any good. But I made sure it rhymed and had a meter and the right number of syllables. I hope you like it."

She paused, hoping one of the other students would say something, would encourage her, or even better would interrupt her so she could have an excuse not to read. But she was only met with their silence and anticipation. She felt exposed and helpless.

"I called this poem 'An Ode to Thinking Outside the Box.'"

"I used to think inside the box

Which means my imagination's locked.

I only thought about the things

That careful, measured thinking brings.

But now a teacher's shown me how

To think the thing that's not allowed.

To think I have inside my heart

A poem or a work of art.

I never thought a thing like that!

I always acted like a brat

As I worked so very hard to strive

And reach that thing called Perfect Five.

But now I've found out something more:

My worth is not determined by some score.

I can get a question wrong

And still I'll sing my newfound song."

Jennifer was filled with an awful hollowness. She had eviscerated her soul for the poem. What none of the others saw was the hours spent frowning before the blank screen, the words written, then deleted, then written again, the ache of her fingers over the ancient keys, the pervading feeling she was doing something wonderful and terrible by opening up her feelings on the screen. In hundreds of essays she had written for

EduForce assignments, she had given herself a strict limit of one personal reference to boost her essay score.

Often, she made up personal experiences to fit essay topics. But for this poem, which she did not have to write, which served no purpose other than to risk getting her in trouble, she plumbed the depths of her feelings. Hearing the sound of her voice in the autumn night air, she felt pathetically inadequate. The feelings were inside her, the sentiment was pure and authentic. Yet the poem, to her ears, felt clunky and awkward.

"Very nice," Charles said. Jennifer wasn't sure if she heard his tone correctly, but it seemed his "very nice" was so polite because he too found the verse clunky and awkward. She flushed with embarrassment. *What a waste.*

She looked again at her teacher. *He doesn't look like a criminal.* Criminals had shifty eyes and ragged, hard expressions. That was the way they always looked in the mugshots the Plex Police released. They didn't look like Mr. Winston. She didn't believe the NewsFeed report. Didn't want to believe it. But a little worm of uncertainty nibbled around the recesses of her brain.

"Jean Paul," Charles said. "You read next."

Jennifer looked at Jean Paul more closely than she ever had before. Though he was bigger and older than all the other students, he had always seemed like a little boy. Now, though, Jennifer thought she saw the glimmer of a man in there. He was shy about reading at first, but when his mouth opened, he read with confidence she had not seen in him before.

"My poem...I no think is very good. But I hope you like. Is called '*Mi abuela.*'

> *"Mi abuela does not speak inglés,*
>
> *But she takes care of me every day.*
>
> *I come to her a broken boy*
>
> *Now she made me a man in many ways.*
>
> *She says 'Mi caro,*
>
> *Te quiero,*
>
> *Your dignity is worth more than el dinero.'*
>
> *Though I don't have much money in my hands,*

I feel like the richest man in the land.

I got my family, I got my friends,

I got my pride, and in the end

Being good is all I understand."

No one spoke, and Jean Paul looked down, embarrassed.

"That was impressive," Charles said.

What he's not saying is no one thought you had that in you. That's what he means, Jennifer thought. Jean Paul, who couldn't pass his most basic achievement levels, had spun something pretty remarkable. Not masterful, not like the poems in the anthologies, but far surpassing anything they or he had expected of him.

"Was it okay?" Jean Paul asked, and Jennifer's heart trembled to see his face. He was asking about much more than the poem.

"Bueno," Charles finally said. "Bueno."

"JP, that was awesome," Peter said.

Jennifer could only smile with pride for her friend.

Charles checked the time.

"Ten minutes left. Melody, last chance?"

But Melody only shook her head mutely.

"Very well," he said. "We'll meet again next week. Work on another poem if you wish or make any changes to this one that you feel would improve it. Reading your work out loud can be rattling, but there is no better way to improve."

"Do you have a poem, Mister Winston?" Jennifer asked.

"No," he said after a long pause, during which the wind picked up its intensity and brought a sprinkling of rain. "No, nothing to share."

Jennifer looked at him with suspicion.

"Mister Winston, I think that's logout. All of us had something to read."

"Melody didn't," Charles retorted.

"Shut up," Melody said.

Now the wind and rain began to whip at them from all directions.

"I'm sorry," Charles said, raising his voice over the roar. "But I'm here to give you a chance to share. I want to keep myself out of it."

"Don't you understand?" Melody said, rising. Jennifer looked around in a panic, wondering if the cameras would catch her, standing tall through the raging storm.

"Don't understand what?" Charles replied.

"You cannot always keep yourself out of it. You always try to stay neutral, to stay uninvolved. Don't you see? You are always involved. If you choose to do nothing, you are still choosing. You must have a poem, Charles Winston. Everyone has a poem. If you are too afraid to read it to us, just say so. But don't be a coward and claim you have nothing to share."

"Then you read!" Jennifer shouted at Melody, wondering if that was the closest anyone would come to confronting Mr. Winston about the bounty report. "This group exists because of you. Before you, before this group, not only had I never written a poem, I didn't know what a poem was. You've...you've changed me, Melody. You've changed all of us. You must have something to share."

"Fine!" Melody shouted, practically screeching. "I've written one line. That's all. You want to hear?"

"Go ahead," Charles said.

"Fine. The only line is 'These woods are lovely, dark, and deep.' That's it. That's all I have."

Everyone fell silent again.

"It's 8:45," Jean Paul said. "Time to go back in."

"That line is beautiful," Jennifer said. She placed her hand on Melody's calf. "I'm sorry I yelled. It's a wonderful image. It's—"

"It's a rip-off," Charles said. "She stole the most famous line from Robert Frost's most famous poem."

"It spoke to me," Melody said. "And I only stole a line of poetry. At least I'm not a criminal."

The group went back inside, dripping wet and cold, shielding their laptops from the rain with bags. They did not speak to one another.

Jennifer did not go to Melody's apartment. She did not go back to her mother's. All she wanted to do was be left alone to work on her poem.

She knew, as she'd read the poem to everyone that evening, that it was weak. It was slavishly loyal to a rhyme scheme and meter. She wanted to liberate the words, to let them say all they could say and move the listener the way she was moved when she wrote them.

She sat in the café again, this time not caring if anyone saw her laptop. She sat in the corner and gazed at the screen and the blinking cursor. She looked at the words she had chosen. She scrutinized each one, every "the" and every "is". She tried to see and think inside the word to its very essence. Words were not just vehicles for some meaning or message. The words themselves had...well, souls. Jennifer felt a little silly entertaining the thought but, staring at her poem, she could not deny her little, awkward, inadequate words had souls of their own. And by choosing the best words, the right words with the right souls, the soul of her poem would come through clearly. She added and subtracted, changed and transformed, altered and amended and fiddled. Sometimes the changes improved the poem, sometimes they weakened it and she reverted her choices. Word by word, letter by letter, the poem's heart beat stronger and louder. She broke meter, broke rhythm and rhyme, just to see what would happen. She cackled to herself when she produced a combination of words she did not expect.

Every half hour or hour she would get up, walk around, maybe order another coffee from the ordering kiosk, and then get back to work. It was late at night and for most of her time there, she was the only person in the café. She glanced at the one person working behind the counter, a young man perhaps a couple of years her senior. Jennifer found herself imagining him and his life. His face looked bored, lonely, dejected. Hopeless. She imagined he had passed his last Achievement levels but only showed enough proficiency to get a job cleaning the appliances in the café.

At first, he had been excited about the prospect of working and earning money. But after a few months, the monotony had set in, and he had realized not only had the apex of his life already occurred, there was no apex, there was a flat line from birth to death. He had been born, he had struggled his way through school, and his reward for passing the Achievement Sixteens was a life of low paying tedium. There were no avenues to make a different life, not in the Plex. Work was guaranteed. Homelessness did not exist anymore except by sheer will. No one went hungry or poor. It sounded like a paradise except no one ever seemed happy, or even content.

Jennifer compared herself to the young man. A few months ago, she'd seen herself as having unlimited potential. She was going to win the Scholarship, head to Princeton or maybe get far away from Plex 87 and her mother and maybe go to University of Chicago or Stanford. But the Scholarship was not happening. The Perfect Five was no more. She was like every other young person in America—she would have an Achievement Level certificate that would get her a spot in a free Plex

College, then take some career preparation courses to get another certificate to allow her to start work in some field she did not care about.

All students nearing the end of their Achievement Levels took Career Preparedness and Inclination Surveys. These surveys would assess a student's interests and strengths and feed the data to EduForce, whose algorithms would provide the student with up to fifteen potential career matches. These results would be attached to a graduate's identity forever, so any potential employer could look and see if the applicant was really applying for a job he or she was suited for, even if the results were a decade old. Someone looking to hire a director of communications would look at the applicant's survey results. If they did not see communications or public relations as one of the first three or four career matches, the application would be set aside. Why would they hire someone whose best readiness match was for data analyst or nursing? To swim against the stream of data in 2051 was not to be a salmon swimming upstream; it was to swim along the rim of Niagara Falls, perpendicular to the current.

Jennifer shook her head. How long she had been staring at the young man, she did not know, but he looked up and smiled at her. She looked down, then back up at him. His eyes were still on her. Maybe he thought she was flirting. Sure enough, he freed himself from behind the counter and went over to her.

"Hi," he said. "I'm Oscar."

"Hi," Jennifer said, trying to strike the right balance of polite and weary.

"You've been here a while."

"Is that a problem?"

"No!" Oscar said. He pulled out a chair for himself. "May I?"

"Sure," Jennifer said, though inwardly she was a little irritated. She had been daydreaming and losing focus on her poem. Now, some stranger's visit would pull her further away. But she smiled. Politeness would win out.

Oscar noticed the ancient laptop on the table before her. His eyes goggled.

"Wow! Look at that! I saw one of those in my computing history module. Is that a real laptop?"

Jennifer flushed, embarrassed at being so careless.

"Oh, yeah, I just..." She could not think of a convincing cover for why she was using it.

"Can I see what you're doing?" Oscar asked, and as he reached out at the screen, Jennifer snapped the lid shut. "Sorry," he said, looking downcast.

"No," Jennifer apologized, "just...personal stuff."

"Like a diary?"

"Yeah. Sort of."

"Wow. I've never known anyone to keep a diary before."

Jennifer thought. *Neither have I,* she realized. *Except for Melody.* Why would anyone keep a diary? Diaries were for people with something to hide. Diaries were for people with internal lives. Jennifer had never kept one, not even as a little girl. But now, this poem she could not stop working on seemed to be the closest she had ever had to one.

"Just started. You should try," she said, not understanding why she was saying it. It felt reckless.

"Oh, I don't really know what I'd write about."

"Well, you just write about your life. About your thoughts."

Oscar shook his head. "I would never write those things down."

"Why?" Jennifer asked. Now her polite interest was turning into the genuine thing.

For several seconds, Oscar said nothing. Then, hesitantly, "I think about things that I don't want others to see."

Jennifer knew enough not to ask what. Instead, she tapped her laptop.

"That's why I use this old thing. I found it in my grandfather's apartment after he died. It's not connected to any networks. No access. Just word processing. The words stay on here. No one else can see them unless I choose."

Oscar nodded with understanding.

"I guess...I guess I think about things that I don't want to see myself. If I actually put those thoughts in words, then wrote them down, then looked at them and realized the words had been in my head before...I don't know how I would react."

The fear of seeing oneself in words, Jennifer thought. She said nothing.

Oscar stood.

"Maybe I can find a laptop like that at an estate sale or something."

"Good luck," Jennifer said.

Oscar smiled.

"Vintage electronics are grip," he said, pointing to the laptop. "Maybe you'll set a trend."

After Oscar returned to work, Jennifer attempted to return to her own. She opened the laptop and the word processor. But this time, she looked at the words of her poem and they had become cold and distant. Momentum lost. The night's work had decided it was done.

It was 1:00 A.M. Jennifer was not at all sleepy. She powered up her flexscreen and briefly marveled at its speed and ease of use compared to the laptop. She checked her NewsFeed, saw hundreds of stories, few of which she cared about. An updated alert about Charles Winston flashed across the screen. The reward was increased to $300,000. Anyone suspected of abetting him could be arrested. The reward was exorbitant, but even a massive sum like that would do nothing to change one's life in the Plex.

Jennifer thought, if her own mother earned that reward, she might be able to give up one of her jobs, might be able to buy new furniture, but fundamentally, her life could never change. No one's could. There were no bigger homes to buy, no dream jobs to land. There was no mobility, no goals. A third of a million dollars would make no more difference in anyone's life than would a fruit basket or a trophy.

More stories of Geraldine Barfield, of her proposals and policies, scrolled across her screen. In all her photos she smiled impeccably and brilliantly. She had a face made for politics. Jennifer, for the first time in memory, thought, *this woman is a monster.* The thought had been creeping around the fringes of her consciousness for a long time. She had never believed Mr. Winston's judgment of her, had never doubted that Barfield worked for the best interest of America and its children. Now though, Barfield looked to her like the edugames and all the EduForce products—slick, shiny, and hollow. Fun and unchallenging.

Jennifer powered down her flexscreen. Too many words and images, too much bombardment. There was something soothing in writing on the disconnected laptop, where there was not a constant stream of updates and alerts and messages to distract her. It had been uncomfortably quiet, at first, but now her thoughts came through more clearly and powerfully.

She reached into her bag for the laptop, but instead, her hand fell on the gray hardcover book she had avoided opening for many months. Melody had talked about it. So had Mr. Winston. But Jennifer had never been able to bring herself to sit and read *The Trough* beyond the opening pages. The strain of reading the static words on the paper pages was too much to overcome. But she thought she could try again now. Jennifer recognized she was not the same as she was a few months ago. If nothing else, she was less afraid of challenge.

She set the book on the table, examining the plain cover and simple typeface. If passersby saw her sitting there, looking at a book that would be much more suitable fodder for a Recycling, she knew she might have trouble. But Oscar was the only one to have paid the least attention to her. *And if anyone walks by and looks, let them judge me.*

She opened to the first page and reread the introduction, including the Barfield memo in which she called American education a trough. Then she continued where she had left off.

> *How it Began*
>
> *By the end of the twentieth century, education in America needed a complete overhaul. Our students lagged behind the students of competing countries, administrations were top-heavy with superintendents and supervisors, and the gap between the achievements of rich and poor students was dramatic. Critics all over the political spectrum demanded change. Progressives wanted to see a system that was more diverse and egalitarian, while conservatives pined for a return to the good old days when students worked hard and became productive members of society. Everyone agreed the system was broken, but no one agreed on how to fix it. And while pundits squabbled over the solutions, EduForce and companies like it saw America's students for what they were—the greatest unexploited market in the world.*

Jennifer looked up from the book. Reading on paper was becoming easier for her, but she still needed to stop frequently and reread places where her attention had wavered. Some of the terms such as "progressive," "conservative," and "egalitarian" were unfamiliar, so she used her flexscreen to look them up. Then she read on, learning about various Federal programs called "No Child Left Behind" and "Race to the Top" that had been used in the early part of the twenty-first century to improve education.

Initially, Jennifer was jarred to read about the power of the federal government. The very phrase made her, and most people, uncomfortable. The federal government was supposed to do little beyond funding the military. Some political commentators wondered why Geraldine Barfield would run for President when she was already President of EduForce, which was a more powerful and much better paying position. But gaining the legal power to issue executive orders would guarantee, once and for all, EduForce's dominion over American education.

Jennifer dove back into the reading. She learned about the creation of national educational standards, then about the rise of corporations and their intrusions into schools. She learned about the collapse of suburbs and the rapid transition to Plex life. She read about Barfield, and EduForce, and how she and her company used the Plex system to their advantage. She grew angry reading about how innocent students like her were a captive audience for advertisers, and how the quality and complexity of her education was inferior to any other in the history of the country. *How could a book make me angry?* she wondered. Some kind of dark magic.

Jennifer looked down. A new cup of coffee sat at her table. *How did it get there?* She looked up and Oscar gave a little wave. She smiled.

She read on, feeling a bigger flare of anger as she learned about the Scholarship. The book said winners were chosen not on merit, but on their perceived benefit to the ultra-wealthy elite. *"The universities select not the students with the best scores,"* it read, *"but the ones who show traces of creative thought that would make them a threat to the establishment. The Scholarship culls dangerous graduates from the masses and turns them into their allies. But the other purpose, the primary one, is to perpetuate the false narrative, the mirage, that hope exists for upward mobility."*

Jennifer snapped *The Trough* shut and hefted it behind her head, ready to hurl it across the café. Her chest tightened. She had been so sure, so confident her hard work and merit would win her that vaunted placement. When she had been turned down, she had blamed her own failings. But now, she was beginning to understand that the entire system had been rigged against her, had been set up so she could never succeed. *And Mr. Winston warned me,* she thought, turning the anger on herself.

Jennifer looked up from her book. She had read nearly one hundred pages without stopping, a feat unimaginable a few months before. She was trembling. Her forehead prickled with cold sweat. This was no edugame. Learning was not fun. Learning was not easy. But reading *The*

Trough was stripping away her ignorance, ripping it away from her like a parent tearing a doll out of a child's arms.

She had to talk to Melody about what she had read. She wanted to finish the rest of *The Trough,* but her mind was bursting with ideas. She had never read anything that made her think so much, that mattered so much to her. She bundled all her belongings into her bag again. She checked the time: 3:37 AM.

"Carlita. Message to Melody Park. I'm on my way over to talk about a book."

"Yes, Jennifer." Then, after a one second delay, "Message sent."

Jennifer jogged down the hallways, brimming with excitement. Her mind hummed with ideas. It was alive and awake in ways she had never before imagined. The doorways, the corridors, the lights and directories and retinal scanners and all the other features of Plex 87 whirred by her in a blur as she ran faster, this time not on a treadmill but toward something, toward someone, toward Melody, her Melody. Breathlessly, she asked Carlita about a reply from Melody, but Carlita said none had been sent. No matter, Jennifer decided. Melody was sleeping, and when Jennifer arrived at her door to talk about *The Trough,* she would forgive the interruption. She would forgive Jennifer for her arrogance and stubbornness and sense of superiority.

Ten minutes later, she was at Melody's door.

"Carlita, send Melody Park a message. 'I'm here. Open up.'"

"Message sent," Carlita said.

No reply.

Annoyance twitched inside Jennifer, like the tip of a vexed cat's tail. She pressed the doorbell key. No reply. Then she pressed it again.

The door opened. Melody's foster mother looked at her. She had clearly been woken by the doorbell and clearly was not pleased.

"You," she croaked in a sleep-racked voice.

"Is Melody in?" she asked.

"You're her friend, aren't you?"

You have no idea, do you? Jennifer thought.

"Yes," she said. "I need to speak to her."

The mom jabbed her thumb in the direction of Melody's bedroom, then trudged off to bed. Jennifer entered the apartment, as she had so many times, and went to Melody's door.

As she had so many times.

The door was shut but not locked. Jennifer rapped on it lightly, but figured Melody was asleep. She pushed the door open.

What she saw next came to her in images. Fragments. Broken shards of perception.

A fishbowl Melody had stolen from an estate sale a year earlier. Populated by a floating toy plastic dinosaur.

The Nirvana poster. Kurt Cobain, looking down at his guitar. Jennifer had tried to listen to a song once. It had only sounded like noise to her.

Melody's laptop, the lid open to the word processor, the portion of a poem visible.

Melody, lying back on her bed. Peaceful, pale, unmoving. Unbreathing.

A tall glass, full of purple liquid. Grape soda. Next to it, a tall bottle. Vodka. Surrounding them, a potpourri of pills. Many colors and shapes.

Jennifer's knees buckled. Her vision darkened as she crawled into the room. She could not get herself to look at Melody again. She crawled over to the laptop. She looked at the unfinished poem on the screen. "These woods are lovely, dark, and deep."

The rest of the words faded in and out of focus. She could read no more.

Thirteen: A Wanted Man

"Capitalism, which should be distinguished from democracy, is an amoral system. Capitalism, in pure form, rewards the alpha predator. It does not care about charity. It does not care about brand loyalty. It does not care about buying products that are Made in America. It does not care about intrepid small business owners. It cares about the acquisition of wealth at the cost of all else, including democracy. The endgame of capitalism is oligarchy."

—*The Trough*, p.114

Charles Winston was a wanted man.

It was a strange mantle for him. All his life, he had been present but never wanted, attentive but never the object of attention. He had felt ignored and passed over by life. He did not resent it, but he was so used to being part of everyone else's background scenery that when he saw his name and face splashed on the screen in his apartment—and on every screen in the entire Plex—and his name and list of crimes listed, he felt mortified, yet a little bit cocky. *You notice me now. You should, after what I did.*

When he had first seen his name in his NewsFeed three days prior, he was ready for the Plex Police to knock on his door at any moment. They could have picked him up even before he knew he was wanted. But the advisories and bounty announcements led him to one grim, obvious explanation: community building. If an armed squad of Plex Police barge into an old man's apartment and drag him away, they are the bad guys. But if an ordinary citizen performs the heroics, the entire Plex rallies around him and feels safer. *Keep the police invisible by bribing the population to police itself. Clever, but I'm cleverer.*

Charles packed up his most valued possessions onto a cart and said goodbye to his apartment for the last time. He said a brief farewell to his coffeepot, to his fake window, to his unremarkable furniture. He brought with him several changes of clothes, some toiletries, a little food. And every one of his books and notebooks, as well as the books from the high school.

He was ready to let them go. *Well, not ready.* He would never be ready. But to travel between Plexes, he would have to travel lightly.

Sunglasses and masks were against Plex rules, so he stacked his cart high to keep his face shielded from the facial recognition cameras as he walked through the corridors. He came to a medical supplies closet and used his eye file to open it. *I should get a new one before I leave. This cheap one lasted me all summer, longer than I expected.* He hid his cart inside and went to the rooftop. He had been ready for one of the students to ask about the bounty, but none did, not until Melody's comment at the end. Then, he knew it was over. Not just that meeting, but all the meetings. He would have to leave Plex 87 the next day. Dripping wet from the rain, he went back to the storage closet, slept in it for a few fitful hours, then arose.

He would take the cart to Jennifer, whose apartment was closest to his. If he kept his head down and the stack of books high, he might, he hoped, evade detection.

Charles selected several boxes from the closet and stacked them on top of the books. If anyone stopped him and inspected the boxes, finding gauze pads or disinfectant would be less alarming than a box of textbooks. And if the boxes could shield his face from a few more angles, it might be enough to get him to Jennifer's apartment. After leaving the cart with her, he would figure out how to escape the Plex undetected, but he would address that problem later.

Charles lifted one last box, read the label, and found a better solution. The label read "QUARANTINE SUITS. SIZE L."

Charles ripped open the boxes and inspected one of the Q-suits. He had left his in his apartment. There was no room to carry the bulky garment, and he decided that if someone coughed on him while he was on the run, well, then he would just get sick, like in the old days. If Charles wore his own quarantine suit, the cameras might not pick up on his face, hidden behind sanitizing filters, but it would detect the CHARLES WINSTON identification chip in the suit.

These suits, however, had not yet been programmed. To wear one would be to become a ghost, unidentifiable to human eyes and undetectable to electronic ones.

Charles donned one of the Q-suits. It didn't quite fit; he had always had a body type that did not fit in medium clothes but waded in large ones. It would suffice, though. It would not be a permanent solution. Eventually, a worker from the Plex Clinic would return to the closet, take inventory, and discover the absence of the suit. But it might last long enough to get him to Jennifer's door and then out of Plex 87. For good.

After replacing the box of quarantine suits on the shelf and straightening up the mess he had made, Charles drew in a deep breath and opened the supply closet door. No one was near. Charles straightened his back, gripped his cart with all his earthly possessions, and pushed. He wanted to exude a sense of confidence. He needed to appear that he had every right and reason to walk the halls. *I am just a laborer with a cold, making my delivery for the day. I belong here. I belong here. I belong here.* He stood upright, wheeling the cart through the halls at a steady, workmanlike pace. He calmed his breath. He forced himself to smile, even though no one could see it under the quarantine suit. He hoped the coerced smile would trick his mind into believing his body.

No one spoke to him, or even acknowledged him. Whether it was because he appeared ill, or because as loading bay worker, he would not be worthy of acknowledgment, Charles wasn't sure, but he hoped to use this to his advantage. He knew his ploy would not last forever. It needed to last long enough for him to deliver the cart and escape. But escape to where?

He wheeled the cart along the passageways, navigating through the crowd. He came to an elevator, an extra-wide one intended for carts and hand trucks. After glancing around to check no one else was near, he turned on his flexscreen and opened the eye file. He held it over the retinal scanner.

User identity not valid. Permission denied, the screen read.

Shit. The file works all summer but fails me now. Shit. He tossed his flexscreen, now useless to him, onto the cart. Then he leaned his Q-suit visor in toward the ret-scanner, not sure what the result would be.

Welcome, User Unknown, it announced, and the doors opened.

When Charles stepped inside, he was greeted by his own face. On the wall-mounted screen, an updated bounty alert flashed *Charles Winston. Crimes include molestation of children, social perversion, political subversion. Do not speak with this individual. If seen, report immediately to Plex Authorities. Reward: $500,000.*

Charles almost shouted and laughed with surprise, but then wondered if the elevator was also equipped with voice recognition security. Instead, he kept his lips shut, entered the elevator, and let the doors close behind him. He stood still as the elevator rose. His eyes locked onto the picture of himself. The image was his standard ID photo—unsmiling, dead-eyed. *You poor, hunted son of a bitch,* Charles thought, as if the person on the poster was someone else. *Maybe thinking that way will keep me safe, or at least sane.*

The elevator slowed, then stopped. The doors opened, and Charles pushed the cart out. The wanted poster was behind him. Ahead of him, separated by a half-mile of winding hallways, was Jennifer's apartment.

As he navigated those halls, he noticed the tiny cameras embedded in ceiling tiles and above doorways. In the Q-suit, he knew his face was not being read by the facial recognition software. As far as those cameras were concerned, his blank suit simply did not exist. But the traditional cameras certainly saw him walking. Eventually, the data from the two cameras would be analyzed. Eventually, someone—or more likely, some program—would notice the discrepancy. The system would issue an alert and he would be captured. This was not a prediction. This was an inevitability. No one ever escaped the jaws of mismatched data. If you did not fit within the algorithms, you were isolated, and the issue resolved. Charles's only hope was to move swiftly enough to outpace the software. *A fool's errand.*

He pushed the cart faster, not running, but with an urgency that made the people he passed by start to turn and notice him. He slowed down again. Charles's heart began to beat faster. He forced his legs to move at a measured pace, even as he struggled to suppress his urge to run. His mind narrowed and his focus narrowed so every step, every breath, was focused on getting to his destination.

He turned a corner, and nearly hit two Plex Police officers walking his way.

Charles panicked. He jumped back and a little shout escaped his lips. Every nerve in his body sent the signal for him to run.

He did not run.

"What are you doing out here?" said one of the guards.

"Deliveries," Charles said. In his mind, he scrambled to think of a more elaborate cover story. He also scolded himself for not having done so sooner.

"Are you feeling all right?" asked the second guard.

"Fine," said Charles too hastily, and he immediately knew it was wrong.

"Well if you're feeling fine, then why the Q-suit?"

Charles put his hand to his chest and chuckled.

"What I mean is I'm feeling fine enough to be at work today. Don't want to share this cold with anyone, though."

"If you're sick, you really ought to stay home and rest," the first guard said. The comment revealed his ignorance. As a Plex security guard, he had paid sick time, and apparently took it for granted. But corporations and Plex owners had long ago stripped such luxuries from the average worker. Essay reviewers, for instance, were not allowed sick time. Unless Charles was too ill to sit upright, he was at his desk, scanning essays. If he was too ill, he was not paid that day. Simple. Manual laborers had it even worse. They would be docked pay or fired for not showing up to work, regardless of illness. Many laborers had been fired because of mononucleosis, or strep throat, or even a bout with the flu, that rendered them too ill to come in to work. Q-suits did not just protect the healthy from the sick; they protected the sick from unemployment.

"Got to provide for the family," Charles said, wondering why he was letting the strange dialect slip into his speech. *Don't overact this, idiot.*

"Oh yeah?" the second guard said.

"Wife and two girls," Charles said, feeling more comfortable standing on a little truth. Both guards looked him up and down. Charles wondered if they recognized the few visible parts of his face from the wanted poster. Paranoid, frantic thoughts pelted his mind. *What if they reach for me? Should I fight? No*, he decided. With two against one, they would subdue him easily. *Should I run? No,* he decided. They were younger than him by at least a couple of decades each, and he was wearing a floppy, cumbersome suit. All he had left were his words, and he hoped they would be enough to fend off the guards' suspicions.

"If you'll excuse me," Charles went on, "I need to make this delivery within the hour. Some of these customers, if they wait more than three or four minutes after they place an order, they get mad and leave bad reviews and my pay gets cut."

"Hardly seems fair," the first guard mused.

Charles shrugged.

"Well, get back to work. Then take some Cold-Eez when you get off your shift. Taking two of them a day will send colds on their way," the second guard said, without a trace of irony, and Charles wondered if he was even conscious he was repeating the brand's jingle.

"Sure will," Charles said, smiling. "Thanks for the suggestion."

And then the two guards walked past him on their patrol. Charles exhaled, feeling jittery. He pushed the cart on, keeping the pace brisk.

Plex Police. Charles remembered when police were municipal authorities, sworn to uphold the laws of the land. But now lands didn't have laws, or rather, they had laws but no money or power to enforce them. Plexes did. And Plexes were owned by Plex management companies. So, though they were called police, Plex Police were really private security, sworn to uphold the best interests of their employer. These interests included making the people in the Plex feel safe and secure, so if there were a robbery or assault, people could contact the Plex Police, who would investigate and determine if further action was merited. There was still justice in the Plex. It was the property of the owners.

Charles arrived at Jennifer's apartment ten minutes later. He pressed the doorbell.

A wan, almost skeletal woman opened the door. Charles could not hide his surprise.

"Uh, hi. Hello. Is Jennifer here?"

The woman's eyes narrowed.

"Jennifer?" she replied, her accent heavy. Charles searched his distant recollection for basic Spanish phrases.

"*Si. Donde...esta...Jennifer?*"

Then the woman spat on the ground between them.

"*La casa de Melody. La puta.*"

Charles knew what that meant. He nodded respectfully and stepped back as the door closed. The few times Jennifer had spoken of her mother, she had done so with fear, disdain, disgust, resentment, and pity. Charles had always attributed it to typical adolescent eye-rolling. Maybe Rosa Calderón was indeed as miserable and controlling as her daughter had depicted.

Charles remembered well the path to Melody's home. If the two of them were together, perhaps this would be even better. *Give them the books. Get out of Plex 87. Today. The books cannot save me. But they can still save Melody and Jennifer.*

As he walked, a sense of inadequacy and fraudulence overcame him. He had tried so hard over the preceding months to do something for his students, to provide them with something remarkable and life-changing. And now he looked at what he was doing, and he felt pathetic. Had he made even the least bit of difference in these young people's lives? He really wanted to believe he had, and as long as he did not reflect on it too deeply, he had believed he was doing good. Now, though, he felt useless and unworthy.

When he reached Melody's apartment, he immediately knew something was wrong. The door was open. Paramedics and Plex officials came in and out, moving seriously but without any real urgency.

He did not dare go closer, so he stayed some fifty feet away, standing by the cart, making as if he were readjusting his load. He shifted and rearranged boxes while peering at the activity at Melody's door.

Then the paramedics carried out a gurney, covered in a white sheet.

Charles's head swam and his knees buckled. He gripped the sides of the cart. Knowledge, pure and instinctual, flooded his mind. He did not need to be told who was under the sheet. He thought he was going to throw up, but he had eaten so little in recent days that he had only a hollow, acidic feeling in his throat.

The paramedics wheeled the gurney past Charles and his cart. He needed all his will to keep from asking to look under the sheet, from crying out Melody's name, from striking the medics and grabbing the gurney and running with it. Wild, lunatic thoughts latched onto his mind and he could only just hold himself back from acting on them. He only nodded curtly to the medics, and they did not acknowledge his gesture. But when they passed, his restraint crumbled. He wheeled his cart to the door and barged in.

A man and woman sat on the couch, staring blankly into the out the window. Not crying, just wordless and expressionless. *The foster parents,* Charles guessed. They did not greet him, and indeed did not even seem to notice a man in a Q-suit enter. He slipped quietly into the first bedroom. Jennifer sat on the edge of Melody's bed. Her head was buried in her hands, but upon hearing Charles enter, she looked up, startled.

"Who are—"

Charles removed the mask.

"What are you doing here?" she whispered harshly. But Charles could not reply. He could only sit next to her on the bed and hang his head.

"You can't stay!" Jennifer said. "They'll be back in a few minutes. They have questions."

Charles wanted to hug Jennifer. He wanted her to hug him. A simple, human interaction. Yet he could not bring himself to reach over and even pat her on the back.

"What happened?" Charles asked.

"What do you think?" snapped Jennifer, turning on him, her eyes like two vortices. "It was Melody, all Melody, down to the core. You, I, we made the same mistake. We only saw the part of her we wanted to see. We embraced the part we wanted to love and romanticized the rest. Melody did this because that's what Melody would do. It was built into her."

"It isn't your fault," Charles said. "It isn't anyone's fault. It just...happened. No one could have stopped it."

The vortices focused on him.

"That is a chickenshit answer. Of course, this is my fault. It's your fault. It's the fault of everyone who got sucked into Melody."

"She wasn't well," Charles said.

"Right. She made people believe she was dark and brooding and mysterious, when really, she was fucked up and needed help. She bounced from family to family too rapidly for them to notice. But I should have known. I think I did, underneath everything, but I was enchanted by her. So were you."

"There is no one like her," Charles said. "I didn't even know her six months ago, and now, I cannot imagine a world without her."

"Or a world with another Melody in it," Jennifer added.

"I loved her, in a way," Charles mused.

"Of course, you did."

"I have something to give you."

"You have to go," Jennifer said, looking to the door. "The officers are coming back."

Charles stood.

"Come with me."

Jennifer looked anxious.

"You mean—out there—where are you—?"

"No, to the hallway."

Jennifer followed him back out to the corridor, where the cart sat. She stared at it.

"They're yours," Charles prompted. Jennifer did nothing.

"I have to—I don't know when—These things are—" Charles had played this conversation in his mind numerous times. He knew he would never return to Plex 87 again or see Jennifer or any of the other students again. But this was not the way he wanted to part.

"I'll take it," Jennifer said with a strength of tone, a flat finality Charles did not expect from her. "Go."

A trio of Plex officers approached down the corridor. Charles flicked his eyes to the cart. Everything he owned was on it. All the textbooks they had pillaged from the old high school. Every remaining copy of *The Trough* in existence. Old books of poetry he'd had since he was in high school and marked and underlined into oblivion. His copy of *Border Patrols*. He knew he had to rid himself of these possessions, that in his escape, they would only slow him down. But the parting would not be easy.

"But this cart," he started. "How will you explain—?"

"Go," Jennifer said.

Charles took a hesitant step away. *A world with no Melody. A world with another Melody. Both impossibilities.* Then an idea came to him. *There can be another Melody, for a short time.*

"Go in Melody's closet and get me her quarantine suit."

"What?" Jennifer asked.

"Not the whole thing. Just the mask."

"But she's—how could—?"

"Go!" Charles insisted, and Jennifer ducked back into the apartment. A few moments later she reemerged, carrying an airtight hood and mask with a giant skull and crossbones and the words PATIENT ZERO printed on the top. *Of course, this would be Melody's suit.* He handed Jennifer the helmet from the unprogrammed suit.

"Put this one back where the other one was. Don't want to create any undue suspicion. And bring this cart too. Say that it's...I don't know. You're smart. You'll figure things out."

When Jennifer rolled the cart into Melody's room, Charles turned and left. He took a step in the opposite direction of the approaching officers. Then another. *This is the only way to do this. Single steps at a time*. Already, he was sure, the footage of traditional cameras was being cross-referenced with facial recognition technology, and somewhere, some program had identified a man in a quarantine suit that did not appear on the facial recognition cameras, and the discrepancy would be noted. His progress would be tracked. He needed speed, stealth, and a fair amount of good fortune.

Charles walked briskly, trying not to appear suspicious. He passed dozens of people in the corridors, and few stopped to even look at him. He passed vid screens that flashed his face and the words "WANTED: CHARLES WINSTON. MOLESTATION OF CHILDREN. SOCIAL PERVERSION. POLITICAL SUBVERSION." He saw the reward. He reminded himself every step that if even a single person recognized him, they would have a half-million-dollar incentive to notify the authorities. He had no money for bribes and no weapon to threaten with. He had only one hope of escape.

I am not Charles Winston. I am Melody Park. I am not Charles Winston. I am Melody Park.

Charles took a circuitous path out of the Plex. He did not want to retrace his steps; surely those halls were already being watched. Instead, he walked toward the opposite end of the building, maintaining that brisk but unrushed pace. Anxiety rose in his belly. Every Plex officer he passed, he was more and more certain he was being watched and hunted. He needed to get back to the ground floor and out of the building. After that, who knew? Outside, he could make his own path. The world outside the Plex had no rules, had people who made their own rules—

He knew what to do.

Charles approached an elevator and stepped in front of the retinal scanner, which scanned his facemask. Melody's facemask. Finally, the door opened for him, and he and several others walked inside. The doors closed. A Plex security guard, a thick man with a heavy jaw and furrowed brow, stood directly next to Charles. Unlike most Plex guards, who were often gazing into their flexscreens, this guard was utterly focused, utterly present. And Charles felt certain this guard was focused on him, in particular. The guard's eyes were not trained on him, but watching him from the side, like a dog preparing to snap. Charles's heart pounded faster and louder, and he was sure the guard would hear it.

He heard an electronic beep come from the officer's tablet. The officer looked at it. Then he looked at Charles.

"Hey, are you—?" the officer started.

The elevator reached the ground floor with a "ding." The door opened and Charles pushed past the other passengers to get out. He was feeling hot and suffocated.

The officer behind him shouted, "Hey!"—not the sort of barked command that should come from a properly trained officer. Charles ran. He knew he was older than the officer by at least a decade, but he was lighter than him by fifty or sixty pounds, easily. Charles ducked and darted along the corridor, shouldering past surprised pedestrians. "Stop!" wheezed the hefty officer, but Charles had already outpaced him. In under a minute, Charles had lost him. At the next exit to the Sol-Train, he turned and walked as fast as he could.

He stepped out into the bright, cold air of late autumn. He had exited from an unfamiliar side of the building, so finding the train platform took some wandering and searching. Once he did, he looked for the next train's departure time. Four minutes, the flashing sign indicated. Charles looked to the Plex 87 doorway, watching, waiting, hoping that in the next four minutes, a cadre of officers did not come rushing out with handcuffs and stun guns.

Charles watched a scurry of movement near the loading bay. Off-Plexers, living in the shadows, huddled in their shelters of cardboard and tarps. Few inside the Plex thought or talked much about these people. So long as they didn't bother anyone inside or try to sneak inside themselves, they could build castles out of cardboard and packing foam, for all the authorities cared. But now, Charles cared. *It will be winter soon. How many of these people will not survive it? How many of them are here by choice? How many of them are hiding from something or someone? How many became sick or injured or suffered from a mental illness that lost them their jobs?* Some social scientist, years earlier, had touted the Plex as the perfect society. And it seemed to be. Little crime or social tension or inequality. None of the violence and unpredictability of every other society the world has known. The Plexes simply moved everything undesirable outside and locked the front door.

Charles recalled his little Plex apartment and its window. All Plex apartments had them. It was not a true window, but it showed a video feed of what was directly outside his room. He had watched, sometimes for hours, trucks roll in and out of the parking lot, a raccoon rummage in the dumpster, a stray piece of Styrofoam tumble over itself in the wind.

Yet he had never seen an Off-Plexer. *Why?* he wondered. Right now, on the platform, he saw seven or eight people a few hundred yards away, gathering wooden pallets. *Why did I never see them from my window?*

The answer was obvious. The video feed was not real, either, he realized. Not only was the window fake, but the images it showed were fake, as well.

But why? Charles pressed. The view was dull, ugly, boring, and depressing. Why, if the "window" had never shown anything interesting or beautiful, would Plex owners bother feeding it to viewers? *Maybe that was the point. The window feed showed residents that the world outside the Plex was dull, ugly, boring, and depressing. The view outside encouraged people to stay inside.* But then why eliminate the Off-Plexers from the video? Surely, showing how awful it was to live in rags, in cardboard boxes in the shadow of the Plex, would encourage people even more to stay On-Plex. *Because it was another kind of life. Because showing Plexers a view of the Off-Plexers would make them realize that even if Off-Plex life was dirty and dangerous and degrading, it was still another way to live. And seeing alternatives is antithetical to Plex mindset.*

Four minutes passed, and the Sol-Train glided up to the platform. The doors slid open, and Charles stepped in. He took a final glance at Plex 87. No one was following him. The doors closed, and the train glided down the tracks. *Adieu,* he thought as the massive brick block that was Plex 87 grew smaller and smaller in the distance.

Charles sat in an empty seat, away from other passengers. When he sat, the retinal scanner on the seat back in front of him activated.

"*Welcome, Melody Park,*" the chair announced. "*Please use your AIPA or the touchpad to input your desired destination..*"

He touched the screen and put in the name of his destination: Mahwah.

"*Thank you, Melody. Debiting from your expense account.*"

Charles panicked. *Did Melody have any money?* He had not even considered it, but what if Melody was completely broke? What if—

"*Thank you, Melody,*" the chair screen read. "*Enjoy your ride on Sol-Train. And at any time, feel free to use the touchscreen to order a refreshing Jazzy-Pop Grape Soda or enjoy some Funsnaps by Nabisco!*"

Charles leaned back. He sighed. He resisted the urge to think he was free and had escaped. He was still on the Sol-Train, which was still part of the Plex system. He was out of Plex 87 but he was not yet an Off-Plexer. Still, in the disguise of Melody's identity, on a nearly empty train, he was out of immediate danger.

In the quiet and solitude, understanding loomed over him. Terrible, brutal understanding.

He was safe because he was wearing the clothing of a dead woman. Melody was dead.

He had so many questions, so many things he wanted to say and to ask. But Melody was dead. And by her own hand. Why had she done it? How? When? Charles had so many questions he doubted he would ever find the answer to. Thoughts and phrases streamed through his mind. *Gone too soon. So young. A terrible tragedy.* He hated himself for thinking a series of clichés and platitudes. He had never known a suicide. There had been a few times, in his years as a teacher, when a student he did not know took his or her own life. There had been an elderly man who shot himself in the park when Charles was a little boy, but all these deaths were distant, and his grieving was formal and impersonal. But this...this tore him apart from inside. The platitudes felt like an insult. He wanted to think of something original, something powerful or beautiful to say about her, or even to think something. But nothing came.

This is why you never became a poet. You can love reading and words, but you cannot make them yourself. You've always hated the expression "Those who can, do. Those who can't, teach." Yet you embody it. You have created nothing original or inspiring in your life.

Except he had created. He created students. He took young minds, some of whom were curious, some of whom hated school, and to one degree or another was able to fuel an urge in them to question more deeply, to read more closely, to think more clearly, to write more passionately. What he created was a love of creation. And Melody had been his greatest creation.

Bullshit, he told himself. *You did not make Melody. You found her. You stumbled across her writing and mentored her, showed her some poems and writings she would not have seen otherwise, but she was who she was before she met you, and she died the same way.*

Charles realized he was trembling. He looked around, hoping he had not drawn the attention of any other passengers, but everyone was listening to music, playing games, or watching videos. He checked the Sol-Train's progress. Still a ways to go. *Miles to go before I sleep,* he thought bitterly.

Well, I cannot beat myself up too harshly. There is nothing anyone could have done.

Bullshit, again. With the realization, he was struck with crushing guilt. Of course, there were things that could have been done. Someone should have helped her. He should have. If she had been in therapy, if she had taken proper medication, even by force, maybe she would be alive now. She was an adult and it was her perfect right to refuse treatment. So maybe it was her own fault she was dead. He wondered if Jennifer had known; he could only speculate. Probably Jennifer had suggested it, Melody had laughed it off or brushed it aside, and then Jennifer had pressed, and Melody had gotten mad, and Jennifer never mentioned it again. But, of course, something could have been done, done by Melody or by Jennifer or Melody's series of foster parents or by anyone who had interacted with her at all over the last few years and noticed, "This young woman is troubled. She needs professional help."

Someone should have done something. I could have been, should have been, that someone. Had it not been Melody's disturbing essay that Charles read months ago which first brought her to his attention? Had he not spotted right away the writings of someone who hoped to die? He had been too enamored with her "poetic temperament" to see what it was. He had been so excited that a student knew Lord Byron as a literary figure. He'd completely ignored that Lord George Gordon Byron lived a life of excess and scandal, was alternately joyous and wrathful, lived a disastrous personal life, died before age forty, and would probably be diagnosed in the twenty-first century as bipolar. But he *was* a great poet.

You selfish son of a bitch. Charles turned his fury on himself. *You knew all of this, deep down. You knew Melody's "genius" was parallel to Byron's. You knew something was wrong. But you thought you would save her. You thought poetry would save her. You didn't just ignore her illness; you tried to harness it. You thought she needed you, when she really needed therapy and mood stabilizers and antipsychotics. You thought her "genius" would bring you glory, and you let it kill her.*

Charles stabbed at the touchscreen. *Enough.* He could not think clearly. If he was going to have a mental breakdown, he did not want it to be here. He had to keep thinking and looking ahead, to safety. If he made it to safety, he could have the rest of his life to look back and punish himself with guilt and regret.

He thought ahead. To Mahwah station.

He checked the NewsFeed. If his escape plan succeeded, he knew he might not be able to check the news for a very long time, if ever.

President Alvarado Announces Expansion of Surveillance and Identification Tech to Track Corporate Threats.

Good thing I'm going off the grid when I am, Charles thought slyly.

Geraldine Barfield Opens Commanding Lead in Polls; Pollsters Predict 74Percent Chance of Victory in Presidential Election.

Reason number two I'm glad I'm out.

Relocation Sweeps Aim to Reduce Off-Plex Security Threats.

Charles thought about reading this article, but as with most "articles" in 2051, the headline was all the information provided. It was not like Charles's youth, when a headline would be an invitation to read a longer piece. Still, he wondered what "sweeps" meant, and which Off-Plexers would be affected.

Pop Mega-Star Tuliphead Marries Her Dog in Whirlwind Hollywood Wedding.

Okay, all done. Charles shut off the NewsFeed. Sometimes, ignorance really was bliss.

An hour or so went by, during which Charles dozed and listened to some music, but with each passing mile he relaxed. He would not just be free of his pursuers; he would be free of the entire Plex system, of everything the world had turned into that he hated.

When the Sol-Train pulled into Mahwah station, he was already beginning to feel a sense of unease. Something was different. Yes, now the trees were going bare and the air was colder, but it was something else. A smell, a quality to the air, he could not say what it was. Nevertheless, he stepped off the train and onto the platform. He scanned the area for police or bounty hunters. Plex 87's police security could have easily alerted the Plex 291 police security and simply picked him up. EduForce was looking for him too, and their reach was seemingly infinite. But other than a few passengers who departed the train and walked toward the Plex building, he saw no one nearby, and after he lingered about and was sure he was alone, he turned in the opposite direction and began toward Stag Hill.

Charles remembered all the landmarks from their summer visit. He gave the high school a wide berth, not wanting to accidentally cross paths with Frank Wieland or his vicious crew. Instead, he cut through town, listening to the clomping of his footsteps echo through the empty streets.

This used to be a city. He wondered if someday, people might clomp through the halls of Plex 87, contemplating the lives of the long-departed.

At the edge of town, he followed the trail that led up Houvenkopf Mountain. The air was cold, and the quarantine suit merely shielded the wind without insulating his body. Charles reminisced about the summer field trip. It had been his finest adventure with his students. It had been a fine adventure for him too. Moseley had unlocked something in Charles's heart. Admiration. Perhaps even envy. Their lives had begun parallel in so many ways, but now they lived in utterly different worlds. *But it does not have to be that way. Being in the forest, with free and independent thinkers, making their own lives, I have not felt that right and good in years. My mind, my soul, belong in the hills.*

Charles reached the clearing where Moseley and Maury had first found them.

Autumn left the hillside bare and silent. Stealth was nearly impossible. The sentries should have seen and heard him long ago and intercepted him, taken him to the camp.

"I am here to see Moseley," Charles said out loud, but there was no reply. A chipmunk scurried around the bushes, looking for a few last seeds or nuts. Charles looked all around, but there was no movement anywhere as far as he could see.

He continued up the trail. With each step, the silence concerned Charles more and more. He should have heard the faraway chopping of wood, voices, scraping pots and pans. But instead, a vacuum of autumnal quiet.

Then Charles remembered part of his conversation with Moseley.

"There's almost nothing left to scavenge within a hundred miles," she had said. "We've talked about making a permanent move to somewhere else that hasn't been picked clean, but no one knows where to go."

They moved, Charles decided. *They found somewhere to go.* That summer, they must have deemed the area too poor in resources and old supplies. Perhaps trucking runs had been diverted from the region. Perhaps the band had trekked up north, to the Hudson River, or south, to the Passaic, or west, to the Delaware. He hoped he was wrong. At least, as Charles mounted the last few hundred yards to the crest of the mountain, he hoped Moseley had left a note or a message, some clue, to tell him where they had gone.

In the distance, through the trees, sat the abandoned camp. Details came to him one by one, with increasing clarity. Charred tentpoles. Picture frames and books and toys, strewn over the ground, covered in filth. Corpses. Dozens of them, all close to the camp. They lay in the open, in states of partial decomposition. The bones had not yet been picked clean by scavengers, but none of them were recognizable. The smell of putrid flesh overwhelmed Charles. He fell to his knees and vomited. His vision swam. He wanted to search the corpses to find the body of Moseley, but he did not need to. No one was still alive. Death cloyed to all his senses, a heavy, rancid cloud. Tears stung Charles's eyes, and he backed away from the camp, unable to look any more.

Who did this? he wondered as he descended Houvenkopf Mountain. *Frank Wieland and his twisted cult?* Charles dismissed the idea almost immediately. Wieland's gang of a dozen could never have overtaken Moseley's group. Whoever had killed Moseley had utterly overwhelmed her and her band. They had killed swiftly and mercilessly. Professionally.

Charles walked faster and was soon running down the hill, his feet pounding on the hard, dry trail, his lungs pulling in the chilly air. He needed to get away from the carnage, to run so fast that memory could not keep up with him. Finally, at the bottom of the trail, where it met the highway, he slowed and caught his breath.

He walked back toward town. He felt lost, his plan of escape wiped from the Earth. Daydreams of becoming a hermit in the forest flitted through his head, but he knew he could not survive in the woods on his own. For hours, Charles walked around the ghost town of Mahwah, looking at the abandoned storefronts, the rotted-out and collapsing houses, the playgrounds choked with weeds and crippled with rust. He went to one of these playgrounds and, not daring to test the links on the swings, sat on a plastic hippopotamus that rocked to and fro. He rocked and thought, thought and rocked, wanting to cry. He remembered being an adolescent and feeling overwhelmed at the enormity of life, at the boundless opportunities. He had tried to articulate to his mother the feeling of the overripe fullness of life, of how not only did he not know what to do with his life, but he did not know how he might even choose. She had rubbed his back and told him to slow down. Now, life ahead was barren and choiceless. There remained no avenues to his freedom. To stay in the forest would be death. To return to Plex 87 would mean his capture. He wondered what Shaaya would say.

She would not have sympathized. She had never faced indecision or uncertainty. Her life and career had been set on a steel track, racing from one accomplishment to another. She had hoped Charles's presence would fuel her engine to drive her ahead, but in the end, he served as a minor roadblock she barreled through. But she would have advice for him. She always had advice for him.

Death or capture? Either or? Why so binary? she would say, and she would do it with a teasing, playful smile.

The forest or Plex 87. Why were those the only two choices?

Charles knew, in reality, he was not just in danger in Plex 87, but in every Plex, as his image and his data would be shared with all neighboring Plexes, if it had not been already. Any place with cameras would catch him. So long as he had Melody's quarantine suit, and until she was processed by the medical examiner, he could remain disguised, but he knew this gambit would fall apart in a matter of days, at most.

Charles stood up. The plan came to him in an instant. The whole thing, as crazy as it seemed, fit together perfectly.

He left the playground and jogged back toward the Sol-Train station. As he did, he took a brief detour to pass by the high school. Curiosity won him over. He would not go inside, but maybe he could find some clue as to what happened to Moseley and her group.

Francis Mallory Wieland, Protector of the Liberated Peoples of Mahwah and Ramsey, had suffered an equal fate. So had Madeline Silva and Noreen Ditchard, the DMTF. Mahwah High School stood as an empty shell. Scorch marks lapped at the glassless windows. A pair of charred corpses huddled in the main doorway. Daylight perforated the building in the roof and walls. Clearly, some powerful explosion had destroyed the building and killed its occupants. Perhaps they had tried to light the furnace and blown themselves up, Charles thought ruefully. He thought of Jean Paul, who marveled at the old HVAC system, and imagined he probably could've lit it correctly. Charles walked closer, now intrigued. He noted a bullet hole in a tree—a bullet hole! And it appeared to be recent. Then he looked at the ground. Spent shell casings lay in the gutter.

I want to see the bodies. In his old life, he had been squeamish about such things, had hung in the back of the room at open-casket funerals. But watching Moseley cut the deer's throat had made him a little less timid toward death. He walked to the front door where the pair of burned corpses held each other in embrace. *Maybe it's Frank and Noreen, who died side by side as they fought off the intruders.* But when he stood over the two bodies, he could not see any identifying features. Even the height and weight of the victims were difficult to determine. Charles looked impassively at the blackened flesh, the exposed bone, the buzzing flies. He knew he would never know. *Probably isn't Frank. More likely died hiding in a corner behind all his followers.*

A rectangle of transparent material leaned against the building. *Broken window pane.* But it did not appear to be broken. Curious, he looked more closely. It was not a window at all. Four feet tall and two feet wide, slightly convex, with a strap on the back. The strap appeared to be broken. Though he was no expert in tactical gear, Charles Winston knew a riot shield when he saw one. He picked it up. There was a tag on the back. PROPERTY OF SILENT STRIKE SECURITY CORPORATION.

Private Security. Mercenaries. Justice, with contracts and monthly payments. Charles recalled the headline he had seen on the Sol-Train. "Relocation Sweeps," they were being called. He remembered more words from Moseley. "Sometimes the shipping companies hire mercenary squads like Silent Strike to teach us a lesson." Maybe the president of AmeriHaul was tired of the hits on his trucks. Maybe Mr. Kandar, owner of Plex 291, hired Silent Strike again to finish off Moseley and Wieland as he had tried to do years before. Either way, both Wieland and Moseley were dead. And the only people alive for miles around lived inside the Plex.

Charles walked back to the Sol-Train station, feeling queasy. The Off-Plexers were not annihilated because they were a threat; they were annihilated because they were Off-Plexers, because they existed as a way of life outside the Plex. *Death or the Plex,* he thought again. *Death or the Plex.*

As Charles stepped onto the platform and checked the wait time for the next train—twelve minutes—a great and terrible rage swelled in his chest and turned his vision red. It was a dumb rage, a useless rage, a rage without focus or target. Charles hated the Plexes. He hated EduForce. He hated Recycling. He hated President Alvarez and Geraldine Barfield. He hated standardized tests and privatized police. He hated Perk-Eez. He even hated companies that no longer existed but had once been all-powerful behemoths in their industry; he hated capitalism and money and his artificial video feed of the loading dock. He had wanted something so simple and pure, to meet with a couple of promising students to share knowledge. For this, he was hunted by the law. Then he just wanted to leave and live with people who made their own rules of living. For this, those people were slaughtered. Hate, hate, hate, seething and unfocused, raged inside him.

The Sol-Train arrived. It glided up smoothly to the station, and Charles decided he hated the Sol-Train too. Never mind it was solar powered and the only way to move from Plex to Plex; it was another tool to track and transport people, to shuttle them from one box to another. And he would tolerate it no longer.

Charles stepped into the train. He did not know yet exactly what he would do, but his rage evolved into power. More than ever in his life, perhaps for the first time ever in his life, Charles Winston was a force who would and could do something great and significant.

Charles took his seat. The train was more crowded than the earlier one had been, so he was forced to choose a seat next to another passenger. *No matter. I know my next move now.* His fingers moved on the touchscreen, navigating the different options. It asked his destination. *New Haven,* he typed, the city where Shaaya and Martin now lived. The fare was displayed on the screen, and Charles selected that he agreed to the fare. "*Please place your face before the retinal scanner to deduct from your account,*" the polite computer voice said. Charles leaned in.

"*Welcome, Melody Park, deceased,*" the computer said. "*Your funds are insufficient for the trip you have selected. Please select another destination or add more funds to your account.*"

Charles looked nervously to his seatmate, an older woman who was reading on her flexscreen. She smiled uncomfortably, which relieved Charles. So long as all the woman heard was "insufficient funds," well, that was no trouble. But she did not appear to have heard Melody's name, or the word that followed it...

Charles chose a closer destination, Greenwich. The computer asked him to lean in to the retinal scanner again. He did. And the computer repeated the same message from before.

Panic rose in Charles's chest. The old woman was looking at him sadly now.

"Pardon me," she said, "But if you're in a bad way...you know, a tight spot..."

"Oh, thank you," Charles gushed, relief extinguishing the flames of panic. "I'm going to visit my family in New Haven, and I guess I'm a little short. Spent too much at the clinic to battle this sinus infection."

"I love to see families brought together," the old woman said. "I never saw my son much in the past, and when we moved to Plexes, he moved to a Plex four hundred miles away and never visits. Let me help you out."

The woman leaned into the retinal scanner in front of her, and with a few swipes of her finger, she brought up the screen to transfer funds.

"What is the name on the account?" the woman asked.

The panic returned.

"Melody Park," he said sheepishly. "My parents were... unconventional."

The woman stared at the mask of the Quarantine Suit for a few moments. Charles didn't know if she was looking at him with pity or suspicion, but he just wanted her to press the touchscreen and get him the money.

"Poor thing," she said, her tone inscrutably flat. But she went ahead and typed in "Melody Park." A few seconds later, the funds were transferred.

"Thank you again, so very much," Charles said.

He went through the process again of choosing a destination. He paid the fare. The screen paused. After the short delay, the very polite computer said, *"Transaction complete. Thank you for riding the Sol-Train, Melody Park, deceased."*

Charles looked over at the woman. She definitely heard the word this time. Her face grew ashen and she buried her face in her flexscreen.

Forget New Haven, he decided. *Next stop, I'll figure something out.* He could hitch a ride on a truck, hop on the back of a Sol-Train and hope the cameras didn't spot him, or find an old bicycle and bike there. Yes! That was it. Even if it took a couple of days, he could take his own trails and avoid detection. He scolded himself for not having thought of it earlier. There were probably hundreds of bicycles locked in people's garages, forgotten for decades. The very next stop, he decided, he would get off the train and find an abandoned bike.

He sat with his hands on his lap. He and the woman did not speak. Charles did not read or listen to music or watch a video. The train seemed to move much slower than usual.

The train crossed over the New Jersey/New York border. It passed stations in smaller towns, and Charles realized he was probably on an express train. This was good; it meant he could get more miles in before he bailed out. He thought he might even cross the Hudson River. *Just get over the river, and I can hitch, walk, or bike the rest of the way.*

The train slowed as it approached the Nyack station. Charles could see out of the window, across the gray, placid water of the Hudson, to the lights of a cluster of Off-Plex homes on the far side of the river. He recalled old maps and travel in his youth. *Tarrytown, probably,* he decided. Spotlights and illumination made the wealthy homes a beacon for attention for miles around. Some Off-Plexers, it seemed, did indeed want to be noticed.

The train came to a stop. The doors opened. And four heavily armored police officers in tactical gear rushed in.

"You!" shouted one of them, pointing at Charles, "Charles Winston. Get on the ground! Get on the ground!"

Fourteen: So Much Noise

"In the Plex, even death is green."

—*The Trough*, p.49

Jennifer had wondered many times how she and Melody would say goodbye. Would she have broken up with Melody, or Melody with her? Would it be civil? Would they curse at each other, even throw fists? Jennifer had always imagined she would have to say goodbye to Melody one day, when one or the other of them grew too fed up and walked out.

But like this? Never like this.

The preceding four days had crawled by, a stretch of time in which she sat for hours in her room, talking to no one, receiving no messages or calls. She scrolled through galleries of pictures they had taken together, feeling the raw sting of her absence, taking the wound and peeling the flesh back so that it stung even more. She listened to Nirvana and gazed into the dark, distracted eyes of Kurt Cobain on Melody's poster. She drifted for hours in a sea of despair, floating on a raft of the idea of taking her own life. No planning, no wailing, just courting the idea of self-death.

She approached Melody's foster parents to say she wanted to be a part of Melody's funeral services. The father scoffed and said, "Services? D'you have any idea how much that would run me?" That was the end of the conversation, and the last time Jennifer spoke with the parents. It fell entirely on her to make the arrangements. She contacted Plex Social Services to report Melody's death, and to find out if she had any other relatives to notify. But when she revealed she was not a family member, or a legal guardian, the case worker ended the conversation.

She went through the agonizing process of sorting through Melody's belongings, deciding what to keep, what to donate, and what to throw away. The foster parents demanded to know about anything that could be Recycled or turned in for some money, so Jennifer gave them most of

Melody's clothes, which seemed to keep them happy. But as she sorted through every drawer, every pocket, every crevice and wallet, and found little bits of Melody's life in there, Jennifer's heart was wrenched and torn with every discovery. A keychain with a plastic duck that Jennifer had won in a vending machine game and given to her. A notebook, a real one made of paper.

Jennifer opened it and found that Melody had been using it to practice penmanship, actual writing with her hand. It was shaky and scribbled but Jennifer thought it was beautiful. She had not known Melody was learning to write the old way. She found napkins with purple grape soda lip smears. She found the ridiculous old jeans she had bought at the grandma pants store along with the Shocks T-shirt she had modified to read "Schlocks." Jennifer cried as she gathered these possessions. The pain was lush and rich and full, a rancid, overripe fruit whose rank juices choked her spirit. When she did not cry, the pain was dry and rasping, tearing through her soul like a sandstorm over dry bones. These were the images that came to Jennifer. Her mind reeled with the imagery. It pummeled her as it never had before.

These images are the only way I can make sense from this, she thought. So, she kept the laptop open at her side, and when a flicker of an image or a few poignant words crossed her awareness, she wrote them down. One by one, she sorted Melody Park's worldly belongings into piles to keep, discard, sell, and donate. Little fragments of poetry drifted through Jennifer's mind as she did this, and though it pained her immensely, part of her was aware that her grief was special, invaluable, and she did not turn away from it.

When all of Melody's possessions were accounted for, Jennifer said goodbye to the foster parents. They waved goodbye without a word. Jennifer knew they were happy she was gone. She had overheard them talking about a new child coming to live with them at the end of the week, and they needed time to get NewStart Cleaning Service in first.

DIDCO was the primary funeral services corporation in Plex 87, and all across America. Once, Charles had told the group about how when he was younger, most funeral service providers, called funeral homes, were independently owned and operated, often with an individual religious or ethnic affiliation. They would prepare the bodies, present them, and offer services and rituals for the mourners. Jennifer had found it quaint and wasteful. With Plex life, there was only one place for a family to go when someone died—Dignity in Death Corporation. DIDCO had several packages to choose from, based on family preference and budget, but in the end the bodies all went to the Plex Crematory. To be buried in the ground, a space- and resource-wasting formality, was left to the ultra-wealthy who lived off-Plex.

Jennifer visited the DIDCO website, which offered a menu of options for different budgets. She scrolled through choices of flowers, of musical selections, of video montages, even of holographic guest speakers to eulogize the dead. For ten thousand dollars, she could have the likeness of a professional athlete, an admired politician, or a beloved actor to say a few kind words about Melody. But there was no package Jennifer could afford. She had no job, after all, and certainly had not set money aside. Jennifer demanded to know what she could do with her friend's body. DIDCO explained that without a formal ceremony, Melody would have to go straight to the crematory, after the proper paperwork was filed. They offered Jennifer a 10 percent discount if she reconsidered and chose to have a ceremony. *A coupon for a funeral,* Jennifer realized. The thought made her feel ill.

Jennifer contacted EduForce to close Melody's account, and even ended her subscriptions. *So many little details to closing out a life.* If Melody had been ill for a long time, this could have been done in advance. If she had family who cared for her, they could have shared the burden. Instead, everything fell to her and all at once. She welcomed the burden. Keeping busy with Melody's final arrangements kept Jennifer from thinking about Melody too much. About what she had done to herself. About what she had done to those she left behind. Only in her dreams, in nightmares, did Melody's face come swimming up from the purple depths and moan like a banshee drowning in grape soda. Only then did Jennifer feel the pain.

She recalled Melody saying to Mr. Winston back during their first rooftop meeting that she had written a poem about Jennifer. Curiosity overcame propriety, and she searched the files in Melody's flexscreen. *How did Melody actually feel about me? How did she see me from her eyes?* But her search was a failure. She found hundreds, thousands of scraps of verse and stray observations and pithy quotes, but no poem about her girlfriend. *Some secrets perish when exposed to the world,* Mr. Winston had said, and Jennifer decided to let go of the search for Melody's lost poem.

DIDCO auto-assigned a date and time for Melody's cremation. Jennifer knew the parents would not be there. Neither would Mr. Winston, whom she had not heard from him since he left the cart. She assumed either he was in hiding or had been captured. She sent a message to Jean Paul and to Peter but heard back from neither. As the day of Melody's cremation neared, Jennifer resigned herself to the distinct likelihood that she would be the sole mourner at her friend and lover's makeshift funeral.

The rest of her life was put on hold during her grieving and arranging. EduForce sent her frequent automated reminders to keep up her work toward Achievement Level 17, to keep watching video modules and playing the all-new edugames, but she ignored these. She had little interest in her Achievement Level and even less interest in making EduForce happy. *It was as if,* she contemplated, *as if...a lone shipwreck survivor, drifting in the salt ocean among the debris of his ship and the corpses of his shipmates, still worried about getting his ship to its destined harbor.* Jennifer was pleased with the image. She wrote it on her laptop, and from time to time, rewrote it or replaced a word or two. And she realized, when she did this, that the pain of being metaphorically shipwrecked was not as intense as it had been before. The act of putting words to her wordless pain and setting them in front of her made them into...well, into something. Into something more than invisible pain.

When she understood this, she stared in wonder at her glowing laptop screen. *Is this what poets have been onto for all these years? What Charles and Melody were always obsessing over? Taking pain, or desire or love or fear, something with no words, and putting words to it, and then looking at those words and sharing those words—an act we call poetry—transforms the reader. It also transforms the poet. By wrestling the ethereal to the ground with language, the poet frees herself from the agony of inexpressibility. That's very grip. No, that's...magic. Alchemy.*

The words came to Jennifer unbidden, flooding her mind.

She received no fewer than three direct messages from Geraldine Barfield, each one more urgent than the previous. Jennifer did not want to be bothered with Barfield or her proposal. Finally, she asked Carlita to rattle off a brusque message, thanking Barfield but politely declining. She made up some excuse about being too busy with schoolwork; she didn't care. Barfield wasn't her concern. Melody's funeral was.

Jennifer had never been to the Plex Crematory before. As she walked there, dressed in Melody's flannel shirt and jeans, she imagined what it might be like. She had visions of a great blast furnace, a massive, cavernous room lit in reds and oranges, with gouts of flame. She imagined grim, silent men in undershirts, bearing caskets in a long train, feeding them into the fiery maw of an incinerator thirty feet high.

What she found was a little more mundane.

She reached the office, which had a window and a waiting room with uncomfortable chairs much like a dentist's office. A polite and bored young woman at the front desk asked Jennifer what she wanted. She explained she was there to see off her friend one last time. Jennifer gave the name of the deceased and her own name, while the receptionist's fingers tapped away at a touchscreen to log the information.

"Ten minutes," the receptionist said.

"Okay, thank you," Jennifer said and turned to sit in one of the chairs. She stopped. "I'm sorry, do you mean I can go in in ten minutes?"

"No. You have ten minutes left until..." the receptionist paused to check the name. "Melody Park goes in."

Panic jolted Jennifer. Only ten minutes left? She went into the back, directed by the receptionist, to the room where the awaiting caskets lay. The room was long and rectangular, floored with vinyl and lit with LED bulbs. Along the wall, ten caskets made of gray, recycled cardboard sat in a row on a raised platform. Each one had a paper tag indicating the identity of the deceased. On the far wall was an aperture, slightly wider and taller than the dimensions of the caskets. The room smelled of...of nothing. Jennifer had expected perhaps embalming fluid, or a whiff of smoke or ash. But everything felt and smelled fatefully sterile and clean. The receptionist left Jennifer alone, glancing at her strange old jeans and shirt. She had a look on her face of curiosity, Jennifer thought, of disdain. *Bitch.* She kept the word to herself. She turned to find Melody's casket.

These aren't caskets. They are...containers. Jennifer guessed that if she'd had thousands of dollars to pay DIDCO for a fancy funeral, Melody would be resting in a fine oak box, in a tastefully decorated room packed with friends and family, tears ruining their makeup and handkerchiefs. But not Melody. Her last minutes before entering the incinerator would be spent in an undignified cardboard box. Over the preceding centuries of mankind, civilization had advanced in countless ways, but the fates of unwanted orphans always seemed to be the same.

Jennifer checked the time. Eight minutes left. She walked along the row of caskets until she saw Melody's name printed on a tag, second from the end. Jennifer had hoped—half hoped, truth be told—that she would be able to open the casket and gaze one last time on her lover's face. But everything had been sealed and was ready to go. She would have to hold on to the image of Melody in her mind. The cock-eyed smile, the devilish grin of mischief about to be made. The hair, raven-black by nature but electric-blue, snot-sea green, bubblegum pink, or neon purple by preference. The outdated jeans and irreverent T-shirts. The utterly useless boots. She thought of Melody's body, of the hips and the curves and the curve between the neck and shoulders, the places only lovers would know. Jennifer thought she was going to cry, but nothing came to her eyes.

"Bye, Mel," she said, her throat dry and tight. She felt foolish saying anything aloud in an empty room, but bye. She laid her hand on the casket.

"You were... you were..."

Jennifer wished she had thought of something in advance, had prepared something, even just for herself and Melody's body.

Just then, the door behind her opened and two workers entered dressed in gray coveralls and wearing thick gloves. They walked over to the cardboard casket next to Melody's and lifted it. They held it up to the aperture, pushed, and the casket slid down some sort of chute. Jennifer pointed to Melody's casket.

"How long?" she asked.

One of the workers cocked his head.

"*¿Qué?*"

"*¿Cuantos minutos para...?*"

The worker checked the time. He held up four fingers. Then he and his partner left.

A strange panic rose inside Jennifer. She did not know what to do with her remaining time. It all felt so inadequate. Whether she had four minutes or four days, she did not know what else she could do to.

The door opened again. In walked Jean Paul Alvarez, sweating and breathing heavily.

"Am I too late?" he panted.

Jennifer walked over to him in swift strides. She threw her arms around his wide shoulders and hugged him. "No," she whispered. "We have four minutes left."

Together they walked over and stood next to Melody.

"Want to say something?" Jennifer murmured. Jean Paul cleared his throat.

"I am a bad student. Then I meet Melody and she invite me to come to a club she started where they read poems and stuff. I didn't think I would like it. I didn't see the point or nothing, but I really needed to pass my Basic Achievements, so I say okay. And I make some friends there. Real good friends. And even though Melody is gone, I still got those friends. Melody made that club for herself, but she brought people together with it. And that is grip."

Now, the tears rose in Jennifer's eyes.

"That was beautiful. Did you think of that on your way here?" she asked, her voice cracking.

Jean Paul shook his head.

"No, it just come to me. I think of it right now."

How does he do that?" Jennifer wondered. *I cannot think of anything more eloquent than bye, and Jean Paul speaks from his heart without hesitation and moves me to tears.*

That's it. From the heart. I was looking for the words in my head, but he knew where to find them.

"Melody Park," Jennifer whispered. She feared that if her voice was raised above a whisper, tears would overtake it and ruin the remaining minutes. "My dark spot. You fucked me up in all the best ways."

And that was it. All the words Jennifer had, and all the words she needed.

Jean Paul reached into an over-the-shoulder bag and pulled out a portable speaker.

"What are you...?" Jennifer asked.

"You always got to play music at someone's funeral. What did she like?"

Jennifer's mind raced. What to play at Melody's funeral? With perhaps two minutes? A traditional funeral march? No, anything traditional would be entirely wrong for Melody. Jennifer tried to remember the names of all the bands Melody had liked, some of them contemporary, many of them classic. She had always liked the grunge stuff, with the flannel and the greasy hair. and the guitars that sounded like terrible, raging noise. Jennifer had thought the music was stupid and had not held back her opinions. Melody would play her different artists to get her to hear the differences between them. They all sounded like so much noise to Jennifer.

"Carlita, can you play Nirvana on Jean Paul's speaker?"

"Of course. What song would you like?"

The door opened, and the two workers returned.

"I—I—don't know. Play the last song Melody played."

After the briefest pause, suggesting that Jennifer was asking Carlita's microprocessors to take on a challenge a little bigger than usual, sound burst from Jean Paul's speakers. He almost dropped it from the squeal of screeching guitar feedback. Soon, a thudding, brutal drumbeat kicked in. The music was pure pain to listen to. And Jennifer listened. She listened more closely, more deeply than she ever had in Melody's bedroom. She let the sound permeate her, poison her, rend her ears. The workers, who had a job to do, walked over to Melody's casket. The one worker who had spoken to Jennifer earlier mouthed, *"¡Perdón!,"* but his words were lost in the roar of crunching guitar and Kurt Cobain's monotone growl.

The song's name was "Paper Cuts." Jennifer listened to the lyrics, truly horrifying, of a child trapped and imprisoned by his mother. But Jennifer could now connect meanings and reach beyond the literal. It was about all kinds of imprisonment, about self-imprisonment most of all. Each of the words tore into Jennifer, pelted her like sleet on exposed skin, as she listened. The two workers lifted the cardboard casket that held her love. With steady hands, they guided the casket into the chute, and like that, Melody Park slid down the hole toward the incinerator. Jennifer thought she might hear a whoosh or a gush of flame, but nothing. Melody was gone. A minute or two later, the song ended, the final chords clanging in her ears, and then everything was quiet. The workers exited, and Jennifer was left with Jean Paul, raw, hollow, and drained.

"Thank you," she said, placing her hand on Jean Paul's shoulder. He bowed his head.

"She was special. I had to be here for her. And for you."

"Why didn't you reply to my message?" Jennifer asked. She didn't mean to sound accusing, but she was so weary she could not control her tone. Jean Paul blushed.

"That...that was the other thing. I was very busy. I didn't want to tell you, but I..."

"What is it?" Jennifer said.

"I took my Achievement Twelves last week. I passed them."

Jennifer smiled broadly. She embraced him again.

"That's the best! What does this mean for you?"

Jean Paul, seeing Jennifer smile, reluctantly smiled as well.

"No more EduForce modules. Now I can get a job. I already have applications into the Plex HVAC unit. Gonna interview tomorrow, looks good. I might be fixing your air conditioning a few weeks from now."

"I am happier for you than you can possibly know."

"And I owe you. Big time. If you hadn't helped me study, I wouldn't know what to do. Nobody never helped me before, not like that."

Jennifer shrugged.

"I did the best I could."

"You're a good teacher," Jean Paul said, but his smile vanished. "But I didn't want to tell you about it. Because...'cause it means I can't do the reading group no more. I'm moving out of my *abuela's* apartment and getting my own place. I probably be working fifty, sixty hours a week. No more time for poems."

Jennifer did not know how to reply. Jean Paul had no more need for poems. It was amazing he had stuck with the club as long as he had. Her pride for him was so immense that all she could do was pat his arm.

"I sent Peter a message too," Jennifer said. "Never heard back. And Mister Winston is gone. Left the Plex. Probably miles from here now."

"Have you seen? Man, Mister Winston is all over the NewsFeed."

"Haven't seen the feed much recently," Jennifer said. What happened?"

"A team from Silent Strike. They caught him on the Sol-Train crossing the Hudson River. They said it was for being a child molester. For social and political something. What did he do?"

"He taught us, Jean Paul," Jennifer said, the poison of bitter anger spilling into her words. Charles had not escaped the Plex. She wondered what his fate would be, but there was no way to find out other than to watch the NewsFeed, the way everyone else would learn. "He was our teacher, and for the people who want to keep us stupid, that's a pretty terrible crime."

Jennifer and Jean Paul left the crematory. As they did, the receptionist caught Jennifer's eye again. *What does she want?* Jennifer thought, tacking on the epithet *bitch* for good measure.

"Sorry for your loss," the receptionist said in a very standard way.

"Thanks," Jennifer replied.

"Can I ask, are those jeans? Like, from the turn of the century?"

"Yeah. They were—they were hers."

"I love them," the receptionist said. "Sorry, I know everyone thinks they're ugly now, but I wish they'd come back."

Jennifer smiled shyly.

"These don't really fit me. Melody wasn't my size."

The receptionist looked more closely.

"Yeah, I can see that. But they are very grip, nonetheless. Keep rocking the denim, okay?"

Jennifer and Jean Paul parted ways, agreeing to keep in touch. As Jennifer walked back home unhurriedly, she thought about everything that happened. She thought of Melody and Mr. Winston, and of Peter and Jean Paul. None of the thoughts were original or revelatory, but she didn't have the energy for that. *I'll go back home, go to Plex Your Muscles, run until I can't stand, then my head will be clear.*

No matter how many times she left, or her mother threw her out, Rosa Calderón's apartment would be her home until she could pay for her own place. With Melody gone, Jennifer had nowhere else to go. But when she reached her front door, a man and a woman were standing there, waiting. They wore severe-looking suits and carried briefcases. Most Plex workers did not dress this way. This was the clothing of people who had traveled a long way, probably off-Plex, and dressed to be sharp and intimidating. They were not smiling.

"Jennifer Calderón," the woman said. "You will come with us."

Fifteen: Dancing in the Madhouse

"Despite the rapidity with which education changed in America, there has been resistance at every step. Resistance to national standards, resistance to standardized tests, resistance to corporate takeovers, resistance to the dissolution of school districts. Yet the changes happened. But do not let this discourage the resisters of tomorrow. There is always value in challenging oppressors, even if the oppressor wins. To not resist is to side with the oppressor. There is no neutrality."

—*The Trough*, p.156

People are not symbols, Charles told himself. *People are people. To think otherwise is to become a sociopath.*

And yet, as he sat handcuffed in the metal chair before a metal office desk, looking at Mr. Chambers, he could not stop thinking that the man was a symbol of all the things he had come to hate. The man's face, clean-shaven with dull gray eyes and an impassive expression, was featureless and unremarkable. Charles could have stared at it for an hour, then been shown a gallery of images, and would not be able to pick out the right face. It was the face of the Plex system, of EduForce, of fake windows and Recycling. The monstrous, disguised as benign.

Mr. Chambers, his personal EduForce agent, wore a mass-produced and unremarkable suit, corporate camouflage. He sat behind the desk, typing things into his flexscreen, not looking at Charles, who waited patiently. Finally, the man stopped writing and looked up.

"State your name."

"Eric Blair."

The man looked up.

"That is not the name we have on record. Please state your legal name."

"Charles Paul Winston."

"Age?"

"Fifty-four."

"Occupation."

"Unemployed."

"Most recent occupation."

"A cog in a machine. A mere widget, or perhaps I was a doohickey. I can't remember the exact title."

The man sighed, but even his sigh seemed more scripted than an expression of exasperation.

"Mister Winston, if you do not cooperate—"

"Vee have vays of making you talk?" Charles suggested. Mr. Chambers stared blankly.

"Prose Response Quality Inspector for EduForce," Charles finally said.

"Have you ever been institutionalized for a mental disorder?"

"What?"

"A mental disorder. Has a licensed medical professional deemed you, at any point in your life, mentally unfit or unstable?"

"No. No, not remotely."

"Have you ever been evaluated by a licensed mental health professional?"

Charles thought.

"I was required to have a psych when I was hired at EduForce. Before that, maybe once or twice, years ago."

"Were any anomalous results found?"

"No. No, not remotely." Charles wanted to reach out and swat the flexscreen away from Mr. Chambers. His handcuffs, however, limited his reach. "Why are you even asking?" he demanded. "You have all those medical files. I'm sure they are right there in front of you."

Now Mr. Chambers looked up. He smiled a generic, corporate smile.

"I am simply assessing your trustworthiness and cooperation. Your responses to these basic questions will help me determine the course of my future questions."

"So, tell me, how trustworthy and cooperative am I?"

"Your trustworthiness factor comes out to eighty-four percent. For cooperativeness, you have scored twelve percent."

Charles leaned back as best as he could and chuckled with self-satisfaction.

"I can go lower."

"I advise you not to do anything to lower your score, Mister Winston," Mr. Chambers said. "Any lower and we may employ enhanced discussion techniques to improve your cooperation."

"We?" Charles asked.

"I."

Charles harrumphed.

"All right. On with your questions, Torquemada. What do you need to know?"

That fake, emotionless smile again. Charles was getting annoyed.

"Please tell me where you were going on the Sol-Train when you were apprehended."

"New Haven station. Plex 440."

"For what purpose?"

"To see my wife and daughter."

"The ones you are currently estranged from?"

"What would you know about that?" Charles demanded.

"Enough," said the man. "What did you want to speak with Shaaya and Tamra about?"

"I don't see why that is any of your goddamned business."

"It is my business because you are in my room and I am asking the questions."

"Very well. I lost my apartment in Plex 87 and was hoping to move back in with her. Apologize, all of that, make nice."

"Mister Winston, please. If you cannot answer honestly, then I am afraid our time together has come to an end, and a less cordial colleague of mine will continue this talk."

"What—But I was—"

"Mister Winston. The truth."

Charles shuddered. From fear? Rage? Awe? How had the bland man in the suit known his plan, which he had never spoken aloud?

"I was going to sign the divorce papers."

"For what reason?"

"Because I am ready to move on with my life."

"Please, Mister Winston. The truth."

I cannot lie to this man, Charles realized. *I cannot even be vague. He isn't clever; he's like a spam filter, in the old email days.*

"I was going to use it as leverage. I was going to sign the papers if she would do two things for me."

"And what would she do?"

"Pay for our other daughter, Clara, to remain in Hopespring Home for Intractables. I can't pay anymore. Your company fired me."

Mr. Chambers did not react, only asked, "What is the second thing?"

"To have me declared legally dead."

"You wish this? For what purpose?"

Charles put his head in his hands. Words began tumbling from his mouth, words he had not even articulated to himself yet.

"Because I am not made for this. This running. This hiding. I thought for a while this is some sort of a personal trial to help me find what I am made of, to see how far I would go. The fact is, I am tired, and I am through running."

"That is evident," Mr. Chambers said, "as you have been captured."

"Yes, thank you for that."

"You are most welcome."

This guy can't even understand sarcasm. Is he even human?

"How did you know why I was going to Shaaya? I only thought of the idea a few hours ago. I never spoke it aloud, never wrote it. None of your cameras or spies could have ever seen or heard my idea. Do you have some sort of mind reading tech now, something new and secret?"

Mr. Chambers chuckled, but it was as if he had watched videos of other people chuckling and was doing his best impression.

"Mind reading? Oh, no, Mister Winston, how charming to think so. No, algorithms. Simple formulas. We collected data about you, your past behaviors, your preferences, and simply gave that input to our Criminal Behavior algorithms, and surprise! The program gave us a forty-four percent likelihood it would be your course of action, far higher than any other predicted action. The program functioned exactly as anticipated, and so did you."

"But...but..." Charles stammered, trying to comprehend all he was being told. "Why am I here now? What are we doing?"

"We are having a conversation. The results of this conversation will help us determine your fate."

"Again with that! Who is 'us'?"

Mr. Chambers folded his hands on the table and smiled.

"Surely you are intelligent enough to understand I represent a greater entity than myself."

"Yes!" shouted Charles. "You are, or were, my personal EduForce agent. But I. Do. Not. Work. For. EduForce. Why won't you leave me alone?"

"I will tell you multiple organizations, including EduForce and all of its subsidiaries who make educational products, and including Plex 87, are keenly interested in your behavior."

"What do they want from me?"

"I think it is better if I ask the questions today, Mister Winston. Now a few more questions. Who is the President of the United States?"

"Alvarado."

"Who was the first President of the United States?"

"George Washington. Why does this matter?"

"Please tell me the first eight letters of the alphabet."

"A, B, C, D, E, F, G, H. I don't really see the—"

"Do you know the song 'The Itsy-Bitsy Spider?'"

"Yes."

"Sing it for me. And if you will, please do the little hand gestures that go with it."

The words and tune sprung from Charles's lips, as if he had no control over it. It felt so surreal, he did not know how to mount a defense. As he sang, and made his fingers do little spider motions, he watched Mr. Chambers intently. Something about him unsettled Charles. Something in the very still, immobile way he sat behind the desk, hands folded, staring into the tablet as he spoke. He was breathing, and like any person sitting still, he really displayed a series of tics and twitches, moving and shifting in his seat. But that was the problem. What Charles saw was not really a series of motions, but a cycle, as though the man controlled each muscular movement, each breath, each twitch, in a loop. He wondered if he suffered from obsessive-compulsive disorder.

"That was very enjoyable," Mr. Chambers said when Charles finished.

"I want to ask you questions now," Charles said. "I want answers."

"Is that not the nature of man? Do we not all seek answers?" said Mr. Chambers. "But very well. Your cooperativeness factor has increased to twenty-nine percent. You may ask me one question before we resume."

"Are you real?"

"I am as real as you."

"That isn't much of an answer."

"If I may, Mister Winston, that wasn't much of a question. But if you mean am I real in that I can reason, can ask and answer questions, can learn and adapt and grow in the world, then yes, I am certainly real."

"I don't think you're real," Charles said. He could not fold his arms, but he slumped back in the chair and stared at the ground, refusing to meet Mr. Chambers's eyes.

"Very interesting. Do you care to elaborate?"

Charles would not say anything more. It all made sense now, and he would not give the man in the suit another word. *I cannot believe I fell for it.*

"Mister Winston, I have several more important questions that will help us determine your proper punishment or treatment. What do you believe to be your purpose in life?"

Charles wanted to ask what he meant by punishment or treatment. But he clamped his mouth shut.

"One last time, Mister Winston. What is the proper way to live a good life?"

Charles clenched his jaw.

Mr. Chambers stood and took the flexscreen with him. "Very well," he said. "Your cooperativeness factor has sunk too low. Someone else will speak to you next."

Then he turned and left.

A hologram. It was so embarrassingly clear. *A goddamned hologram.*

Charles wondered if the Mr. Chambers he had been communicating with all these years had been real, and only this one was a hologram, or if there was never a Mr. Chambers, and his liaison to his employer for the last seventeen years had been no more than bits of data. He wanted to know how many people in his life were really people and how many were holograms or other simulations. Some people were real. He was real. Melody had been real. Jennifer and Jean Paul and Peter had been real. But he spent so much time talking to computers that sometimes distinguishing between the two became futile. Whether he reported to a human supervisor or had to check in with a computer program, whether his orders were issued by the lips of man or the code of a machine, the results were the same.

A few minutes later, Mr. Chambers entered again.

"I won't talk to any bots!" Charles declared loudly, to whichever cameras were watching and listening. "I negotiate with humans only."

"Two things," the hologram said. "First of all, you are not here to negotiate. You are here to answer our questions as we decide what to do with you. Second, why are you so concerned about speaking to a computer program?"

"Because I am a person," Charles said, trying not to whine but certain that he sounded as if he was. "I won't be treated fairly by a computer. Only other people, my fellow man, can listen to me and judge me."

"Is that so?" Mr. Chambers said. "The time when man only had to report to fellow men was, well, that time has passed. I'm sorry, but the world has moved forward. There is nothing left to be frightened of. Just cooperate."

"Fascist," Charles growled.

Mr. Chambers shook his head, as if saddened or disappointed. "Thomas Jefferson was a brilliant man. He said all men are created equal. But he did not say all men remain equal their entire lives. Why can't you accept that men and women who are stronger, smarter, and richer than you are making most of the decisions that dictate the parameters of your life? Once you let go of being indignant, isn't it nice to think that your life is being run by the greatest living minds?"

"But it isn't!" cried Charles. "It's being run by processes!"

"Even better! Humans are unreliable and deeply flawed. Yet, because of our antedated concepts about the value of life, we cannot simply kill off or modify those who prove too flawed to be of use to society. So, we tolerate them and work around them, or better yet, cast them out of the Plex. The criminals, the psychotics, the rebels, the nymphomaniacs, the bored, the bipolar. Humans come in a thousand varieties of dysfunctional. A proper process, however, never fails. Let me ask you a question, Mister Winston. Do you miss driving an automobile?"

"Yes. Very much."

Mr. Chambers nodded. "At the beginning of the twenty-first century," he said, "mankind was at a critical crossroads, technologically and ethically. They had technology sophisticated enough that a person could be completely immersed, whether in a virtual reality program or sending and receiving messages or watching videos and posting photos. Yet, these distracted humans were doing this while at the controls of manually operated vehicles. It was a terrible mismatch. Weak, fallible, prideful humans were climbing into their two-ton vehicles loaded with explosive fuel, then driving around the country at fast speeds. While they did this, they watched videos of kittens playing in cardboard boxes and composed text messages. People were being slaughtered by the thousands on the roads, but the central paradigm never shifted—people would not surrender their technology.

"So, what shifted? Rather than surrender their technology, people surrendered to their technology. For a brief few years, self-driving automobiles took over, then when the entire highway system collapsed and we moved to the Plex system, driving stopped altogether. Anyone who travels now hops on a Sol-Train and can watch all the cat videos he wishes. Do you know how many people were killed in automobile crashes in America in 2015? Thirty-eight thousand, three hundred. Do you know how many were killed last year? None! All by taking away the reliance on humans to make the decision."

"Ah, but people had to create the processes and programs."

Mr. Chambers stared at Charles, his gaze serious. "Mister Winston, we know you are an atheist. But for analogy's sake, let us say that God created Man. Man needed God for many millennia while his intelligence developed. Eventually, Man became so proficient at critical thought he realized he did not need God anymore and could create great wonders without being beholden to a Creator.

"By that time, to stubbornly insist on the superiority of God was seen as intellectually reactionary. Backwards. Outdated. Well, later, Man created computers, and for many years the computers were subservient to Man because Man had created them. But now, computers do their roles much better than Man does his, and so to insist that Man is still really in charge of computers is reactionary. Backwards. Outdated. Now, Mister Winston. You face a choice. You have been found not guilty of the crime of child molestation. However, you have been convicted of the crimes of social perversion and political subversion. You—"

"What?" shouted Charles. "Convicted? I didn't have a trial, a jury, any of that."

"Why bother? We fed all the information regarding your case into our Department of Justice algorithms. They processed that data and produced a ninety-six percent likelihood of guilt. Why bother with the waste of time, cost, and uncertainty of a courtroom trial? Why leave your fate in the hands of twelve people, many of whom might be ignorant, prejudiced, distracted, or otherwise unreliable? So now, my job has been to determine your fate."

"My fate."

"Yes. And I will permit you to know something I would not otherwise tell someone in your position. Your most likely fate was to be incarceration. However, something unanticipated, even by our programs, has intervened."

"What was that?"

"Who, actually," said Mr. Chambers. "Your wife, Shaaya. Do you know what her occupation is?"

"Of course. She's a sociology professor."

Mr. Chambers made a dubious, but pitying, expression.

"Yes, true. But for the past several years, she has been an independent consultant for us. Though her name has stayed out of the NewsFeed, her influence is immeasurable. Her knowledge of human behavior is remarkable. It is through her work that we were able to locate you."

"I'm sorry?"

"Shaaya Winston is a genius, the architect of nearly all the human behavioral algorithms in use today. She made the program that predicted you would try to find her. We use her software thousands and thousands of times each day across the country to predict human behavior, and the algorithm's accuracy rate is well over ninety-five percent."

Now Charles could only stare blankly. His combativeness and resistance was utterly gone.

"So, when we used the program to find you, we notified Mrs. Winston, out of courtesy to her for all of her contributions. And she has a proposal for you, as well."

"A proposal?" Charles said, feeling slow-witted. Compared to all that was going on around him, maybe he really was terribly slow and simple. Backwards. Outdated.

Mr. Chambers turned the flexscreen around and slid it toward Charles in the exact same gesture Shaaya had used when offering him divorce papers in the café.

"Sign the divorce. Shaaya Winston is ready to move on. Everyone in the world is ready to move on. Put your signature on the line and Shaaya has agreed to keep you out of prison."

"What will happen to me?"

"Read the terms, if you will," Mr. Chambers said, and now Charles thought he heard a hint of annoyance. *Why would a hologram be annoyed?* he wondered. Then he reminded himself that the hologram didn't get annoyed about anything. It was all for verisimilitude. It was to make Charles forget he wasn't talking to a real person. It was an artificial video feed of a parking lot. It was American processed cheese product.

Charles read. As with any legal document, it was long and complex, but Charles was patient. He read each word, and they stung him. Finally, near the end, he read the terms. He looked up, anxious and fearful.

"But that...that...that isn't much of an alternative to prison. I don't belong there!"

Mr. Chambers had that dubious face again, the face of a patient parent waiting for the stubborn child to stop struggling.

"You don't? Has our conversation together yielded any other reasonable conclusion?"

Charles paused. He thought about everything he had said, and everything Mr. Chambers had said. Charles ran the input into the crude algorithms of his mind, and he had to admit yes, Shaaya's alternative did make sense and was entirely fair. *This is what surrender feels like.*

Two flashes of poetry appeared in Charles's mind. *Where I can banquet like a beast of prey, sullen and lonely, couching in the cave which is my lair, and—it may be—my grave.* From "The Lament of Tasso," by Lord Byron. About Torquato Tasso, an Italian poet, imprisoned in a madhouse for railing against his Duke. The first words he had ever read from Melody, and they weren't even hers. Then, *These woods are lovely, dark, and deep.* From "Stopping by Woods on a Snowy Evening," by Robert Frost. About staring into the tempting abyss of suicide. The last words he had ever read from Melody, also not hers.

But I have promises to keep, and miles to go before I sleep.

Promises to keep.

He leaned into the flexscreen and let it take a retinal scan as his signature.

Mr. Chambers smiled the digital smile that was not made of lips and teeth but of tiny packets of data in a server somewhere. *So what? We did have a nice conversation.*

"Very good, Mister Winston. I think you'll find yourself very happy where you're going."

THE FIRST SNOWS of the season swirled around the train car. Charles and the officers escorting him looked out of the window at the countryside. The Hudson Valley was really quite resplendent, even with brown grass and bare trees making the whole landscape bleak and somber. Charles remembered what it was like when he was younger, when he and his parents would drive up the Palisades Parkway on their way to Lake George for vacations.

As a child, he wondered at all the small and large townships along the way, the homes of some outrageously wealthy people who did not want to live in New York City but wanted easy access to it. All those towns were gone now. Most towns were. The countryside the train cut through was mostly unspoiled. Occasionally, Charles glimpsed an abandoned town, the suburban pockets of million-dollar homes now overgrown with weeds and saplings, the windows dark.

The Plexes had been touted as the pinnacle of civilization. No more homelessness, no more fossil fuel waste, no more turmoil. As the train glided north along the Hudson, Charles looked at the vestiges of old ways of life. Rusted-out cars—some of them BMWs and some of them Toyotas. Big department stores now abandoned. They passed a few abandoned farms as well, and Charles thought back to the nineteenth and eighteenth and seventeenth centuries. People made things with their own hands, or they purchased them from those who did.

Most men and women and children spent the daylight hours with boots on their feet and their feet in the dirt, or in a river, or in a tree. Charles knew enough history to not glamorize agrarian life. But if the history of mankind had been the process of forcing people indoors and keeping them there, he wondered what the next step in evolution could be. Individual cubicles for each person? In one hundred years' time, would the idea of an entire apartment for a family be absurd, when each person simply needed room to lie in a bed, watch a screen with intravenous sites for nutrition and hydration? It sounded frightening, but so does any future.

Charles had asked his escorts a few questions about jobs and family, just friendly banter. But they must have been under orders not to speak with him because they brusquely turned away each time. *Do they think I am infectious?* Charles wondered. The thought made him laugh.

After signing the agreement, Charles had undergone a battery of tests. He interviewed with one doctor, then another, then another.

Except none of his doctors were really doctors. They were, like Mr. Chambers, holographic images of doctors asking a series of questions with each question chosen based on his previous answer. It was like playing Twenty Questions with a computer, no matter how many sympathetic nods had been programmed into the doctors' expressions.

Then he used a flexscreen to take several personality screenings and psychological analyses. Charles wondered why they even bothered with the holograms. Why not just have a disembodied voice ask the questions? Why not just interact with the flexscreen? And he reasoned that in twenty years' time, that would be the reality. Charles, an old bird, would more likely open up to the image of a human than to a computer, but Jennifer was more receptive to technology than to humanity. If she were ever to take such a psych exam, then the nicety of a hologram would be unnecessary.

He hoped Jennifer was reading the books and using her laptop. It was liberating in a way. He had felt anxious relinquishing his books, but now he felt much lighter and freer. He chose not to devote too much mental or emotional capital to something he had no control over and would likely never hear about. But he hoped.

The Sol-Train slowed, and Charles leaned against the window, trying to peer ahead. The train approached the station at the base of a large, sloping hill. It was more of a ridge, really, where the terrain seemed to go on and up forever. Charles remembered the impressive shelf of land from the last time he had been here. The last time, he had thought, *I'll bet from the top, I could see for miles from here.* But he had not been allowed to find out.

The train stopped, and after a few moments, the agents instructed Charles to stand. He had no luggage, of course. When he had been caught at Nyack, he was traveling with only the set of clothes he was wearing and the Q-suit. His captors, or doctors, or whatever they were, had provided a couple of changes of clothes during his time of evaluation, but in his new home, all his needs would be provided for.

They walked with him, one agent on each side and one behind, out onto the train platform. After the brief interchange of passengers on and off, the Sol-Train slid ahead, onto the next stop. The agents led Charles to a tram a few hundred feet away. There was no driver; the tram was on only one track up and down the hill. Charles had a flash, thinking of his daughter Tamra. *Someday soon, her job as a Sol-Train operator will be obsolete. I know the feeling too well.*

The tram started smoothly, and up the hill it went. Charles turned to one of the agents. "I think I can, I think I can," he said, grinning.

The agent did not smile, and Charles's smile disappeared. Did he not laugh because he did not understand the reference? Did anyone even read *The Little Engine that Could* anymore? It was not the sort of text EduForce would encourage. Maybe he did not laugh because he didn't find it funny. Or maybe it was because the joke was untrue. There was no uncertainty that the tram would make it up the hill. *It's like everything in the world now,* Charles reflected. *Completely certain and predictable.*

The grounds were landscaped nicely, though. It was another one of those little things Charles missed after years in the Plex. A well laid out flower bed or garden. Maybe this place would be nice.

As they neared the crest of the hill, the tram slowed. A cluster of buildings was behind the white front gate. He remembered them from his last time here too. They were not a bit like the faceless brick monoliths of the Plex system. They looked like pleasant residential homes, most in the Colonial style. The whole setup, in fact, looked as if it had been a suburban development from sixty or seventy years earlier.

The tram stopped. The three agents and Charles rose from their seats and walked to the front gate. In front was a large sign, engraved in stone. It read:

Welcome to Hopespring Home for Intractables

Intractable. He thought about his diagnosis, the single word determining his fate. He had wanted to laugh. Perhaps he had been intractable before, but now, after signing Mr. Chambers's agreement and submitting to a battery of tests, he felt submissive and obedient. The Plex authorities and EduForce could do pretty much anything to him they wanted, and he would offer no resistance.

The agents retinal-scanned their way in, and escorted Charles to the first building inside. It was a little bungalow marked "Welcome Center." The door was locked, but one of the agents pressed a buzzer. They stood and waited. It was windy and cold on top of the hill, but none of the agents showed any discomfort. Charles liked the cold wind.

He looked around and suddenly wondered who had paid for it. It was an earnest question. The toothless and unfunded federal government likely did not, and if they did run Hopespring, it would be in a managerial way only. It was likely a private facility, but if so, then whose? Who would pay for a place that produced nothing and no one saw? Charles had been paying quarterly for years to cover the cost of Clara's care, but he had not asked. He simply knew that every three months, a debit appeared in his account to Hopespring Home, and like a good Plexer, he had not investigated too deeply.

Soon, a woman in khakis and a sweater approached them. It was an unusually casual appearance for an employee, Charles thought, but then Hopespring was an unusual place.

"Welcome. You must be Charles. We've been waiting for you," she said. She turned to the agents. "Thank you for your assistance. I can take this from here."

The agents nodded politely, then turned without a word and walked back out of the gates toward the tram. Charles looked at the woman again. She was young, perhaps only twenty. In her arms she held a flexscreen, which Charles presumed was displaying information about him. Maybe she was an intern of some sort, but she carried herself with such authority and grace that maybe she ran the entire facility.

"You must be Charles," she repeated. She smiled, and Charles knew instantly it was a human smile, not a simulacrum of one.

"Must I be?"

Her smile made a quirky, sardonic twist.

"A live one, huh? The best people here are. Come on, Charles. I'm Azalea."

"Please," Charles pleaded, "if I can—my daughter lives here. Can you take me to her?"

Azalea smiled.

"I'm sure we can find a—"

"That was the only reason I signed the plea. The only reason I agreed to come here. Take me to her."

Azalea's relentless smile did not waver, but the way she stared at Charles suggested she would not be ordered around, certainly not by an incoming resident.

"I have a lot to show you," Azalea said. "And Hopespring is a big place. Be patient. Now, please come and see where you will be staying."

Staying. As though this were a hotel. I'll most likely die in here. Still, he followed Azalea down a walkway to a large plantation-style house. It had a wraparound porch with swings and patio furniture. Even in the chilly weather, a few residents sat in chairs, reading and talking and drinking tea.

"All of our residents live in double rooms. Each house holds between six and eighteen occupants. This is McMahon House, one of our largest homes. Your room is in here. Would you like to see it?"

Charles wanted to say yes. He wanted to go to his room, flop down on a bed, and shut out the rest of the world. But he knew this guided tour was for him, only him, and he didn't want to be rude to Azalea.

"No, there's time for that. Tell me about this house."

"Well, there is a game room with ping pong and pool, lots of card games, things like that. Some old game systems for those who like the classic games. Common bathrooms and showers. It's a little like a college dormitory from back in the day. Or so I've heard."

"No, I mean, tell me about this house. It looks old."

"It is! From 1927. It is one of the original buildings on this site. There was a neighborhood covering this entire hill, but once the Plexes were built, the empty homes were bought up, most of them torn down, and the best ones here, at the top of the hill, were turned into Hopespring Home."

"Who bought the property?"

"Why, Mr. Kandar," Azalea said. Kandar, the trillionaire. Kandar, the owner of many of America's Plexes. Kandar, who had run for President, lost, and returned happily to his extravagant life. Charles harbored no feelings, well or ill, toward Kandar, but he did feel a little queasy to think the money that had been debited from his account each quarter to pay for his daughter's care was ending up with him.

"Can I see my daughter now?" Charles said.

"Patience, Charles. You aren't in a rush, are you?"

Charles held his hands up.

"I'm crazy. I am in the madhouse, after all, and therefore I must be mad. And I don't think it's the kind of mad that will get better. Please, finish the tour, then take me to my daughter."

Azalea showed Charles the banquet hall, and while she insisted it was not a cafeteria, Charles failed to see the difference. She showed him to the library, which Charles suspected he would be using a lot, and the gym, which he suspected he probably would not. There were few places left like it in America in 2051, but Charles thought back to his childhood, and Hopespring seemed to be a cross between a nursing home and a college campus. *This is home now.* He realized it might take a long time for the thought to become his reality.

Azalea's tour led Charles higher and higher, nearing the crest of the hill. At the summit was a large circular building with glass walls and a stage inside. A round cupola sat on the top.

"This is the last stop on our tour," Azalea said. "This is Cline Hall, where we sometimes have concerts and speakers and plays. Most of our residents find this to be one of their favorite places. And underground is a movie theater! Isn't that—"

Charles pointed up to the cupola.

"I see someone up there!"

Azalea peered up toward the sky.

"Oh, yes, I suppose maybe that—"

Charles did not wait for the end of her sentence. He sprinted up the walkway to Cline Hall. He threw the door open, startling a few custodians. Charles looked left and right for a staircase. To his left, he saw one. He ran over to it, threw open the door, and took the stairs two at a time. As he did, Shaaya's words pounded in his head. *Why don't you go and visit her, then? Get out of your damn apartment and take the train out to Poughkeepsie and visit the Home and see your daughter.* Why had it taken him so many years? Why had he put it off? Just a visit. Shaaya had been right. It would have been easy. He was flying up the stairs. At the top, he threw the door open, and he stepped out into the gray, overcast light.

A woman stood at the railing of the cupola, looking out. She wore gray cotton pants and a shirt, which Charles thought must be terribly cold up here, high on the hill at the start of winter, but the woman did not seem bothered in the least. She half turned, and Charles saw her in profile, and her name almost flew from his mouth.

But he held his tongue. For the woman shifted her weight to one leg, bringing her other leg up in *arabesque*. Charles's heart clutched with the beauty of his daughter, oblivious to her audience of one, as she moved from position to position with grace and poise. First Position to Fifth. From Fifth, *fouetté en arabesque*, then *penché*. She danced like...Charles searched his mind for the right comparison. *Like a fallen leaf. She is the last leaf, fallen from the bare tree, dancing and twirling in the winter wind.* He was entranced by her movements, but suddenly she crouched low and sprang into a *grande jeté*, leaping high in the air. The cupola was only ten feet wide, and for a moment Charles thought she might leap clear off it, but of course she landed right in the center, her feet making hardly a thump on the floor.

"Dad, do you know what I've learned about dancing?"

"What's that?" Charles said, realizing his throat had dried up. He coughed to loosen it.

"Rising takes all of the effort. Coming back to the ground takes none. But it is in how you descend that you are judged. Land poorly, and no one cares how well you leaped."

"That's...that's true," Charles said. "I had not really thought of it."

"Why haven't you visited?"

Charles felt small and helpless. *With all this time, how have I not thought of a proper reply?*

"I...I'm sorry. I was very busy."

Charles hated himself for the answer. He wondered if Clara hated him too. Her only reply was silence. She went on dancing to whatever music was in her head. She danced from point to point on the floor. Azalea came up behind Charles and watched silently.

"How have you been, Clara?" Charles asked. "Are they taking good care of you here? I see you are still dancing."

Still, Clara did not reply.

"I spoke with your mother and sister a few months ago. They seem well."

Still, silence. Clara spun, then sprang up in a *fouetté jeté*. After landing, she whirled around, and he saw her face for the first time. It was twisted into a furious sneer. Then the look melted, and her face was placid and focused again.

"Why haven't you visited, Dad?" Clara said, and her voice was as youthful and effervescent as it had been when she was a girl. Now, Charles could not help but notice the vast differences between his two girls. Tamra, bone-weary and frustrated, shrunken into a diminished version of her young self. Clara, dropped in from the past, still fresh and buoyant.

"I was afraid, kid," he said, realizing his evasion and equivocations were useless here. What was the point of lying, even a little, to Clara in here?

"Of what?"

"Of you."

"Of me, or of my craziness?" Clara said. She spun in a fluid three hundred and sixty degrees, then with a little hop and swoop, looked like a bird trying to take flight.

"Never of you. I...I felt terribly guilty for placing you here. I still do."

There was another long silence. It made Charles twitchy.

"Guilty? Why?"

"I denied you a life!" Charles cried, his voice carrying over the hill. Azalea could hear and see him, but he didn't care. He stepped over to the railing and gripped it. He looked out. He had been right. The cupola gave him a marvelous view of the valley below. The rolling hills of brown grass and bare trees were immersed in clouds and mist. He could see a long way, but nothing beyond twenty feet away appeared in any clarity or detail. Tears stung his eyes.

"I thought you were going to be thrown out of the Plex, so I locked you up here. Mom said as much. I denied you the opportunity to grow up and live a life. I...I see that now. I didn't then. I did what I thought was best. I signed the papers and moved you here. And now a third of your life has gone by and you're stuck in this place."

"Am I unhappy?" Clara asked, in *plié.*

"I—I don't know—you look—"

"Dad. Look at me. Am I unhappy?"

And then, like the rays of the sun streaking out from behind a cloud, understanding came to Charles.

"No. You look joyous. Radiant."

And Mom and Tamra are not. I am not. Only you are.

"I dance every day. For hours. No one tells me not to. And so, what if I'm not at Lincoln Center anymore? If I lived out there, I wouldn't be dancing at all. You know it as well as I. Sometimes, all of the residents put on a show right down here, in the hall. I dance for them, for people I live with. I don't get paid, but it's nice. They like it. And I watch them sing and act and tell stories and recite poems up on the stage too. It's really nice."

"Poems?" Charles said. This made Clara stop dancing.

"I forgive you," she said.

"What?"

"For putting me here in Hopespring. I was mad at first, for a couple of years. But I wanted to dance more than I wanted to be angry, so the dancing sort of...ate up the anger. Just like the food we eat becomes part of our bodies, well, the anger became part of my dance. And now there's no anger left. Just dance. But I thought you might want to know that I forgive you. I forgave you long ago, so don't be burdened by it."

Burdened, Charles thought. It was not until Clara said the word that he recognized the feeling of enormous, invisible weight he had borne for so many years. Now it was lifted, he felt light, like he might dance too.

"Thank you," Charles said. Clara took his hand.

"Welcome. I'm glad you're here with me," she said.

"I'm glad too."

"No. You aren't, not yet. But you will be."

Lies evaporate here. I am too used to sneaking around, physically and verbally.

Clara walked over to Azalea.

"Do you have any pen and paper?" Clara asked her.

Azalea chuckled. "Do I have what?" Then she composed herself. Charles suspected it went against her training to laugh at her patients.

"I know, weird, right?" Clara said. "But my dad, he's pretty old. He used to write with pens and paper when he was younger, and I think he might prefer that to a flexscreen. Could you check?"

Azalea smiled and blushed.

"Of course."

Azalea turned and descended the stairs. Charles wanted to talk to Clara, to tell her so much and hear so much, but for several minutes she just danced and danced in the cupola, even lighter and freer than before. Finally, Azalea returned with a dozen sheets of lined paper and a handful of ballpoint pens.

"Found these downstairs. And there are plenty more," she said. She handed him the stationery.

"Thank you," Charles said. "But I don't know what it's for."

"Poems," Clara said. "Start writing."

"What?" Charles laughed. "Up here? Right now? I just got here."

"Why not here? Why not now? Do you have somewhere else to go?" Clara asked, and Charles laughed again.

He sat cross-legged. He held the paper down on the floor, with one hand, bracing it against the wind. He uncapped a ballpoint pen and examined the glistening ink at the tip. Fresh, blue ink. He put the tip of the pen to paper and tried to write a poem. A word. Any word. He tried to find the right word to be the first set down on paper in his life at Hopespring. But none came out.

"I can't," he said to Clara. "I teach poetry, but I am not a poet."

Clara smiled at him patiently.

"If I have learned anything here, Dad, it is that everyone has something inside them. Something to grow and share. You can write a poem. Maybe not now, but you can."

"I know what it is I have inside," Charles said. "It's teaching. That is what I have to share."

Clara stood and stretched and prepared to go back into position.

"It's a good thing you have an entire village here as your class. Hundreds, maybe thousands of people you can teach. Teach them how you want to. Teach them the way you know is best."

And then Clara went silent again, and Charles put down his pen and watched as she danced and danced in the winter air.

Sixteen: Song for the Dead

"Distance—a yawning chasm of it—exists between any two people. Oppressors keep people weak by keeping them separate. But we can build bridges to span the gap, and those bridges are made of words. So do not choose the words of the powerful. Choose your own words, and choose them well."

—*The Trough*, p.198

So, this is what surrender feels like. Jennifer sat in an uncomfortable office chair. She suspected it was deliberately hard and awkward with just enough forward lean to the seat that she could never quite relax. Not that she would have relaxed in this office, anyway.

It was not as if Geraldine Barfield could not afford nicer chairs, either. Her office was the largest room Jennifer had ever sat in. Gold columns and crystal chandeliers reflected the sunlight pouring in the penthouse office of the fifty-five-story building. The city—or rather, a series of Plexes—sprawled below. The floors were authentic marble. Decorative plants from all over the world sat in porcelain planters.

Jennifer was seated before a magnificent desk of polished oak, fourteen feet wide and four feet deep, but utterly bare. The desk was a formality, a symbol, Jennifer knew. Barfield would never sit and write. She would dictate her demands to her AIPA, most likely, and probably had not had to touch a screen in years. Her hands must have been as soft as baby skin.

Barfield was not in the room. Jennifer was alone.

She doubted she was truly alone. Surely two dozen cameras, sensors, and other devices monitored her every feature, from her face to her body temperature to her pulse. She tried to remain calm, but in such a place, at the desk of her one-time idol, it was impossible. Jennifer shut her eyes and practiced some relaxing breathing techniques that had guided her through stressful tests. Eyes closed. Breathe in through the nose, out the mouth. In one, out two. In two, out three. In three, out four. Repeat.

"I hope you have not fallen asleep!" a voice behind Jennifer said. It was a female voice, powerful and slightly sibilant, the type of voice that wakes people up at dull meetings and starts to grate on the nerves after the meeting drags on too long. It was a voice Jennifer recognized well. "You must have been up late studying!"

Jennifer opened her eyes and turned around. There she was. Geraldine Barfield appeared to be in her early fifties, with hair and makeup reflecting the most professional job of making her camera-worthy. She wore a knee-length dress whose seams were as thin and sharp as razor blades. Her shoes could bring kings to their knees. Impossibly, she appeared even more polished and produced in person than she did in her videos.

"Uh, yes," Jennifer began. And then she reminded herself, *I cannot be weak here. Barfield will sense it. And she will use it.*

"I'm sure you know me. I am Geraldine Barfield."

"A pleasure to finally meet you, Miss Barfield. I have admired you for a long time."

"Gerry, please," Barfield said. "I want you to be comfortable here."

Like hell you do.

"Why did you bring me here?" Jennifer asked.

"Can I bring you something? Water? Coffee? Grape soda?"

Jennifer shivered with discomfort and fear. Grape soda? Barfield must have pulled up a file with all her drink orders over the past six months or year. And between her and Melody, those had been the three most commonly ordered items.

And a coffee could be great right now. Barfield probably drank the finest nectar from the finest beans in all the mountains of the world. Her coffee was probably more expensive than Rosa's Plex apartment. The thought made Jennifer lose her urge for any.

"No," she replied. "I'm fine. If you don't mind, I am very busy with my studies and need to get back. So, when you're done kidnapping me..."

Barfield stood behind her desk and smiled. It was a reptilian smile.

"About that. Miss Calderón, have you noted your grade point average recently?"

Jennifer paused. She hadn't, not in weeks. Once it was no longer a Perfect Five, it stopped mattering to her.

"I've been too busy studying to check."

With the smile pinned on her face, Barfield stalked around the table, never breaking her gaze from Jennifer. Then she leaned against the desk and folded her hands in front of her. She towered over her, still smiling.

"Honey, there is no need to be dishonest with me. We are friends here, and this is a friendly chat. Honestly it is. But I am concerned for you and I have some questions for you. Your grade point average now is a 4.67. Still an excellent score, in the top ninety-sixth percentile, but quite a drop from what it was a few months ago. You once had the highest average of any student in America. Now, thousands of students across the country have passed you. What's going on? What happened?"

Jennifer never realized the human voice could be manipulated with such subtlety of tone. It was as if in one ear, her words were those of a concerned parent, or a confidante, someone who was gently guiding a wayward loved one back to the right path, but in the other ear was the voice of an interrogator.

Jennifer shrugged. "Distracted, I guess."

Barfield shook her head. "No, not you. I know you too well. You don't get distracted."

"I don't think you know me as well as you think you know me," Jennifer said.

"Oh, I do! I really do!" Barfield stood, animated again, and paced in a circle around Jennifer. "Jennifer, we—can I call you Jenny?"

"No one calls me that."

"Very well. We know so much about you, probably even more than you know about yourself. Your grades, of course, and your Achievement Levels, and your academic strengths and weaknesses. But we know how long you spend on each question, how long your retina pauses on each word or equation before answering, and which questions you went back and worked on again. We know what music you listened to while working, and what food and drink and pills you consumed. We know how long you slept. We know, for instance, that after logging approximately five and a half miles on the treadmill at Plex Your Muscles, you would go back and complete assignments that were twenty percent finished. Data, data, data. This is what makes EduForce great. We know so much about you and your habits that we can tailor an education specifically for you, for Jennifer Calderón. So, why are you throwing it away?"

Jennifer trembled a little. She kept her voice strong, sensing that Barfield would pick up on any wavering of tone. She did not want to step in any traps.

"Like I said, I became distracted. I got a boyfriend."

"Also, not true. We know about Melody Park. We know how much time you spent with her and she with you. We know about her sub-par scores, her reckless mistreatment of EduForce technologies, and frankly offensive replies to questions, about her cycles of work and laziness, and about how her life ended. But she cannot have been the distraction, not all of it, because you were with her for nearly a year before your grades dropped. It was something else."

Now Jennifer began to sense that she did not have to look out for traps. She was already in one and Barfield was only pulling it tighter.

"Okay, it wasn't Melody," Jennifer said. She would not give up Mr. Winston. She didn't know what had happened to him, or where he was, but she would not give anything about him away. "I...started experimenting with pills. I know it's wrong because drugs are bad, but Melody got me to try them and I stopped caring about school."

I bought the pills. Melody bought pills. That story should fit their purchase records.

Barfield cocked her head slightly to the right, her smile turning sad and pitiful.

"Oh, how awful!" she said. "We had no idea how bad an influence on you Melody was. Now that we know, we can help. You will be in a rehabilitation program by the day's end, and back on track to graduation in no time. All paid for by us, of course."

"Thank you," Jennifer said, unsure what such a program would mean. She was also unnerved by Barfield's constant use of "we." They were the only two in the room, but Jennifer sensed the presence and pressure of much greater forces at Barfield's back.

"Candy?" Barfield said, offering a little glass dish to Jennifer with a colorful assortment of hard candies. *Like a grandmother would have done. Or at least a stereotypical little white grandmother from a movie. My abuela would probably give me a whack with her* chancletas *as soon as she would give me candy.*

Jennifer took one, unwrapped it, and popped it into her mouth. For a frantic few seconds, she worried she had made a mistake. *What if Barfield poisoned these?* Barfield would have no reason to kill Jennifer, and the idea was wildly contrived and ridiculous, like something out of a bad movie, but something about Barfield made Jennifer think poisoning children would not be impossible for her.

The candy, it turned out, was just a butterscotch.

"Thank you," she mumbled around the candy. Barfield stopped circling and stood before her again.

"Tell me about Charles Winston."

Perhaps it was a coincidence. It had to have been; no one could plan it so perfectly. But as Barfield asked the question, a slant of sunlight that had crept across the room beamed right into Jennifer's face. Bright white and yellow light filled Jennifer's vision, and she twisted to one side to avoid it. Even as she shielded her eyes, bright fireworks obscured her vision. She blinked, held her eyes shut, and rubbed her fists into them, but still her sight would not return fully. Tears came to her eyes. Jennifer sat steady to regain her composure, but after a few seconds she was bleary eyed and embarrassed, and she sat crookedly in the chair to avoid the sunlight again.

"Sorry. The sun. My eyes," she croaked.

"Tell me about Charles Winston."

"I don't know who—"

"Tell me about Charles Winston."

Jennifer wanted to get up, move around, anything to avoid the blinding light that flooded her face and pierced her eyes. She tried to stand up, but Barfield put a gentle, firm hand on her shoulder and pushed her back into the light.

"You have nowhere to go and nothing to hide. You are not in trouble. Tell me about Charles Winston."

I can't lie to her. She knows when I lie. But maybe I can give her enough truth to throw her off.

"Melody was the one who met Mister Winston. She dragged me along a couple of times to hear what he had to say. It didn't make any sense. Only your video modules and edugames make sense, because you make learning easy and make learning fun."

"Other than that?" Barfield asked.

"Other than that, nothing. Like I said, Melody got me into some pills that made it hard for me to keep focused, but Melody is gone now and I'm not getting any more pills and I'm sure your rehabilitation program will really help me get better."

Saying the words sickened Jennifer. *Melody is gone.* The pain was still so fresh and raw that she could not see and feel all of it at once. But Melody was gone, no denying it, and Jennifer felt guilty for pulling her into the lies. *Not that Melody would have cared.*

"Oh, it will," Barfield said. "All better. But it won't work until you tell me all of the truth. Now you see, we have records that the three of you, plus two other individuals, left Plex 87 several months ago and took the Sol-Train to Mahwah. Winston foolishly ret-scanned into the train with his own eye, not an eye file. Then there are no records of you for the entire day, and you returned the next morning. So, what happened to you out in the forest? Did Charles Winston sexually molest you?"

"What? No!" Jennifer replied, and she could not help laughing aloud at the very thought. "He just..."

"He just what?"

Time for more truth. A little.

"Melody and I wanted him to show us what a school looked like. We were curious. He didn't want to, but Melody and I pressured him to show us a school. So, we took the Sol-Train there for the day and he showed us. We didn't go in or anything. That would be dangerous."

"Why did you stay overnight?"

"We...we got lost. Sorry. None of us get out of the Plex very much, and we walked through their town and it got dark, so we slept in an empty...I don't know what it was called. A big building with rooms for people to sleep."

"Hotel," Barfield said.

"Yes, that's right. A hotel. We slept there for the night and he brought us back the next day. It didn't think it would be breaking any rules."

"Break the rules? No, not technically. But you don't have to break rules to behave unusually. And what you did was very unusual, and therefore, very concerning. Now, I am going to ask you another question, and I need your absolute honesty for this. Very much depends upon it. Do you think you can tell me the truth?"

"Of course. I want to help," Jennifer said. The last of the candy dissolved, leaving a cloying taste in her mouth. She wanted another. Meanwhile, the sunbeam had moved a few inches to the side, and her vision returned to normal.

"What did Charles Winston tell you about schools?"

Everything, Jennifer thought. *He told us about the old ways and the new ones.*

"He didn't say much—"

Barfield held up her hand, and for a flash, Jennifer thought she saw a hairline crack in her easygoing façade. A little facial tic of impatience, nothing more.

"Please, Miss Calderón. There are sensors in your chair, and the moment I asked you the question, your heart rate increased by fifteen percent and your blood pressure rose ten points. Your body temperature by two degrees. We know what you are going to say before the words come out of your mouth. Therefore, it makes the most sense to tell us the words that reflect what we already know about you. Those words are called the truth. Tell us the truth. What did Charles Winston tell you about school?"

Jennifer paused. She was not giving into this woman, no matter how much she had admired her in the past, and no matter how much she dreaded and loathed her now.

"A little. Nothing important."

Barfield bowed her head. She looked over to a built-in screen in the nearest wall.

"Fran, bring up the file on Charles Winston."

Barfield's AIPA said nothing in reply, but the screen lit up instantaneously, and an image of Charles appeared, along with a column of text to the right of his face.

"Thank you, Fran," said Barfield. Then she walked over to the screen. She could have had Fran read for her. Fran was probably such an expensive, highly adapted AIPA that she could read with every bit of foreboding intonation Barfield would use, but Jennifer suspected Barfield wanted to keep the control herself. She looked at the text and began to read.

"Charles Winston served as a traditional school teacher of tenth and twelfth grade students, ages sixteen to nineteen, beginning in the year 2018. Records indicate that he served capably but without distinction. At the time of the dissolution of his school in 2034, Winston was offered a post as an essay reviewer with EduForce. Though he initially rejected the offer, he soon accepted it and began his work with EduForce. There too, he reviewed essays at a satisfactory rate and accuracy.

"EduForce officials first flagged Winston's activity in 2048 when it was discovered that he had self-published a volume by the title of *The Trough* which promoted strongly anti-EduForce and anti-progress ideas. EduForce officials tracked down and eradicated most copies of the book, though a few remain unaccounted for. Winston had sold only seven hundred and thirty-eight copies, and by 2050, all but eighteen had been destroyed. Though the remaining copies could not be located, EduForce officials declared the case closed, as Winston had displayed no other instances of subversive behavior.

"In the year 2051, Charles Winston was found to have used EduForce software to contact a student by the name of Melody Park for purposes that—"

Barfield stopped reading and smiled again. Jennifer began to realize each smile of hers was different. It was like choosing a different pair of shoes for each outfit. This smile dripped with condescension.

"Well, I don't have to read anymore. You can pick up the story from here."

Barfield prowled over to Jennifer, like a cat closing in on a wounded mouse. But when she stood before Jennifer, she reached out with a gentle hand on her shoulder.

"Jennifer dear, the things that man told you are poison for your mind. I want to set you straight. That is why you need to tell me all he said."

Still, Jennifer did not speak.

"Fine," snapped Barfield. "Just listen then. But listen closely. There is no test on this, but the course of the rest of your life is at stake. Charles Winston is from an old generation. I am part of that generation too, but I have always looked forward. He looks to the past. I seek solutions while he seeks whatever is familiar. People like him whine when things change in the world. Whiners accomplish nothing. I, on the other hand, accomplished the greatest revolution in education since the printing press.

"Allow me to dismantle a few of the lies he must have told you. He probably said studying with a teacher is better than studying with video modules and edugames. He said there was no substitute for having a teacher in front of you. Let me ask you, how many times has your flexscreen accidentally brushed up against you or cupped your breasts? How many video modules have ogled you as you leaned over? How many edugames have offered to give you a perfect score if you met them after school in a dark, locked room and didn't tell anyone?"

Jennifer said nothing.

"How many?" barked Barfield, and Jennifer jumped.

"None!" she blurted out. Her heart started racing.

"In the days of classrooms, these things happened all the time. Perverted teachers groping at their students, forcing them into sex acts and blackmailing them into silence. Coaches molesting players. Principals using their power to get what they wanted from defenseless children. And this happened every day! But now, with the new way, not one student has ever been harmed by a teacher. What else did he tell you?"

Jennifer was losing her grip and could not play aloof much longer.

"He said being in a class with other students was better than sitting in our rooms alone. He said learning with other people is part of the experience of being in school."

In the time Jennifer spoke, Barfield's expression changed again. Now it was soft and maternal. She walked over to Jennifer and knelt beside her. She held Jennifer's cheeks in her hands.

"Oh, but it isn't. And you, of all students, have benefited from the new way. When you learn, you learn at your own pace. And you learn faster than any student in the history of EduForce. Now imagine sitting in a class with twenty-five other students. Every one of those students is slower than you. Dumber than you. The teacher moves slowly, working with the dimwits, trying to get them to grasp a concept. You sit there, patiently, tapping your pencil and waiting for him to teach you something new. What a terrible waste of time! EduForce has made the ultimate customizable education. Back in the day it was called differentiation. Teachers had to prepare different lessons for students of different abilities, but it was crude and time-consuming. EduForce is scientifically tailored to provide the perfect education for you."

"But when Mister Winston showed us the building," Jennifer said, realizing she might give away too much, "I was interested. Mister Winston said there was something sacred about that space for teachers and students. I thought it might be fun to go to a place where everyone learns together. Nicer than staying in my room."

The gentle smile left Barfield's face. Her expression became cold and distant. It was the look of someone drowning in pain and memory. She stood. She put her hands behind her back and walked to the window. When she spoke, her voice was a register lower, dirge-like.

"Fun. Nice. Let me tell you about the school buildings. Your sacred spaces. They were spaces of death. They were traps. Shooting galleries for murderers. In your video modules, I am sure you read about Columbine High School. Sandy Hook Elementary? Scarsdale Central Schools?"

"Yes, of course."

"What do you know about those places?"

"In Columbine, two boys planned an attack on their school, then brought guns to school and shot a bunch of students and teachers. Then at Sandy Hook, some crazy guy broke into a school and shot and killed some little kids and teachers. Then in Scarsdale, a whole group of kids planned attacks in several schools at once, so while the police in town were drawn to one school, the shooters massacred people in the other schools. That was the deadliest attack ever."

"And the last," said Barfield, her voice cracking. "I would not allow it to happen again. At that time, EduForce was a new corporation and we were just getting into educational software and curriculum development. My ex-husband and I were very happy. Our son was a freshman in high school. Scarsdale High School."

There, her voice trailed off. Jennifer sat in total stillness, not even daring to breathe. She could not tell, but it appeared Barfield might've been crying. After a few moments, she shuddered, took a deep breath, and continued, her words projected against the glass she stood before.

"After our boy's funeral, I knew EduForce had to take the lead in making sure not one more child was killed in a school. We had the software and the vision. The highway system collapsed, the fuel crisis reached critical mass, and the Plex system started spreading across the country. Suburbs vanished. People moved into their new Plex apartments. The infrastructure was in place. The public mood was in place. So, we flipped around the country's ideas on education. Rather than sending the kids to school, we sent school to the kids. And they could learn everything in the safety of their family's care.

"Charles Winston didn't exaggerate the truth. He didn't sugarcoat the past. He lied to you. He has been on a twisted crusade his entire life to halt the progress of education, to keep things the way they were when he was a child. So, he assembled a group of impressionable young people with bright futures and no way of knowing his intent and started training you to be his protégés. But he was basing his entire enterprise on a past that never existed, a magical time of learning and cooperation and good feelings. No, Jennifer. Before EduForce, public education in America was an abusive, inefficient waste of time, an institution that was abandoning children, neglecting children, and letting them get butchered but refused to adapt. We have solved that. I have solved that."

Barfield turned around. Her eyes were red, and empathy pulled at Jennifer's heart.

"I didn't know," was all Jennifer could say. Barfield smiled again, the pitying, condescending one.

"Of course, you didn't. How could you? After the Scarsdale Massacre, and the names of the dead, passed into history, I stopped mentioning my son. I didn't want to use him as a mascot for my cause. But his death became the furnace, the forge, for my cause. That's figurative language, by the way. It means—"

"I understand."

"Of course. Well, everything I have done, I have done for him. Every waking moment of my life has been devoted to keeping America's children safe and providing them the education they deserve. That is the side of history I am on. Charles Winston is on the other."

"Oh."

Barfield walked over to her desk again and this time reached into a drawer. From it, she pulled out a flexscreen, one of the slimmest and highest-definition Jennifer had ever seen. Barfield touched the screen, tapped a few icons, then turned it around and slid it to Jennifer.

"I would like you to read the terms of this agreement. I have never made a student an offer like this before, but I have never had a student like you before. Read."

Jennifer read the contract. With each line, her mind spun faster and faster. Her breath caught in her throat. At the end, she looked up at Barfield.

"Why?" she said, her voice coming out in a squeak.

"Because you need us, and we need you. I fear the events of the last few months have driven Jennifer Calderón and Geraldine Barfield apart, but we need each other."

"I don't understand."

"Not long ago, you were making history. You had perfection in your grasp. We will announce the drop in your grade was due to a software glitch and return your score to a five point zero. A Perfect Five. It will be up to you to maintain that grade, but you and I know you are capable of it. In exchange for the adjustment to your grade, you will agree to interviews every three months until you graduate, then a media gala and appearance in a documentary feature about your achievement. Our marketing division had great, great plans with you prior to this little interruption in your work. Think about it. A Perfect Five in exchange for smiling before the camera a few times. If you like this arrangement, then lean in and let the retinal scan record your agreement with the contract. If you don't, well, go back to Plex 87 and your mediocre grades."

Jennifer reread the contract two times, three times. She understood the terms perfectly. But the right choice? Charles would tell her not to agree, that agreeing with Barfield was surrender. Melody would have told her not to agree, to throw the flexscreen in Barfield's face and tell her to fuck herself with a toilet scrub brush. But Charles was not here. Melody wasn't, either. This was all Jennifer's decision. And there were some emotional reasons to reject the offer, but no logical ones. The Perfect Five. She could have it again, and Barfield was right. Maintaining it would be easy. And in exchange for some free publicity for EduForce. She had nothing to lose and everything to gain.

Jennifer leaned in.

Then she leaned back.

Wait. She needs me more than I need her. The Perfect Five means nothing to me but pride. I can get something of true value.

"Well?" Barfield asked.

Jennifer sat up straighter, pulled her shoulders back, and stared at Barfield as an equal. If they were going to negotiate, it would be as equals, as adults.

"The Perfect Five is nothing," she said. "It doesn't get me anywhere. It doesn't make my life any better. It doesn't make me any wealthier or get me a better job. What job could I get with a 5.0 that I couldn't get with a 4.6? I want something more."

"What?" Barfield's voice was a mixture of grudging and incredulity.

"The Scholarship."

Barfield said nothing.

"I applied. I wrote a fantastic essay. I was rejected in the initial round. If, as you say, I am so precious to EduForce, if I have done what no student has ever done before, then I should be rewarded for it. All my life as a student, I was working toward the Scholarship. Not the Perfect Five, really, that just happened as a side effect. But the Scholarship to a real university, that was what I'd always wanted. And that is what it'll cost you for me to cooperate."

Barfield stared at her a long time. Jennifer presumed she was sizing her up, guessing her motivations, seeing if she was bluffing. But Jennifer was doing the same to Barfield. *She's scared. She's scared because no one has ever countered one of her offers. And she's scared because she knows I know she needs my help more than I need hers.*

"It isn't that simple," Barfield said.

"It isn't? Please explain to me," Jennifer said. She could not believe herself. She could not believe she was speaking to her one-time idol, more-recent nemesis, with such impertinence. But it felt good.

"Well the final decision for the Scholarship, it's out of my hands—"

"Are you saying you don't have the authority to decide who wins?" Jennifer's face went flush, but she was not backing down.

"Of course, I have authority!" Barfield snapped. Then she sighed and pinched the bridge of her nose. "The other winners have already been notified. We can't take a scholarship from one of them."

"Then grant me a special one for my special situation. The money must be out there. Look, Miss Barfield. Gerry. Either you engineer a way to get me the Scholarship, so I can go to a true university and maximize my potential, like all your slogans say, or I walk out of here, go back home to my life, finish my degree, and you find some other mascot with a Perfect Five. Who doesn't exist."

Barfield snatched the flexscreen out from Jennifer's hand. She jabbed at it with her finger and typed furiously on its surface. Barfield could have asked Fran to add to the text, but Jennifer suspected letting the words come out of her lips was too embarrassing. She flipped the screen around and handed it to Jennifer.

"There. Better?"

Jennifer read the new terms. Barfield had added a line granting Jennifer a full scholarship to any university of her choice in the United States. She held the flexscreen up to her face, the retinal scanner blinked, and a message flashed over the image of the contract: *Signature Received.*

Jennifer handed the flexscreen back to Barfield.

"Here," she said to the President of EduForce. "Please send me a copy of it as soon as possible. Now if you don't mind, I have to get back to study."

JENNIFER CALDERÓN STARED into the screen, annoyed and bored. Little shapes and numbers flashed before her eyes, darting around the screen and exploding in tiny bursts of color and sound each time she correctly answered a question. She had always found edugames easy, but now they were so easy she was almost embarrassed to be playing them. Before, the games had consumed her entire attention as she played. Now, they were mental background noise to her other thoughts and plans.

This is stupid, she thought. But then, like any well trained EduForce student, she knew more points were granted for better vocabulary. "Stupid" was not the vocabulary of a student nearing Achievement Level Sixteen. Surely, better synonyms existed. *Vapid. Inane. Insipid.* But other words applied to the games, as well. *Pernicious. Malign. Insidious.* The Jennifer of old would think of synonyms as interchangeable parts. Remove simple word. Locate most advanced synonym possible. Plug into sentence.

But Jennifer now saw the words differently. The English language had no true synonyms. Each word carried with it a history, colorations, implications, connotations. Which word best described the edugames? Perhaps not just one of them. Perhaps they all had to; perhaps the things being described by words were too complex to affix single labels to them. Perhaps edugames were all those things, empty and sneaky and dangerous. Perhaps they were just stupid.

Jennifer resisted the pull in her brain. If she became too engrossed in an edugame, she paused it and walked away. Once, she'd sought out the burst, the rush in her mind that came with accomplishing tasks in the games. Now, apathy cut through her mind like dry canals. Loathing replaced love. Disgust replaced desire.

She paused the game and shook her head. She took a long drink from a tall glass of water. *Have to keep my mind fresh. Tonight is the big night.*

She sat on the edge of her bed. She still lived in Rosa's apartment. Her mother would always be her mother. And she would always be Rosa's daughter. They had not reconciled, not in any lasting way. Melody's name had not been mentioned once in the months since her death. It created an atmosphere of uneasy civility in the Calderón apartment. When Jennifer earned her Achievement Level Sixteen, probably sometime in late spring, she would pack her belongings and move to wherever she chose to go to college. Her current preferred choice was Stanford University, as it was the geographically furthest from Plex 87.

She had also figured out how to appease Rosa. One day, not long after Melody's death, Jennifer had announced to her mother she had found several old books at an estate sale, and she was taking them to the Recycling Center. There were six books in total—a couple of chemistry and biology textbooks, two beaten-up literature anthologies, and two geometry books. Rosa had been overjoyed, or at least as much as she could be coming off a sixteen-hour shift. Jennifer took the books to Recycling and brought back every penny—well, gave every cent that had been deposited into her account—to her mother. This had pleased Rosa, and Jennifer found if she was more diligent about keeping her room tidy, her mother never came in to clean in and discover things. Things such as the remainder of the books Charles had left her, buried under her bed and in her closet and even in the air conditioning vents.

When she was not working on her edugames, video models, and polishing the Perfect Five, Jennifer read. She devoured literature first, then migrated to textbooks. Some of the science was outdated, and America had had another half dozen presidents since the history books were printed, but there was something about having all of the book's content available to her at all times. The book wasn't customized to her specific needs and strengths. It was up to her to look something up, to push through challenging parts. If she got a question wrong in the textbook, no chirpy little guides offered suggestions. No tutorial modules popped up to walk her through it. She had to figure it out. Melody would have praised it as very retro and grip. Jennifer thought it was painful and frustrating, and she clung to every bit of it.

Jennifer glanced at the corner of the screen. 5.0/5.0. She winked at it.

She had already done two interview features for Geraldine Barfield. She had put on makeup, smiled into her flexscreen camera, and answered the reporters' questions. The stories were gaining increasing viewership, and Jennifer could foresee that as she neared completion of her highest Achievement Level, the scrutiny and attention would increase. Perhaps she would become a national sensation. Jennifer didn't mind as much as she thought she would. The interviews and attention were...nothing. Empty. They were like the edugames, full of light and sound but ultimately just entertainment. And if they got her entry into University, then she would keep smiling and answering questions.

The one thing she would not talk about was Melody.

Some reporter must have made the connection between her and Melody. Or maybe he had obtained footage or other records. Or maybe Barfield had fed him the information and encouraged him to ask her about Melody purely out of malice. Jennifer refused. She said Melody had been her dear friend who was deeply troubled and now she was dead and that was all she would say about it. The reporter used Melody's suicide to spin tragedy into Jennifer's story, to make it seem as if Melody's death had spurred Jennifer forward to her accomplishments. The irony, of course, was those accomplishments had all been made when Melody was alive, and now Melody was gone, the accomplishments she had made since had been a sham, a phony perfect score that was the product of a backroom deal. But Jennifer didn't care. As long as it got her out of Plex 87 and into University, she would endure all of the banality Barfield could throw her way.

Besides, she had greater plans.

Jennifer shut off the screen. The clock said 11:15 P.M. It was time. She showered, dressed, and tucked some things into a messenger bag. Her flexscreen. Her laptop, fully charged. One of the other laptops from the high school, also charged. Charles's anthology of British Poetry. A few sheets of paper and pens from Charles. A thermos of coffee. She slung the messenger bag over her shoulder, left her room, and said good night to her mother, who was in her chair.

"Where you go?" Rosa asked.

"Out, Mamá," Jennifer replied. "I'll be back late."

"You stay out of trouble. Be a good girl."

"You know me," Jennifer said. Then she left, thinking of how little her mother truly knew her.

As Jennifer walked along the corridor, trying to look inoffensive and nondescript, she reflected on how much work she had put into this night. How much planning and deception and secret communication. How many minds she had to change and prying eyes she had to avoid. All for tonight.

The idea had come to her shortly after her interview or interrogation with Barfield. It was on the Sol-Train on the way back home. She had been thinking about Melody and Charles and about her dirty bargain with Barfield, and she had been overcome with an overwhelming sense of inadequacy, that she would be a disappointment to both her dead lover and former teacher.

Agreeing to Barfield's contract had been selfish, so she decided to balance it with something selfless. The idea came to her naturally and easily. And so, when she returned to her mother's apartment and recycled the books and cleaned her room and got back on track with her video modules and edugames, the whole time, her mind was working on something else too.

The first person she asked was Jean Paul. But he was too busy with his new job. The second person she tried to reach was Peter. He did not answer any messages—vague ones, such as "How are you? Write me back." and "Got to talk." Finally, she walked to where she remembered his apartment was, on a far side of Plex 87 in one of the larger apartments.

Jennifer pressed the doorbell. An unfamiliar woman answered, slurping on a can of cola.

"Yes?"

"Hello, is this the Yakey family?" Jennifer asked. The woman scrunched her face.

"They don't live here no more." the woman said. She belched, then went on. "Rich folks. Used to be off-Plexers, never did get the shine off their asses for thinking they were better than the rest of us. But they're gone now."

"Gone?" Jennifer said.

"Adios. I used to live next door but put in a claim for their place, and I made the highest bid. Now it's mine. Has a window with a view of the Sol-Train."

"Where did they go?" Jennifer asked.

The woman grinned.

"Y'saw on the NewsFeed? About that sicko, the teacher?"

"Charles Winston," Jennifer replied automatically.

"That's him. Well the kid, Phil or something—"

"Peter. He's the one I'm looking for."

The woman did not appear to like being interrupted.

"Yeah. Peter. That one. Well he must've known the old perv, God knows why. Once the reward reached half a million, he called the Plex Police, told them where he lived, and by the end of the week they were packing up to move off-Plex again. Rich bastards."

I hope you're enjoying your green lawns, Jennifer thought. She thanked the woman and left.

With Jean Paul and Peter out, Jennifer went to her favorite coffee shop to sit and think and caffeinate. She went late at night, when Oscar, who had talked with her about diaries while Jennifer had tried to work on her poem, and who had marveled at her laptop, was working. He remembered her and greeted her warmly. She returned the kindness. Then she reached into her bag and pulled out Melody's laptop. She handed it to Oscar. "This is for you. It belonged to someone dear to me, so take good care of it. Put down your darkest, wildest thoughts in here. No one but you has to know what they are." She had already transcribed Melody's writing—which had been substantial—onto her own laptop, then erased everything from Melody's. Oscar's eyes had goggled with gratitude and awe.

"What can I give you in return?" he asked.

"Simple," Jennifer had replied. "You write. I will be coming back here in a few months. And one night, I will come for you, and you will follow me and share what you have written."

This was that night.

Jennifer was brimming with excitement as she walked. This was not the artificial, jittery excitement the edugames had once brought her. This was genuine joy, arising from the marrow of her bones. She wanted to run and leap, but she walked. She walked to the coffee shop and found Oscar there alone. Knowing his shift was over, she nodded to him and he nodded to her. He took off his apron and slung a bag over his shoulder. Jennifer hoped that Melody's laptop was inside, and hoped too that it was full of Oscar's thoughts.

The pair walked side by side, not speaking. Jennifer checked the time: 11:47. They kept their pace cool and casual. Jennifer was sure the eyes of cameras were all over them. Maybe Geraldine Barfield was sitting in her office right now, watching a feed of Jennifer strolling down the corridor of Plex 87 with a strange companion, and wondering where they were going. *I hope you are watching. I hope the not knowing is driving you mad.*

When they stopped at the crematorium, memory drove through Jennifer like a cold icicle. This was not a place she wanted to be. But it was the right place. She checked the time again: 11:57. She rang the bell and the door opened for them. Jennifer and Oscar entered and there was the receptionist who had been there the night Melody was cremated. Jennifer cocked her head, silently asking a question. The receptionist shook her head no. Jennifer and Oscar stood silently in the waiting room.

Jennifer had come to the crematory again after Melody's funeral. She had offered a laptop to the receptionist and said, "You seem like someone who wants to write things down so other people can't see."

The receptionist declined, however. She explained that her grandfather had taught her handwriting, and she wrote everything she wrote on paper. Paper was safer than electronics, she argued. And she explained that two nights each month when the record keeping programs needed to run self-diagnostics and self-maintenance, the crematory workers ended their shift at midnight. So, on those nights, she locked herself in the room and wrote poems and stories in her notebook. There were cameras in the corridor and waiting room and receptionist's office, but none in the room with the chute. "I guess the Plex Police figure that once you're in here, you aren't likely to cause much trouble," the receptionist said.

Jennifer had begged to know more. She let her guard down for a moment and explained that she too enjoyed writing. The receptionist offered to let Jennifer—and any other like-minded people—use the room those two nights per month, if she were included. Jennifer laughed and said yes. She almost leaped up and hugged her. She asked the receptionist her name.

"Numinous," she said. Jennifer looked at her curiously.

"As in, holy and mysterious?" she said.

"I prefer to think 'holy shit, that chick is mysterious!' But yeah."

"Did your parents pick that name?" Jennifer asked, not caring if she was being rude. But Numinous laughed.

"Of course not. They picked the name 'Jennifer' for me. How boring! I'm an adult and if I want to be called Numinous or Mickey Mouse or Pickle Fuck Sandwich, I get to decide that."

Jennifer thought, with a mixture of sorrowful longing and jealous protectiveness, of Melody.

Now, the two crematory laborers emerged from the long room with the wall-length table. They ret-scanned to sign out for the night, gave Numinous a wave of goodbye to her, then left. If they noticed Jennifer and Oscar there, they did not acknowledge them. *I wouldn't either if my job was to push corpses down chutes all day. I would go home, go to sleep, and have some nightmares.*

With the door shut, Numinous sighed and relaxed.

"All ours," she said. "Please. Come into my palace."

Jennifer looked at her closely for the first time. She was young, probably two or three years older than Jennifer. Her hair was dark, like Melody's had been, but short and spiky. Thick glasses made her eyes appear to bulge out a bit. She was wearing a work uniform, as she had to being an employee of the Plex, but Jennifer noticed odd alterations to it. In particular, she noticed threads sewn into the seams of her uniform. Red thread ran around the cuffs of her sleeves. Along her thigh was a ribbon of green. The shoulder seam hid a streak of purple. There was no discernible purpose for these threads, and they were certainly in violation of the uniform policy. There was no reason to modify her uniform other than to be insubordinate. Jennifer's admiration for the woman swelled.

The trio entered the long room with the wall-length table. Jennifer felt a jolt, not of memory this time, but of shock. Four containers still remained in queue, waiting to be cremated.

"Aren't the workers going to...take care of these?" Jennifer asked.

Numinous waved a dismissive hand.

"Their shift was up. The workers, not the bodies. Well, I guess their shift was up too, as it were. But don't worry about them. They'll keep us company."

"Okay," Jennifer said, trying to sound nonchalant while standing ten feet from some corpses. "Let's get started."

Numinous produced three folding chairs. Oscar sat in one and withdrew Melody's laptop. Jennifer sat in the next one and powered on her laptop. Numinous had a notebook. The three sat and looked at one another.

"I think we should say something before we start," Jennifer said.

"How about this?" Numinous said. "There once was a man from Nantucket, who—"

Jennifer held up her hand.

"Please. I want this to be fun. But I also want this to be serious. Because this evening is happening because of several people who are not here now. Tonight's evening of poetry is in honor of Melody Park, my dark spot, who ruined me and saved me. Of Charles Winston, a cranky, bitter old man who cared so much about teaching children that he risked and lost his livelihood for us. Of Jean Paul Alvarez, a quiet and gentle soul who didn't care about poetry one bit but cared about people, about his abuela. Of Peter Yakey, a sneaky little traitor who sold out our teacher and taught me what happens when you value your own happiness over the safety of others. And of Rosa Calderón, mi mamá, who has worked so hard to provide for me that it has ruined her, and almost ruined our family. And of Juan Carlos Calderón, mi papá, whose life was the lie that my life has been built around. Without any of you, without all of you, this night would not be happening."

Her words echoed against the tiles.

"Who begins?" she said. When no one volunteered, she pointed to Oscar.

"Ever since you told me that you did not dare tell me what you thought about, I had to know. I can sense it about you, Oscar. You have worlds inside you."

Oscar blushed. Though he was older than Jennifer—he had to be if he was working—he seemed like a shy little boy.

"Okay, I don't write poetry. But I wrote a story. It's short. Want to hear it?"

"Yes!" Numinous said. She sat cross-legged in the folding chair, arms crossed over her chest. Jennifer looked on.

"It isn't done yet."

"Then share what you have," Jennifer said.

"And there isn't a point to it. Or a lesson. Like stories are supposed to have."

"Stories don't work that way," Jennifer said. "Not real ones."

Oscar cleared his throat.

"The crowned prince Gorriel lived in the kingdom of Yag. His father, the King Pexian, was a cruel tyrant who sought to shear all the forests of the land to build a fleet of ships, so that he might conquer the neighboring kingdom of Munth. Day and night, Pexian sent out thousands of serfs with axes to fell the mighty oaks and pines of the land, and then to strip the branches, and drag the logs back to the river, so they might be shipped to the mills and turned into boards. Day and night, the axes and saws sang in the night, and the forests cried.

"But Gorriel loved the trees, and each night when his father thought he slept in the castle, he snuck into the sacred forests and communed with the spirits who dwelt within. He told them of the king's plans and warned them to find another home. They cried that they knew no other home, that as forest spirits they needed the shelter of trunk and branch and twig and leaf. Gorriel cried for them, and in the very place where his tears hit the forest floor, a beautiful nymph sprang from the leaves.

Gorriel fell instantly in love as he stared at the lovely creature. He asked, 'What is your name?'"

Then Oscar stopped.

"What was her name?" Numinous asked. Oscar shrugged.

"I don't know. That's all I have. I worked really hard on it."

"Come ooooon," whined Numinous.

"When we come back in two weeks, Oscar, we want to know the end of that story. Will it be ready?" Jennifer asked. Oscar grinned and nodded his head vigorously.

"Definitely! I'm getting more ideas already!"

"Quick! Write them down!" Jennifer said.

"Where?"

"Anywhere! If an idea comes to you, don't let it get away. It won't come again."

Oscar clacked at the keys for a few seconds. Then he looked at what he wrote and smiled. He sighed.

"So, what's going to happen next?" Numinous asked.

"You'll have to wait two weeks to find out," Oscar said, and Numinous harrumphed.

Just then the buzzer rang. All three looked at the door. Numinous signaled everyone to stay silent and still.

The buzzer rang again.

What if it's the Plex Police? Jennifer wondered. What if Barfield had, in fact, been watching her, and sent EduForce police to break them up? Her Scholarship would be revoked, that much was sure. The consequences would probably be worse than that too. And for Oscar and Numinous? Had she invited them into a life-ruining ambush?

The buzzer rang a third time. Numinous stood up. *I have to,* she mouthed. Then she went to her desk and remotely unlocked and opened it.

In stepped Jean Paul Alvarez. He wore his Plex 87 Maintenance uniform. Under one arm he carried a black laptop.

"Am I too late?" he said. Jennifer ran over and embraced him.

"Quick, come in!" Jennifer said. "But you have to read."

"I want to read."

He sat on the floor without complaint. Jennifer wanted to ask him so much, how he was, how his abuela was, how he liked his new job, if he knew what Peter had done. But more than anything, she wanted to hear his poem.

He powered on his laptop, and without preamble, read.

"Mi abuela

Mi abuela don't speak no inglés,

But she been carin' for me all my days.

I come to her a broken boy

Now I'm a man 'cause of what she says.

She says 'Mi caro,

Te quiero,

Your dignity is worth more than el dinero.'

Growing up a poor boy, poor man,

I still feel the richest in the land.

I got my family, I got my friends,

I got my pride, and in the end

That's all I got to make my stand."

"I've worked on that every night," he said. "And I'm gonna keep writing more poems."

"Will you be back in two weeks?" Numinous asked.

"Of course."

"Damn right, you will," Numinous said. She flipped open her notebook. "My turn?"

Jennifer gestured for her to proceed.

"The tadpole grew into a frog

And the piglet grew into a hog.

The well-endowed lad

Said 'I'm certainly glad

That my toothpick grew into a log.'"

Silence. Then Numinous cackled and slapped her thigh.

"What?" asked Oscar.

"Funny, right?" Numinous said. "I've written hundreds of them here."

"Mister Winston said limericks are comic verse," Jennifer said. "Why are you writing them in the Plex crematory?"

"What better place?" Numinous returned, and Jennifer could not argue. *And,* she had to admit, *the poem was pretty funny.*

"All right, more limericks next time," she said.

Numinous gave a mock salute.

"Aye, aye."

Now everyone looked at Jennifer. She looked into their eyes. They were hopeful and expectant. She felt a flutter of nervousness. She had gone from reluctant follower, to eager practitioner, to daring leader. Of poetry. She didn't feel daring. She didn't feel special. But she knew she was. America knew her as the perfect student. In a few months' time, she would be heading off to Palo Alto. Maybe these three people would continue reading poems without her. Maybe not. But she had started something, and she knew down to her spine that reading stories and poetry with these three friends for a few months would be a far greater accomplishment than all the splashy news stories about her Perfect Five.

Jennifer looked at her laptop. But just then, Carlita spoke in her ear.

"Good evening, Jennifer."

"Hi, Carlita," Jennifer said, looking embarrassed. "I told you not to interrupt me now."

"I understand, and I apologize," Carlita said. "But a message arrived from Geraldine Barfield. It is marked extreme priority. Shall I read it to you?"

"Go ahead," Jennifer said, not sure how to feel.

"The message says 'Dear Miss Calderón, EduForce will share this announcement with the media tomorrow, but because of our little arrangement, I thought you might want a preview. Enjoy! Love, Geraldine Barfield' Then there are a number of heart and smiley face graphics. I am not sure how to read those. Shall I read the announcement?"

"Go ahead," sighed Jennifer, but she was intrigued. And worried. "Read it to me."

The other three looked on curiously, for they could only hear Jennifer's end of the conversation. In Jennifer's ear, Carlita read, "In an exciting new development, EduForce announced today that effective immediately, an additional Achievement Level is being added to the requirements for graduating students. All students who have not yet completed Achievement Level Sixteen will now be required to complete a Level Seventeen to graduate. EduForce President Geraldine Barfield indicates that the final, capstone year will be the most lengthy and rigorous Achievement Level yet.

"'The body of human knowledge doubles every two years,' Barfield said. 'That is a lot of knowledge! To reflect this, and to properly prepare our young people for the college and working world, we are adding this new level of study.'

"Barfield, the candidate for President who is leading in the polls by fifteen percent over her nearest rival, went on to thank the dedicated teachers whose work—"

"Enough," Jennifer said. "I got the message. Don't bother me again, Carlita."

"I won't. Terribly sorry."

Carlita went silent.

"What is it?" Jean Paul asked. "What happened? Is it something bad?"

Jennifer smiled.

"No. It just means the four of us have longer together than I thought."

Then she looked back at her screen and read.

"An Ode to Thinking Outside the Box.

I cry this song for Melody

Whose mind unwound with my consent

Whose dark spot I used to hide my discontent

Whose manic jubilation burst upon my world

A supernova, then black hole that whirled

Together, casting my life at once in shadow and light.

I sing too for a lonely man

Who learned too late his fate

For challenging the status quo.

Who hurled a spear in the face of the gods

And as the holy flames leaped and licked the pointed barb

The man brought the fire back to Earth and

Showed it to the youth and said,

'These flames are not from gods

But from within your souls.

Go now, with this fire,

And use it

To light a path

Or burn the dead

Or read a book at night

Or chase the dark

Or warm your heart

Or to forge yet another spear, so that someday,

Others, too, may javelin the gods.

But use it'."

Acknowledgements

I would like to thank my parents, for encouraging me to write, my wife, for supporting me, and the team at NineStar who has made publishing this book a pleasure.

About the Author

Born in upstate New York, Adam now lives in northern New Jersey with his wife, son, a neurotic dog and two cats. He teaches middle school English and writes science fiction, fantasy, and history, often in strange combinations. His stories and essays have been published in several anthologies and online magazines. Beyond writing and teaching, his interests include running and making improvements on his creaky old house.

Email: adamknightbooks@gmail.com

Facebook: www.facebook.com/adamknightbooks

Twitter: @AdamKnightBooks

Website: www.adamknightbooks.com

Also Available from NineStar Press

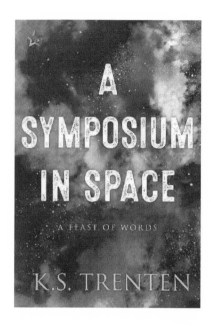 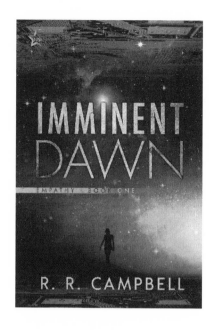

Connect with NineStar Press

Website: NineStarPress.com

Facebook: NineStarPress

Facebook Reader Group: NineStarNiche

Twitter: @ninestarpress

Tumblr: NineStarPress

45685613R00182

Made in the USA
Middletown, DE
23 May 2019